TONY KLINGER

under god's table

LOVE - HATE WAR

LONG.42.5   LAT. 33.3

Typeset by Jonathan Downes,
Cover and Layout by SPiderKaT for CFZ Communications
Using Microsoft Word 2000, Microsoft Publisher 2000, Adobe Photoshop CS.

First published in Great Britain by Gonzo Multimedia

c/o Brooks City,
6th Floor New Baltic House
65 Fenchurch Street,
London EC3M 4BE
Fax: +44 (0)191 5121104
Tel: +44 (0) 191 5849144
International Numbers:
Germany: Freephone 08000 825 699
USA: Freephone 18666 747 289

ISBN: 978-1-908728-70-8

Dedication

This book is dedicated to Avril, my wife. Thank you for reminding me that I am, after all, a writer. I love you; and thank you for kicking me up the ass when necessary!

Tony Klinger, Northampton, April 2017

... And Tyre did build herself a stronghold, and heaped up silver as the dust,
And fine gold as the mire of the streets. Behold, the Lord will impoverish her, and he will smite her power into the sea; and she shall be devoured with fire. Ashkelon shall see it, and fear, Gaza also, and shall be sore pained,

And Ekkon, for her expectation shall be ashamed; And the King shall perish from Gaza, And Ashkelon shall not be inhabited.

THE HOLY SCRIPTURES,
Chapter 9 - the Prophecies of Zechariah

.... If thou art rich, thou'rt poor; for, like an ass whose back with ingots bows, thou bearest thy heavy riches but a journey, and death unloads thee.

WILLIAM SHAKESPEARE,
"Measure for Measure"

In the name of Allah, the beneficent, the merciful, Abundance diverts you
Until you come to the graves. Nay, you will soon know,
Nay, again, you will soon know.

Nay, would that you knew with a certain knowledge! You will certainly see Hell.

THE HOLY KORAN
- Chapter 102 - the abundance of wealth.

Prologue

E hud's ancestors, the Jews, dispersed from the biblical land of Israel by the tides of war and trade, had settled in Iraq more than two thousand six hundred years ago – about six hundred years before Christianity, and one thousand two hundred years before Islam. The family had inhabited a town called Hillah, not far from the ancient site of Babylon.

The original Jews found Babylon, with its nourishing Tigris and Euphrates rivers, to be a land of milk, honey, abundance and opportunity. Although Jews, like other minorities in what later became Iraq, experienced periods of oppression and discrimination depending on the rulers of the period, their general trajectory over two and one-half millennia was upward.

Under the late Ottoman rule Jewish social and religious institutions, schools, and medical facilities flourished without outside interference, and Jews were prominent in government and business.

That was then and *this* is now, and inexorably our future is bound up in the fulcrum of the world, a small part of it known as the Middle East, stretching between the Nile and the Euphrates rivers, humanity's ultimate enigma.

BOOK ONE

"Two Tribes"

Chapter One

Basra, Iraq
18 March 2003

Ehud scampered through the narrow space between the buildings. He heard the noise of the other, bigger, pursuing boys, they were shouting and laughing. But Ehud was clever, quick and nimble, as he charged into the market, the busy Kasbah full of traders selling everything from gold to spices. Gradually the noise of his pursuers faded as they lost sight of their young target. Ehud's small boyish frame went largely unnoticed by the market traders, who were more intent on their daily battle to make a living.

'Why do they chase me? thought the young boy, 'what did I do to them? Ehud was nearly eight years old and therefore didn't yet understand that his place in this Arab city was imperiled by his having been born a Jew. He especially did not understand what his friend, Mo had meant when he said that the Jews had insulted the Prophet Mohammed. Ehud didn't remember insulting anyone, not his friend, nor the Prophet with the same name, in fact he didn't know who the Prophet Mohammed was, or he would have apologised to him at once.

The first time he understood the depth of his insult to the Prophet came when the bully Abdul had punched him on the nose. Ehud had run to Mister Christian Applethwaite, the teacher from England, who was one of the two foreigners who taught at what had, long ago, been the Hebrew School of Basra, but was now the Saddam Hussein School for Boys. Mister Applethwaite listened impatiently to Ehud explain what had happened, then said, "Wipe your nose young man, you're dripping blood on the floor." Ehud didn't have a handkerchief so he used his sleeve to stem the flow of blood, "But Sir, Mister Christian Applethwaite, I didn't do anything to Abdul or the Prophet but he still punched me!"

Ehud was outraged, and his little thin voice was raised in anger. His teacher got up from his wooden chair and loomed over the boy, he was a very tall man, in his thirties and disappointed in his own achievements, and everything around him. He especially didn't like Jews.

"Will you stop sniveling, I'm confident you had something to do with your own fate, you people are very good at being victims are you not."

Ehud knew the teacher had said something nasty, but didn't know what he meant. "But he hit me sir!"

Mister Applethwaite stood up so he towered threateningly over the little boy,

"And one can safely determine that you must have perpetrated some mischief to deserve it, Abdul is a fine boy. In any event your people also insulted the Lord Jesus Christ, so if anyone was going to give you a bloody nose this pleasure should be reserved to our Christian brothers don't you think? Now get back to class and I do not want to hear one further word on this subject."

Ehud tried hard not to cry in front of the Englishman, but it wasn't easy. He felt some tears on his cheeks but he was determined not to let anyone see his distress. He wiped his face on his sleeve and left the room. It just didn't seem fair to the little boy, this world in which he had insulted both the Prophet and the Lord Jesus Christ, both of whom he had never met nor insulted!

Waiting outside was his best friend, Mohammed who everyone knew as Mo. As usual it was his friend who comforted Ehud, putting an arm around his scrawny shoulders. "Don't worry my friend, I will always be here for you, he's just a big ignorant infidel."

"Is he?" asked Ehud,

"Yes, that's what mom said he was."

Basra was not a hospitable place for Ehud's family, who were amongst the last Jews in Iraq's once thriving and large Jewish community where the people of the Book had lived for thousands of years despite the occasional cataclysmic tsunamis of local hatred.

After school, Ehud had regained his good humour and walked to the big river, which flowed into the estuary and the sea. He was full of fun and an electric energy, but was able to calm down sufficiently while he sat on the big rocks by the busy port and dangled his long fishing line into the water far below.

As ever, the small boy wore sandals and his sun browned skinny bare legs stuck out from his baggy shorts. He was wearing his treasured Manchester United shirt, unaware and uncaring that it was a cheap fake. He dreamed that one day he might travel to far away England and play football in front of huge crowds in the Theatre of Dreams, his centre of the universe, Old Trafford. He knew this to be a fact; he had seen the huge stadium and its magic on the television for sale in the window of the shop at the corner of his street. He saw those young men from the four corners of the world who played their football in Manchester, and he spent every spare moment practicing with the ball he had fashioned from used Coke paper cups. He could keep the ball up for nearly nineteen kicks in a row, and thought that when he could manage one hundred, he would be ready to find a way to make the journey to the football Mecca.

He liked the feeling of the breeze from the water on his feet at this late part of the day when the sun wasn't too hot, and everything was a bit drowsy, lazily and slowly getting ready for the night.

Ehud thought about his parents and whistled as he worked with his clever little hands on the rudimentary home made fishing equipment he had created. The worm he gathered from the earth, the hook he had fashioned from the old metal coat hanger he had rescued from the rubbish outside the dress stall in the market, and he attached this to the plastic washing line he had bundled up in his pocket, which he had recently requisitioned from the washing line hanging between two nearby apartments on the opposite sides of his alley way. The big lady on the other side of the alley had nearly caught him in the act of washing line liberation but had given up the chase when she realised that he moved like an eel, and was impossible to grasp.

He knew from hard-won experience that he would probably not catch any fish but he was philosophical and liked to sit in the early evening sunshine, before it got too hot, and watch as the sea birds wheeled in the sky above the scuttling smaller boats which plied their various trades between the gigantic oil tankers and huge variety of cargo ships. He sat on the scrubby, nearly bare patch of grass between the small, straggly gathering of palm trees overlooking the vast, mostly rundown buildings on the opposite shore of the estuary leading to the open sea.

Ehud wasn't sure nor did he care what they did in the big buildings but he saw the men in uniforms with their black guns, and he wished he had one, but his mummy forbade him from even a toy gun. She was always calling him her "soft lovely boy." and although he was becoming too big to be cuddled and spoilt like a little boy, he still secretly enjoyed her comforting warmth and clean smell.

Ehud loved to imagine where they all came from or where they would go; his favourite game was to pretend he was a sailor journeying around the world. He longed to know more about what was out there. But his family had always stayed where it was, and were proud to have done so. They could trace their roots in this town back into the ancient times. They were one of the last Jewish families to live in the port city of Basra. Jews had lived with their Arab neighbours here for three thousand years.

During the time it took Ehud not to catch any fish, he was joined by his best friend, Mo, the boy whose family lived next door and who sat next to him in school. The two boys were the same age, and many people who didn't know them jumped wrongly to the conclusion that they were related. The two boys loved each other without reservation, as only two small street urchins could do. Their eyes lit up when they saw each other, unaware that their being Jewish and Muslim might make their friendship appear strange to many others.

Mo sat next to his friend and punched Ehud on the arm affectionately.

"Catch anything?"

Mo knew the answer before asking the question, but it was their standing joke, Ehud answered,

"I caught a sea monster, it was four metres long, as tall as two and a half giants standing on each other's shoulders, and when I pulled it out of the water, after a four hour battle it spoke to me."

Mo enjoyed Ehud's rich imagination,

"Oh yes, and what did this colossus say?"

Ehud warmed to his theme as he smiled to his friend,

"He opened his huge wide mouth, and showed me that he had four sets of very big sharp white teeth, each one was bigger than the fingers on my hand and said, what's your name little master fisherman, and so I told him, I am Ehud Ben Avram of Basra, and although I am small I have caught you despite your being very large, and he said, are you going to eat me sir?"

Mo was wide-eyed, he relished the way Ehud told him stories,

"And I said, no, because my friend Mo would think I was being greedy, and possibly you are a fish that is forbidden to both of us because we have to be careful we eat only the correct animals, me eating only the most pure Kosher food and my friend only the very best Halal food; and the fish stopped and thought for a moment, and then said he understood such things, as he only ate small boys who were Christians for the same reason, him being a religious fish who wasn't sure whether he was Jewish or Muslim, so we said our farewells and I tossed him back in the sea, where, even now, he watches us from close by to see what we're going to do next."

Mo knew his friend was joking, but nevertheless he warily eyed the murky deep water before him, checking for the sea monster, which might still be hungry. Mo liked the moment of fear, of the unknown, when he didn't know what would happen next, but when he turned to look at Ehud he saw that his friend was smiling broadly. They both giggled and then it boiled over into the kind of laughter without restraint that only the innocence in children can share. They hugged each other as tears rolled down their cheeks.

"You should have seen your face Mo, it was a picture!"

Ehud looked at the sun-dappled water rocking the small boats speeding about their business and smiled. One day he would be a sea captain, or perhaps a pirate. Then he wouldn't need to spit on any floor, because everyone would be scared of upsetting Ehud, and when they heard his name, they would spit on their floor. He sighed when he thought of the days to come, when he would be big and grown up and could look after his mother and brothers. It didn't matter who was bigger or older to the small boy, he was certain that he would be the one to fight their battles and bring home their food to feed their hungry bellies.

"Come on, Ehud. Mum sent me because it's dinner time and if we don't come home right now she won't let us eat any of that delicious baklava your mum made us for dessert!"

Ehud didn't need any further encouragement as he loved the sweet-tasting food and before Mo could say another word, his friend was packing up his rudimentary fishing equipment and sliding his feet into his sandals, scampering down the path towards their homes. Mo was bigger, but he had to rush to keep up with Ehud who, as ever, was looking straight ahead, never deviating from his chosen path, whatever the distractions.

They marched through the neighbourhood, captivated by the hustle and bustle, the rich aromatic smells and the never-ending tides of humanity as it flowed past them. They made a game of walking very fast, but not breaking into a run, their little arms pumping as their little legs whirled like windmills.

The two boys had homes next to one another in the poorest section of the town, which had many similarly poor areas. They practically lived in each other's homes. The slum was in the suburbs, in a district called Gzeiza, which was as poor as any third world shantytown. But not to the boys, who thought that the place was a palace of adventure and fun. Almost everyone who lived there was unemployed, or worked for the government's endless bureaucracy, many doing jobs like opening doors, or if things were really slow, closing them. The overcrowded, poor inhabitants lived in half-built or half-destroyed dwellings, intersected by open sewers. The boys didn't notice the mud and trash that was everywhere in the dirty grey and brown landscape, it was just the place in which they had always lived.

Saddam's army guarded the entrance to these districts. Many outsiders refused to enter fearing for their lives. But the boys were young and had no idea that they were particularly deprived. The rumor was that it had once, many years before, been a prosperous district, but that was generations before. Now it was for those far beyond any forlorn hope of economic salvation.

The paradox of this city was that it contained some of the poorest places in the world, sitting on top of vast oil wealth just a few miles from Iran, and cheek by jowl with the hugely important Shatt Al Arab waterway. Basra could never be safe until the gap between downtown Basra and the slums was overcome, and on this day, this was far from being accomplished.

The mothers of both boys supported their large families but neither had a man to help with this. The reasons were very different, but the results were disastrous for the economic wellbeing of both. The houses were crowded with a chaotic mix of the generations of both their families. Aunts and uncles came and went all the time, to visit the boys, their mothers and their grandmothers, two very old ladies who never spoke with one another, but for exchanging insults over long-exhausted battles. Every time one of the boys passed within reach, they were either smacked,

"Just in case he should be thinking of doing something wrong!"

....or cuddled

"Just because he is so beautiful".

Sitting in the corner chair, never moving, but smiling quietly, was Ehud's grandfather, Poppa Sam, a man who was so old that the boys calculated he must have personally known the prophet Abraham.

Ehud's father had vanished before the boy had been born. The man was a legend to all in the small, tight Jewish community of Basra, except for his wife Sarah, who yearned for his support, his strength and the heat of his body in her lonely bed. She enjoyed sharing the legends about the shadowy giant of a man who peopled Ehud's imagination more like a superhero than a father. No one seemed to know where he had gone, or what he was doing, but when other boys gossiped that he had run away and left his family, Ehud would fight to protect the good name of the man he had never known.

Mother repeatedly cautioned her son that everything she shared about his father was a secret, which Ehud honoured, except with his friend Mo. The boys shared every secret, dream and hope. They were closer like only small boys who become blood brothers can be. What could be wrong about his very best friend knowing that Ehud's father was a Zionist, whatever a Zionist was?

His father's name was Benjamin and he was a giant. Literally, his mother told him, more than two metres or six feet six inches tall and so broad that he filled the entire room with his magnificent physique. Too big not to be noticed in the sea of hostility surrounding him and his family. Benjamin had simply disappeared one night, vanishing from their lives, and no one thought he was still alive, except for Ehud's mother, and Ehud.

The boy had heard the whispered rumors that his father, the great Zionist, the handsome young giant with Ehud's mother in the pictures on the wall, had helped smuggle many of the Jews of Basra the short distance to Iran, and from there to Israel years before. Ehud didn't quite understand what smuggling meant, but he knew it was a good thing to do if you were a member of his family or simply were a Jew of Basra, but equally was a mark of great shame and danger if the same facts were discussed with the local Arab neighbours.

In return for this carefully-guarded secret, Mo had shared his very best mystery with Ehud. One night in the recent past, while Mo pretended to be asleep, his eyes screwed tight, next to his mother in the bed that they shared, she had allowed the rent collecting man to kiss her on the mouth, then she opened her mouth and their kiss became bigger as the tongues of the two grown ups explored each other, which Mo thought was vaguely exciting and fascinating at the same time. He told Ehud that his own penis had grown to two or three times its normal size as he watched. Then his mother had carefully climbed out of the bed, this allowed the rent collecting man to pull up her nightgown, they kissed more as he felt her body intimately, he turned her round and bent her over so that her face was close to Mo on the bed. The man had pulled down her knickers, and then grabbed hold of her big breasts, which had hung down from her chest like ripe fruit from a tree. Then while the Rent Collector pulled at his mother's nipples with one hand, he opened the buttons on the fly of his trousers with the other. Mo saw that his penis was huge, much bigger than any he had ever seen before, standing up as a penis sometimes does in the morning, but bigger. Then Mo's mother and the man fiddled around and then they both sighed and started to rock back and forwards and made some very curious groaning noises while their bodies slapped together; her face went all pointy and she started to grunt and sweat and the man cried out to the Almighty as they did what Mo had seen dogs do sometimes in the alleys near their home.

Mo told Ehud that he had tried to keep his eyes screwed up tight and had pretended to be asleep but when the noise coming from his mother became like screams, he had jumped up to defend her from the man who seemed to be trying to attack her bum with his penis.

"Why would he do that?"

Asked Ehud.

"I don't know,"

Mo answered,

"But I leapt like a hero onto my mother's back to punch the man in the face."

Everyone and everything went crazy. Mom seemed embarrassed then shocked, and she straightened up and dumped me on the floor and ran from the room screaming. I continued to hit the man who shouted at me, telling me to stop hitting his head, and it was funny because all the time he was trying to pull his clothes together."

Eventually the Rent Collector had gripped Mo by the wrists to stop his attack and had shaken his head sadly.

"What do you think you just saw, young man?" Mo had tried to pull his hands out of the grasp of the man, but he was too strong to be resisted.

"You were hurting my mother!"

He shouted defiantly, but the man shook his head with infinite sadness.

"No, I was helping her. It is our secret that I help her once a week, with a little problem we both have. Do you understand me?"

Mo had no idea what the man meant, but like all small children he liked to be treated like an adult occasionally.

"What little problems?" He asked, beginning to be calm.

"I am sent here by the man who owns this place to collect rent every week from your mother, but she prefers that you eat, so I help her with the rent; in kind, do you understand?"

"And what was his problem?" Ehud asked, always keen to understand the little details of life.

"He answered that he had an itch on his penis, and that he liked to put it somewhere nice and warm to give it a scratch, once a week, or more often if possible."

Ehud thought about this for a few moments, and then nodded, as if satisfied. "We all get an itch there occasionally, perhaps that's a good way of making it better?"

Mo nodded and then remembered how he had looked at the serious man for a long moment, the man had released him, and the boy had rubbed his wrists, sizing up the situation.

"What does 'in kind' mean?" He enquired politely.

"Don't you sometimes get a reward when you do something for your mummy?"

Mo thought for a moment. "Yes, sometimes I get something nice to eat when I help clean up."

"Well, it's like that then. I'm just exchanging something for something with your mommy, and we're both very happy. I'm like an uncle, coming to visit. OK?"

"Oh, you are my uncle? Because uncles give presents to their nephews, and you've never given me a thing, uncle?"

The man smiled and pulled out a large banknote that he gave to Mo.

"I am indeed, just like an uncle. Now shall we keep this our little secret; just between us, now and forever?"

Ehud and Mo kept their secrets from anyone else, just like they had promised – everyone, that is, except each other.

"What do you suppose a Zionist is, Mo?" Asked Ehud.

"Something like a Communist, I suppose," Volunteered Mo,

"But to do with Zionist stuff. What do you think about my mum and the Rent Collector?" Mo asked.

"Oh, they were fucking each other," Replied Ehud.

"Fucking each other?" Mused Mo.

"Does it hurt?" Ehud didn't know for sure.

"Maybe a bit if it's by a Rent Collector, or even more if you're being fucked by a Zionist. I guess it hurts more to be fucked than to fuck, what do you think?"

"I don't like the sound of doing it to someone else, but I wouldn't mind it being done to me," Whispered Ehud quietly. "That seems like a friendly thing to do."

Mo wasn't much interested either way. Ehud had noticed that his friend always had become quite excited when he accidentally on purpose went a little too far with the girls at school when they played with them, stealing a glimpse of their private parts when they did dares in the art supply cupboard, a game many of the girls played with the art teaching fellow with the sweaty hands.

Ehud was always very popular with girls for this game, but he would like to play it with other boys rather than girls, who he found very uninteresting. Something in his mind warned him not to tell Mo about this, as something told him not to share his preferences.

The two boys were not aware of the big world outside, the richly-textured but narrow world they inhabited. The big issues were whether they could convince the chocolate and candy stall holder, Ibrahim, to allow them a little credit so that they might purchase a little delicious flaky milk chocolate each, that came in that clever wax paper which stopped the perfect chocolate from melting. Preserved in its paper, the flake could be pinched between chocolaty fingers and swallowed in a transport of delight. But their main occupation on this day was to obtain the two chickens from the big old Chicken Lady, who had her noisy coops just a few stalls away from the chocolate and candy man in the same market. The woman was known as the smelly woman with the chickens, for obvious reasons, but no one dared to cross this angry lady. The boys hated a visit to her stall just as much as they loved going to the chocolate shop. First there was always a haggle over price – it never seemed that they had sufficient money to satisfy the Chicken Lady. Next came the handover of the chickens. The boys always hoped that they had enough money for the Chicken Lady to snap the chicken necks, and to pluck them straight after their slaughter, because otherwise they had to carry the birds home and this might involve them in "doing the necessary", as their mothers would call the messy and noisy business.

Today was a good day, the Chicken Lady, who was sitting on a blue wooden three-legged stool in the oppressive heat, fanning herself, saw them coming and put out her hand.

"You have my money?"

Ehud counted out her money, coin by coin as she grabbed them.

"You have our chickens, nicely slaughtered, cleaned and plucked?"

Asked Mo, who she cuffed around the ear, leaving him holding his head and screeching in pain.

"Why, are mummies' hands too precious to get dirty?"

Ehud folded his scrawny arms and stood his ground, staring at the Chicken Lady, with his best effort at intimidation. She also folded her arms and stared back at him.

"Well, are our chickens ready?"

He demanded. She laughed, and produced two chickens from on top of the crate behind her.

"And these chickens are Halal?" He demanded of her, as he took possession.

"Your family are Jewish, what do you care?" Ehud sighed, this being a discussion he had often had with the Chicken Lady.

"It is written that where there is no kosher food, we have special permission to eat Halal food, just as Muslim people can eat kosher food where Halal food is not available. It is written!"

The Chicken Lady nodded, as if this were the first time she had ever heard this information. "It is written? This is very interesting. I hope you enjoy my almost kosher chickens as long as it is written. Oh, I have one more thing for you to take with." She leaned forward and Ehud did the same, expecting some free chicken eggs, which sometimes were given as a bonus for the chicken soup, but instead he received a ringing smack on his ear.

"What was that for?" He yelped.

"Just because!" She cackled, handing him a little bag with the chicken eggs.

"Just because you two make me laugh. Enjoy and send my best wishes to your mothers, they deserve some good luck and the best fresh chickens, bringing up two monkeys like you without the benefit of a strong man."

Neither boy was aware, nor would they have much cared, that their country's leader, Saddam Hussein, had angered many other countries with his ill-judged bravado following a decade on from his ruinous attack to the south, when he had invaded Kuwait, and that the rest of the world was readying itself to punish him and his country yet again by doing the same to their country that the Rent Collector had just done to Mo's mother.

The two boys delivered their precious chickens to their mothers who were preparing their supper in Sarah's warm and busy kitchen. The boys moved to that part of the accommodation where people would sit and wait for food, talk and socialise. They greeted Ehud's old Poppa Sam with a kiss on his whiskery cheeks. He sighed with pleasure, and smiled, his eyes full of life and joy at seeing his family congregate. The boys were still gossiping quietly about what they had seen Mo's mother, Amina, doing with the Rent Collector. Poppa Sam, who heard everything but said nothing, as he sat in his chair, listened to the boys chatter, and looked with new appreciation at Amina and wished he was a decade or two younger and a bit stronger. Now he could only smile and dream of her hidden pleasures, wishing she had owed him some rent money.

Ehud in all his nine years on the planet was sublimely indifferent to the political tectonic plates shifting around the world. All he knew was that whenever his mother heard the name Saddam Hussein, she would surreptitiously turn to the side and furtively spit three times onto the floor. When he asked her why, she said that you should spit on the floor to keep the evil eye away from her family, which was a habit he copied unselfconsciously.

The boys sat at the huge and solid table inherited from Ehud's great uncle's great uncle Solomon and his wife Miriam. He didn't remember as they had both gone to heaven long before he had been born, but he always did as he was taught when he heard their names mentioned, and mimed three quick spits to the floor, keeping the evil eye well away from him and his friend. He said the words,

"A thousand blessings from the Lord."

While Mohammed seriously intoned,

"Allah the most merciful."

Neither having a clue what either religious incantation meant.

Ehud rubbed the smooth rich dark texture of the wood, enjoying this sensual connection to the past but not understanding why; he had often been told the mythological story of how this particular table had been passed down to his mother by many generations of their family and it was, he was told, a fact that this table was carved from the actual wood of Noah's Ark, the second most holy of all woods, only second to the wood containing the Ark of the Covenant long-since vanished from the Second Temple after it was destroyed by the cursed Romans two thousand years before, but this was wood even thousands of years older and so solid that it was heavier and mightier than rock. Poppa Sam told them the family had always called it God's Table because it was a gift from the Almighty and they thought it was their duty to be its custodians for future generations.

Ehud had never understood the ancient riddle Poppa Sam always repeated to him as they sat at the ancient piece of furniture,

"If this table is carved from Noah's Ark, how come there are not two tables?"

But the little boy dutifully laughed with the rest of the family. But this wasn't enough today, because his grandfather was looking intently at the two boys playing and called them both over to sit, one on each of his knees.

"Did I ever tell you the story of Jacob and Esau?"

He asked, the two boys looked at each other and feigned an interest, but like youngsters all over the world they weren't very interested in the silly stories of very old men, but Poppa Sam was not one to be deterred by their indifference,

"Two boys, just like you, but a very long time ago, one grew up to be a hunter, hairy and strong, the other more gentle and maybe more subtle, clever with more guile.

Which is which?" He asked, tickling them to solicit a response. The boys laughed without answering, enjoying the gentle old man's warm familiarity.

"I tell you that you're a Jacob."

He kissed his grandson on the cheek,

"And you're definitely an Esau!"

He hugged Mo, who loved the old man as if he was his own grandfather. The boys jumped from his lap and scampered off to play.

Ehud enjoyed hearing his family tell him how he reminded them of long-dead relatives, how he looked a bit like one ancestor around the eyes, another around the mouth, but he didn't yet have any of the old men's double chins, which he would suffer only when he was old, if he became too heavy.

Best of all the many stories recounted how his uncle Tal, who had long since joined the angels in heaven, had looked after everyone as the first volunteer fire officer in the district, a man revered by everyone for his considerable bravery and huge belly. Perhaps, thought Ehud, nana was right and their family was blessed because they had done much good, that was the reason that, despite being very poor, the table was miraculously always covered in a vast array of rich aromatic food, and, tonight as ever, surrounded by their noisy and rumbustious families.

The two young friends had long ago arrived at the shared conclusion, God's Table was clearly a magical thing, endowed with mysterious powers direct via Noah. Their families and friends might sit together to start to eat, but the miracle was that once you'd eaten you might get up but your belly stayed in the chair. No one ever got up from sharing a meal at that table without feeling full up and happy.

The boys looked at one another and smiled guilty little secret smiles, full of the knowledge and fun that only small children share, and which made their confidences and friendship deeper and more important.

The two families shared more than their kitchen and the food that came from it, they also trusted and loved, cried and laughed together.

Their mothers, Sarah and Amina, were of similar age to one another and were in their way, as close as their sons, brought together by shared circumstances, experiences and adversity, doing what they had to in order to survive. The boys wouldn't have been able to tell you how old these women were. 'Very old' would have been their opinion. In fact both women were just approaching thirty. Both were dark haired and had big eyes; Ehud's mother, Sarah's, were wide spaced large cornflower blue, which looked striking against her dark brown skin. Mo's mother, Amina, had kindly deep-set dark brown eyes. Each of the women wore loose-fitting flowing Jilbabs that camouflaged the fact that both had slim but voluptuous bodies. Sarah, although not a Muslim woman, had, in the recent traumatic past, taken to wearing a full-face veil so that no one could see her eyes, so different to most other people in the city, often attracting unwanted male attention.

Amina's husband, Uday, had abandoned her when she was pregnant with the twins, after she had been raped by the secret police who had briefly arrested the students at her university class. Uday did not want the responsibility of more mouths to feed, especially if someone else could possibly have fathered them.

No one at this table had an interest in, or appreciation of, the broad sweep of Jewish history in Iraq even though their families had been part of it right from the beginning.

Ehud and his family had all been born in Basra, one of the last Jewish families of a once- large and bustling community. After the State of Israel had been formed, the Jews had found themselves forced to flee or face persecution. Like most of the others, the family members who did emigrate were initially dispossessed refugees in Israel. They didn't fit in well with the bustling Western leaning, technologically-driven young country. They spoke Arabic at home and thought like Arabs, not like the former eastern European idealistic socialists who originally led Israel.

The boys passed some bread under the table to the fat dog, Shah, that lazed there, eating scraps of their unwanted food and farting noisily, indifferent to the smell and confusion he caused everyone, and the giggles the boys enjoyed with his noisy interjections. The twins just cried for their food to be fed to them, which their mother and her friend did while continuing to chat and other than wiping their messy mouths and noses, the twins were, as ever, ignored by everyone.

"You remember I told you about my special arrangement, me with the rent man, did I tell you what happened?"

Whispered Amina, giggling like a naughty schoolgirl. Sarah nodded.

"Yes, you did. Why, what happened?"

Amina with her mouth half hidden behind her hand, described the wild situation in her bedroom. Sarah tried to listen sympathetically, but her smile soon became a grin, and then she was laughing uncontrollably.

"Stop it, or I shall wet myself,"

She pleaded, herself in a stage whisper, but Amina went on to describe how she had no alternative but to run out of her bedroom.

"But then what happened between the gentleman and the young fellow?" Sarah whispered. Amina nodded theatrically.

"That's just it, I don't know and when I asked, they both tell me that a gentleman never tells!"

"You didn't leave it like that?"

Amina, who had the good grace to colour in embarrassment, and indicating the two older boys with a sideways glance, replied,

"I told him fun was fun, but there would have to be new, more private arrangements, if you know what I mean."

Sarah laughed.

"Yes, I think something a little more private might be better, but then again, we don't have many options."

Amina laughed also.

"Not unless we want our bits to heal up!"

Noticing the boys watching, they switched the subject.

"What about you?" Amina asked.

"Are you going to wait forever? I tell you the truth. I worry that he's never coming back."

Sarah sighed, her perpetual cloud of concern obscuring her beautiful smile.

"I know. You're right in my head."

Her hand went to her breast. "But here, here in my heart it feels like he will come back, one day, and anyway, what choice do I have? Even if you're right, how many other Jewish men my age are there in Basra for me to choose from?"

Both women sighed, resigned to their insecure and unpredictable futures. They tried to switch the subject to something less personal, so they sought to discuss the situation of Iraq without either of their sons understanding. This was not an easy task when the two boys were so bright and eager to know everything, but it was essential, because if either of the boys ever mentioned their shared intimacies in front of the wrong people, the women could be arrested, brutally interrogated, tortured and even be butchered by the hated and much-feared secret police. The women, who both spoke fluent French, switched to that language, as they always did when their boys, with their big ears, were too close for discretion. "What do you think the Yankees will do?" Amina asked.

"I'm not sure they know, so how should we?"

Sarah smiled as she added,

"I don't know who's right or who's wrong, but I do know that when the fighting starts we, the poor people will be the ones who suffer."

Amina nodded, knowing intuitively that her friend was right. It was always the poorest who suffered the most!

Ehud had climbed surreptitiously under the heavy old wooden table and was rolling around with Shah, the dog, who wagged his tail in appreciation. Sarah bristled as Mo joined in their rough and tumble, creating a riot of giggling boys, the yelping

dog, and food falling from the over-full table. Shah let out a mighty fart, the boys roared with laughter, but before Sarah, who was suppressing her own giggle, could begin to reprimand the boys, Amina, also smiling, gently put her hand out to her.

"Let our lovely boys enjoy themselves. How often do people like us laugh?"

A sudden thunderclap of noise crushed their world to a moment of silence just an instant before the room exploded as the huge bomb hurtled into their home, destroying every surface, evaporating anything exposed so that later no one could tell which body parts belonged to Jews or Arabs.

Sarah had been blown across the room, and looked as if she were just shocked, with no apparent damage, but inside her body she had been irreparably damaged while her lovely friend Amina had been blown into small unidentifiable pieces. Sarah looked at what was left of her friend and knew with certainty that their souls would soon be fused together from this instant from hell, that Amina would be made even closer in death's immortal embrace than they had ever been in life.

Sarah looked around the room. The only thing miraculously left in one piece in the once- humble home was the table, and under it the two young boys, one so suddenly orphaned, the other, Ehud, soon to join him in this suffering, but both were physically untouched by the cataclysm.

Shah the dog shook itself free of the dust and let out another mighty fart, but this time there was no one who wanted to laugh. The dog looked at the scene of devastation and stood guard over the boys, terrified and traumatised, but ready to kill or die defending them.

There was a moment or two of silence; nothing moved, everything a horrific freeze frame, then, just as suddenly, that moment was broken by the world re-booting; sounds came flooding back, people screaming, groaning, crying out for help in surrounding buildings. Flames licked the dark edges of the night, seeking something to burn, something that hadn't already crumbled to dust.

Ehud returned to consciousness. Though still confused and disoriented, he saw Mo stir in the debris next to him, he seemed all right. He felt himself falling asleep and then a gentle hand smoothed his brow. He re-opened his eyes to see his mother smiling down at him. He returned her smile but then saw her grimace. He tried to sit up but she hushed him.

"What happened Mama?"

Sarah tried to smile through her own pain but she was finding it hard to breathe. "I don't know, but I think that the world is a little bit crazy sometimes. I want you to do something for mummy. Do you think you can keep a secret?"

Ehud loved nothing better than secrets.

"Yes, mamma. What secret?"

She took off her fine gold necklace with the treasured wedding picture of Ehud's father in the locket, and secured it around her son's neck.

"There is one secret you must never tell anyone, ever, unless they can give you the other half of this picture, the bit that has my picture on it, do you understand?"

She grimaced in pain, her breath now coming in a tortured gasp.

"Yes, Mama, are you OK?"

She smiled again.

"Very soon I shall be going to heaven, and I shall see my momma and daddy.

It will be fine, we shall have a party together."

He started to cry and she reached down to kiss his cheek, again she gasped in pain.

"I don't want you to go, Momma, I shall be left all alone."

He cried, desperately holding on to his mother's neck as she bent over him.

She hushed him again.

"You have to be a brave soldier now. I will always be watching you, I promise. Now do you remember that secret I told you about?"

He nodded, trying to be brave, to suppress his tears.

"When someone gives you the other half of this picture you will tell them these numbers. You can remember some numbers. You're very good at numbers at school, and these are very important numbers."

But Ehud wasn't certain he could remember the numbers.

"What will happen if I forget them, Momma?"

"Pick up a knife and scratch them into Noah's table for me."

Ehud did as his mother asked, picking up a knife from the litter strewn over the floor and reaching to the underside of the table, he began to scratch the numbers as Sarah told her son the exact location of Iraq's weapons of mass destruction, where they were hidden, deep under the desert, waiting to be discovered, and possibly used.

Sarah didn't tell her son what these numbers meant because he would be simply too young to understand or to tell him that she had been passed this information by her teacher, Abu Saif, her Professor of Physics, before he had been arrested by the secret police and then vanished without trace.

As Sarah finished, she asked her son to repeat the numbers, and he did so without a single mistake. He was so proud when she smiled and said,

"You're my very best boy!"

But before he could say anything more to his mother she sighed and, with a smile still on her face, gently subsided to the floor, dead. Neither of them had seen Mo was conscious and, despite his own shock was trying hard to listen to their every word, the sound of their voices muffled by his burst eardrums he watched Ehud carve the numbers into the ancient wood unaware of the meaning of his friend's action.

Ehud looked up from his task and saw Mo looking at him and pretended that he was doing nothing of consequence.

"Are you hurt my brother, can I help you?" He asked Mo who shook his head and smiled.

"No my friend, we'll be OK, nothing can stop us when we have each other."

The neighbours rushed to help rescue anyone left alive from their wrecked home, but were too late to do anything other than take the boys away to a place of relative safety. No one knew exactly what to do with the boys, who simply wouldn't let anyone break their embrace.

The next day the Rent Collector came to collect his due and was upset to find the building was wrecked and the families gone. He shrugged philosophically, after all it wasn't his building and there were always new opportunities, but he had enjoyed his time with Amina. He would miss that more than a little; such sweet afternoons.

He looked through the debris, realizing there was nothing for him to collect in lieu of rent on this day. Then he spotted the big old near-black wood table knocked on to its side, covered in dust and decided that the solid-looking furniture might find a use in his home. There were a few men standing around discussing the loss of the two families and he gave them a few coins to help load the table onto his small flatbed truck. He would clean up the table and his wife would be very happy with her new possession once he removed the few scratches under the table that he saw as he inspected it. Mind you, who looked under a table, maybe his wife should just polish the top.

Mo watched as the Rent Collector drove God's table away.

Chapter Two

Children of Christ Orphanage, Basra, Iraq
1 December 2003

*E*hud and Mo had been the only survivors from the bombs that fell on, and wiped out, both their families. There was no one else to give them comfort or familiarity – it was as if a giant had simply extinguished their previous existence. There was nothing to remind them of the past, not a picture, not a keepsake, a piece of clothing, nothing. They hung on to each other, getting over the immediate shock very slowly, hardly noticing that they had been taken to a new home, a place full of other children orphaned by the war.

The passage of time could be measured by the increasing number of other children rapidly filling the squalid buildings. Each new child had stories of horror and shock that they were compelled to keep to themselves; who wanted to listen when each of them had their own recent trauma to deal with and overcome? Soldiers would call their suffering 'Post traumatic stress syndrome', but these were little children, and they were unable to put a name to their nightmares.

Days turned to weeks and even the worst, most terrible memories fade to less harsh pastel shades with the distance of time. The boys had each other and most of the other inmates of their strange new home had no one at all.

A few months went by and a group of boys, bombed out from another part of town, decided to levy a tax on the candy money they were each given to spend at the little stand the nuns set up each Thursday afternoon. As Ehud went past their leader, a burly eleven-year-old named Mehmet, he whispered,

"Give me half your money and we won't beat you up, Jew!"

Without any thought, Ehud hit him on the nose, which started to bleed. Mehmet began to cry as his blood spilled onto the floor.

"Look what the Jew did to my nose!" he screamed.

"He broke my nose!"

Some of his friends who were prepared to join in an easy attack moved a little back, cautious not to get too involved if this meant a bloody nose for them.

Mo walked over to Mehmet and stood just inches away from him, their faces almost touching.

"You touch my brother, and I shall hurt you."

Mehmet backed away.

"I only asked for half the Jew's money. He could have kept the other half, and anyway, how can you be an Arab and brother to a Jew?"

"Because that's what we want,"

Replied Ehud, just as Mo kicked Mehmet in his groin, sending him to the ground clutching himself.

This proved to the entire orphanage that the boys were as tough as anyone else in the place, and there were two of them, one always watching the other's back. This placed them at an advantage with everyone else, and they were left alone by the other boys and girls who remained nervous of them. The staff either had too much to do elsewhere, or simply didn't care.

After that day in Basra life had taken a very strange turn. They had been placed in the orphanage run by the American charity, "Children of Faith", for the orphaned Christian children of families ravaged by the bombing and warfare, who were considered sufficiently devout by their community. No one was quite certain what to do with the two boys who continued to be inseparable. They clearly loved one another, but who, in living memory had ever heard of a Jew and an Arab who were like this?

Of course the small Christian community had all heard the ancient stories about how the two other ancient communities had once been so close, like long lost brothers, but those days were so long ago that they were now considered just to be myths. The priests were nervous, aware that their community was surrounded by hostility, but determined, nevertheless to do whatever was necessary to maintain their beliefs. Their leader, Father Louis Saaker, had taken one look at the two boys and decided that whatever the consequence, their families' faith or the cost, his orphanage would give them a home. The Christian Father of the community was not a man for practical considerations. He often said, "God will provide." when his Muslim assistant, secretary and general factotum, Abdul, asked how they could afford to give any more charity when they had so little themselves.

A few months passed, and the British had now seemingly taken control over the city of Basra. They had fought briefly with the local militia, but the superior conventional firepower, equipment and training of the British soon saw them triumph in the brief asymmetric war.

Or so the British had thought when they relinquished their metal war helmets and replaced them with their red berets, settling down for what they thought would be a relatively comfortable occupation.

This was deemed an invitation too good to miss by the fighters of the militia who began to systematically subvert the British army at every opportunity. They booby-trapped the soldiers' foot patrols and their lightweight vehicles with improvised explosive devices. They ambushed and harried until the Brits were forced back to their barracks around the town's airport.

As time passed the local militia allowed the Brits to keep to certain areas of town, while they controlled everywhere else. It wasn't what either side of the conflict wanted, but a battlefield compromise, a way they could mutually exist.

The American General Staff in Baghdad was furious at the Brits, who, after winning the battle, were, in their view, losing the war simply by walking away.

The Americans decided to send their marines to fill the void left by the retreating British, now almost encircled in their Basra air base. It wouldn't be long before they would replace the British, who would remove their soldiers and redeploy them to Afghanistan.

"Lions led by donkeys!"

The American general said to Major Max Roman, quoting a German derogatory comment about the British army in the First World War, commending the incredible bravery and ferocity of the British infantry while insulting their terrible leadership.

"Go sort this mess out, Major, and we can still win the peace, you guys from Civil Affairs can wander around with your loose cash and goody bags like it's the Wild West and we get to keep to the rulebook."

The general added before sending Max to liaise with the British to co- ordinate the American takeover.

Roman was the man in charge of the intelligence group attached to the 1st Marine Expeditionary Force's First Battalion command that had taken over their town after the British had lost control to the Shia militia. Prior to that, during his first tour, he had been attached to the British first invasion wave when they had come into Basra, Iraq's second city with their own major battle group and plenty of the right attitude. Time and budget cuts from the Ministry of Defence in Whitehall, London, had taken their toll and as the Brits ratcheted down their military presence, the local militia had done the reverse, with the help of the Iranians just across the border.

The Major was massive, made ever larger satisfying his huge appetites, he was sometimes called the Russian bear behind his back, almost as broad as he was tall, a giant, he seemed to fill a room. Unable, or unwilling, to control his ferocious food intake, he had an equally massive ego. Although Max was an American officer, he still had his thick Middle- European accent from his Polish birthplace that no amount of private lessons, or practice, had managed to fix; so when speaking his fractured English, his vocabulary was soon more than sufficient, but his syntax and grammar was idiosyncratic. He had joined the American army because he believed he could quickly make money, connections, and a future in its vast overblown and richly financed infrastructure. After dealing with the Soviet police state in which he had reached maturity nothing scared Max who believed he could achieve anything he set his mind on, and today he wanted a child to send home to his barren American wife.

Max's unconventional and eccentric uniform was his impression of how an American military man should dress, included a well worn, large black Stetson cowboy hat, a leather flying jacket he wore in all weathers, the finest black leather boots, and army issue handguns with his own customised pearl handles in his belt. He entered Basra's one Christian orphanage.

The interpreter, Abbas who was also the priest's general assistant, summoned the boys from the classroom where they were making necklaces with coloured beads.

Although a young man, Abbas looked old before his time. Swarthy, his face appeared to permanently have a growth of a couple days' stubble. He was always sweating, even when it was cold, had bad breath and a limp, and, as the ever observant Mo had noticed, one eye that didn't appear to work. Ehud his friend, sensing that this man could be trouble, had instructed Mo to always talk to the eye that did work, out of courtesy, and to not look at the dead eye, and never to mention it.

"Allah," Said Mo, "Forbids mocking the afflicted."

Ehud nodded with great solemnity. "I have noted he is also a very ugly man, but I'm honour bound not to mention it."

Mo agreed. "Not good at all, especially in an interpreter who must deal with strangers, who must find his stinky breath, wonky eye and unshaven face very difficult to talk with.

Allah the merciful must be very happy that such afflictions are never mentioned."

Abbas brought them down the corridor of the dilapidated building, and paused when they got near the door. He bent down so that he and the boys were about the same height, and he talked to them with his good right eye close to their faces. The boys tried their best only to look at his good eye, and to ignore his gargoyle-like face and his extremely bad breath, Abbas was blissfully unaware that the boys were suppressing their laughter.

"This is an American that Abbas is introducing you to,"

He explained, "The most extremely biggest very important person. Remember what Abbas tells you, your name Mo, is now Moses. Moses is your name. You are no longer

Mohammed. Now you are Moses for Abbas. You understand, Moses?"

Mo pretended not to understand.

"My name is Moses?"

Abbas sighed, aware that the boy was toying with him, but insistent that this was not to be left to chance.

"This is too important for you to play being silly, you understand Abbas? Your name is Moses."

He held up his hand as if to smack the small boy, as he said this to Mo, who nodded.

"Moses was always your name, people call you Mo. You can remember this for Abbas, yes, Mo?"

Mo nodded again.

"So, Abbas asks of you your name, what it is?"

At that moment, Mohammed became Mo, for the first time he was serious.

"My name is Moses."

Abbas smiled.

"Excellent. Remember it is Mo that people call you, OK, Mo?"

The older man turned to Ehud,

"You also?"

He turned to Ehud who also nodded,

"If you want to live in America, in a big house, you will be brothers, and Moses was always Mo and will always be Mo, OK? You understand, nothing else must you say, never, if you want to live there in palace, you will have to live like your friend, as his brother, as one of two Jewish boy. Yes, you understand what Abbas tells you?

This way you will grow up both to be lovely fat American boys."

Mo managed to keep a straight face. "Where is he from, sir, this important person?"

The older man stood up to his full height. "Are you stupid? America. He comes from America. He is a special type of soldier."

He stopped for a moment, and taking that opportunity, Ehud asked his question.

"What kind of American soldier, what part of America, it is such a big country sir?"

Abbas rubbed his forefinger and thumb together, in the age-old sign for money.

"We have found you a rich Jew soldier, not like you poor Jewish Basra always has here, no good waste of time poor Jewish, how is it our Jewish is all poor and a waste of time without pot to piss in? This Jewish he comes from a place called New York State, and you will smile at everything Mister New York says, and we will all nod our heads, is this clear?"

The boys looked to one another, not sure how to react, but before they could say anything, Abbas raised his hand as if to strike them. "Is clear?"

Both boys nodded eagerly. "Yes sir, clear!" They chorused then followed Abbas down the long corridor, past the torn, old furniture and fly-blown posters of the old Iraqi regime, extolling the virtues of Saddam Hussein, now on the run.

In the bare grey interview room, they were confronted by a huge American soldier who spoke differently to all the Americans they had ever seen on their town's streets or on the television.

"Them boys are bigger than you said mister supervisor. Don't we got something a size or two smaller?"

Max struggled to make his English sensible, unaware that the fact he'd learned it from cheap crime novels and bad American cowboy movies and television cop shows made him sound like an old gangster.

Mo and Ehud smiled and nodded, unaware of what the giant was saying to the interpreter Abbas, who responded in English to the big man.

"Abbas is assuring you that apart from these two lovely boys, all available adoption Jewish babies is not available no more. This two piss poor selection is all we can show. The others is already in America or similar other countries, Major Roman.

There is only this two cute, very cute, lovely Jewish boys in whole of Iraq, and we is very lucky that they is very good-looking, top of class in school, already no mess makers and helps plenty around house!"

"We can buy a shiksa Russian maid from the old country. We want good boys who will make my Mrs. Roman happy," Max said in his odd colloquial English.

"They're very dark for Jewish boys."

He studied their handsome but small, swarthy faces.

Abbas had also noticed the major skin colour difference between the American and the boys but had an answer ready for him. He had no way of knowing that the big

American Jew was in fact half-accursed Russian.

"They are Sephardim."

The American held up his big hand.

"Me also, I'm half Spanish Jewish heritage myself. My mother, may she rest in peace, her people they come from Turkey to marry my daddy, a good Jewish man from the eastern part of Europe, so I know from this, but still, these boys, they could both pass for Arabs."

He said this to the Arab man as if looking like an Arab was undesirable, but what he really meant was that he wanted his children to look a bit like him and his wife. At

least the one called Ehud promised to grow up and be a big guy like Max, even if he was a bit too dark. The other one, well, as they said, he and Nancy would have an heir and a spare.

Abdul nodded, thinking this was a bonus for these boys, both of whom he thought very handsome, handsome enough to cause them trouble if they were to stay in the orphanage.

Max looked at the two boys with what he thought passed as a friendly smile, but his smile never reached his cold eyes. Like children everywhere, they sensed when an adult might be dangerous underneath a carefully-constructed edifice. Both boys were unnerved when he opened his mouth and gestured for them to do the same, but they smilingly obliged. He held both their small jaws and looked deep into their mouth, inspecting their teeth, like the itinerant horse dealer his father had once been. He nodded and grunted.

"Good strong teeth. Clean them up and have them ready for me after lunch."
The boys looked at one another in discomfort and then to Abbas who smiled at Max.

"And the major remembers the very special private arrangement with the 'umble Abbas?"

"You have proper kosher papers, the official papers, so that I can take them home legal as nice present for Mrs. Roman?"

He turned to the boys and showed them a photograph of his wife, Nancy,

"This lady will be your new mom, she's very thrilled you come soon."

The boys smiled, and Mo reached out for the picture, which Max gave the boy to look at, Mo thought she looked friendly and this time his smile was genuine, he missed having a mother.

Abbas opened a transparent plastic folder and withdrew a slew of documents in Arabic;

"Abbas has every paper, all in an order that is very good !"

The major's two big weaknesses, which he saw as strengths, was an inability to recognise anyone else's point of view, and a liking for way too much after shave, he used a bottle of the stuff every week, and it was cheap and smelled strangely feminine. Although the agency handling adoptions in Basra were never to be sure of the paperwork surrounding the two young boys, Max had preferred to hear the version of events he liked best. Although he could have soon ascertained that these boys were not brothers, he took the view that if that's what they wanted, then that's what they would be. After all, there was no proof to the contrary, was there? All the records in that part of Basra had been destroyed and no one much cared about these two poor orphans in any event.

Max smiled and thought it oddly appropriate that the little Arab interpreter didn't appear to mind dealing with the Jewish man when discussing money. Max produced the largest wad of cash that the orphan's custodian had ever seen and handed it to the interpreter.

The wily man couldn't believe his luck, and didn't know whether to bow or count the cash. He did both simultaneously, unaware he was doing so.

Max didn't tell the Arab that the money he had been given came courtesy of the United States government. It was earmarked for a totally different purpose, being a small part of the first fifty million dollars in bribe and pay-off money courtesy of the Central Intelligence Agency targeted to pay off some of the more pliable terrorist groups in the Basra region. Who would know that Max Roman had diverted a minute portion for personal use? Max's job did not involve the writing of receipts.

"Get all my papers ready, then Abbas gets other half when we pick them boys up, like we agreed, all right?"

He tapped the revolver on his hip to emphasise the point.

"Very good, Abbas very happy," he replied, taking the cash and smiling.

"Come on boys, is shower time, everyone very, very happy!"

He followed the confused boys as Abbas led them from the interview room after that strange first meeting, neither of them dreaming that the fate of the entire world was set to change because of the series of events they had unleashed that day.

The boys were confused by what had happened, but excited about the idea of going to America, the land of baseball and Disney, where all the movie stars and Big Macs came from. Ehud looked forward to their new life despite being repulsed by the big, smelly American. Mo was hopeful that their new home would be warm and comfortable and that their new mother would look after them well.

Chapter Three

Poughkeepsie, Duchess County, New York State, U.S.A.
7 August 2006

Once in America the boys fast became Eddie and Mo. Their former identities of Ehud and Mo had been adapted to suit their new American lives. Soon even they began to forget their roots as they did their best to fit in with the society around them. Like all kids, they wanted to be as much like the other kids as soon as they could.

The boys were given no alternative but to fit in with the views of their tough, dominating adopted father, Max Roman, a man known not to humour idiots or tolerate inadequacy of any kind in anyone.

When the boys had time alone they talked about the strange man, who they found very odd but were too intimidated to ever ask him, or anyone else, anything about his past, unless he occasionally told them some nuggets of information about curious, cold snowy lands in a place called 'Europe' where he'd apparently come from.

To the boys, Max seemed like two different men; one, the quiet man at home, almost silent, never smiling, but always plotting and planning how to get what he wanted. The other Max was the public figure, always charming and gregarious, a joke teller, and a man with his meaty arm around the shoulder of the world. He seemed like a man always in motion, never still, always about to leave or arrive but never in the moment unless it was a deal or a monetary pleasure to be devoured.

Instinctively, the boys knew his public good humour was just a façade, but they learned never say this to anyone for fear of his private revenge. He could, without warning or provocation, slap the boys around the head and knock them to the floor, as if was swatting a troublesome fly. His rage, when it came, was like a volcano erupting – the best way to survive was simply to run for cover since Max would hurt anyone who got in his way if he lost his temper. When he was angry no one was safe around him, and when he was quiet, a wise person would carefully watch for signs of his terrible anger.

Eddie developed a nervous squint and would automatically duck whenever he saw Max become angry, scared he would receive another painful slap on his face. Mo tried to defend his new brother, readily defiant and brave even against overwhelming odds. He would find a way to stand between Max and Eddie, but it didn't work because their new father would simply pick up Mo, slap him and then slap Eddie.

Max never thought long about any decision, movement or word he uttered, not seeming to care whether they were appropriate or would embarrass the boys, or anyone else.

When he had returned from the war in Iraq he had somehow, almost miraculously, been transformed into a very rich man. No one knew how. In fact he had systematically stolen cash from the vast sums he had been entrusted with by his real masters, the CIA, to bribe the various warring factions. There were no receipts. No one else was aware of the reason for this sudden and inexplicable increase in his wealth, but the war had also given Max indispensable trade and business connections around the world.

Nancy, like everyone else, happily and simply accepted Max's story about the adoption of the two handsome little boys. Nancy was a quiet and mousy and Max had satisfied her one wish and that had been to be a mother. She adored her man for making this possible, however he had achieved this miracle of bringing these two handsome young boys to her. Her life was governed by her need to please her domineering husband. In return, he felt obliged to give her toys, because everything Max did in life was some kind of bargain, and in fact, anything that would make her smile made him feel he had provided for her adequately. It was a strange system of give and take, but it worked for the odd pair. Nancy had been unable to have children, or so she thought. In fact it would have astonished both her and Max to discover it was his sperm that were infertile; lazy swimmers. Like everything else in their life, Max found a way to fix the problem.

He spent every moment working, scheming and struggling to become an even bigger success in the way he understood what that meant. His power grew inexorably, but without him realizing or caring that the small degree of warmth and humanity he had once possessed was diminishing in direct inverse proportion. His obsession and preoccupations were work and money. He saw everything as a battle to be won or lost – there could be no happiness unless he won and everyone else had lost, and knew it.

Mo and Eddie found that they could communicate with Nancy, and that she could smooth any bumps out in their volatile relationship with Max., a man who never explained nor apologised for any of his actions.

Both boys quickly became fluent in English. It was almost as if they had been born in America. Their clothes, mannerisms and tastes in food, television and opinions all adapted to their new friends in school and their seductive new environment. Like kids everywhere they wanted to fit in with the other kids around them.

Within a year it was hard to believe the boys had ever lived overseas. Their past lives in Iraq faded into a sepia background hardly ever discussed, even in private between themselves. The only thing they had failed to adapt to was the weather; in the winter the snow was at first a wonderful plaything, but they soon realised they were too cold for months without end during the winter, and they missed the sun beating on their backs that they were accustomed to in their hotter homeland.

Time had passed pleasantly enough as the boys had begun their journey toward adulthood in their comfortable home, and now they vacationed in Israel. Everyone who knew them called them "the boys", no longer Eddie and Mo, and they had become fused in everyone's minds. So close, and such great brothers and friends that they were almost like twins. Like all brothers there was the odd argument, but nothing serious except for a growing jealousy that Eddie felt. He watched but said nothing as Mo became, in his opinion, the favourite of Nancy. He wasn't able to show his maturing emotions so easily as Mo, who was more tactile and charismatic. It gnawed at his core like poison, growing more virulent and putrid as time passed.

Chapter Four

Las Vegas
4th July 2007

I wanted you to see where you boys will celebrate your bar mitzvah," intoned Max seriously to his boys, as they stood next to the full-scale replica of the centre of the old city of Jerusalem that was a temporary feature outside the Caesar's Palace hotel on the Vegas strip. "This is the most special place in the world for us Jews, this old wall, which was once part of the Second Temple, and you two will say your coming of age prayers right here. So make sure you keep up your studies or you'll shame us all. Understood?" Max instructed the boys, who stood looking up into the glaring sun, craning their necks and squinting to see the top of Jerusalem's huge ancient Wailing Wall, that had once buttressed the Jewish Kingdom's sacred second Temple. Neither boy thought it odd that their father had brought them to the other side of America to see this replica when he could have taken them to see the real thing, but he had thought of that.

"I didn't want to spoil it for you when it is time for your bar mitzvah, so you don't get to see the real thing until it's time."

"And you get to gamble," said Nancy

"And I have some business to do. What's so terrible? The boys get a vacation, and you get to shop."

He answered "And you always have some business to do."

"Why do they call it the Wailing Wall?"

Mo asked as Nancy sighed and fanned herself in the oppressive desert heat.

"Because when the Temple was destroyed by the Romans the people all wailed, I guess."

Responded Eddie. "What does wail mean, crying?"

Mo asked. Eddie looked over at him to test whether he was being sarcastic and decided he wasn't.

"Yeah, crying and shouting and lamenting, that's all wailing; they were all wailing."

"Shut up and pray!" Max said quietly, but with threat in his voice,

"Or you'll both be wailing!"

They looked at their mom and dad and although the other people looking at the replica were chatting and taking pictures they had no alternative but to do as they were told.

The boys bowed their heads and appeared to be praying. Other vacationers stared at the two boys and whispered to each other, embarrassed for them. Three teenage girls began to giggle as they watched the boys pray, despite their parents hushing them.

"Don't they know it's only a model?"

The oldest of the girls asked her parents. Max moved toward them and their family immediately backed away, "Show some respect or do you want trouble?"

He said it loud enough for them to hear.

"No offence man," the father of the girls quickly responded as he led his group away.

Eddie was hugely embarrassed, he hated it when Max behaved like that. In any event he was beginning to doubt that there was a God, so he never really prayed, unless to pretend to placate his adopted bullying father. Mo was a total contrast as he still believed, without question, in Allah. He still secretly practiced as a good Muslim, although his memory of the Koran and what he should do was now becoming very sketchy. So he discreetly prayed to his version of God without allowing anyone but Eddie know he was doing this.

The boys were now inquisitive, rumbustious twelve-year-olds and in almost everything important that they did, they appeared to act like non-identical twins. Although it had happened only a few years before, the boys barely remembered their former lives. It wasn't of much consequence and the only thing that they ever talked about in private of that time were their mothers, who they both still missed and in quiet moments talked with as if they were still with them. But like most young people, they had an amazing gift of being able to move forward, to block out unpleasant memories, to close out conscious thought about things too difficult to deal with.

Perhaps it was the sheer intensity of Eddie and the huge exuberance of Mo, because these were the names by which they had become known.

The boys were no longer Mo and Ehud to anyone, not even each other. If you asked the boys, they barely remembered anything about their early, much harder lives, so different from their current affluent existence with the big American officer and his small, quiet wife, Nancy.

The boys thought that their adoptive parents were very strange. Max and

Nancy, the big white man and woman, with their pasty skin, his strange combed over thin hair always covered by some kind of hat, and her hair, that strange blonde colour, some kind of awful wig, she called it a sheitel. Orthodox Jewish married women such as Nancy believed that their religion obliged them to wear so that no man other than their husband should see something so intimate as the actual hair on her head; another man would realise that this woman was not available, was a married lady, if she wore the sheital. Nancy's wig was like the colour of wheat in the fields they saw in the countryside surrounding their big new house.

Max only ever allowed a carefully measured time allocation for the boys. He loved and cared for them, especially, despite himself, the rough and tumble and quick wit of Mo. The boy was always laughing, telling jokes, playing sport, and rapidly adapting like a chameleon, he seemed capable of blending in any background, quickly becoming an all-American boy. Eddie still retained something of the middle-eastern streets.

Max wouldn't have been able to identify the emotion he felt when either boy achieved some positive outcome from their school or sports, but if he had, he would have known some pride. The boys showed all the signs of growing into fine young men, despite, not because of, their adoptive father's strange ideas on parenting.

Max never understood that Eddie had become progressively more compulsive about his friend Mo. In fact he had, without realizing it, become infatuated with him. Eddie thought he loved Mo in the same way he had always loved him, but in fact he really did love his friend, and didn't know what to do with that love. When Mo had been playing with him and had fallen over, he cut his face and when Eddie tried to stroke his friend's cheek, Mo had instinctively pulled away. There were progressively more awkward, untidy moments like this between them.

Eddie had never heard the word homosexual, and wouldn't have known what it might mean to him if he had, whereas Mo was starting to notice the girls at school as a few of them began to blossom prematurely into young women. Eddie had no such enthusiasm, and in reality he only had eyes for Mo, whom he adored. Something instinctive told him to be cautious about exposing these feelings, but they were bubbling to the surface with increasing regularity and Eddie didn't know what to do, or how to deal with them.

Max was blissfully unaware of these problems and still thought he had all the answers. He considered Eddie was far too serious and self-confident for a little boy, and Max also didn't care for the fact that, despite his insensitivity, he could feel the boy judging him as if he was lacking in some sense. Max would catch the boy watching him, almost weighing him up. Max could never bring himself to ask the boy what he thought of his adoptive father, but he sometimes saw the handsome, almost beautiful, boy stare at Max as he set about his studies. He knew that Eddie was different in some way, but he was unaware of what set him apart.

If Max had known how Eddie had fallen in love with his adopted brother, he would have killed him.

The Vegas vacation, passed by without further incident, the unusual family going largely unnoticed in the unique city.

In Basra the Rent Collector was very pleased with his table, so pleased that he found himself quietly humming a little song when he caressed its smooth dark surface. Sometimes he thought of the lovely Amina wistfully as he did so, taken so wickedly by the American bombs, but then he reminded himself that she was now at the right hand of Allah and that made it easier. He was proud that it was now his family who enjoyed their food on the fine old piece of furniture. He shared the stories about it being Noah's Table and everyone was suitably impressed. His wife liked the table but insisted that the only problem with it were the odd scratches and blemishes it had picked up over its long life. The marks on it annoyed her although he thought it gave the old table character, an echo of a long-forgotten past. She told her husband to get it fixed up or it would have to go and he would have to buy her a brand-new table.

"I'm not a rich man."

He pleaded, but she was insistent, perhaps, he thought, we should smooth it down and make it perfect, like new again. When I have time I shall see to it.

Chapter Five

Manhattan, New York, U.S.A.
Christmas 2007

The Roman family prospered. They now lived in one of the best houses in town. They were very rich. Their mansion had once belonged to one of the Rockefeller family who still owned huge financial interests. Max felt he'd arrived because he owned this prestigious property.

As the boys approached their teenage years they competed with progressively more ferocity. Both seemed compelled to come first, to beat everyone else was wonderful to each of them, but to beat their best friend, their brother, was the ultimate. Because they were different to the other kids in their elite school and amongst their friends, they had unconsciously reached the decision that they would get their revenge in first. Once both boys realised that they could beat everyone else then came the really big battles, against each other.

Sometimes it seemed to Mo that he caught Eddie letting him win some of their contests, and he never understood why this should happen. The reason never occurred to Mo, and, in truth, Eddie didn't consciously understand his own motivation either.

Each boy was the leader of their own set of friends, quite distinct and separate. Mo had become a jock, more naturally athletic, he was being considered for their High School's Varsity Football team as the quarter back while Eddie was in the school's chess and debating teams. Eddie loved to play with the school computers, and at home he took Max's old PC apart and almost managed to put it back together. He took a beating for failing to do so, but it didn't deter him. He wanted to know how everything worked, fascinated by taking every mechanism apart and then putting it back together to see if he could make it operate more effectively.

The scale or nature of the boys' victory didn't matter; a game of checkers, a swim meet, or a math test, each always wanted to win. Eddie had a wonderful and prodigious memory, he remembered the lyrics and tune of every song he heard, every fact embedded itself in his large creative mind.

Mo was becoming wirier and lean, his endurance almost remarkable, whereas Eddie was blossoming into a bigger, but less natural athlete. Their schoolteachers predicted a creative future for Mo, and something like science or engineering for Eddie. They each found it very difficult to accept that their brother was better than them at anything, but were genuinely proud of the achievement of the other.

Nancy was proud of their every success. She never tired of celebrating each of their many small triumphs. She no longer worried about being ignored by her husband as he went about conquering the world and flirting with every desirable woman he met, she had her boys. They were more precious to her because these two wonderful boys had come to her when she had thought that she was destined never to have any children of her own, and here they were; beautiful boys, loving and kind, both of whom were appreciative of everything she did and unfailingly affectionate to her. It was as if she lived for their hugs, their kisses every time they left or entered their home. Their spontaneous smiles were meat and drink to this woman whose emotional life had been desiccated by years of pained neglect and lack of warmth. No one had hugged Nancy except for Max, and that was only when he had wanted her sexually. Even then, his warmth had been fleeting and even those occasions were becoming very rare.

The boys wanted nothing more than her hugs, warmth and emotional security in return for their deep love. They were now her sons, and all three of them knew it. Max had been aware of this and if he had bothered to evaluate his stunted emotional response, he would have understood he was jealous, but he considered such a response to be a weakness and therefore he suppressed it, burying these moments deep within, never allowing anyone to see inside the high wall surrounding his soul.

Chapter Six

Jerusalem
9th.August 2008

Max and his family stood by the Western Wall of the once-great Second Temple in the golden city of Jerusalem, destroyed two millennia ago by the Romans. This time it was the real thing and they were attending the boys' bar mitzvah – they were thirteen – and instead of a big party back home, the boys agreed to this form of celebration which had been Max's long held dream.

They were about to be welcomed into the Jewish faith as men, like every generation of Jewish boys, ready to take part in religious services as an equal to any other man. Once they had read their portion of the law they were deemed capable of being counted in a minyan, the minimum number of ten men necessary to pray together in public.

Mo didn't appear to have any inhibition about his bar mitzvah, to him this was the natural result of his now assuming the identity of a Jewish boy, and in his mind there was nothing wrong with this. He remained indifferent to race or religion, not thinking any group better or worse.

On the other hand, Eddie was never religious and, in fact, was becoming more distanced from the rituals of his religion. He was uncomfortable praying, he found it silly and awkward, and was near to formulating his resistance to his being required to participate. The contradiction to this was his adoration for all things Israeli. A silly smile crossed his face as he dreamed of being a soldier in a commando unit, or a pilot defending the skies above. He looked with awe at the young men and women with their clear sense of purpose in this vibrant little country and contrasted it with his vacuous friends back home.

Ironically, it was Mo who encouraged his friend and pseudo brother to carry through his studies so that he would be able to read and sing his portion of law in

Classical ancient Hebrew, as the service required. However, each session stuck in Eddie's throat and he found the constant prodding by Mo and their adoptive father infuriating. He tried to argue with them but was unable to convince them.

Eventually Max had sat down with both his sons after yet another ineffective rehearsal. "So tell me my impetuous boy, Eddie, what's your problem with this?"

Eddie thought for a moment; this was his chance to make his family listen. He thought that Mo was sneering at him having sided with their father against him. "I just don't believe in this stuff, so why should I have to pretend to pray to something I don't believe is there?"

Max turned his attention to Mo, "Is that what you think Mo?"

Mo shook his head and smiled. "I think Eddie is being dumb. We should be happy to do our bar mitzvah."

Max considered the situation with due seriousness, remembering the same arguments he had once had with his own father many years earlier.

"I'll tell you something my father once said to me. Imagine there's a golden thread, leading from one of the generations of our families to another, for thousands of years, and now that golden thread has gone to you and is now in your hand. Are you going to be the person after one hundred generations of Jewish men to drop that golden thread?"

Eddie hadn't considered this, and it did make him think. Something about it had touched a chord deep within him, and he looked hard at Mo who almost telepathically understood what his friend was considering and it terrified him.

"So the truth and customs are as important as the religion?" Eddie asked Max.

"Of course," he replied. "The truth is that we are nothing if we don't know where we come from, what we are, that's what forms us."

"I tell you what, if there's a God somewhere let him strike me down, here and now!" Eddie shouted at Max.

Before the man could raise his hand to strike the boy it was Nancy who stepped between them. She turned to face Eddie, "Apologise to your father, right now!"

Eddie understood she was trying to protect him, but he remained defiant, he was at that age.

"Cool it Eddie, you're out of order!" Mo tried to keep the peace.

Eddie turned to him. "Do you think dad's right?"

He asked, emphasizing the word, Dad, to an almost ridiculous extent. Mo was, for a dreadful moment, unable to think of the words that would stop Eddie, and his defiant spirit got the better of him.

"Dad is right. We are all the bits of our heritage, whether we like it or not."

Max turned from one boy to the other, not sure what the subtext of this conversation was, but knowing there was one.

"Does someone want to tell me what the secret is? You know what it's very important that we are truthful with each other."

Both Nancy and Max thought this was some boyish prank, but were interested enough to clear it up. Eddie didn't turn his stare from his friend.

"Do you want to tell Dad our secret, the truth is very important?" Mo shook his head, "You mustn't do this, please."

Eddie was to regret the next moments for the rest of his life. "He's not Jewish, so why should he have his bar mitzvah?"

There was a moment of silence, frozen, no movement, as they looked at one another, understanding that they had opened Pandora's Box but not yet aware of what horrors might fly into their lives.

"What did you say?"

Asked Nancy, as the two young boys stared at each other. Mo ignored her for a moment and turned to his adoptive father, intuitively understanding that now his only hope lay with honesty.

"It's the truth. I'm not really Jewish."

Max shook his head. Nancy said

"You shouldn't say such things, even as a joke. You're young, you just mean you don't feel Jewish. Your father felt the same way when he was a boy in the old country. That's what you're trying to tell us?"

Eddie now began to realise the enormity of his revelation. "Let's stop this. I was only kidding, I was just mad."

Max towered over everyone, demanding of Mo, "What does he mean?"

Mo started to cry with the pressure, unable to deal with his father's intense stare. "I'm an Arab."

Nancy gasped as if she had been punched in the stomach;, all the air seemed to go out of her. She sank to her knees, instantly understanding the enormity of the moment. Max turned to Eddie.

"Get your stuff, we're going home." Eddie was scared of the way his father addressed him and the manner in which he ignored Mo, who also stood up and tugged at Max's sleeve, but he appeared not to notice.

"What should I do, Dad?" He asked Max who turned to Mo, tears in his eyes, but icy. "You're nearly home right here, aren't you? We'll make arrangements for you, but you're never coming back to our house. You're a cuckoo in our nest, so it's over. I'll say goodbye, Mo. I wish you good luck. You're a good boy really, but you're an Arab, and you lied to me, it's what you people do, so it's over. You stay here and I'll have someone come and pick you up. I'll make arrangements for you to have some money."

Nancy tried to step between Mo and her husband, trying to calm the situation, but even as she did so tears streamed down her face because she despaired of changing Max's mind.

"But he's a good boy, he's our son, we love him, give him a chance, maybe we could arrange a proper conversion, he's a good boy!"

He simply ignored her begging and turned away, Mo was horrified.

"We both lied, both Eddie and me, but we're real brothers. We've been together all our lives. Whatever we did I'm sorry. I don't want your money, I want to come home with you and our mom. We're family, we all love each other, you can't walk away from your family."

Max shook his head,

"You don't have no home and no family. You'll make a new life; this one is over. You don't belong to this family and we don't belong to you. It's oil and water, it don't mix. You're an Arab so I'll tell them to find you a nice Arab family." He turned his back and walked away, ignoring Mo's forlorn attempt to hold his arm, which he easily shrugged away. Mo turned to Eddie who couldn't look back into his friend's eyes.

"I'm sorry," he said.

"I never meant for this to happen. I didn't realise. Dad will get over it, you know how he is."

But Mo understood that whatever had been their lives before, was now over, permanently. He felt the colour drain from his face as he realised that he wasn't wanted in his own home, that he'd been dispossessed.

Nancy looked deep into Eddie's eyes and then, without warning, slapped her remaining son across his face as hard as she could. Eddie stifled a sob. Max watched as Mo spat at Eddie's feet.

"I hope you don't die until I can kill you; you just destroyed my life."

Max called back to Eddie and Nancy, "Get here now!"

They dutifully joined him, he paused for a moment and then he also slapped Eddie with tremendous force around his face. "That's for lying to me, and that's for informing on your friend. Don't ever do that again."

What he didn't add was his thought, and that's for taking away my favourite son! Eddie tried not to cry but couldn't hold back the tears as he followed his parents away from the big wall, and turned back one last time to Mo, who was now left standing alone in the crowd.

"What's going to happen to Mo?" he shouted, but no one would answer.

Unseen by them Mo was soon ushered away by Max's driver, and within moments it was if he had nothing to do with the Roman family. Mo didn't have time to think about his fate. One day he was part of a family, however dysfunctional and strange, they were his, and then they weren't. Now Eddie and the rest of the family had simply left his life.

He hadn't been left destitute; Max had been as good as his word about money. Mo had been reclassified as Arab and Muslim, and handed over to the men who ran the East Jerusalem Islamic Orphanage and Vocational School for Boys.

He didn't realise that this apparently bad luck couldn't have happened on a better day. He was dropped off at the big stone building in the Old City that had largely been funded by an Italian Corporation's Emergency fund for a number of years, and that money was running out as the Italian economy went into free fall. Although it was near to the Al Aqsa school, it wasn't as well funded or stable, and Mo saw that this was obvious as he was shown to a bed in a dormitory of other boys about his own age. They swarmed around him as if he was an American movie star, but he could see they were envious of his western designer clothes and curious about how he got to be in this situation. Before he could acclimatise, the old man who ran the place came into the room. He was called 'The Old Man' by all the boys and reminded Mo of Yoda, the Jedi Master in the Star Wars movies. The Old Man was small, wizened and seemingly able to float a few inches over the ground. Everyone in the orphanage appeared to love the man. They ran around him as he threw boiled sweets to the boys who happily grabbed them. Mo simply sat on his bed as the Old Man quietly ordered everyone to sit.

"Today we have much to thank Allah the most merciful for. Today we say welcome to Mo, who joins our little family."

The other boys turned to face Mo and smiled in his direction. He felt uncomfortable, he fidgeted, his fingers secretly scratching at his trouser leg, but he enjoyed the boisterous and spontaneous friendliness of the other boys. The Old Man held up his arms for their attention and they all fell quiet.

"And also today we are going to have some very important visitors to our home. These people will be joining us for prayers and then will have dinner with us.

Everyone will be on their best behaviour. It's very important, OK?"

Mo raised his arm to request a word with the Old Man, who smiled and nodded. "Sir, will I be living here with you now?"

The Old Man smiled benignly, and he nodded.

"Yes, Allah has placed you in my care and I shall be honoured to do his bidding."

Mo was relieved to be in the care of such a kind- hearted person. At last, he knew where he belonged, and that felt good. When the Old Man left the communal area, the other boys crowded around Mo asking him a million questions about how come he, clearly an American, was now amongst them. Mo soon managed to convince them that he was actually an Arab boy, just like them. He didn't tell them how he came to be there precisely, or that he had been living as a Jew. Instinctively he know they wouldn't have understood or approved. Like the rest of his new roommates, he was also interested in who their visitors would be. As the sun set, one of the other boys called out to the rest to look out of the windows from their second level dormitory.

Outside, several black four-wheel drive vehicles, with darkened windows pulled up. From the first and last vehicles, two teams of armed men in smart suits jumped out and formed a protective guard around the occupants of the middle car, a beautiful Rolls Royce limousine, like the one Mo had seen the Queen of England in on the TV. A man in snowy white robes swept from the car. He was tall and erect, his face hawk-like and severe. Accompanying him was a female. It was hard to know any more about her since she was hidden by her all enveloping robes, even her face was covered. They entered the orphanage. Mo turned to his new friends.

"Who are they?"

The general consensus of the boys was that they were very rich and very powerful to arrive like that. Even the Israelis treated these particular Arabs with the correct amount of respect. A voice rang out and the boys started to make their way noisily out of the room. One of them called to Mo, "That's the call for prayers, follow me."

The people living in the orphanage congregated in the small mosque, together with the mysterious visitors. Naturally, everyone was soon praying but Mo fidgeted, not knowing what to do to pray in the true way, it had been such a long time. The Old Man included Mo into his prayers, aware that the boy was unable to understand the ritual.

"It has been a long time for you, yes?" he asked Mo, knowing that the boy had been away from his roots for as long as he could remember. The boy was comforted as the Old Man put him at ease showing him quietly and kindly what to do, letting the boy mimic his actions without letting anyone else be aware of this.

Mo looked up and saw that the tall man in the white robes was also smiling at him, not in a bad way, but supportively. The man nodded, and Mo felt even more as if he belonged. He didn't notice the girl watching him from a small section of the room, which had clearly been roped off just for her. She had also heard the boy's story and felt sorry for him. It was her idea to make her father break away for an hour or two from his talks with the Israelis instead of simply writing a cheque for a donation to the orphanage. Her father was the King of Saudi Arabia and he could never say no to his daughter, Princess Leila Aziz.

Afterwards, the same room was converted for use as the canteen and again, everyone was on their best behaviour, aware that their guests were both important and powerful, but not who they were. While they were eating, Mo was aware that he was being watched by the new arrivals, but not why he was the centre of attention. As the meal ended, the Old Man signaled to Mo to follow him as he led their important guests out of the room.

They filed into the Old Man's chaotic study where he forlornly tried to clear some space among the piles of books and papers covering every space. The King sent his men out of the room and started to help the Old Man.

"Here, let me make a space, sir."

Following his example, the Princess and Mo began to make piles of books on the floor, creating room on the chairs opposite the desk. The two youngsters found themselves glancing at one another. Mo was nervous but the Princess smiled behind her face veil, seeing but not being seen. The young man would have blushed had he seen her frank appraisal.

Soon there was enough space for the King and his daughter on two chairs, leaving Mo to stand to their side, all facing the Old Man who was seated on his rickety chair on the other side of his desk, barely able to see over the still-overflowing papers.

"We are great admirers of your work here,"

the King began. The Old Man smiled in appreciation, not expecting this visit and unsure of what came next, "and we would like to show the appreciation of our people in the proper manner." He clicked his fingers and one of his security men, a giant, gave the King an envelope, which he passed to the Old Man. He was unsure of the protocol, so although he desperately wanted to open the envelope he held it nervously in his hands. The King noticed his discomfort and nodded. The Old Man opened the envelope and gasped as he extracted the note and cashiers check, he quickly read the figure to confirm it was for ten million American dollars.

The Old Man almost couldn't breathe but was so excited that he jumped up from his chair to embrace the King, but before he could reach the monarch, he was restrained from doing so by his sense of protocol. He subsided back into his seat and turned to Mo who found that he was smiling in happiness for the Old Man, but who was still unsure why he had been summoned into the room to witness the King's generosity.

"Of course," said the King, "we would expect to work closely with you wisely and judiciously through the years to come."

The Old Man nodded vigorously, but the King held up his hand, stopping him from interrupting. "To mark the start of this relationship, and to celebrate the occasion we believe we can show the way forward and make a difference by our personally adopting a child, to try and change the course of his life, as Islam teaches us, we should give a loving home and family to an orphaned or displaced child. Are we not encouraged, as believers, to nurture the children who are without parents and to treat them as our children, while always making sure that the child knows their true biological origins."

The Old Man was still nodding in agreement when it dawned on him that the King was looking at Mo while he was talking.

"The orphan taken into the care of your Majesty would be fortunate beyond comparison."

The King continued, as if he hadn't been interrupted,

"What do you know of the Kingdom of Saudi Arabia, young man?"

Mo nodded but he had only a vague idea who this man was and where he came from. Back home in the middle of America there was very little talk of exotic countries far overseas unless America was fighting them or playing against them at sport. He didn't want to look stupid as everyone was looking at him in dismay, not able to believe that any Arab boy could not know of the richest Kingdom in the entire world.

"I could describe it to you, Mo, but better still we can show it to you. How would you like to be part of our family, you will have your own man to look after you in every way?"

He indicated his own bodyguard,

"This is Nafti."

The silent, ageless giant looked at the boy and inclined his head, a slight smile on his face. Mo liked the big guard instinctively but found he couldn't speak in the presence of the King, this clearly powerful man made him so nervous. He didn't have the maturity to realise that what scared him was that the King reminded him of Max Roman, not in looks or background but in the way he imposed himself on everyone around him. He dominated his environment, used to instant obedience without his autocratic decisions ever being questioned. He wanted to say no, he wanted to stay with the Old Man who he instinctively trusted. He looked at the Old Man who was watching the exchange of the orphan and the King, with his smile beginning to fade, sensing that the enormous donation he had just received might be in jeopardy.

The King was unused to the surly responses of a growing boy.

"You don't understand me, Mo. We are offering you a place in our family, for the rest of your life you will be a Prince of the royal house of Saud. Equal to all other Princes. Don't you want that?"

Mo felt trapped; he looked to the Old Man for guidance. The man reminded him of Poppa Sam, who was like his own lost grandfather. The idea of being a Prince meant very little to the boy. He had never met a Prince nor anyone royal until today, and he didn't understand what it meant, except that it would take him away from the first people he had felt comfortable with in many years.

"Do you want to talk with the young man for a few moments?"

The King asked the Old Man, more as a command than a request.

"We will remain here while you convince the young fellow where his best interests lay."

The Old Man led Mo out of the room where the Princess had been hugely enjoying this exchange, hidden behind her veil. She had anticipated the boy would jump at the opportunity to be the public flagship for her father's generosity. For sheer mischief, she richly enjoyed it when anyone defied her father. It mystified her that the boy appeared hesitant.

Outside the room the Old Man turned to face Mo. He smiled at the boy who was doing his best not to cry and hating his lack of self-control as he felt his eyes water involuntarily.

"Why do you want me to go away, I like it here, why doesn't anyone want to keep me?"

The Old Man hugged the boy and felt the tension in his young shoulders.

"SShh, it's OK, it's going to be OK. I promise you this is for the best. How many boys are lucky enough to be wanted for a son by a King, to become a real Prince?"

The tension drained from Mo and he cried for the first time in years, all the pent up frustrations and hurt and humiliation came out of him. The Old Man simply embraced him, waiting patiently for the emotion to abate, and eventually it did. The Old Man straightened his arms slightly and took half a step back, looking into the eyes of Mo, and extracting a large white cotton handkerchief from his pocket that he handed the boy.

"That's it, dry your eyes and have a good blow,"

He instructed Mo, who did as he was told.

"You're going to be a Prince, maybe one day you can even be a King. This isn't a punishment, you know, it's a fairy story, like Ali Baba and the Forty Thieves!"

Mo looked up at the Old Man quizzically.

"Who's that?"

The Old Man sighed.

"I can see you have been educated in the United States. You can probably build your own website but don't know the work of Dickens or Shakespeare or any of the classics."

The Old Man squeezed the boy's shoulders.

"But if you take advantage of your great good fortune, you will have every opportunity and the best of everything. This is a very easy choice, everything you ever dreamed of; riches, education and a wonderful home or a hot, crowded and insecure orphanage, what is there to even think about?"

The answer to Mo was obvious, here in the orphanage he felt loved for the first time since he was a small boy and this was worth more than all the riches and palaces in the world, but he instinctively understood that the Old Man needed him to say yes for the sake of the orphanage and all the other boys.

"Is it what you want, for me to go with the King?"

The Old Man nodded, feeling sad that he had to think of the greater good for the greater number and that this wasn't what the boy wanted to hear.

"Yes, it is honestly for the best. Go with the King, become a Prince, and you will never have to be afraid again. Other people will be afraid of you instead."

And so it was that a street urchin from the bombed ruins of Basra, Iraq having been a Jewish "Prince", became an actual Prince of the royal house of Saudi Arabia, known officially as Prince Mohammed Aziz, but to his close friends he was still Mo.

The years rushed by and Mo almost forgot his humble beginnings and the time he was an American Jewish boy as if it were all a series of wild, bad dreams. He was expertly taught the necessary subject for the Common Entrance Exam by British tutors in the royal palaces of the desert so that he could take up the offer of a place at the best school in England, Eton, the same school where his adoptive father, the King had studied.

He was looked after by Nafti; his ever present servant. It was the giant guardian who quietly made sure that any scrapes the Prince got into were never too dangerous. He regularly reported the boy's progress to the King who was satisfied with his choice of the exceptional boy from the orphanage. The story of Mo reminded him of the tale of Moses being found and brought up in the palace of the Pharaoh; although this time in reverse!

No one thought it odd that Mo was sometimes violently abusive to servants or anyone that questioned his authority with the sole exception of Nafti who could still terrify him with just an admonishing look. The King made sure Mo was given leeway, believing these were just the wild ways to be expected of a boy growing to manhood.

When the King decided it was time Nafti supplied a compliant and beautiful prostitute from the Ukraine so that the Prince could enjoy reaching manhood. The Prince very severely beat her for no reason other than his sadistic pleasure. She was paid two hundred and fifty thousand dollars in cash delivered with a complimentary Hermes Crocodile handbag, itself worth tens of thousands, and received the necessary plastic surgery at a luxury Swiss clinic. But these gifts couldn't compensate for the terrible physical and psychological abuse the Prince had inflicted on the woman.

There were whispers among the Royal Court and the Diplomats of the Government that there might be charges against the Prince if he ever behaved that way again. It was considered wise by the King's advisors that he should dispatch his beloved but wayward adopted son overseas more permanently so that, if he got into any mischief it wouldn't be on their own doorstep.

Mo was duly sent for an interview at Oxford University. He had turned down an opportunity to attend Harvard. Declining their offer purely on the basis that it was American and he now hated everything from that country. He was unaware the King had arranged multi million dollar donations to those colleges in both countries so that either would have been more than happy to accept the Prince as a very honoured student. After all, the King reasoned, this was an investment in the future running of his country, since he had decided that Mohammed was the young man with the passion, drive and commitment to lead Saudi Arabia forward when his own time at the helm was over.

The fact was that the Prince had never been interested in being an academic high flyer at Eton. He wasn't worried since he already knew what he wanted to do and was certain he could do it. But no one else knew of his secret plans. Both the King and the Prince would have been very surprised by the other's plans.

His time at university as a student Mo wasn't academically spectacular, but he made friends with the future leaders of the world, and that was his aim. He raised his profile as a hell raiser that hadn't proved difficult being a young, rich and extraordinarily handsome man. Like many Arab royals, once they were out of sight of their homeland they earned their reputation for partying. Drink, drugs and women spiced up by fast cars and access to the best boats and planes. The only thing that kept the Prince from real trouble was the ever-present Nafti, always lurking in the shadows, making certain that the mess the Prince left behind was cleared up without too much fuss.

After just about managing to graduate Oxford Mo surprised the King when, instead of returning to Saudi Arabia, he asked permission to follow other members of his family into Britain's foremost military academy, Sandhurst. It remained one of the world's leading officer training schools and would be the perfect place, thought the King and his advisers, for the Prince to round out his education. After all, it had also been good enough for the leading members of the British Royal Family.

Here, for the first time, and to the surprise of all that knew him, Officer Cadet Mo excelled, both in tactics and strategic thinking; even armed and unarmed combat proved no obstacles and he appeared to know no fear. He enjoyed demonstrating to Nafti that he had found his element at last. But he would never dare push the big man too far as something told him that to do so would be foolish.

At his graduation, the Prince had pleasantly surprised his family and their advisers as he was placed just two positions from being the most outstanding officer cadet in his entire graduating class. Only Mo knew that this was at his own choosing, as he didn't want to be too highly profiled by coming out top. Those that knew him were shocked that he had stuck to his task so well and achieved such a prestigious result so superior to any academic result he had ever received previously.

The King and Princess Aziz attended the traditional passing out ceremony, both swelling with pride at the achievement of the Prince. At dinner that night, the King gently suggested that royal duties now awaited the Prince back home in Saudi Arabia, but he was surprised again when the Prince said that he now wanted to learn about policing in the U.K. The King was astonished at this turn of events.

"Why would you want to be a police officer?" he asked.

"When I am in possession of the best knowledge of both the army and the police, I shall be perfectly equipped to protect our Kingdom father."

The King took this at face value, because he never suspected that such knowledge could also be used against his beloved homeland.

Again the time passed quickly as the young Prince went seamlessly from military training, breezing through the graduate fast track programme for the high-flyer university graduates entering London's Metropolitan police force.

Mo opened up the video diary connection on his cellphone. He was clearly in his element with technology. He smiled as his fingers flew over the controls. He checked his reflection as the camera showed him his own image like a mirror that adored him. He smiled since he knew that was one of the reasons for his popularity, his smile. Bright white straight expensive teeth in a wide jaw, his eyes were described as the brightest in the blogosphere, chocolate brown and over large like those of a happy baby. Women found his eyes appealing, and Mo used every tool in his armory, such was his training and natural inclination.

"Hi Copper Cam followers, this is Mo, and I'm here outside the famous Hendon

Police Training College in a suburb of London in England."

He turned the camera around so his viewers shared a picture of the College that took up several city blocks of the quiet district of London's suburb, Mo turned the camera back to his own face as he jumped from his car and walked towards the studio.

"I'm the Arab American Brit who today qualifies top of his class as a policeman, and what do we say? Onwards and upwards!"

He posted the message via his iPhone knowing that his five thousand 'friends' on Facebook and twenty-five thousand followers on Twitter would be celebrating his meteoric progress. None of them would know that he had any other agenda.

Chapter Seven

Tel Aviv, Israel,
General Military Headquarters – 15th June 2020

The year 2020, what a great date, Max thought. Something resonates about that date. Was it that the twenty-twenty simplicity of it, or perhaps it was that it sounded important somehow, like something tremendous was bound to happen on such a date?

His mind wandered when he was not fully involved, and right now Max was not in the present. He was thinking about numbers, how much was a trillion, would he really be worth a trillion dollars if he was successful, what could he do with a trillion dollars, he already had six palatial houses on five continents, and three jets. They had names, but for Max they were simply a big one, a medium sized one and a small one for when the other two were too large for a small runway. There were also the four super yachts, each bigger than anyone else's. And that was important. Equipped with anti-missile defence shields, crews trained to sail them and defend him, and the last numbers he was thinking about were the measurements of the serious young woman in uniform that he was studying. He was calculating what it would take to get her into bed with him. Was it money, jewellery or something else that would get her naked with her long legs wrapped around him? There was always something.

Max was used to getting what he wanted. He shifted awkwardly in his chair, although comfortable for a normal sized person, it didn't meet the needs of this bear of a man who boasted he was two metres by two metres, with everything else in perfect proportion – big – or as his women who had enjoyed his horizontal company were more inclined to say, very heavy, like having a wardrobe on top of you with a draw out!

Max was now proud to be an honoured citizen of both the U.K. and the U.S.A. He had never lost his liking for hats to keep his big shaven head warm. Max Roman had become famous for wearing different hats for every occasion; it was his trademark. Today he was wearing his American navy captain's cap, the one with the gold braid, which perfectly fitted his state of mind.

What am I doing here? Max asked himself. Do I need this aggravation? He removed his spectacles and cleaned them on the small cloth he kept in his jacket pocket. It served two purposes: it gave him time to think, and it cleaned the glasses.

By dint of his extraordinary energy, drive, native wit, cunning, luck and chutzpah, Roman had become super rich, with his stocks and shares and fast growing portfolio of other holdings. This huge wealth derived originally from his ability to exploit the de- nationalization of oil and gas in his original east European home territory in the 1990s and then he had re-invested constantly, firstly in the burgeoning property market of the newly- independent Baltic Republics then media on the Internet. His was the single biggest company in the new frontier. He liked to be first at whatever he did. He was the richest oligarch in the world, and proud of his political links with the world's leaders, including the Kremlin that had made this possible. When his Russian friends and associates had resumed practical control over their former Soviet Union colonies he had quickly made yet another fortune. Why would Russia's rulers stop such an efficient man from making his fortune ever larger when he did the same for them.

Max spotted business opportunities before anyone else. He was also very clever and brutally honest about everyone and everything, except about himself and the very select group he loved. If he had been, he would have known about and dealt with his women, who were his weakness, his indulgence and his folly.

One, a mistress called Orla bedded every man or woman who took her fancy. Max appeared blind to her infidelity. In reality he knew what she did; pretending not to because he was terrified of losing this woman he was so crazy about. In truth he wanted to kill her for not being afraid of him like almost every woman. Instead he found her sexuality with others stimulating and erotic. This small whiplash of a woman born to peasant Russian stock could dominate him when no one else could. Max had a discreet member of his staff pay the tawdry but lengthy parade of Orla's young sexual partners to disappear. The truth was Max hopelessly loved Orla.

Roman's other major attribute was that he had the ear of the leadership of the U.S.A. He was especially close with the new-elected American President Pollaci, the first woman to be elected to lead that country. Max had worked tirelessly for the President in his own electronic universe. The brilliant but flawed colossus of new media had done a powerful and ultimately successful job to get the woman elected. It was these powerful connections, more than Max's eminence in the smaller Jewish community that made him the world's ultimate power broker. The general public might know that less than ten percent of America's population is Jewish, and less than half that number actually voted for the incoming Democrat President Pollaci. What almost none of them understood was the fact that nearly three quarters of all funding for the Democrats came from their Jewish donors, and number one in that group was Max. This made him one of the most powerful figures in American politics without his even casting a vote.

Sitting opposite Max was General Mordecai Zvi, Chief of the Israel Defence Forces, who thought Max Roman was a disaster for the image of all Jewish people. In the general's opinion, the huge American was typical of the kind of self-made man who bought his way into positions of power and responsibility in the global Jewish community. The general was convinced that such men believed that their money and power entitled them to dictate the policies of their large and generous charities and organizations. Worse still for the general, these rich Americans were determined to dictate policy in Israel.

Zvi had assumed a special responsibility for relations with the Jewish community overseas; the Diaspora; so he tried hard to be diplomatic and deal with such men, but it didn't mean he had to like this aspect of his job.

The general was lean and angular, this hardness accentuated by his tightly cut crisp beige uniform, his grey hair closely shaved, the antithesis of the American. Zvi, despite being in his mid fifties, still did two ten kilometre runs a day wherever he was, and this was preceded and followed by a full hour workout and full contact practice of Israel's own self defence system of hand-to-hand combat, known as krav maga, of which he was an expert.

The general addressed his guest with familiarity but no warmth. Zvi didn't care for the nature of their relationship and didn't like the man.

"We have information, Max, incontrovertible evidence, that there is going to be another very large scale attack on civilian Jewish targets on America's West Coast.

We believe your own private Jewish Security Service has done a remarkable job looking after all the buildings and events in the community. But we're anticipating a military style terrorist attack."

He paused, "We have a long-standing understanding, entered into before you took over the JSS. When there was this kind of threat, we would quietly assume responsibility for security of our entire community in the U.S.A."

"The community in the U.S.A. is American and Jewish, not Israeli." Max responded.

"A figure of speech." said the General.

Roman didn't like the Israeli summer heat, despite the ultra efficient air conditioning of the Tel Aviv military headquarters. In fact everything about Israel annoyed him. It was a place that was way too anarchic for his taste. He was used to getting his way either because he was usually the cleverest and richest man in the room, or simply because his reputation and economic power generated such fear. All the Israelis seemed to think they were as clever as him and none of them showed fear, or even respect. The general looked at the oligarch and found him wanting. He was an old school Zionist, a man with left of centre politics and an example of modern muscular Judaism that Max simply didn't understand.

Max peered at the general then smiled towards his nubile young aide, Captain

Naomi Kaplan. He looked at the trim and serious girl and thought he'd like to screw her. She returned his look frankly, feisty and unimpressed by him, unaware how he liked a challenge like her. Why don't they make Jewish girls like that in Los Angeles, he thought? Maybe he'd send her some diamond earrings later, see how she reacted.

Roman patted his forehead dry with his large handkerchief, sighed, then continued to talk.

"So you're saying we need to import some of your shtarkers, the hard men. I ain't so sure we want those kind of trigger happy guys wandering around our synagogues and events. We have our own people and they're polite, well dressed and perfectly competent."

"You don't have a need for such men in America, Max. We have them, already in place. They know what they're doing. Leave the heavy lifting to our boys and girls."

He smiled, but the message was clear to the big man, who understood that the skinny brown-skinned, tough military guy was patronizing him, and he didn't like it.

"With money," he said, "I buy muscle."

The general held his stare and then nodded.

"But brains and motivation can be lacking. Trust me, Max. We know how to deal with these situations. It's what we do. There is a clear and present danger. We have a great deal of practice. We're in a tough neighbourhood and we don't panic. This is for real. We have intelligence that Islamic State plus Al Queda and various other Jihadist groups are going to attempt some joint spectaculars together; outside the Middle East. Will you listen to us?"

Max nodded.

"I'm listening. Tell me what you want me to do."

Chapter Eight

Los Angeles, U.S.A.
16th June 2020

Eddie exercised with all his normal vigor at five in the morning, before first light, as he always did. Two hours of stretches, yoga, and then the brutally tough work out regime that had become a part of his life since he was eighteen and officially served with the Israel Defence Force's Paratroopers.

His extraordinary gifts had been quickly recognised and he was quietly encouraged to apply to another unit, the even more elite Sayeret Matkal. It had been brutal at first. He had thought he was tough and then found out what being tough really means.

Once admitted to the unit, he had undergone an additional eighteen months of training. He became expert with small arms, martial arts, navigation, camouflage, reconnaissance and other skills required for survival behind enemy lines. He had completed the seventy-five mile Red Beret March in the final four days with his fellow graduates to win their coveted red beret. Four months of basic infantry drill, held in the Paratroopers base; it was all part of the regular Paratroopers basic preparation routine.

There had been a further two months advanced infantry training, within the unit. Three weeks parachuting course in the IDF Parachuting School. Five weeks counter-terror course in the IDF Counter-Terror Warfare School, followed by more inner-unit CT training.

The rest of the training was dedicated to long-range reconnaissance patrol training, and especially to navigation, which is of vast importance in the unit. While most of the orienteering exercises were undertaken in pairs for safety reasons, as in every other unit in the IDF, Sayeret Matkal is one of the handful of IDF units which conducts long-range solo navigation exercises. Although Sayeret Matkal has its own insignia, it is also one of the few units in the IDF whose soldiers are not allowed to wear it in public due to its classified nature. Ironically, this lack of insignia often leads to Sayeret Matkal operators being recognised as such, as the fact that Matkal troopers don't wear insignia is well-known.

Eddie looked in the mirror and shaved with great care, making certain he left a light bristle on his pronounced jaw line. He noticed that there was the faintest of lines beginning to appear at the corner of his eyes, but he winked at his own reflection, satisfied that the face his lovers always seemed to adore, still had the magic. His eyes were powder blue, and maybe it was the contrast with his coal black hair that made him stand out in any crowd. By any standards, he was a very handsome man, and some found his face beautiful. He carefully put on the blue latex gloves and looked around to see if everything was OK. It seemed to be. Everything was quiet, and here that passed for OK, at least no one was complaining, and that was just great. Eddie didn't like it when they complained, not that he cared too much, but it was dealing with the managers when they had to field the complaints and laid it all on him, like it was his fault. As if!

He was never right. Sure that, all his life, except for the one thing, it was always him getting it wrong. In that one thing no one argued, he was the best.

That one thing he could really do, he had to keep to himself. He had to keep his expertise secret except for the few people who needed to know, and they kept this information to themselves, until they needed Eddie.

Today he was baking little biscuits, rolling the dough with the two raw eggs, into the flour, then cutting out into smaller pieces with a cookie cutter. He measured some sweet chocolate into some of the little balls that he then flattened and then made a small indentation with the back of his fork, placing a small amount of raspberry jam into the space he had created. Then he put these small masterpieces onto large baking trays, which already had oven paper on them. He took them to the large, already-heated ovens and put the tray inside, closing it with a satisfying clunk.

The elderly men and women, who had been vacantly watching him, smiled when he smiled, understanding only that there would soon be some warm tasty cookies to eat. They didn't know that Eddie's real name was Ehud, and although he was good at baking, he had other, less obvious gifts.

A little later Eddie drove his hybrid car in the already-busy very early morning traffic up the Wilshire corridor, passing the High-Rise buildings between Westwood and Beverly Hills in the seemingly perpetual Los Angeles sunshine. He was talking on the telephone that was connected by Bluetooth into his car. As he pulled up at the traffic lights crossing Beverly Glenn, a middle-aged woman in a Bentley next to him tooted her horn. As he turned, she smiled. He glanced and then resumed his attention to the road in front of him as the lights turned green, and sped off, ignoring the woman's open invitation.

Another woman, this one much younger, also blonde, in her late twenties, was watching from the window of her office overlooking the street. She smiled, then donned her robes. She was known as Rabbi Dorothy, and was one of five ordained rabbis in the bustling, huge Temple Beth Shalom. The Temple served one of the richest and most generous Jewish communities in the world. Rabbi Dorothy's origins were in the pleasant and ancient Israeli town, Safed. Set high in the north, it had been a sedate but stylish artistic community for over a hundred years, and home to mystics, rabbis and scholars for millennia before that. Her mother was a painter who had met and strangely fallen in love with a Yeshiva student. After they were married, her mother had continued with her art, opening a small gallery in the town. Her father had become an expert on comparative religion. The Rabbi had not been religious at all, but had been selected by others to follow this path when she was undergoing her military service.

Eddie drove into the big white building's car park after satisfying the two armed and serious looking Latino security officers that he should be allowed entry. The building took up an entire city block and was seven floors above ground and five below. Eddie drove down the wide ramps and parked his car, taking the elevator back up three flights to the Temple halls.

He entered the smallest of the three halls, which could still hold more than four hundred people in its rich star-shaped interior. This morning there were no more than sixty men and women preparing for the early morning-prayer rituals. Eddie stood bathed in the lights of the huge stained glass window that depicted the exodus of the children of Israel from their bondage as slaves in Egypt that encircled the room.

From a small cloth bag, Eddie extracted two black leather boxes with straps. One he placed on his arm, the other he carefully removed from a plastic case. With his right hand, he put the box onto his left arm, rolled up his sleeve so that the box was in direct contact with his arm. He put his arm through the loop formed by the knotted strap. He then placed the black box up on his biceps, just below the halfway point between the shoulder and the elbow, right across from his heart.

Eddie said, "Baruch Atta Ado-nay, Elo-hainu Melech Ha'olam, Ashair Kidishanu, B'mitzvotav, V'tzivanu L'haniach Tefillin."

Rabbi Dorothy was alone in the row of seats in front of Eddie, praying quietly as she also wore the Tefillin.

"Good morning, Ehud," she said to him in Hebrew, blending it with the sounds of the prayers all around the hall.

"Good morning, Rabbi," he responded, in the same way.

He tightened the strap around his arm, mindful that the knot stayed in direct contact with the box.

"You are ready for your assignment?"

She asked, as ever unsure how seriously this rich young man was about his duty and his ancient homeland. He felt her discomfort, and he was sensitive to it, but didn't allow this to show. He had trained himself to toughen up.

"What is it?" He continued to wrap: two more times over the strap-socket of the black box and around the biceps, then seven times around his arm and once around the palm of his hand, leaving the remainder of the strap loose. She duplicated these actions. He shook his head as he watched her go though these rituals.

"Why do you want to be a man so bad?" he asked, both of them knowing that in orthodox Jewish rituals women were forbidden from these practices. She ignored the question and continued, "You will soon get an opportunity for a business trip overseas."

He frowned.

"I get many such opportunities."

Next, he removed the head of the Tefillin from its plastic case. The box went on to his head, just above his forehead, centreed in the middle of his head above the point right between his eyes. The shaped knot left to rest on the base of his skull.

"This trip is to Saudi Arabia."

This made him smile, because Eddie liked danger, it excited him, and there were few more dangerous challenges for a Mossad agent than penetrating the royal Kingdom of Saudi Arabia.

"You will return to your offices in London, and we shall arrange the rest from there."

"What about my mission here?"

"History, forget it. We want you in London. When we're ready we'll call."

She responded.

His attention reverted to his hand. Wrapping the remainder of the strap three times around his middle finger: once around the base, then once just above the first joint, then one more time around the base. He had some strap left over, that he wrapped around his palm, tucking in the tail end.

He cleared his throat, and then, in a clear, bell like voice intoned the words that all practicing Jews say the world over,

"Hear, O Israel, the Lord is our God, the Lord is One.

Blessed be the name of the glory of His Kingdom forever and ever.

You shall love the Lord your God with all your heart, with all your soul and with all your might. And these words, which I command, you today shall be on your heart. You shall teach them thoroughly to your children, and you shall speak of them when you sit in your house and when you walk on the road, when you lie down and when you rise up. You shall bind them as a sign upon your arm, and they shall be for a reminder between your eyes. And you shall write them upon the doorposts of your house and upon your gates."

He turned to say yes to the young Rabbi but while his attention had been on the Almighty, she had vanished.

In Basra the years had been kind to the Rent Collector and his family. It had grown so much that when they all came to eat together they filled almost every place around the big old table. If you kept your head down the religious lunatics, both the Sunni and the Shia and the maniacs from Iran left you alone and you could make a living again.

It was a blessing, he thought, this table, since we had it here we had only good luck, and tomorrow I shall pay that useless son-in-law of mine to sand it down, and make it like new. That way he would make both his nagging wife and moody daughter leave him alone for a day or two. Neither he nor anyone else in the family had bothered to look at or examine any of the many scratches in the table but soon that wouldn't matter as they would all be gone and his wife would shut up.

Chapter Nine

Cave Complex, Tora Bora Mountains, Afghanistan
& Tel Aviv, Israel Military HQ.
17th June 2020

Bahir Ali San, Supreme Caliph of the Islamic State finished his first morning prayers at exactly the same time as normal, at 04.30; he liked to keep military hours. He wanted to control this part of his life because there wasn't much else in his environment that he could control. He had been running from the Imperialist forces of Britain and the Great Satan, the Americans, for more than half a decade now. He grunted as he rose to his considerable height, and every centimetre of him ached, probably from the damp, or was it his increasing age? He looked around the cave he called home and considered the day ahead. His plans were epic in scale and by the end of today, he would have changed the world forever.

At the other end of the same continent, the Israeli air force chief of staff, Moshe Barak continued his summing up for the new Prime Minister, Shira Lipna. She smiled as she listened to Moshe. She remembered their days in university together, when they were just two youngsters making their way. There had been that one particular evening, but neither of them ever mentioned it, especially not now, when things were as serious as they could ever be for Eretz Israel.

"Let's cut to the chase Moshe,"

She interrupted her general.

"Can we do it?"

He paused before answering, knowing the dramatic moment would find its way into the memoirs of several of the war cabinet members sitting round the table, if they survived.

"Yes."

He paused again.

"We can take out the Iranian nuclear capacity. We could have done it years ago, should have done it years ago, when it was easier. The majority of our assets, our boys, might not make it home."

"You will do your best to suppress their air defence systems. For every victory there is a price. We had to wait, just like our predecessors. We needed proof of the threat

Moshe you know that, or we'd be like the British and Americans in Iraq when they couldn't find the weapons of mass destruction, we'd be cast as the villains forever.

So this time my question is can we take out all of it, their whole nuclear threat in one hit without causing an accident between us and our American friends?" she asked.

"I can't guarantee that, but we will put the Iranians back at least five to ten years, to when they were just in development,"

He responded and the Prime Minister nodded, but he continued,

"But our intelligence is that they will retaliate. They have moved long-range missiles into position and there's no guarantee we can take them all out with our Iron Dome 2 and our counter measures when they launch."

The Prime Minister looked back at her general, and then at the men and women around the long oblong table. This was her first major decision since she had got rid of the old man, the indecisive one; she called him in public, whereas in private she called him the relic.

She reflected on the military man telling her that Israel's own anti-missile missile system, although brilliant was not one hundred per cent reliable. She had read the statistics and knew that it would knock out about ninety to ninety-five per cent of the incoming missiles, but if the remaining five to ten per cent of the incoming missiles were tipped with nuclear or chemical or biological weapons, it would deal a hammer blow to her small country and its densely populated belly around Jerusalem and Tel Aviv.

Remembering that her main selling point was her willingness to make the tough decisions, she addressed the members of her innermost emergency team.

"I want your votes recorded on this one. Everyone in favour of our launching an attack on all the Iranian nuclear facilities with immediate effect, please vote yes."

Shimon Mendel, the dignified Minister for Housing interrupted.

"Prime Minister, surely, as custodians for the security of all our people, we must consider what the Iranian response will be, before we act impulsively."

The Prime Minister turned to him, her temper only visible from the rising colour on her cheeks. "This impulse has been more than a decade in the making. The question now is what do we do, not what the enemy might do afterwards. That's another matter, already being dealt with by our air defence people, in collaboration with others. The question before this group remains the same; do we launch Operation Big Strike now?"

Mendel looked around the room for support but didn't see much sympathy for his more cautious approach. A bead of perspiration rolled down his podgy cheek. He had never adjusted to the heat in Israel, after spending the first twenty years of his life as a dissident in his native Russia.

"It sounds like the decision has already been made. How close are we from launching Operation Big Strike?"

The Prime Minister sighed theatrically and then allowed one of her famous megawatt smiles to fill the room. She knew that she could win most men over with that smile, and a glance at her great cleavage, which had already distracted the leaders of many a country, when she had so ably represented Israel as its Minister for Foreign Affairs.

"One hundred and twelve of our aircraft are in the air right now, and could be over the target in less than two hours. Now your votes – your country has already been waiting for far too long for us to protect them."

In the White House the telephone rang discreetly on President Pollaci's desk. She was also new in her office. She had won the election against all the odds. She'd beaten the great black hope, Senator Al Shipton Junior, at the last hurdle. All had seemed lost, but her rival's colourful past had finally caught up with him. He was no Obama, and didn't have the old man's sure-footed political common sense.

Who would have guessed that Shipton, the man who had everything: great wife, family, career also had a string of indiscreet lovers. The President chuckled as she recalled how the great Shipton election bandwagon had come to a sudden, juddering halt and collapsed just days before voting on election day. She had crushed him at the ballot boxes like the bed- hopping bug she knew him to be.

The President picked up the telephone and smiled as the connection was made and she heard the voice on the other end. She found the Israeli Prime Minister very attractive, now if only they were both single, gay and she was thirty or so years younger.

"Hi there, Madam Prime Minister. How'd it go?"

At the other end of the line, the Prime Minister also smiled. She really liked the President, and wondered if she would ever learn that it was her American Jewish supporters, directed by Max Roman, who, through third parties, had discreetly paid Shipton's ex lovers six-figure sums to tell their stories. They knew that she would be a better friend to Israel than the inconsistent man.

"Our birds are flying Madam President. Now it's over to you. We throw, you catch like we agreed."

The Prime Minister spoke so quietly the President had to concentrate to hear her. When she did, she nodded.

"We keep our word, rest assured, Madam Prime Minister, just like I promised, woman-to-woman, leader of one great democracy to another."

The elected leader of the State of Israel said,

"Thank you, shalom"

And replaced the receiver. She looked at her weary and worried colleagues. Even the men she didn't trust or like, she respected. Her lawyer's training had taught her to be objective, and she realised the time was right to say something memorable to match the moment.

For a few moments, her mind was blank but then she remembered her history.

"You are all aware that the President of Iran and other leaders of that country have repeatedly threatened to wipe Israel from the face of the earth as if it never existed. This President is the same man who repeated the denial of his predecessor that there was ever a Holocaust. Despite these mad denials, the last time our people ignored the entire world. Now we are not refugees hiding in cellars and attics, but a proud nation, with the means to defend ourselves. We want peace, but like Gold Meir, said, 'not the peace of the graveyard'. As Chaim Herzog memorably said to the United Nations, 'For us, the Jewish people, this is but a passing episode in a rich and event filled history. We put our trust in Providence, in our faith and our beliefs, in our time hallowed tradition, in our striving for social advance and human values, and in our people wherever they may be'. Gentlemen, l'chaim, to life!"

Her colleagues were silent for a long moment, and then led by Mendel they started to thump the cabinet table with their fists, shouting and cheering, "To life!"

Chapter Ten

HM Prison Doncaster ('Doncaster Hard'), Doncaster, England
17th June 2020

In Britain, Special Measures prisoner Richard Sullivan was furtively passed a note from the heavily-bearded young Asian man in the exercise yard. Sullivan glanced at it and nodded so that the other man would realise it had been understood.

Thanks be to Allah, the all merciful. His time had come. Sullivan silently exulted. He couldn't help smile.

The guard watching over the inmates in the new maximum-security jail, Her Majesty's Prison, Doncaster 1, or 'Doncaster Hard' as the inmates named it, called to his fellow office on the gantry.

"Here take a look at that. Laughing Boy actually smiled."

The other guard looked down at Richard Sullivan and whistled through his teeth. "By heck, someone must have died to make that sod smile."

Sullivan felt their stares and looked up, his face having resumed its proper and serious Muslim countenance. He was relieved to know the day of decision was finally upon the world and that all his allies were in place, with their leader ready to lead the jihad across the infidel world in the great and good name of Allah, the all merciful.

It was an insufferably hot in Basra and Farouk, son-in-law of the Rent Collector wiped the sweat from his brow. How could anyone expect him to work in this heat? He decided to have another bottle of Coke from the refrigerator before he took to planing the table surface and re-varnishing it. He could still charge the old rich bastard for a whole days work even if he did it in less than half the time. Just so long as the bloody old table had no marks on it they'd be happy and he'd get paid.

Chapter Eleven

Iran
18th June 2020

T he first of Israel's seventy five F15s and F16s arrowed across the vast desert joined by twenty five F351 Lightning 11 Eagles at less than four-hundred feet through the darkness, unseen by all but a lonely shepherd and his small flock of hardy sheep.

The fast combat aircraft had swept over several Arab countries who had covertly given their blessing to this action. They were all more scared of a nuclear Iran with a lunatic at the helm than they were of Israel.

War makes strange bedfellows.

The engines of the fast jets were pushing the aircraft in excess of the speed of sound as they entered Iranian airspace. It wouldn't be more than a few more minutes until they were over their targets. No interceptors or incoming missiles had yet been launched. The Israeli umbrella of air suppression aircraft circled high overhead, their electronic signals punching a black hole in the outdated air defence system. The Revolutionary Guard's leadership had assured the Islamic High Command the system would detect the long-anticipated air attack. They were wrong. The hated enemy, who they called the Imperialist Zionist entity, Israel, was about to deliver a hammer blow.

Other jets, these launched from the American aircraft carrier Nimitz, were nearing the western deserts of Iran and had already received the go signal to launch their bombs and cruise missiles at their targets. The advice given to the American President was that, under International Law they were allowed to take this action as the Iranians had breached their treaties. This was considered sufficient provocation. Patience had long since run out.

On the ground British Special Boat Squadron Special Forces with their American Navy Seal colleagues, painted their targets with their sophisticated laser guidance equipment. This meant that when the approaching warplanes unleashed their bombs they would all hit their targets.

Hovering above, unseen by anyone, were the tiny drone camera planes, looking for enemy threats. Slightly higher were the bigger drone craft, these armed with Typhoon missiles.

All the drones were being 'piloted' by British technicians based thousands of miles away in an air force base near Las Vegas. These technicians were skilled 'virtual' pilots. They sat in dark air-conditioned rooms, half a world away. They watched on giant screens the Iranian targets in real time as if they were in the craft. Observing the area below, guarding the backs of their colleagues on the ground.

Even higher than this, in the near reaches of space, the ever-watchful Israeli, American and British satellites observed everything from their geo-synchronous stationary orbits over the Iranian part of the earth's surface. Each of these systems had their own autonomous abilities but today they silently shared their information.

Young men and women in Nevada, Northwood and Tel Aviv all watched with intense concentration today. They knew that this was special. History was being written, and every action would be examined later.

It was at 05.30 GMT hours that the pilots heard the final confirmation command and unleashed the first of their weapons.

There was no turning back now.

The armada of fighter/bomber aircraft split into groups and flew toward their targets, the Russian-built light water reactor in Bushehr, the giant underground uranium plant in Natanz, and the two vast water facilities at Arak in which the Iranian scientists converted uranium dioxide into weapons grade plutonium.

The first time that the Iranian Military High Command in their control centre bunker in Tehran realised something was wrong was when the screens in the centre went blank. At the same instant their communication systems went down.

The backup transmission lines became operational, with barely a blink; this was a system of fibreoptic cable buried in indestructible conduits made of concrete far underground. It was invulnerable. That was why there were some very shocked faces in the bunker when that system only lasted a few seconds before it also became fizzled into indecipherable static on the screens. No one in the bunker had even the slightest knowledge or suspicion of the SAS teams who had successfully arranged this complete sabotage of all their communications after having been inserted across the border from Iraq three weeks before.

Iran's military leadership was blind and deaf!

The Shohab 3 missile system, with its twelve hundred-mile range was targeted onto Tel Aviv. These missiles were located in the Western desert. They were supposed to launch automatically whenever there was any such interference. But something jammed their launch command. It was as if a giant electronic hand had switched off all the command systems in the Iranian High Command.

This was being achieved by the American fleet of MC-130E Combat Talon I and EF-18G Growlers, an electronic warfare version of the F18, plus the super-specialised 'Wild Weasels', the nickname for aircraft of the United States Air Force tasked with the suppression of enemy air defences.

To add to the confusion of the Iranian Military Command, their entire computer controlled system linking all command and control elements rapidly unraveled.

The Iranians had never suspected that their German computer systems supplied so diligently and methodically maintained, had actually been designed by some very clever viral engineers in Israel. They had long planned for the day when they had to activate the computer virus and turn Iran's computer defences against the Iranians.

Despite the Herculean efforts of the best Iranian programmers and coders, they could do nothing to stop the Israeli super virus from eating their computer network within minutes, rendering the whole system useless.

Senior professional Iranian military men immediately understood they were under an extraordinarily well-organised coordinated attack. However their colleagues from the watching Islamic Revolutionary Guards refused to listen to their urgency. Instead the religious warriors waited for word from the Islamic High Council who they had been trained to accept as the only givers of the truth. No earth bound source of command could ever be trusted above those given divine inspiration.

The Revolutionary Guards other principle weakness was that these were men not used to reacting quickly to fast changing military situations. They were still being summoned to convene and discuss the political and religious implications of what was happening long after their air defences and computer systems were being torn to shreds.

Iran was now a country without any effective control and command, just as their enemies had planned.

The Israeli jets screamed to their targets and bombed the suspected nuclear sites with the enhanced bunker-busting bombs supplied just weeks earlier by America after years of delay. These hugely destructive weapons not only destroyed their hardened targets but everyone within them as they penetrated reinforced sites, and then sucked out the air, suffocating any survivors who hadn't already been blown to bits.

The supply of these super weapons had taken a special, top-secret dispensation from the American President. Her husband, Hank, was a twice-decorated, former U.S. navy pilot. He had urged her to release these weapons to the Israelis from the American stockpiles. He had agreed with the Pentagon's analysis that if the mission was to be a success, the scientific elite of Iran had to be decapitated while their existing nuclear capacity was demolished. The alternative would allow a repeat of the same problem. No one in the leadership of the Western allies could continue to tolerate an Iran armed with nuclear weapons they were prepared to use. This was a one time only opportunity to delete that possibility.

Madam President wasn't sure about the military commanders but she absolutely trusted her husband. She had given the green light.

The missiles, rockets and bombs wreaked their carnage with precision and devastation at each of the Iranian sites, even the ones that the Iranian High Revolutionary Council had been confident that no one had suspected.

Spies that Israel had planted many years before had done their job well.

After less than fifteen minutes, there was no remaining Iranian nuclear capacity and many of the scientists who had led the research and manufacture lay dead amongst the ruins.

As a bonus the Americans and Brits had taken out over one-third of the Iranian attack plane capability and almost all their advanced long-range rockets in the desert. The allies were not going to repeat the mistakes of their war with Iraq. This time they had known where the weapons of mass destruction were and had kept track of them throughout the long period of waiting before the attack.

The Israeli support Squadron Commander smiled at the reports coming in. He sat comfortably in his command plane, a converted Boeing 737, circling high above the air battlefield.

He communicated with the American and British command aircraft in their sectors. Satisfied, he transmitted via the Israeli communication satellite home to Tel Aviv.

"Hello, Madam Prime Minister. I am proud to report, mission accomplished."

In Tel Aviv, the men and women assembled in the Israeli command centre saw their leader's famous smile as she heard the reassuring message over her headphones. They held their collective breath, waiting for her affirmation. The Prime Minister cried and laughed simultaneously, then jumped in the air and shouted, "Yes!"

The rest of the men and women in the hardened bunker, normally so controlled and professional, leapt in excitement.

Arab leaders in the region who were discreetly kept informed by the Americans quietly celebrated this news, relieved that the Iranian threat to their own borders had been obliterated for the foreseeable future.

In Iran, twenty-five men and women were arrested, tortured into signing confessions of their complicity and summarily hanged after they were all found guilty of spying for Israel's intelligence service, the official Irna news agency reported.

They were all Iranian, and executed inside Tehran's Evin prison, according to judicial officials. This had been filmed and was conducted in accordance with such practice in the People's Republic of China and the United States of America. Espionage is punishable by death under Iranian law.

The Iranian Revolutionary Council alleged the group was in contact with the Israeli spy agency Mossad for several years, and had passed on information about Iran's military activities.

The group was arrested when trying to leave Iran with their families. It was reported that the Iranian-born prisoners had confessed that they had transferred information to Mossad about Iran's military activities, adding that each of the supposed traitors had "received between sixty and one hundred thousand dollars to give classified information to the Zionist regime".

They were accused of providing details about Iran's military bases, fighter jets, training flights, air crashes and missiles. It was not clear from the Irna report whether any of those executed was a government employee, or how they had obtained their information.

These "spies" allegedly met their contacts from Israeli Intelligence during trips to Turkey, Thailand and the Netherlands.

In 2008, an Iranian telecoms engineer, Ali Ashtari, had been hanged after being convicted of spying for Mossad. Tehran had a long history of routinely accusing Israel of conducting hostile activities against Iran, including espionage against its armed forces and nuclear programme. The truth was different. The group that the Iranian regime had executed had nothing to do with espionage for Israel. Instead, they were part of the Iranian opposition and their mass execution was just an excuse to get rid of them.

In increasingly hostile Turkey, the President, a short and irascible marionette like man called Kamal Celal, condemned violent protests, while seeking to detract attention away from his country's failing economy, saying the attack on Iran by Israel and her allies was "not acceptable", and vowed to punish rioters and the Zionists, who he compared to the Nazis. The country, secular since its modern founder, Attaturk, was teetering on the edge of a populist Islamic regime.

He said the demonstrations, which have been held mainly by graduates, would hit tourism and jobs. Many thousand of protesters took to the streets of Turkey on Monday to demand jobs and an end to corruption. Twenty-two protesters were shot dead during huge and violent clashes in the capital, Ankara.

"The use of violence in the streets by a minority of extremists against the interests of their country is not acceptable," President Celal repeated in a speech broadcast on Turkish television. He was turning into a more extreme version of his predecessor, President Erdogan who had died of a massive heart attack the previous year.

"It will have a negative impact on creating jobs. It will discourage investors and tourists, which will hit jobs. We believe the attack on Iran was provocative and an insult to the followers of Islam. We are recalling our ambassador from Israel and will consider future ties to that country."

According to the AP news agency, he added that the law would be "applied in all firmness and rigor" to punish anyone found to be instigating violence and disorder.

However, he also said that he would seek to find a solution to the problems of international relations, unemployment, and simultaneously to improve the standard of living.

Demonstrations were sparked by the mass suicide earlier that day of an entire class of university students in front of television cameras outside the Presidential palace. This soon went viral globally on YouTube and Facebook.

The students, average age nineteen, had congregated illegally within sight of the Presidential Palace. The protestors were members of the banned Islamic Brotherhood. Public protests were once rare in Turkey and dissent was routinely repressed. According to the Turkish League for the Defence of Human Rights, they doused themselves in gasoline then set themselves alight before the police could react.

"We will not show you this incident as we consider it too disturbing for our viewers," said the network television journalists.

The same day, in Paris, another group of young Islamic men and women, no one was later able to work out exactly how many, blew themselves up below the Eiffel Tower. Other young Muslims duplicated such protests across the world.

As if by some invisible signal the trouble started to escalate and spread still further. It began in Her Majesty's Prison, Doncaster in England's forbidding North. There were growing protests of extreme violence around the world by radicalised Muslim prisoners. Prison guards were attacked, some even beheaded.

So many prison buildings were set on fire that the emergency services were unable to cope and, as a result, the buildings were allowed to burn to the ground.

Other prisoners used the breakdown in law and order to attack the prison guards, settle scores with other inmates or attempt their own breakouts.

Law officers were rushed to the prisons in all the countries affected, which included the U.K., U.S.A., Germany, France, Germany, Sweden, Israel and Italy.

As the hours dragged by, just when it looked as though the situation was coming under control, the majority of men and women of the Islamic faith serving in the military and police forces of the world began to refuse orders, pitting them against their comrades. This made certain units of the forces susceptible to breakdown. The commanders had no alternative but to draft in reserves and pull out all Muslim men from their front line reaction forces in case they weren't loyal. This only increased the pressure on those remaining. It caused increasing tensions that fermented mistrust and paranoia.

The governments of the countries affected did their best to suppress this information from reaching their civilian populations, but it was too big a story to be handled using old- fashioned methods. It soon leaked and went viral when the news got to all forms of social media, with videos of the terrifying attacks on the guards at various prisons shown on YouTube before they were forced by the authorities to remove the horrifying footage.

The civilians of each country saw their police officers and prison guards being systematically butchered, and their revulsion caused an instant wave of unjustified reactionary violence against the local, almost universally innocent Muslim population, now spiraling out of control over the city streets of Europe and North America. The holy men of each religion prayed together for calm but their words of wisdom were largely ignored in a world gone mad.

Chapter Twelve

Trafalgar Square, London, England
20th June 2020

The huge crowd had been rapidly assembled in the evening's last light. They filed neatly into the square from the surrounding streets, under the close supervision of London's Metropolitan Police, with whom the route of the protest march had been decided just hours before. As agreed, the parliamentary section of London, including Whitehall, Downing Street and Parliament Square were strictly off limits to the giant gathering.

There were protesters of all political persuasion in their vast number. They chanted, "Stop the war, stop the war, stop the war!"

Endlessly, in a mighty rumble of noise. Although the group filled the square and all the surrounding area, no one knew just how big the protest was. Estimated figures varied, but everyone agreed, somewhere between one and two million people had rushed out on London's streets that night, with one voice, to stop the fighting in Iran before it spread to the rest of the Middle East, and maybe the world.

Most of the people attending didn't realise that they were a very strange set of bedfellows. The majority of those present were well intentioned, left of centre liberals, but also in the vast crowd were Fascists, Marxists, and most worrying for the forces of law and order, the hard boys and girls from the revolutionary Anarchists had infiltrated them. As ever, the black-clad Anarchists were looking for trouble. Police spotters specially trained to scan crowds knew that these were Anarchists because they followed the usual pattern of covering their faces with black scarves and their heads with helmets or hoods of the same colour, their clothes completing their ominous black uniform.

Police snatch squads readied themselves as the evidence of looming trouble became obvious when the anarchists started to chant, "Kill the pigs, kill the pigs!"

The police were using their "kettling" strategy of forcing the wilder, more dangerous sections of the crowd into smaller sub groups, and channeling them into side streets which the police then blocked at both ends, this effectively imprisoned the sub group in the open air until either the crowd had calmed down or for as long as the forces of law and order required or, if that didn't work, to arrest their leaders with snatch squads.

A burly police sergeant spotted the danger of fires being lit by some in the crowd and shouted an alert to his fellow officers over the megaphone he was carrying. "Get your bloody fluorescent jackets off now, they burn like fuck!" The policemen and women who heard him removed the easy-to-see yellow jackets understanding the danger. There were other colleagues who kept the jackets on, unaware of this additional threat. Some of the police officers readied their pepper sprays, checked their telescopic metal batons and removed or obscured their police identification numbers, aware that these numbers were one of the few reliable methods by which the crowd or the watching media could identify them later. If this riot were to spin out of control with the inevitable inquiries were to follow, it was against their standing orders, but who had the time for those endless inquiries?

It is a fallacy that the police in the UK are unarmed. There have long been armed units ready for emergencies and the years of terrorism, starting with the anarchists more than a century earlier had been confronted by the men in blue bearing guns. This need had grown during wars and more recently with the quasi military campaign against the IRA leading on to Islamist terror.

A group of several hundred protestors rushed the police officers guarding the front of the large iron gates protecting Whitehall, leading, several hundred yards away, to the home of democracy, the Houses of Parliament. The recently-installed high metal gates, huge new steel bollards and iron fence were massive new safety measures, which electronically rolled into place across the wide street to safeguard against just such circumstances. This would be their first test.

The thin blue line of one hundred and fifty policemen and women formed into a defensive perimeter exactly as they had been trained to do. Almost in unison, as the order rang out,

"Raise shields!"

From the office commanding, they lifted their large round transparent plastic shields, "Prepare to hold position."

They then flicked out their telescopic metal batons. A few feet behind them, behind the gates, another police unit, the armed response group, turned off the safety switches on their semi- automatic guns. They were discreetly hidden by their vehicles but anyone who saw them in their dark blue uniforms, their faces hidden by black face coverings would be rightly nervous of their paramilitary preparations.

"Steady, boys, steady!" shouted the police sergeant, making certain that none of his men opened fire.

The U.K.'s police armed response units are under the control of local police commanders, and are in no way used for, or by, politicians. The armed officers were present as a final resort, to protect the public and the politicians, whatever their politics. The country's leading police authority, London's Metropolitan Police Commissioner, had publicly declared that he would not tolerate any incursions into the mother of Parliaments after recent protests had become semi-permanent eyesores in London.

The protesters rushed the barriers, not deterred by the police, and seemingly out of nowhere a volley of flaming petrol bombs were thrown at the officers. Many of them, who hadn't heard or had ignored the warnings were still wearing the dangerous yellow jackets and these men and women were instantly engulfed in flames; they were like Roman candle fireworks, they screamed in agony and shock as they began to burn alive. Most of the invading crowd paused momentarily, shocked by the results of their actions, but the crazies whooped and hollered their delight and continued the charge, someone screamed,

"Burnt pork, burnt pork, burnt pork!"

Others joined the chant. Many of the unharmed police waded into them with equal violence, their anger revulsion and fear overwhelming their ingrained discipline. Now it was a pitched battle, every person at the barriers was fighting for their lives.

Some less extreme protestors tried to calm the situation but were overwhelmed by this shocking escalation of violence. The first police line tried to hold, to resist, but were soon overwhelmed by the ferocity of the attack, and the men in blue suffered vicious beatings as they fell before the crowd's fury. The reserves of police behind the gate looked to their officers to allow them to fire their weapons in order to disperse the raging mob and rescue their comrades, but their commanders knew that would escalate the situation still further and they hadn't received any order to turn the battle into a massacre by indiscriminately opening fire.

Senior police commanders observing the scene were quick to realise that their lines of defence were starting to crumble and that there were officers down and others' lives in real danger or already forfeit. They had to get their men and women away from the rampaging crowd who were attempting to snatch police hostages using tactics they had learned from the police.

Seeing the leaders of the mob charge start to climb the vast iron gates, the police commander, who had just received clearance to use deadly force as a last resort, barked out on his loudspeaker, "This is the Police Commander. You must immediately back off or we will open fire. This is an official police instruction you are to back off immediately or I will have no alternative but to order my officers to use deadly force!"

There was a momentary pause in the riot as his warning registered with the crowd, but now the crowd had become a mob, like a single-cell animal; feral, dangerous and ready to ignite at the slightest incident and that came when a young woman threw a long burning wooden pole at the Commander, forcing the senior police officer to pull back. The rioters sensed the uncertainty of the police, and didn't believe that they would open fire, so carried on climbing to the top of the railings ignoring the armed police officers as they aimed their weapons, each picking a target. The young woman who had thrown the pole at the Commander, screamed back to the rest of the mob,

"They aren't going to shoot at us!"

Another police officer, a long term Sergeant realizing how close this situation was to a total disaster screamed, "Get down NOW!"

But the young woman pulled up her loose T-shirt to expose her naked left breast, "Go on then, shoot me in the heart you cowards!"

The crowd roared and charged along the line, and as they came at the police, the officers fired a ragged volley of shots. The young woman and several others fell from the gates to the concrete below, while others were left hanging like dead fruit on a macabre tree.

There was a moment of stunned silence, but the blood lust of both sides; a mixture of raw fear and aggression was raised beyond reason. A policeman, inside the gates, seeing his colleagues were at risk of being killed by the vengeful mob, forgot his standing orders of keeping the gates locked shut in an emergency situation, pressed the electronic release button to try and rescue his colleagues who were trapped on the other side.

Instead of being able to get his fellow officers to safety, the rest of the hard men in the crowd raced to the small gap and fought a vicious hand-to-hand battle with the officers in order to get beyond the open gate, with thousands pushing forward against a few hundred trying to block them.

Now the hidden agenda of some of the anarchists and fundamentalists was exposed as they pulled machetes and long knives from concealment and stabbed, hacked and thrust at the police officers who were in the front line, unable to back away or do anything but fight for their lives. The people behind the front of the mob pushed and jostled forward, most of them not comprehending the terrible carnage happening in their name just a few yards ahead of them.

At about the same time, and aware of the situation and the escalation of the level of danger, the Commissioner for London's police contacted the COBRA Committee Liaison Secretary from his state of the art command centre.

"Patch me through to the Prime Minister. Code Red Alpha!"

"Putting you through, sir."

The woman recognised both the urgency in his voice and the recently-adopted code the Police Commissioner was using for the first time. Previously she had just heard it in exercises, but her training kicked in and so did that of the Prime

Minister's personal staff, who switched this call as an emergency.

Atrocities in the past had taught the British authorities that they had to be able to respond instantly if they were to contain civil emergencies. Every emergency had to be imagined and thought through, and every response by the Government pre-planned and packaged, ready for instant deployment with just minimal customization for particular circumstances. This situation had been gamed, simulated on computers and finally rehearsed using units of the SAS and their highly trained counterparts in the police. These were men and women who received refresher courses for all armed contingencies every six weeks within their normal workload. Seconds later the U.K.'s Prime Minister, James Ostler, came on the phone.

"Yes, Will?"

The Police Commissioner, Sir William B. Kouric, framed his next sentence carefully. "I believe we need to move to national Security Condition Red, sir. Do I have your permission to act accordingly?"

The Prime Minister thought for a moment, aware that this would mean the gloves would come off once he gave the go ahead. "Give me a quick situation report, Will."

The most senior police officer in the UK, Kouric considered how best to answer. " I have reports that the security in Whitehall has been breached. Armed men have been spotted infiltrating the demonstration, and there have been fatalities. So far, we have reports of at least three dead, two of them police officers, and about two hundred injured, from both the crowd and our officers, some critical."

He stopped, trying to keep his report brief and objective.

The Prime Minister barely paused. He was sometimes mocked as the ditherer in charge, but today he was determined not to go down in history as the man who let the maniacs get control of the asylum.

"Yes, go ahead. You have my permission. You are to go to Security Condition Red. Keep me posted and go with God."

Britain's Prime Minister turned to his Permanent Private Secretary, the almost cherubic- looking Sir Dickie Dowling.

"I want a blanket ban on all media coverage of this situation under the Special Powers Act, with immediate effect. Make it so Dicky!"

Dowling, an old school snob, hated being called Dicky by anybody, especially disliked being addressed that way by someone who didn't have a double first from Cambridge, even if the oik was the PM.

"Yes, of course, sir, straight away. It shall be so, indubitably!'"

He almost whispered in his most officious-yet-oily manner for which he was, as he knew only too well, lampooned mercilessly by most members of the government, behind his back, as they would never dare offend such a powerful and vengeful man to his face.

The leader of London's police, Sir Will Kouric receiving the orders from the

Prime Minister was the first Commissioner of London's Metropolitan force in nearly a half century to be more of an old time copper than he was anyone's political appointee. He knew, and feared that once he gave the word, there was the distinct possibility that the trouble could swiftly degenerate into an all-out civil conflict, but he was confident that there was no other decision he could have recommended. As he always did in moments of crisis, he thought of what Winston Churchill would have done in these circumstances and decided that he would have acted with vigor and determination, and hang the consequences!

The Commissioner turned to the Junior Communications Officer in his command truck. "Patch me through to all command and security centres."

"Putting you through now sir," said the junior officer as she pressed some buttons, and nodded at the Commissioner, indicating she was ready.

"This is Police Commissioner Kouric. Please switch to secure net one immediately." He paused as his officers did as they were told, his communications aide turned to him after switching the transmission to the previously-unused emergency communication channel, supposedly impenetrably encrypted and unknown to both the media and either professional or amateur hackers.

"Be advised that we have moved to National Security Code Red under the direct orders of the Prime Minister and Her Majesty's Government. I repeat, we have moved to National Security Code Red. You are to act accordingly. You know what to do, so let's take back the streets."

All his listeners knew this meant that they were authorised to use deadly force, effectively martial law had been declared. Men and women who had spent their professional lives maintaining order with the minimum application of force were now instructed to forget everything they had ever been taught. Many of them loved the idea and a few were troubled by the implications. They were almost all loyal and proud officers of the law, and would do as they were ordered. The consequences were for others to consider.

Today, they were, for the first time, being used in an almost-military role, and were disciplined, loyal subjects of Her Majesty the Queen, and the one hundred and thirty-five thousand people dressed in blue around the country beginning with the thirty thousand policing the streets of London would do as they were told.

Chapter Thirteen

Nana Rosen's Apartment, Moortown, Leeds, England
20ᵗʰ June 2020

There was hardly a sound except for Nana Rosen's beautiful and dainty playing of her piano, she loved the works of Beethoven.

She was now a very old lady, or as she sometimes joked to whoever would listen, an ancient relic. Her hands were a little arthritic and weak but she could still master the classical music she loved. As she played the Moonlight Sonata she was transported and didn't know what was happening in London, Israel or Iran, since she didn't want to know. She didn't watch television or listen to radio, and computer communications were unknown to her. All the nonsense in the world upset her so she preferred not to know. She was an old lady of almost one hundred who liked the peace and quiet of her life, and the piano was her joy. Each new day brought her special pleasure as she played with slightly less dexterity than she had nearly ninety years before when she first played it.

Well, she thought, if I can't do it anymore I can, at least, think about it. A smile came to her heavily-lined, but still pretty, face. Now in her early nineties, no one including Nana Rosen knew for sure exactly how old she was. She remembered the days when the young men wanted to be with her, and make her smile. In the days when she was a little girl it wasn't so important how old you were, just that you survived Hitler's Europe. None of her family or friends had done so.

Her memory of the concentration camp came unbidden as she continued to play. There were two reasons she survived; her music and her beauty. She didn't like to remember because it was too painful. But no, she would never hate, because that would make her like the people who murdered. She would bless every day with her music and the music would bless her.

As Nana Rosen played the wonderful music she looked around the small room and sighed If only they could have seen where she came from, what she came from. How had it happened? How did she end up like this without her lovely family, all dead in the camps, but always alive in her heart?

Oh dear, never mind, it was best not to think about it so much. It was funny now, she no longer thought in her native German, but in English. She couldn't figure out how long it had it been? Many decades had rolled by; where had all the years gone? When did she become a Brit? She played on, the music her peace, giving her tranquility.

Once Nana Rosen had been known as Kathrin Rosen, then she was the well-brought-up daughter of Doctor Peter Rosen and his wife Bertha, both born and raised in Hamburg. No one she knew had seen that monster, Hitler, coming? Well, very few had taken him seriously. He was an Austrian corporal, a bit of a silly joke with that funny moustache and imperfect German. But it wasn't long before Nana Rosen and her family was ripped apart.

One day she was attending the music conservatory and the next she was unceremoniously dispatched onto a train full of men, women and children and sent to the showcase concentration camp at Theresienstadt, together with her son and husband.

There the Nazis pretended to the Red Cross and other international agencies that they were treating the Jews with kindness and respect. They even brought in the cameras to record their fabricated largesse as the Jewish inmates were made to perform music, play sport and to look well fed and happy.

But as soon as the cameras were gone the Germans resumed their normal barbarity that had resulted in over thirty thousand deaths in the camp, including Nana Rosen's young son and her husband. Sometimes when she was tired she couldn't quite remember their faces with clarity. Robbing her of this memory was the only thing she found hard to forgive but she knew hatred would eat her soul whereas music and love gave it nourishment.

She never saw the rest of her family again. It was many years later, well after the war, that she was formally notified by the Jewish Agency that her husband and little boy had perished in Belsen. She stifled a tear. It had been so many years and she was more tearful about her mother and father now than she had been when she was a youngster. Perhaps, she thought, the nearer I am to joining them in heaven, the more I miss them.

Apart from one torn picture of her parents, she had nothing to remember them by, no keepsakes, not even a button, no grave to go to between the High Holy Days, nothing.

She understood the need for memorials, but they weren't personal to her.

No one could understand except someone else who had suffered the same loss, which she wouldn't wish on anyone, even her worst enemies… well, perhaps them. They did, after all deserve it.

But then Nana Rosen smiled again. What enemies did she have? The Nazis were gone, every one who had ever started with her or her family was in the ground somewhere. Hardly anyone had ever had a cross word for her. All her life, she'd done right by everyone, and mostly they'd done right by her.

For almost all her life, since she'd settled in Moortown, a mostly genteel, almost sedate and quiet Leeds suburb she had been at peace. People surrounded and cared for her.

A lifetime working as a music teacher had brought with it a pleasant and cosy little house, and the respect of the community. More important, it had made her the grandmother, or Nana, to thousands of children who had been her students at St. John's Primary school. There had never been the luck to meet another man and create another family, but what did it matter if a whole army of children took the little lady to their hearts and called her Nana Rosen.

During the last years of her teaching Nana Rosen's boss, Mrs. Lonhghurst, had serious doubts about her age. What was the women's real age? she pondered, but then sighed and shook her head. Although Nana Rosen was visibly older than the official retirement age of sixty there was, she insisted, a give or take ten or twenty years elasticity to her vintage. Besides which, no one wanted the wonderful old teacher to leave her school, where everyone loved her.

Staying on as head of music had kept Nana Rosen young at heart, and she was well into her eightieth year before an incoming new head teacher insisted that it was time for her to officially retire. There was an emotional reaction to the announcement of her leaving, and the other staff, the parents and the students, new and old, gave her a wonderful retirement party. It was even reported on the local television news. The memory of the event made Nana Rosen smile and now she was retired, she had to admit, if only to herself, that she was really enjoying the long-deserved rest.

She was still smiling with the sweet and sour reminiscences and therefore didn't see, or at first understand what happened next. There was a loud noise, he heard something; it was the sound of a group of boisterous youngsters as they rushed past her house.

The words she heard made her flash back to her long-suppressed childhood memories. "Jews out, Jews out!"

There was the noise of breaking glass as a petrol bomb smashed in through Nana Rosen's living room window. Then a second and a third petrol bomb came into the front room. Nana Rosen looked at her curtains and furniture, and she understood that her home was on fire and she was in danger. She tried to stand up, but her legs were unable to react quickly enough to this life or death emergency. She was still conscious when the flames began to lick up around her feet and legs; fortunately the poisonous fumes put her beyond her agony and terror as the raging flames stripped the skin from her body.

Nana Rosen didn't live long enough to see all her neighbours who loved her without reservation, fight to come to her rescue. Her immediate neighbour, a young Asian man, Yussef, risked his own life to try and get her out.

She was the best teacher he'd ever had, he owed everything to her, he was first violin in the town's orchestra because of Nana Rosen.

Two of his brothers and their father saw what he was trying to do and joined his rescue attempt. Yussef told anybody who'd listen that he owed his career to that wonderful woman. But it wasn't enough to save his own home from being burnt to the ground by the rampaging mob of Muslim youths who were seeking revenge against any

Jew, of any kind, they could find in retaliation for the attack on fellow Muslims in Iran by the State of Israel.

The Hindu and Sikh population in many British cities realised that they were being attacked by both their old Muslim enemies and their white Christian neighbours who didn't know there was a difference between these various brown-skinned groups. These groups of people from the Indian sub continent formed their own neighbourhood level self-defence, resulting in a growing series of pitched street battles.

Vigilante groups of armed young men of every type and group dragged cars and trucks and anything else that could help make a barrier across each of their roads and set fire to them to keep other mobs away from their homes.

The ferocity of these local battles astonished everyone involved. What started with a few lobbed bricks and stones soon degenerated into a bloodbath. Rumors of deadly attacks, rapes and burning carnage went viral within minutes. People were using their cell phones and computers to show burning buildings, people on fire and others being ferried in cars to hospitals already unable to cope with the sudden and dramatic upsurge of casualties.

The leaders of France and Germany, having seen the results of what they considered lax and late reactions by the British police forces, decided to deal with the same threat much more harshly and with immediate effect.

The leaders of the two close allies had, as always, conferred on the best tactics, and as usual, the French leader took their signal from their German counterpart. Police snatch squads in both nations began making preventive arrests of their known Islamic ringleaders and troublemakers. Within an hour, three thousand and forty- eight men and women were kicking their heels in previously-unknown holding areas housed in old military compounds which had long been prepared for just such civil unrest. The French were unusually talented at long-winded bureaucracy and were supremely confident that their methods of delay and prevarication would defuse their local hotheads. They had, they thought, withdrawn any provocation to the large, vocal hard right movements who had been spoiling for a fight with the large Muslim minority who numbered about ten per cent of the entire population, but in some ghetto areas surrounding Paris were actually a large majority.

In Germany, most of the people arrested were of Turkish origin and had long worked in the country but had never been granted citizenship despite their feeling that they had fueled the latest German economic miracle. The Turkish population in Germany was substantial, and couldn't fail to notice that their country had not been afforded the warm welcome to the European Union that other rising countries had received. In fact, some of the members of Parliament in both countries had made it very clear that the reason for not wishing to allow Turkey membership of the European club was the fact that it was a Muslim country and would irretrievably change the nature of the basically white-lead Christian collection of countries. The local Turkish people felt deprived of the same rights that they believe should be theirs, and only needed the slightest spark to explode.

The balance of the population had lost faith in the status quo when the results of the ultra liberal immigration policy for refugees under the past leadership of Angela Merkel had resulted in an additional two million new inhabitants of the country. This led to her losing her position in the elections and in much the same way the strong lurch to the right in French politics had unleashed a reaction to the increasing Muslim population from the hard right parties led by Marie Le Pen now undisputed as the most popular leader in that country.

Many people of the Muslim faith in both countries witnessed the attacks on Iran, the uprising in Britain, and then heard unconfirmed rumors that their own leaders had been arrested without trial.

Their cautious elders, normally treated with respect by their community, were ignored when they pleaded for time so that they could talk with the authorities. The anger of their mobs couldn't be contained by anything other than victory on the streets of their cities and towns.

The young who felt they had been victimised for simply being brown skinned saw this as the chance to avenge a million wrongs, large, small and imagined. Now it was their opportunity to show everyone what it was like to be pushed around because today they would start pushing back.

The general population of these two countries had not, in fact not been particularly bothered by the rising tide of immigration when it was fuelling their huge economic gains of the previous forty or fifty years, but they didn't like to feel threatened.

When their televisions showed the beginning of the riots spreading across Europe, they were at first bemused, and then this changed to shock and anger. The results were cataclysmic as very large gangs of white young thugs rushed to help the police combat the Islamic youths despite being asked then instructed not to do so.

These mobs were soon getting in the way of the authorities and seeing the Muslim neighbourhoods on fire, the white youths sabotaged the fire services' equipment in the hope that they would have no alternative other than to let the high-rise apartment slums burn. Some unconfirmed social media reports claimed that many thousands of occupants of these vertical neighbourhoods were burned alive. The news footage of people leaping to their deaths rather than wait to be cooked was soon seen around the world. But nothing defused the rapidly-worsening debacle. Various political leaders, like the previous President of the USA, Donald Trump, Tweeted that the barrage of news items were fiction and couldn't be trusted, but no one listened to his discredited voice since he'd so narrowly escaped prison after he plea bargained his way out of the ultimate punishment following his impeachment.

Muslims seeking revenge set fires in the surrounding districts and there was no longer anyone available and no equipment to stop the spread of wild fires across whole districts. It was only at this stage that the army was ordered out across the streets of the main European countries, with orders to shoot to kill anyone now that a twenty-four hour curfew was imposed.

Most people saw the rapid arrival of the trucks carrying armed troopers, and returned to their homes to survey the wreckage and to help begin the tidy up. A few people waited in hiding for the next round of the battle to start, not believing that their soldiers would open fire on their fellow citizens. But they had misjudged the situation; the soldiers were well disciplined and hardened by varying tours of duty in theatres of war over the previous decades. They weren't nervous of using their guns if that was the order they were given. Of course it helped that many of the young men in uniform shared a very prejudiced and unreasoning antipathy to the Muslim question. As the U.K. tabloid, The Sun, screamed in a huge headline, 'The gloves are off – At last!'

The situation was portrayed as a crusade by the worst elements of the gutter press, which kept the pot boiling and sold a record number of copies. The media made it seem like the military was the underdog in its uneven conflict with the rapidly-vanishing mobs of Muslim youths. It was as if there was a civil war happening across Europe, and most threatening for the allies of the powers of this part of the world, was the fact that the countries most affected were amongst the richest and most stable in the world.

The Russians and Chinese were confronted by their own Muslim minority rebellions but they had long since decided on their own ruthless suppression of anything perceived as harmful to their respective economic miracles. Nothing would stand in the way of their continued growth and they crushed their own small insurrections within twenty-four hours. More difficult for them to handle was the growing troubles emanating from the Muslim countries pressing against their vast borders.

The orders went from Bejing and Moscow to roll the tanks and heavy weapons to these potential trouble spots, and the world held its breath.

Now the tactics of the disaffected Muslim youth in Western Europe shifted to an expanding series of acts of terrorism that included bombings, kidnapping and murder. Only in the United Kingdom was order restored quickly as the authorities brought in their draconian War Powers Act, which gave the forces of law and order total power, arrest without trial and the cessation of habeas corpus.

Once arrested, the prisoner's whereabouts were not made known to their family or representatives. No lawyers were permitted to file any defence on their behalf; the simple expedient being that, in most instances, the prisoners had not been charged with a specific offence, but were simply shunted off to heavily-guarded camps on the Isle of Man, cutting them off from the rest of the country and any contact with the outside world.

Chapter Fourteen

The Boleyn Ground Football Stadium, Upton Park, East London, England
Former home to West Ham United Football Club
19th June 2020

Grant, a man with pure white crew cut hair and a black pseudo military uniform entered the room with two huge bodyguards, All three men dressed identically. As he entered the room everyone gave the infamous one-armed Fascist salute. He stood smiling at the head of the table acknowledging the moment. He waved them to their seats.

"Gentlemen, take your seats. There is no time to waste!"

His voice was guttural, and oddly accented, as if English was not his first language. The group of men sat around the long table in the starkly-lit room in the disused stadium's bowels, listening to the man known simply as Grant; or simply "The Leader".

The stadium had been abandoned to the developers when West Ham Football Club had been granted the use of London's Olympic stadium a couple of years previously. A property development hated by protests from local fans and businesses who had since missed out on the income from those fans on match days.

No one except a security man, friendly to the cause and who looked after the old stadium had a clue that the extreme far right held their clandestine meetings in this otherwise-secure environment.

There were thirteen of them, including Grant. He had an aura of electricity about him, a tension, like a coiled spring of unreleased energy. Even his white hair was chopped and crew cut, erect in salute.

"This is it, men. This is our chance. The useless idiots who run our precious country, the so-called government has totally lost any semblance of control. Muslims are attacking the Jews and our boys are breaking heads to protect our nation because there's chaos everywhere and no one is looking after our people so we have to do it for them. The police have lost control and there's a power vacuum. Now's our chance and we've got to take it. Do you agree? Are you with me?"

One of his men, Trebor spoke.

"There's one call I should be making. Do I have your authority to make the call Leader. It'll take one minute?"

Grant nodded curtly and wiped his mouth with the back of his shirtsleeve. "Quick, Trebor, move your fat ass. We need to act immediately. I want answers in minutes not hours and seconds not minutes!"

Trebor left the room as Grant addressed the gathering. "We ain't got many windows of opportunity like this. We've got to take it when we can or we're fucked."

The rest of the group nodded and Grant continued, "Anyone else got something to add?" The other men remained quiet,

"We've got good reason to expect that our actions tonight will be successful. Don't ask me why, but we have a very good feeling indeed."

As he spoke, the door opened and Trebor re-entered the room, smiling broadly, exposing the fact that he had lost all his front teeth from continually sucking on his extra strong Trebor mints. He raised his thumb in triumph to his leader.

Grant was exuberant; "This is what we've been waiting for men. Our Zionist allies have joined us in the common cause. Cry havoc and let slip the dogs of war!"

Some of the other men didn't recognise the Shakespearean quote but nevertheless jumped to their feet, giving their usually unseen Sieg Heil Nazi salute.

A very tall dark haired man joined them in the room. He was so thin he appeared almost emaciated. He was clearly a serious man. He wore a white shirt and plain dark blue suit. He sighed theatrically, he was wearing a multi coloured skullcap. He was Jewish. Grant warmly shook the newcomer's hand as the rest of the group became almost silent. The newcomer was clearly reluctant to be friendly with the other men in the room.

"Where's a proper welcome for our ally Mister Andy Landau, the leader of the Zionist Opposition Group, or ZOG. His fight is our fight, and together we can take on the Islamists and defeat them!"

The other men roared their approval. Landau allowed himself a small smile and held up his hands to quieten the room while he spoke. "Together we are strong, divided we're weak, together we can win, together we will win!"

He shouted in American-accented English, betraying his Brooklyn, New York roots. He quietly turned to Grant and whispered, "It's Andrew, not Andy."

He then turned back to the other men, as unseen by him Grant mouthed the word, "Prick!"

Landau continued, "I can't stay with you tonight but you have our full support. We are together and together we will finally stamp out the Islamist scum, together we will win!"

The Neo-Nazis roared their approval for their Jewish visitor and before he left the room Grant and Landau shook hands and then raised their arms together in triumph. The other men surrounded Grant as he led the group out of the room. None of them appeared to see the irony in a group of Nazis supporting a Jewish ally.

Grant knew that this was his moment. He led the group on the long walk through the dimly lit corridors into the huge arena and watched the news on the big screen televisions with a sense of destiny and stood on the stage of the huge cavernous space looking out onto twenty thousand of his followers. Dressed in his plain black uniform, it was reminiscent of the black shirts worn in Nazi Germany. Like everything else about him, carefully thought out for maximum effect.

Hiring such big expensive facilities had only been possible since Grant had met with close American friends of ex-president Trump and they had financed his ambitions with the assistance of Russian banks who in turn were prompted to advance almost unlimited loans at low interest rates by their political masters in the Kremlin. Only a very few of his inner circle knew Grant had enjoyed warm private meetings with both Trump and Putin who had both expressed their support for his movement. He understood it was still too toxic for global leaders to meet with him publicly. But his day would come, he was sure of it.

Flanking him were the men and women who represented the hard right organizations of England that he believed he would forge into what he considered an unbeatable force. They had previously been the leaders of extremely violent gangs of football thugs, the rump of the National Socialists, the British Empire movement, the English Defenders of Faith plus the old National Front, and the English, Welsh and Scottish Defence Leagues. What they had in common was their visceral hate and contempt for what they regarded as the foreigner, the stranger, the other.

These were the people he would forge into an alliance to regain the country for its original inhabitants. He would dominate and be their leader. He knew that his dream of a purified England harked back to a legendary time that had never existed in reality. England had always been a nation of immigrants and invasion. There had been waves of invaders, refugees and immigrants, the Celts, Picts, Romans, Norsemen, Vikings, French, Germans and others too many to list, all of whom had fused over the centuries to create the typical Englishman.

Added to this in the last century or two had been the Jews, West Indians, Asians, East Europeans and finally the waves of immigration from the wars in Afghanistan and across the Middle East, both legal and illegal and those simply looking for a better life in the UK from many parts of the world.

Grant, who was expensively educated, knew these facts, but he chose to ignore or manipulate these facts as they suited him.

Underneath his populist exterior he was a politician much like most others. He would say or do anything to get power, and once he had it, he could be as political as the next conviction politician to hold onto it. Nevertheless he carefully concealed the fact that his family were middle class, aspirational senior managers, both involved with Employment Law and Human Resources. As his mother would often say to her friends "After all what are the real differences between my little lad and a Thatcher, other than for the fact that she foolishly believed in democracy which is a proven failure."

There were race riot reports coming in from all the major towns in the country. The nations reactions to the Muslims burning the old Jewish woman to death were made to order. They couldn't have been better. Grant couldn't have dreamed this up if he tried. The general population, even those that didn't particularly like the Jews, didn't like the idea of Muslims going on the rampage in Mother England and murdering a defenceless old lady in her own home.

Now the English smelled blood. Long-pent-up fear and loathing burst from deep within the normally polite and reticent English population, still more than ninety percent white and now determined to re-impose their version of old England that only existed in nostalgic dreams.

Grant knew from his extensive research of historical revolutions that they don't need a majority to spark them off. No, to fan the flames just a few unafraid and determined people were essential. Then their revolutionary ideas had to take hold with enough people to set society ablaze, and the movement would become unstoppable. This was just such a moment. He led the leaders of his crusade to the temporary stage in the middle of the packed stadium. He watched the huge crowd carefully. He was aware it was like an animal, ready to either roar its approval and follow him to the ends of the earth if his message resonated with them or to swallow him up if it didn't.

Grant looked around the vast crowd, drew himself up to his full height and puffed out his chest. He looked around and screamed.

"Friends!"

Grant knew how to speak to his legion of followers to grab their attention; it was in short staccato bursts that they could understand and be excited by, and he carefully concealed his own impeccable accent to mirror those around him.

"What is our aim? Victory, victory at all costs, victory in spite of all terror; victory, however long and hard the road may be; for without victory, there is no survival. This was first spoken by a hero to every member of our sacred English race, Winston Churchill who said these words in our Parliament in 1940. The same is true today. These are historic times. As you know we have nothing against Muslims. We have Muslim members of our organization."

Grant paused for dramatic effect, his audience ready to rebel when they heard words that could be considered too conciliatory from their supreme leader.

He continued.

"Some Muslims are acceptable, those loyal to our monarch and country. Those that were born and raised among us. They accept our culture; support our national football, athletic, rugby and cricket teams. We object only to those followers of Islam that preach hatred of us, of the country we all share; they are traitors and should be hanged! Those Muslims who burn our churches and synagogues, they have to be hanged!"

The crowd was now roaring their approval.

"Those Muslims who murder innocent old ladies, our old ladies, they must be hanged!"

The crowd erupted from their chairs, clapping and cheering as their leader paced a couple of steps back and forth along the stage, unable to control his excitement.

"We will never allow the green flag of Islam or the black flag of ISIS to fly over our castles and palaces or the mother of all parliaments, the House of Commons. We are the English and we are proud to be English. The best nation on the planet!"

The crowd again roared its approval.

"This is the hour, this is the day! Tonight our men will be out on the streets!" He was almost screaming.

The crowd was reaching fever pitch, shouting,

"England, England, England!"

It was like a big football match where the national team was triumphant!

Suddenly, a group of hooded young men rushed through the crowd towards the stage, shouting,

"Allah Akbar!"

They charged towards Grant but before they could reach him, they were counter-attacked by a waiting phalanx of large guards dressed in brown military-style uniforms, all of whom were carrying telescopic batons. The battle was short and bloody, the hooded men outnumbered, and although they had weapons, they weren't trained in their use. The guards beat them back with ruthless efficiency.

Grant rushed to the attack, his reputation with a razor blade was legendary, but his fellow leaders pulled him out of the way. The stadium was in uproar as the battle spread into the hall, where more counter demonstrators were ready and willing to battle with the followers of the far right.

Grant stood by the microphone and started to sing: "Land of Hope and Glory, Mother of the Free, How shall we extol thee, who are born of thee? Wider still and wider shall thy bounds be set, God, who made thee mighty, make thee mightier yet, God, who made thee mighty, make thee mightier yet." As he sung, the battling protestors were beaten into submission and the rest of the huge crowd began to sing with him the words to England's unofficial national anthem, Land of Hope and Glory.

"See how we will crush the enemies of a free England. We cannot lose because we have right on our side." He paused, and grabbed his own chest, as if touching his heart. He continued, now standing on his toes, screaming hoarsely at his followers, "We have won here and tonight we are going to reclaim the streets from those people who are the enemy of England, but it wouldn't matter who wins or loses this battle tonight, if we win we win, and if we lose we win because tomorrow, when the English finally wake up to the fact that their sons and daughters get beaten and scarred by those who don't deserve to be in England, they will rise up in revenge for us all. We will win this war. Do you hear me? We will win, do you hear me, we will win, we will win!!"

The crowd had now been turned into a giant beast, with one mind and one thought, to win. They bayed back to Grant,

"WIN WIN WIN!"

Now Grant was shouting loud enough so that everyone could hear him, and the crowd was so pumped up, it was hard not to be swept up in the emotion of the moment.

"England, England!"

He roared.

"ENGLAND, ENGLAND, ENGLAND!"

They roared back at him in a tidal wave of fervor, grown men wept, swept up by the emotional torrent. They felt they were finally unashamedly allowed to be patriotic after so many years of pussy- footing political correctness.

"This is the night that lights the spark to set England ablaze. The Muslims who attack us will be the reason their mosques will burn, not you! I want the glass in every window of their houses and businesses to shatter in a thousand pieces. I want them bastards out of their businesses, their cars and homes ruined. I want them out of this country. I want them out of OUR country. If they like Pakistan and Bangladesh and India so much, we'll lay on the ships to take them home." He paused for effect. "And we're kinder than they are; we won't even charge them for going back where they came from. They can all go back where they come from for free!"

The crowd laughed, then cheered and stamped their feet in unison Grant's plans started to unfold.

"This is not the end of the road. This is not even the end of the beginning, but it is a first step, the start of the beginning, and nothing will make us deviate from this path, to make England English again!"

He held his arms aloft and the crowd roared their approval. When they leave you will get their houses and businesses at an especially low cost. All of it will go to eh people, FREE!

The crowd erupted and Grant knew he had started the long march to power.

Chapter Fifteen

Mo's Apartment, West India Quay, London, England
19th June 2020

Mo played with his new twins, Faisal and Zafar on the floor of the apartment. He laughed and they smiled back to their father. The apartment overlooked West India Quay set in the heart of London's new, second financial district of Docklands.

Becky, his blonde life partner, was in the kitchen where he thought she belonged, making him his dinner. He was happy that his 'shadow' Nafti had gone home early because, for what he'd planned, he needed privacy.

He cared that his dinner was late. He believed a man should be fed as soon as he got home. After all that was the woman's job in life. She'd better get used to it. Becky had found it difficult to adapt to Mo's foreign, old-fashioned upbringing. But she was a delicious paradox, a thoroughly- modern liberal, left wing western woman who was willing to subjugate herself almost totally for love to this exotic, strange, compelling man. He enjoyed these sexually submissive progressive women. They almost always let him have his way and obviously enjoyed his abuse.

She sung to herself as she made hummus and goat cheese salad for their supper. Becky was blissfully unaware of how strange it would appear to friends from her previous jobs and university that she, the biggest feminist of them all, was not just willing, but eager to adopt to such an old-fashioned life. Perversely she found it satisfying to sublimate her identity to that of her man and their common faith in Islam of which she was now a devout follower.

She could hear the television's 24-hour news channel that Mo enjoyed to have on all the time, like visual wallpaper. He wasn't really watching, but keeping it on, in case something relevant was to catch his attention.

A vacuous red haired girl was on screen gabbling on with the day's gossip when an item caught Mo's attention.

"Today, in London's glitterati we witnessed the changing of the guard. American

Sir Max Roman, seen here on his super yacht somewhere in the Mediterranean was out of town, while his son, the super cool Eddie Roman, attended the opening of the new Rothko exhibition at London's Tate Modern Gallery which his daddy sponsored out of his multi billion dollar inheritance. He refused to comment on rumors that there is a continuing rift between him and his father."

Mo snorted. It upset him to see his erstwhile family, and his anger boiled as he continued to watch. He hated everything they represented, particularly the western decadence, the filthy democratic weakness, the excess, these people, and above all their arrogance. How dare they even dream that their ways, their system, was even the equal of the true way?

He reserved his special hatred and contempt for Eddie, the pederast. He could pretend to the world that he was a normal man, but they both knew the truth; he was homosexual, always was and always would be. And that bastard Jew, Sir Max Roman, with all his money and toys, such men as these would discover soon enough that Islam was superior.

The only Jew he loved was Nancy, his one time mother, who he adored. He kept track of her although there had been no direct contact for many years. He knew she was now divorced from the pig and had gone to live in Israel where she had an apartment. Maybe, he thought, one day I can see her again, that would be nice.

He stabbed the remote, which turned the set off. He couldn't tolerate watching for another second. If it hadn't been for the kindness of his benefactors and the men at the Madrasah, a fundamentalist Islamic school hidden deep within the fabric of his Riyadh mosque, he might not have found the true path so quickly.

He didn't know how or why he had been singled out for special attention, nor would he have cared. All he did care about was that he was given the love of Allah and respect of this community, not for his money, but for himself.

The sheikh in charge of his school paid him more attention than any other pupil. He initially thought that it was because he was the adopted son of the King but they had an ulterior motive. They nurtured him, gave him one-on-one teaching, singling him out as a star pupil. But there were reasons, it was clear to the men who ran the organization that here was a perfect weapon. Mo had the true background they required.

He possessed an Arab's honest anger at being part of a martyred family suffering as a consequence of the Big Satan, the U.S.A.

The young man was a handsome, athletic and clever boy, who spoke English like a native. As a bonus, he particularly hated the Americans and the Jews but would be trained to conceal this. He was tailor-made for their long-term strategic purposes. He knew, and they thought, he understood the enemy intimately.

The men who nurtured him were clever enough not to ever mention his personal relationship to the King nor ask him any questions about the Royal House. They were subtler than that; they were playing the long game. These were men who were members of the ultra secretive Muslim Brotherhood that had spawned almost all the extremist, so called terrorist organizations, such as Al Qaeda. It was from these sources that nineteen of the twenty one men who took part in the 9/11 massacre came from his adopted country, Saudi Arabia.

To Mo's surprise it transpired that Nafti was also committed to the coming Caliphate. Although his giant shadow was loyal to the King he was also a devout follower of the Islamic war to be unleashed on the West.

That was the reason he could vanish off the radar sometimes, accompanied by his guard who would attest to their being in some secluded and decadent fleshpot. But every vacation was actually spent at various advanced armed training camps in rural Pakistan, which had taken him back to his true roots as an Islamic warrior. Here he had been trained and indoctrinated even further and deeper to achieve an enhanced knowledge of how he could help Islam gain control for eventual victory over the infidel in the coming battles.

When he was a young man of eighteen he had been whisked off to London to continue his schooling. He was a conscientious soldier of Islam long before he ever fired a shot. He never met the movement's leaders at this stage.

He knew he could never have achieved his present prominence without his exposure to the Higher Education he gained studying criminal justice for his first degree at Portsmouth University, followed by a prestigious M.A. in Criminal Justice at London University.

Unlike many of his working class English friends, he never had to work on outside jobs to give him enough money to continue the course or simply to have fun. In fact, his benefactors insisted he participate in the general revelry of his fellow students as they would expect of a young Prince with unlimited means.

Now a devout Muslim he genuinely didn't want to do this, he found it fun to drink and whore with those he pretended to befriend. He found it disgusting that the young women he barely knew were willing to fornicate with him within hours of meeting. He enjoyed ravishing them, treating the girls as if they were disposable whores for his pleasure, to debase them.

Even in this regard, he was instructed what to do by his instructors from a back room located in a remote wing of London's Central mosque. These were the wise young men in their early twenties who monitored everything he did. From the way they spoke Arabic, as if it were their second language, he guessed they might come from Iran, but he would never knew for sure.

They smiled with benign indifference as he admitted to his behaviour, and they taught him that to achieve a greater goal, it was sometimes necessary to sacrifice an individual belief momentarily for the greater good.

The enemy had watchers who would never suspect his true motives as a warrior of Islam if he continued to behave in the same depraved manner as the infidels. The wise young men were able to convince Mo that Allah, the all-knowing and the all merciful, would understand. He would even applaud his actions.

He never forgot this lesson, nor its true purpose. He existed to create the conversion of this heathen place to the true religion, bringing it into the eternal Caliphate.

If a few possessions or personal beliefs or people had to be sacrificed in the name of Allah, the merciful, then these were all a price worth paying. Not only was his life dedicated to Allah, his handlers carefully and quietly stoked the fires of his hatred for Eddie and his stepfather, Max, and all the other decadent, depraved Jews until it was a roaring fire.

It had upset Mo even more to give his boys such a stupid, decadent western upbringing, but it was essential for his task, as was his selection of the blonde woman in the kitchen. At least her features were pleasing and her body pliant and eager. These western women were such whores, he thought, but Allah would forgive him for he had only used her to further his holy duty. He had used her body regularly until the whore had bred him the boys that were necessary. Given time, they would fulfil their obligations and duties, their path though life was already carefully mapped for them.

He had to admit that they were handsome babies. The combination of ethnicities strangely did produce wonderful-looking people. Mo picked up the boys and studied them. So helpless, so innocent of the world around them, they gurgled happily as he walked out to the balcony.

It was time for the next stage of the plan to unfold. He had made sacred promises many years before to the men who had given him faith and a new life, and he knew the time had now come to pay his debt to Allah, and his representatives on earth.

Becky looked through from the open-plan kitchen. She held her breath, unsure of what he was doing with their children. He had frightened her recently. She tried to suppress her sniffles from Mo. He quickly became angry when she cried. But it was hard not to when he hit her, especially in front of the kids.. She must be doing something wrong. She tried so hard not to upset him, but whatever she did, it wasn't enough. Just the way she stood, or looked could set him off.

Becky wished Mo still loved her like he did when they had first met in the office where he had both worked as an intern playing at being a journalist while she did the same before he had joined the police.

It was a simple affair at first. Everyone had warned Becky that it wouldn't lead anywhere, that all he wanted was a new woman, to supplement his many other conquests. Becky knew about the many affairs he was rumored to have had; he was famous among his co-workers as the office Casanova.

When their relationship started she found his reputation exciting, she never admitted it to anyone, but she was more than a bit stimulated by the idea that she could tame him when all the other women couldn't. She would deliver that extra something in bed that would stop him from looking at other women, she had thought. Becky believed that whatever made two adults happy in bed sexually was fine with her as long as no one was hurt.

She caught her reflection in the mirrored surface of the big American style metallic refrigerator and realised what a mess she looked. "Pathetic woman," she mouthed to herself. Although she covered her hair and wore demure clothing, she knew she didn't conform to Mo's desire for a devout and comely Muslim woman. She knew she didn't satisfy his requirements as much as she tried.

The TV caught her attention as it cut from the program about the Royal gardens to a newsflash. There were images of riots and flames being beamed into the studio from all over the country and suitably worried-looking newsreaders.

A tired-looking Prime Minister spoke from his office in Downing Street.

"You will have all seen the terrible pictures of the public disorder happening in various parts of our country, particularly against our Muslim community. We call upon everyone, from all our communities, for calm and restraint. You will notice an increase in the police presence on the streets. I have ordered all leave cancelled and presently there are an additional fifty thousand specially commissioned officers to protect you, your homes and businesses. The forces of law and order are there to protect and serve all the communities that make up the rich fabric of our society. To those of you breaking the law, you should be aware that this government will, very shortly, restore order, and anyone breaking the law will be brought to justice and face the most severe penalties. The waving of flags, unauthorised marches and demonstrations will not be tolerated. The law will be enforced. We have called upon the services of the Army Reserve and declared a National State of Emergency under the Emergency Powers Act. This means that there will be curfews imposed in certain parts of our country until the situation has been brought back under control."

Becky called Mo: "Have you seen what's happening? The whole world's going potty!"

As she watched the Prime Minister speak, there was a red roller of further information appearing at the bottom of the screen adding further news. 'The Iranian government claims their missiles have hit the centre of Tel Aviv – Israel makes no statement.'

The Prime Minister, looking more drawn and sallow than ever, continued. "The news from overseas is very grave, but we remain resolute in our conviction that this country remains a United Kingdom for all its citizens. We will not stand for any attacks on places of worship, businesses or individuals, and these must cease immediately." Becky heard the phones in the house start to ring at once. She rushed to pick the one up in the kitchen.

Mo held his twin babies in his arms as he stood on his balcony, looking out at the excellent view of the Thames far below. He ignored the incessant ringing of his mobile and that of the landlines inside.

Becky picked up the telephone and listened for a moment. "I'll get him at once."

She rushed out to the terrace.

Mo held up his children. "Look at the life I am giving to you, my children. Your souls will live in Allah to see the black flag of the Islamic Caliphate fly over this land, and your sons will be able to rule it in the name of Allah."

He smiled, knowing how his fellow senior officers in New Scotland Yard would interpret his statement. Especially since he was a Deputy Commander, in day-to-day charge of monitoring anti terrorist activity and the strategic planning for rapid reaction.

He laughed as he held his two babies aloft, as if in prayer, so that each one of them was suspended out over the harsh ground far below. Holding each of them just under their arm by his hands, it was as if Mo was listening to instructions as he nodded.

Becky saw Mo suspending their two baby boys without any security other than the strength of his hands.

"If you want my children, Allah, remove my strength and take them to your bosom. I submit myself to your will."

Mo held them as his hands began to shake with the sustained effort. He felt his grip start to lessen in his left, weaker hand, and he thought to himself, maybe it is Allah's will that I should lose one of these babies, but not the other.

Mo didn't hear Becky come out onto the terrace after him and her children. She'd heard the boys start to cry, their pain and confusion evident to her. She saw the situation as soon as she came out but didn't dare breathe or speak or even move.

Becky understood the terrible danger they were in, and for a fateful moment, was frozen in indecision. She loved her husband Mo, but her babies were her very core. Her existence hinged on those two children; there was nothing she wouldn't do for them. She heard Mo mumble to someone unseen, but who, she instinctively knew was Allah. "Give my hand strength, Allah, or take my sons as my tribute."

Mo looked up and both his arms shook with the effort of holding his grip.

"Mo," Becky called so gently to her husband that he, at first, didn't hear her. His eyes were still closed in prayer, and now his left hand was shaking so violently that he could barely control it. Becky edged toward him until she was very close.

She reached out to Mo's face, and stroked his cheek with great care and tenderness. "Can you hear me, Mo? Are you OK?"

He opened his eyes and turned to his woman with a smile spreading over his face. "I have been given this test by the all-merciful, all-seeing, Allah."

She nodded, reaching toward the baby in his left hand. He then uttered the words, "Talaaq, talaaq, talaaq."

""What are you trying to say Mo?"

"I divorce you, I divorce you, I divorce you."

Becky was so concerned for the safety of their children she wasn't able to process what he'd said to her, although she knew it was the Muslim custom in parts of their religion that these words meant she was now divorced from her husband.

"Mo. I don't know what I did to upset you but everything is OK. We can fix this. Allah doesn't want either of our babies right now, OK?"

Mo opened his left hand, letting the tiny child fall, as he did so, Becky caught the baby's hand in her own. There was a moment of elation as she held it before she felt Mo's hard shove in her ribs, sending her and the baby over the balcony. Becky didn't even have time to register her shock or scream as she vainly sought to protect her precious baby by trying to put her body first as they both dropped like stones to the unforgiving concrete far below. Neither would ever know why they had been murdered.

Mo turned away as he held Zafar, the remaining baby in his arms and happily sung him a lullaby.

"You witnessed that little one. She was no longer my wife. I would never harm my wife. Everything serves a purpose little one, everything and everyone. Now your weaker brother has joined Allah with his mother, I can give you three times the love. We will all grow stronger through every sacrifice. We will win because we embrace death, and the infidel is weak and just loves life."

Chapter Sixteen

COBRA Committee Room, London, England
20th June 2020

The men and women of the COBRA Committee were seated around the very long brightly-lit heavy glass table in a room buried far beneath the streets of Whitehall. The air conditioning was, as ever, making the room uncomfortably cold to the exacting specification of Marjorie Bull-Spier, the most recent of several, ultra efficient and tough ladies to lead the United Kingdom's Special Intelligence Service. She was focusing her remarks primarily towards her ultimate boss, the Prime Minister. He looked tired and, as ever off camera, scratchy, mean spirited and irritable.

"Prime Minister, ladies and gentlemen, this COBRA Committee is the United Kingdom's emergency response team for national crises. An acronym for 'Cabinet Office Briefing Room A', COBRA's membership includes the head of MI5, the police, and the civil contingencies secretariat, as well as other senior ministers. I need not remind you that our prime function is to attempt to co-ordinate responses across government."

She paused, making sure she had the team's total attention, then continued when she saw that she did.

"COBRA may have met at 10 Downing Street or, if the Whitehall area was thought to have been in danger, as we have been re-located, to the Citadel – which as you can see for yourselves is the prime secure underground complex below our government buildings in the area." The other members nodded, realizing that she was making sure the minute takers of this meeting would register that she was doing everything by the book for the forensic enquiries that were certain to follow these historic upheavals.

"You were summoned to this emergency meeting as soon as the enormity and seriousness of the riots became clear during the last twelve hours."

She paused again before continuing.

"I repeat this for those of you who have never previously faced such situations. In the past, COBRA was responsible for managing the response to many difficult emergencies. COBRA has also responded to the alleged terrorist plot uncovered on tenth August 2006, foot and mouth scare and the fuel crisis in 2000. The Prime Minister can convene the COBRA Committee at his or her discretion."

The Prime Minister used her pause as his moment to interject. He stood and cleared his throat, as was his habit when nervous.

"Thank you, Marjorie.

As you know, in the past day there have been large-scale, uncontrolled and continuous riots taking place throughout the big conurbations of our country. There are many reports of casualties and widespread damage. However, what is not known to you is that we have been feeding friends in the media with very deflated figures as to the scope and nature of this carnage. We took this decision in the inner emergency cabinet to stop copycat actions and counter strikes by various sections of our society. This, I can report, has only been marginally successful. We have also turned off mobile cellphone communications and internet connections with the full co-operation of the operators, using the pretext of sabotage at several power and communication hubs. We were compelled to take this regrettable, and some would say, undemocratic action, for the benefit of the majority of our population, and history will judge us. But that's for later. Right now we have a country to sort out."

The men and the women in the room were silent and nervous, realizing that the situation in the country had apparently spun out of their control.

"Before I continue, I would like a situation report from the police service from Sir Will Kouric. Sir William?"

The Prime Minister resumed his seat as the gigantic figure of the Commissioner of the Metropolitan Police lumbered to his feet. Sir William Kouric's shuffling, bumbling demeanor and avuncular speech pattern hid two things, his razor-sharp intellect and secret loathing of anything that was not English. This included his Scottish-born Prime Minister who he considered both a socialist threat to his country and someone who should be living north of Hadrian's Wall, as far to the north as he could travel. In the cold North sea would be excellent.

"Thank you, Prime Minister."

He nodded to the man on his left. They smiled, despite their mutual loathing. "The disturbances are, as you say, widespread and ongoing. So far, we have witnessed major damage in many instances, total destruction of more than two thousand Mosques, and the ransacking of tens of thousands of Muslim businesses and homes. I have estimates of several hundred fatalities and many thousand severely injured. I'm afraid that, at present, we can't be more precise. We just don't have total or accurate information." He then deferred to Harriet Wells. "I believe the Minister for Health has something to add."

She smiled nervously at the Prime Minister and read from a briefing paper, without looking up.

"The Health Department is simply overwhelmed with the number of injuries and deaths being processed at present. We have put in place our emergency response procedures at the nation's hospitals but, regrettably, these are, at present, simply not keeping pace. As the conventional treatment centres have been overwhelmed, we have used our pop-up field hospitals and mortuary facilities, and this has allowed us just enough capacity to deal with the initial numbers, but I have to warn the Committee that we don't have enough staff, medicines or backup facilities if this mayhem were to continue another twenty-four to forty-eight hours. However, we do appear to have enough body bags, and burial of the victims will be, I am informed, both swift and hygienic."

The Prime Minister was thinking this woman was both a dimwit and a lightweight on the edge of hysteria. He might have to replace her and she'd make a great sacrifice. The light on the telephone on the long glass table glowed red, which interrupted her dry delivery of facts.

Kouric, the police chief picked up the receiver impatiently.

"Yes, this is Sir William. Tell me."

He nodded as he listened, the rest of the room remaining respectfully silent.

"Oh dear, yes, understood." He disconnected, his face ashen.

"Get on with it, Will," said the PM, displaying his famous impatience.

The police chief sighed and then looked up after gathering his thoughts. "It appears as if large and growing numbers of militant Islamic youth groups have begun to retaliate against Christian, Hindu, Sikh and Jewish targets in sections of Luton, Bradford, Sheffield, Northampton, Manchester, Birmingham and London. Whole streets are ablaze, as are churches, synagogues where there are non-Muslim minorities in predominately-Muslim neighbourhoods. This is a catastrophe. The number of victims, dead or injured, and property damage is beyond counting. We need to call in the full backup of the entire military apparatus and we need to do this immediately, sir. The police service alone can no longer hold the line. We're being overwhelmed on all sides. We need more armed men and women on the streets with immediate effect or we will not be able to regain any measure of control."

The others in the room were silent as the Prime Minister pondered his response. The Deputy Prime Minister, Jack Harrison, saw the opportunity to put his position on the record. He interrupted the quiet moment with his bluff Yorkshire accent.

"Prime Minister, there is no doubt that the police Commissioner, although well intentioned, is having to deal with devastation none of us has ever previously experienced. He's advising you to the best of his, very considerable experience, he means to do the right thing, but do we really want to alienate an entire section of our community? We're talking about several million Islamic people here…"

The old windbag, thought the Prime Minister. "We can't tar the whole Muslim community with an extremist brush," The Deputy Prime Minister continued, "But who's to know whether this is sage, whether or not the best thing to do is to engage in what the master, Noel Coward, called some masterly inactivity. This whole situation might well blow itself over like a candle in the wind if we've just the courage to have faith, and wait, until the people involved sort themselves out like good folks of this country normally happen to do."

The Prime Minister looked on with ill-concealed disbelief at this political dinosaur he had inherited from the hard left of his party. He was a sick joke of a resignation gift from the previous Prime Minister. They were both going to resign from office as a package deal to placate a fed-up public, but at the last moment there was a change of plan and he was left in despair having to humour this idiot. The Prime Minister looked at his Deputy to check whether the old windbag had stopped talking. He appeared to have done so. He smiled at the man, trying hard not to patronize him.

"The whole world is ablaze, Deputy. I truly don't think benign neglect is an option in such a situation. I have here a report…" He rapped the document he was holding onto the table. "This is from the Assistant Commissioner,"

He peered at the name of its author, "Mohammed Aziz. Good name in the circumstances don't you think."

"In which he makes various forecasts as to how such situations will develop."

Sir William Kouric raised his hand at once.

"Can it not wait a moment, Will?" asked the Prime Minister, but the Commissioner of Police shook his head and coughed to clear his throat.

"If I may, Prime Minister, just a quick point here." The red telephone lit up again, and Sir William picked it up. He stood after listening for a moment then handed the receiver to the Prime Minister, who, in turn listened, his face flushed deeply red as he listened.

"Yes, Madam President. That's a very kind offer indeed from our most important ally, really much appreciated, but no thank you. We really don't require any help from the United States to keep order on the streets of the U.K., but it is most kind and considerate of you to offer your assistance. Again, we thank you very much."

It was as much as the Prime Minister could do not to explode with fury as he hung up from the American President. He looked around the room,

"Bloody woman, as if we can't control our own bloody streets. Hell will freeze over before we need their bloody help, delete that from the minutes would you. Jesus, do they think we got out of the bloody EU just to become the fifty first state of the USA? Don't you bloody minute any of that!" he instructed the Cabinet Secretary.

The Cabinet Secretary asked the question they had all wanted to ask. "Was that the President of America, sir?"

The Prime Minister turned on him.

"Well, it wasn't the President of the bloody Board of Trade offering me fifty-thousand bloody Yank troops to keep order on our bloody streets, was it?"

He quickly realized that he sounded a bit hysterical. "Bad day all around, yes. Let's get this back under our control, shall we?"

The Deputy Prime Minister asked, "Why isn't this other Police Commissioner

Aziz here then, if he's the chap with the anti-terrorism expertise?"

Sir William smiled, without a trace of sincerity "Thank you for that, sir. Assistant Commissioner Shah has unfortunately been unavoidably detained on personal business. Very tragically both his wife and one of his baby boys have been murdered in his home. It appears that subversive anti Islamic elements broke into his home and after a struggle. The Assistant Commissioner was only able to save one of his twins and himself. Of course there is a full ongoing investigation as to the circumstances. In light of this, I shall be posting a permanent security detail on all the members of COBRA for the duration of the emergency powers being in force."

The Deputy Prime Minister bristled at this. "Oh, for God's sake, we don't all have a need for these measures. It's so unnecessary!" He spluttered to a halt.

Sir William continued with another of his most insincere and patronizing smiles. "I'm sure the security details can be discrete, if that's your concern, but whatever our personal needs, we must take action now, Prime Minister."

The Deputy PM jabbed his finger towards the policeman. "Are you making a stain on my escutcheon?"

The Senior Police Officer smiled and continued. "If I knew what that was I am confident I wouldn't be doing so, sir!"

The others around the table laughed nervously, breaking the tension slightly. The Prime Minister banged his hand on the table bringing silence to the room. "There's no way that this meeting is going to become personal when our whole world is burning. Now, let us get back to the business at hand. Commissioner, thank you for your input, but this is one of those times when I, as the leader, having listened carefully to many options, and having read many position papers, have to take the lead and make a decision."

He looked at the large electronic wall clock that read 09.37 and sighed. "Under the War Powers Act, I am, in my capacity as Prime Minister, declaring both a state of emergency and martial law. The army and the emergency services will immediately position themselves as required by our contingency plans, there will be a forty-eight hour curfew. Anyone on the streets after mid-day today will be arrested and locked up at Her Majesty's pleasure. Anyone caught looting or such like is to be shot on sight. Let's not go down in history as the men who bickered with each other while our country disintegrated."

The other men started to get up, but the Prime Minister raised his hand. "Just a moment to reflect please," he commanded. There was an awkward silence as the others in the room, mostly modern agnostic men of the liberal left intelligentsia, paused, unsure of how to react to this devout man's implicit call to prayer. Seeing their hesitation, he led the moment,

"May God grant us the wisdom to guide our country to a safe harbour, amen." Everyone in the room said, "Amen!"

For this one time they meant it.

Chapter Seventeen

The Embassy of Israel, Kensington, London, England
21st June 2020

The embassy was in lockdown mode, as secure as the Israelis could make it within the leafy confines of London's Kensington. The embassy staff were well prepared, armed with the best weapons, trained and psychologically conditioned to deal with trouble, but when it came they were still shocked. It just wasn't what a person would expect from lovely, hip, and cool London town.

Despite the fact that there were widespread and continuing riots throughout the major cities of the world, these had been kept far from the gates of this luxurious, quiet part of London, commonly known as 'Embassy Row'. So when the crowd of several thousand chanting people burst into the normally quiet street it was a shock for the vastly outnumbered additional police officers that had been stationed at the street's entrance. Their resistance was quickly overwhelmed when it became clear that the crowd had turned into a mob. Initially the policemen and women tried to turn the crowd back with their mounted officers but someone in the crowd had a gun and within moments there was the sound of shots. Several of the horses were injured and stampeded into the crowd without control. Soon there were seriously injured littering the concrete like war victims.

Inside the embassy, there were hard young Israeli men assessing the bloody riot outside and evaluating their chances of being able to keep the building, its people and information secure. Yitzak Perl opened a line of communication on his secure satellite mobile to Tel Aviv. "It is a red line situation, sir. Yes, we will."

The craggy voice on the other end of the line was Meir Sol, the chain-smoking general who ran army intelligence.

"Do your best, like always, and good luck. You know what to do in such a situation. We trained you for this contingency. You'll be fine. Shalom"

Yitzak cut the communication and made sure his ten tough young men had their weapons loaded and ready. He smiled to each of them, trying to give them confidence he didn't feel. He checked that the door area, made of solid steel, was sealed. He turned to his Sergeant, Ronnie Yacov, and they exchanged a knowing look, "We've been in worse situations," he said to the older man, a veteran Israel Defence Force non commissioned officer of too many bloody conflicts to remember.

"Yes we have, but this one isn't going to be no day on the beach, Yitzak."

They embraced unselfconsciously, not having to prove any masculine credentials. The other well drilled young men formed a huddle then broke apart, like a sports team needing that small intimacy to cling on to, that moment that told them, yes, there was someone else standing at their side. They were not alone.

The other embassy staff, mostly young diplomatic professionals looked to the military man for their leadership. Like most Israelis, they had confidence in their military men and women. They knew they were bright, tough, well trained and motivated to survive.

Yitzak kept an eye on the CCTV screens which were monitoring the growing mob rioting outside. He could see they were rapidly overcoming the London police guards from the special protection squads.

"This building is legally part of Eretz Israel, and we are all soldiers for our country, every one of us, and this includes every single one of you. Remember your training. You are all about to be issued with weapons. Everyone here will follow my orders without question, including the Ambassador. Understood? You will use these weapons without hesitation if that's what I tell you we have to do. This is not a polite debate about the peace process or a negotiation. You kill them or they will kill or capture you. We will not accept any hostage situation here. This is our place, and we will fight to keep this little bit of Israel. If we can hang on a while, I promise you, help will arrive. In the meantime, your instructions are to stand and fight. Today the front line to Jerusalem is this front door."

He pointed to the solid steel door and as he did saw they all heard the hammer blows against the door. Sergeant Ronnie Yacov called out;

"It seems like someone wants to pay us a visit!"

There was a wave of nervous laughter.

"Hear, oh Israel,"

Said Yitzak, knowing the end was possibly very close for them all he said the prayer many Jews call out to their God before they go to meet their maker.

"The Lord our God, the Lord is One!"

The rest of the embassy staff had joined him in this prayer, said by most Jews in the final moments before their death. They looked at each other, seeking some comfort and hope; but knowing that their end was probably going to come very soon, without even the chance to say goodbye to loved ones.

They waited and watched the door as the sound of the baying mob grew louder and more insistent, knowing that even a reinforced steel door to this, the supposedly safe 'secure room', would break when it was hit by enough explosive, and it surely was just a matter of a few more minutes. Many of the men and women hoped that the end would come quickly if the door was breached, but others swore to take as many of their enemies with them to their deaths.

Chapter Eighteen

Temporary Intelligence HQ, Tower Bridge Road, London, England
21st June 2020

Marjorie Bull-Spier sat opposite Mo as he blankly stared at her, seemingly distraught and distracted.

"I'm very sorry for your loss. We all are, of course."

Mo barely acknowledged her presence. They sat in the leather armchairs of her otherwise ultra-modern office overlooking the Thames, just upriver from the Houses of Parliament. She looked at the police officer closely. He in turn looked away.

"You shouldn't worry about your son," she continued.

"He's under the closest protection… Now, while it's fresh in your memory, I would very much appreciate it if you could walk me through what happened."

He nodded, as he slumped in his chair.

"I really appreciate you dealing with this personally, Marjorie, especially in light of what's happening right now."

He wiped a crocodile tear from his eye as she looked on with what she hoped passed for some warmth. She had long ago heard herself described as the Ice Maiden in bugged conversations. Oddly enough, she could deal with those inaccurate slurs from the men rather easier than she could from the few women who had travelled up the ranks with her.

She had been very discrete about her more intimate relationships, she trusted her special female friends to behave well toward her, and they knew just how intense and passionate she could be in private moments.

"Mo, we have to look for links, perhaps there is some connection between the terrible attack on your dear family and the wholesale disturbances around our country. So, can you take me through the matter once more? I realize how hard it must be for you, but it's vital I gather whatever information possible for the Security Services while it's still fresh in your mind. I know this is an intensely personal and private time but as a man with training in your position, you will understand why we have to do this."

He nodded. "Of course."

"From the top, in your own time then."

He looked at her once more before repeating the same story for the umpteenth time. He knew her reputation for brilliant analytical skills, the double first at Oxford when she took her degree after working her way up on the fast track reserved for the best and brightest, first as an office girl and then in administration and management. He wondered if it was also true that she owed her first promotions to her gifted work on her knees with the senior officers in the Security Services. It wouldn't have been too hard. He repressed a smile at the thought of this grey-haired and tough-minded woman giving oral sex to the bland, grey-suited men who ran the Security Services.

Mo couldn't help look at her lipstick-red lips with renewed interest as he retold his version of events.

"As I told our fellow officers, I haven't got a clue who they were. I was playing with my beautiful sons when these guys burst into my home. They said I must die. They called me a traitor to Islam, to the Caliphate. I tried to fight them but it was hopeless, altogether hopeless. They made me go onto my knees and then they tried to drag my boys, my precious boys, out of my arms. I don't remember the rest, it all went blank."

Marjorie smiled with a contrived look that she thought passed for sympathy. But as many enemies of this formidable woman would attest, she didn't do sympathetic.

She studied the man who had been promoted from relative obscurity as a Deputy Commander to Assistant Commissioner of London's Metropolitan Police with impossible speed. The rumor mill persistently credited this to his adopted Saudi royal connections but she'd checked this out and it was apparent to even the most cynical and jaundiced mind that he was a brilliant officer. But what was it that stuck in her throat? What was it about him that she didn't like, didn't trust? She couldn't quite put her finger on it, but she had always liked that American phrase, 'If it looks like a fish, smells like a fish and swims like a fish, it's a fish!' That's how she felt about Mo. She wished she were allowed to slip him some mind control drug to find out, without having the biggest racist inquiry ever, when this mess was all over.

Perhaps now was the time to use all those very interesting emergency powers and sort out some long-overdue mess, here and elsewhere. She considered the exact reason why Mo's tears failed to convince her of his sincerity?

Was there the faintest whiff of the racist in her make-up, she pondered, but decided that on balance, she thought not, seeing that the big love of her early life was her Oxford don, T.P. Patel, who taught her that a woman's age was no bar to how she could make love. A quiet shiver of long-repressed sensuality shot through her as a small smile came to her mouth unbidden. Mo noticed this but didn't comment. He was confident his story would suffice, but for some reason this woman made him nervous.

Chapter Nineteen

The Embassy of Israel, Kensington, London, England
21st June 2020

The battle between the police and the mob in Embassy Row quickly and violently escalated. The police met the first charges confidently; their training at Hendon Police College against just such a mob had prepared them well. They raised their transparent plastic shields and pulled down their visors, keeping close order as their drill sergeants had constantly drummed into them following the police debacle of the riots of 2011 that had started so suddenly in North London's Tottenham district.

Senior police chiefs had vowed never to be caught unprepared again. They pulled together into their well-practiced wedge formation, to try and arrest some of the most dangerous ringleaders from the mob. They screamed as they charged, and the crowd began to pull back. The young police officers would have laughed if anyone had told them that their shield formations had a traceable history reaching far back in time to when used by Roman legions fighting some two thousand years earlier, at some long forgotten battles not far from the same location.

The first people to approach the front of the separate Israeli diplomatic mission building easily broke through the smaller police cordons at that position. This second group of policemen evaporated without any real resistance, as if by the command of some unseen leader. The mob's run to the big, forbidding building stopped when the people at the front of the crowd realized that they were about to step onto new, uncharted territory.

The anarchists amongst them had reconciled themselves to their hard left and far right fellow travellers on this momentous day, but some of them hated each other far more than they commonly hated the Israelis. These were the class enemies of a generational battle. The young Fascists were uncomfortable with the lefties and the Muslim radicals, but unconsciously they acted on the old saying, the enemy of my enemy is my friend, and they all bowed to no one in their unreasoning hatred of the Jew Zionists!

None of these realized that a small hard-core group of the young British Muslim men were, in fact, highly trained sleeper operatives originating from the secret service of Iran's Revolutionary Guard. Some of these men had learned about armed combat in Afghanistan or the Syrian Civil War and conflicts in Libya, Lebanon, in fact anywhere there was trouble in the Middle East.

Before they returned to their British birthplace they had been recruited by the Iranian secret service. Most of these men didn't know who their eventual masters were, just that they would be given their chance to strike at the Zionists. This was their mission; attack the Zionists. These angry young men had been waiting in England a long time for this specific purpose and were determined to succeed. They smelt blood.

There were thirty of these highly trained and motivated men, three sub-groups of ten in each unit, all of whom had made it this far without more than some scratches and bruises. The group's leader, Cyrus Mostofi, smiled, paused and caught his breath.

Cyrus especially enjoyed the fact that he and his men had broken through the police lines using Krav Maga, the self-defence and military hand-to-hand combat system developed in Israel. Well, as he thought, one should learn from the enemy and use that strength that comes through knowledge against them. Krav Maga had come to prominence following its development from within various Israeli Security Forces and was now used by military and law enforcement personnel, as well as civilians, around the world. Of course, he and his colleagues never mentioned the fact that this method of unarmed combat originated from the hated Zionist entity. They never used the hated word, Israel.

He looked back at the police officers about a hundred yards away, regrouping near the police backup vehicles parked in the road near the barriers they'd erected on the entry way between Kensington High Street and the House of Fraser Building. He and his unit would soon be ready. The truck had to be in position, but so far it wasn't . He looked around with growing desperation. The mission was in danger of turning into a disaster.

Chapter Twenty

Marjorie Bull Spier's Office, London, England
21ˢᵗ June 2020

Mo was tiring as the day wore on. He knew the techniques and games these people played yet they persisted in treating him, a man who should already be Commissioner of Police for London, as if he were an ingénue.

How ridiculous, how pumped up with self-importance a woman like this was. She should be at his feet, licking his shoe leather. Instead she was trying to browbeat him. Clearly she was part of the group of white, middle-class idiots who hated Muslim men, like him, who were cleverer than they were, and whom they saw as a threat.

He had learned his lesson well over the years. Smile, nod, say things like, "I hear what you're saying", and then do what the hell you wanted. While you had brown skin and they had white skin, they wouldn't dare do anything to you, not really. Oh, they might posture, and pretend, but the truth was that they were still paying for hundreds of years of oppression and theft and rape of the empire. Now it was payback time.

Mo's smile was not convincing Marjorie at all. She was encouraged to see a very slight nervous tick in his left eye as he sat there, hunched slightly forward, his body language signifying a willingness to appease to be ever so humble that his crafty eyes belied.

He'd probably received rapid promotion because he's a Saudi royal. More than likely he doesn't know his ass from his elbow, she thought.

Marjorie stood, she wasn't tall, but she was very upright. She made every one of her five feet and six inches count to their fullest extent. He noticed that, despite her demure Hardy Amies twin set and pearls, he could see the swell of her breast pushing forward half-hidden in her off-white blouse. He knew what it meant as she caught his straying eyes and pulled her jacket together in an involuntary and modest gesture. He knew she would love to have him between her legs, riding her for all she could take, begging him to do it again and again, just like that white whore Becky he had finally been able to shut up.

He licked his lips like a wolf before a tasty meal, with the thought of what he could do to this overrated, self-opinionated career manager of spies.

If he had known her better, he would have understood that Marjorie would use anything that gave her any advantage, fair or otherwise. Mo's lurid and varied reputation with women was well documented in his files, as was his use of the race card at every opportunity. She didn't much care who he screwed or how often, and she didn't care if he liked to look down her top or up her skirt, it didn't do much for her either way. Well, that was not strictly true, as despite the passing years, she did like to think that there were still men who thought of her in that way. It still sent a little tingle to her. Marjorie paced around the room, seemingly to stretch, but also to toy with him just a bit. She did some mock stretches that had the effect of pushing her bust forward. He couldn't help but notice her prominent nipples poking through her surprisingly dainty bra. How was he to know that she had tried both men and women but had long ago chosen the latter?

"Is there anything else?" he asked as he shifted in his seat a little uneasily.

All these Western sluts were so obvious. He tried not to stare at the woman's brazen display, but it was difficult, he had to shift uncomfortably in his seat. Did she expect him to fuck her over the table?

"I understand how hard this must have been for you. Will you be staying with the force?"

He sighed and responded, "I shall be taking an extended leave of absence back home with my family."

"Of course, would you like some water? We won't be too long and then you can go." she asked.

"That would be very nice, thank you."

"I'll be back in a moment," she said, and left the room.

Let the arrogant bastard sweat a bit. She really didn't like or trust the man and she wished she could turn that feeling he was somehow guilty into proven facts.

Chapter Twenty-One

The Embassy of Israel & The Israel Consular Mission, London, England
21st. June

The men inside the Israeli Embassy distributed the weapons to the rest of the staff as the perimeter team herded the more desk-bound diplomats into the supposedly impregnable 'safe room'.

No one in the Embassy was entirely certain that the safe room was actually either safe or impregnable but when the Israeli embassies in Egypt and Tunisia had been previously attacked, the safe rooms in those buildings had saved the lives of all the Israeli diplomats in them until the civil forces of law and order had eventually been sent in to hurl back those rioting mobs.

Almost every Israeli in the building had undergone their compulsory military service, and thereafter fulfilled their regular annual training periods each year in the reserves. None of them were nervous around firearms, but there was some grim gallows humour as they waited to do battle.

Even the older men and women were fairly fit and able to look after themselves. They were familiar with battle conditions when in their military service uniform. But they all realized that this was about to be a defining moment in their lives, and could go either way.

Yitzhak looked up at the bank of screen monitors and saw that there were still a few press people outside. Where was the mob? Had the Israelis suddenly got lucky? Most of the mob who were supposed to be outside had simply vanished.

Yitzhak pressed the buttons, which revealed more images, and then the realization dawned, there, in front of the consular section building, that was where the mob was. He saw a group of black-clad men moving with military precision towards the nearby building. He knew immediately that the attack was well led even if it was aimed at the wrong direction, but was very dangerous.

There were too few defenders at the Consular building. The expectation was that the crazies would only be interested in the embassy. After all why would anyone want to attack an administration centre?

The young women in the consular section were trying to dial through to the embassy. Briskly determined to hold their own, they wanted clear and explicit instructions as to what action to take if and when the mob broke through.

Shira Livna, the assistant head of security was well drilled, but nothing really prepared you, she thought. The nearest thing to this she'd encountered was dealing with the attempted bombing at her El Al posting in Los Angeles International Airport seven years previously. She'd learned then to appear confident, calm and firm, it helped. That time she had felt that the young man with the excellent manners and ready smile just didn't "feel right" to her. As he'd talked to her for the security check, she summoned help by pressing a secret button linking her to a superior officer.

That day he had whispered into her tiny earpiece, and his words stayed with her.

"You know it costs the airline millions of dollars if we pull this flight and you're wrong. So, Shira, are you certain?"

She had looked at the young man with the American passport in the name of Steve Ronaldo, and spoke into the small microphone.

"Code Alef" was all she'd said, and before anyone said another word, Steve Ronaldo had six Israeli border guards dressed like tourists overpower him.

Two of the security men had taken their target down to the ground, pinning his arms and legs so that there was no possibility of any movement. Another two of their associates had their pistols aimed at him, and the remaining two had their pistols raised at the crowds nearby. Almost immediately, another team of guards had cordoned off the area before the LAX security had even realized there had been an incident.

As the local airport police had begun to approach the sanitized area, it became clear to them that the man, the security people, in fact the whole area had been swiftly transformed into a secure area.

Shira remembered that long ago feeling of deep anxiety as her colleagues carefully checked the suspect's bags and initially found nothing at all. The suspect maintained his cool exterior as he was questioned, giving nothing away.

Shira had remained certain about the man. There was something very suspicious about him. She didn't accept his story that he was a Christian Arab of Lebanese descent going to Jerusalem to research the Holy Shroud of Turin for a television documentary movie for British television. It was just too elaborate, too clever and glib. She had begun to feel sick when her colleagues confirmed that everything in his bags backed up his story.

Her boss, Bobbie Yetchansky, discreetly shook her head when she came to join the suspect's questioning.

"Mister Ronaldo. It will go easier with you if you tell us where you have hidden the explosives. We can do a deal. The prisons here will be a great deal more comfortable for you than those we can provide."

Ronaldo had smiled and shaken his head.

"I don't know where your head's at lady, but there's nothing to tell. I'm just producing a documentary on the Holy Shroud, like I told you."

Bobbie Yetchansky found herself not liking the younger man, and took another look at his passport. She said to Shira in Hebrew, "My turn," then switched back to English. "Mister Ronaldo, how comes you have Lebanese Christian heritage but a Latino name?"

There was no pause as Ronaldo responded,

"My father was from Venezuela and my mother was from the Christian part of Beirut."

Bobbie thought for a moment, and then smiled as if he'd just thought of something. "We're a very liberal group here. We have some sympathy for people that fight for their heritage, we can understand that. How do you feel about the Middle East conflict?"

Ronaldo smiled again. "It really isn't my-" Before he could finish the sentence one of the young security men came bursting into the room. "Shira you just got yourself promoted!"

She smiled but was unsure what was going on. "You've got the best instincts of the lot of us."

She shook her head. "Why?"

The security man calmly sat down next to Ronaldo.

"You think you're a clever bastard, don't you?"

Before Ronaldo could respond Bobbie smacked him hard across the face, leaving a clear palm print on his cheek.

"What are you doing, sir?"

Bobbie turned to her junior officer and tried to re-assure him,

"His bag. The entire bag is made from plastic explosive, shaped to look like a bag. It was already set to go by an altimeter. Very clever, Mister Ronaldo."

Ronaldo looked very scared. "I'll take the deal. I'll do my time in America!"

It was the Israeli officer's turn to smile as she shook her head. "No, that offer is gone from the table. Now you'll be entertaining my friends back home, big time. I hope you like it nice and hot."

With a shock, Shira returned to the present and realized this was her second great emergency. Perhaps this was to be her ultimate test as she witnessed the angry mob on the monitoring computer as the leaders hacked at the doors with axes.

The rabble was soon knocked aside by other men, organized, drilled and dressed all in black. Her first thought was that these were anarchists, dressed in their normal riot clothing of all black, their faces ominously hidden by scarves, black motorcycle helmets protecting their heads, but then she noticed that these men moved like a military unit, with precision, and were probably obeying pre-set orders. It made her still more nervous.

The other members of her team were looking to Shira to be calm and show leadership. The phones went dead, along with the electricity. Then the emergency system kicked in as the spare generating capacity kept the building illuminated. Her small mobile communication device was still working as she contacted her colleague in the embassy.

"We are under professional military attack. These men look like they're Hezbollah or even Iranian Special Forces. Repeat; this is no longer a crowd incident. Please advise. We need immediate assistance."

At the same time a truck full of explosives smashed through the flimsy cordon at the top of the street and without any lessening of speed it rushed towards the Israeli building smashing through the crowd, friend and foe alike. It happened too quickly for the law officers to react. Before they could do anything the young man driving the vehicle gunned the engine and the men clad in black made way for the truck.

Shira saw the big vehicle smash into the front door. The driver screamed, "Allah Akbar" and there was a huge explosion as Shire pulled her women colleagues back from the door as it burst from its hinges. The women left standing raised their weapons.

"Shoot to kill!" Shira screamed.

The Israeli women who had survived unharmed were regaining their feet. Two of them were horribly wounded but readied their weapons from the prone position; the other two crawled onto their knees and pointed their guns as the smoke began to clear.

Some of the people in the crowd outside were too shocked by the huge explosion to react. The bearded man in the all-black outfit jumped onto the railings near the door and pointed at it, shouting, "Death to Israel!"

His men allowed others in the mob to lead the charge into the building's entrance.

Waiting for the first people into the narrow entrance was the concentrated firepower of all the Israeli automatic pistols, firing indiscriminately into the screaming mob. In seconds there were more than twenty rioters groaning on the floor, as the bullets thudded into them from the Consular defenders.

The attack team who had been well trained by the Iranians waited, one step back, until there seemed to be a lull in the firing. Then they ran in throwing their stun grenades in a well-rehearsed fusillade.

"Let's take some of the bastards with us!" Shira screamed as she fired her weapon and led her group of women in a desperate counter attack. Knowing that they had no fall back position, there was nowhere to run except at the enemy; she would rather die than be taken a prisoner by them, for even one minute.

The two groups crashed into one another, the well-trained Iranian attackers had not anticipated having to fight with women, their training had not included that possibility and for a fatal moment they hesitated.

That was the moment that Shira traversed her Uzi gun in automatic firing mode across the charging men, mowing down their first and second waves, sending about fifteen people to the floor in a bloody mess as almost simultaneously. The brave young woman and her companions were bludgeoned by the impact of the stun grenades, which had the effect of making both sides pause for a moment. Both sides were unable to see or hear clearly in the fog of battle.

There was nowhere to hide as the advancing rioters, infiltrated by the Iranians, realized that they were in a real fight to the death. This wasn't empty rhetoric, these bullets were real and so was the blood that was already spreading like spilt thick paint over the floor, making it sticky and slippery. The men and women of either side were now fighting hand-to-hand, and the frantic melee was made worse by the screaming and hysterical British rioters who were frantically trying to get out of the killing room.

The Metropolitan Police strategic reserve officer, Commander Lucy Hunt, aged forty- two and previously head of London traffic management, heard the gunfire from inside the Consulate. She panicked and wasted precious moments trying to find out if the sounds were coming from their own, British counter insurgency forces.

When she was told that no order to fire had been given and realized the implication, she radioed for permission to intervene with deadly force on what might be legally considered foreign sovereign territory.

The question took more than two minutes for her question to travel up the chain of command and reach the Prime Minister and for his response to come back down the chain of command. This was much faster than had been the case in previous emergencies but not quickly enough for the pile of wounded and dead combatants, innocent or otherwise laying in the Consulate.

The anguished groans of the wounded had decreased in volume as the police officer on the loudspeaker shouted to make himself heard.

"We're armed police, Put your weapons down – we're coming in. Any sudden movements will be met with deadly force. Everyone put your weapons down now!"

Very tentatively a group of nine London police officers heavily armed with powerful semi automatic weapons and dressed in dark blue full-body armor, entered the area. They held their machine pistols cocked and ready to fire in front of them, searching for targets, but nothing moved.

It was far too late for the officers when one of the Iranians lying motionless screamed, "Allah Akbar, God is Great!" and pulled the pin on the massive high explosive bomb he was wearing as his suicide vest.

The high explosive blast decapitated the man, his head flew high into the air and as it spun, it appeared to look down at the carnage, its eyes still open as if in surprise, and in that split second, the concussive wave reached out with deadly impact, destroying everything in its path, indiscriminately, without regard of anyone's race, religion, age or gender. It swallowed them all up in a hole with a thirty-five feet circumference and nearly ten-feet deep at its centre. Into this pit fell all the mixed body parts, which had, until moments before, been a group of individuals, each with different hopes, ideals, dreams and aspirations. Now all life in this charnel house had been extinguished, and an awful quiet calm claimed the area, with no one left to fight.

Chapter Twenty-Two

Jewellery Shop, Babylonia International Hotel, Baghdad, Iraq
28th June 2020

Alimah had once worked as the manager in the small, but luxurious, jewellery store off the main foyer of the Babylonia International Hotel in Baghdad. She'd loved her job and found it easy to smile at everyone who visited her shop.

She dressed in the fashions of London, New York and Paris without losing her modesty. She was no fool and understood her striking good looks had got her this much-sought-after job against stiff opposition. She knew how to tread the line that was the divine balance of a young lady being able to retain her modesty while still flirting with male customers just enough to give her huge success at the shop. Her abilities, charm and physical attributes combined to encourage sales from the rich Arab clients who visited the store to shop for their wives, girlfriends and mistresses, sometimes all at once.

Alimah would never step over the line and risk her married virtue. Her family back in her Basra hometown would have been shocked and upset by such a thought, and she was happy with her husband and young family. She was a good girl from a family of solid Muslim values.

The first thing that she noticed about the Saudi Prince was his smell; the most wonderful aftershave shrouded him. He was probably no more than in his early thirties, much taller than her, his face handsome and cruel, he was wearing a elegantly tailored, obviously expensive Saville Row suit that didn't disguise that he was a fit young man.

If she had been a single woman she might have found him very attractive, in fact, even as a married woman she did think he looked exciting, but of course, no interest to her other than as a customer.

She noticed that he had four armed guards with him, one of who was a huge man, but a rich man with guards wasn't very unusual in Baghdad at this time. The man looked at her and smiled, but there was no warmth in that smile.

"What would you recommend I buy for the most beautiful woman in Baghdad?" he asked.

She smiled. "What's the occasion?" she asked by way of a reply.

"It's by way of payment for making love."

Alimah didn't like the way this conversation was going.

"We don't have anything like that here," she answered.

"Perhaps the sheikh would like to try somewhere else, I can recommend wonderful shops who will provide you with an excellent discount?"

She edged towards the panic button under the counter. If necessary, she could summon help from the two British guards who had once served with the SAS in her country. The man smiled and shook his head.

"I've been watching you, and there you are showing yourself to anyone who wants to look, so don't give me a hard time. This can be easy or hard. What would you prefer?"

He walked closer to her, and while she was looking at him she hadn't noticed that one of his men had gone behind her and she squealed as he grabbed both her hands and pulled them backwards. She was unable to stop another of his guards from pulling the blinds shut and turning the sign on the door to 'Closed'.

Another guard, the biggest, locked the door. He was a giant of a man, and for a moment she thought she saw a flicker of humanity and decency in his eyes, but before she could plead for help, the third guard taped her mouth shut.

Prince Mohammed nodded as she struggled.

"I like to see your body as it squirms. I can see your big tits moving, and I can think how I'm going to enjoy sucking your nipples. I might even let you cum. I bet you never do that with your western customers, you cheap whore. If you behave yourself and pleasure me, I might not cut you up afterwards. I would enjoy cutting off your nipples, nose and ears as a souvenir of the moment."

His hand reached into his jacket and he pulled out a wickedly sharp knife. Amina shook her head. Two of the guards picked her up and placed her on top of the counter as if she were weightless. She had never been so scared but despite all her efforts she was powerless to resist. The Prince came closer to her and lifted the hem of her skirt with the blade of his knife; he stared at her bottom half and then gently placed the knife on her knickers. She hardly dared breathe and now

"Look at you with your naughty little thong. What decent respectable Arab woman wears such a thing and shaves her natural hair. You're naked there, like a little girl, that's disgusting for a grown woman. Next time I take you, I want you to have proper hair like a woman should have."

He seemed genuinely angry and moved the knife to her blouse, where he seemed hypnotized by her breasts squashed flat by the tight material as she lay motionless.

"Let's take a look here, to see if you're at least decently covering your chest with proper modesty."

He cut the buttons of her blouse, which allowed it to burst open, exposing her black lacy bra. "I thought it would be like this, just what I expected to see. Look at this whore!"

He instructed his guards who did so, but showed no expression. "Let me see, I bet."

He cut the centre of her bra and her breasts were now exposed to all the men in the room, her nipples were large and distended, as they normally were.

"You see, she's excited by what I'm doing to her. She's just a bitch in heat!"

His hand was quivering as he placed it on her breast, and pinched her nipple hard, she squealed in pain.

"Do you like it bitch?" She nodded. She didn't want to die, so even tried to smile. "Take the tape from her mouth."

He instructed the nearest guard, the man ripped it off, "What do you want bitch?"

"I want you here, now, on this floor, but you don't need to tie me up, and you don't need these men in here. If they go out I can do things with you that you've only ever dreamed about."

He wasn't sure straight away, but he liked people to obey his every whim and fulfil his fantasies, and here she was, begging for it! He tore the little clothing she still had from her voluptuous body and delighted in seeing her laid out in front of him like a delicious meal. He felt himself stir and stiffen as he traced her curves with the knife, gently caressing her with the sharp, deadly metal.

But Alimah was a very intelligent woman and she guessed intuitively that what turned on this crazy Prince was the struggle. If she did the opposite, it might save her life. So she wet her lips with her tongue and smiled up at him.

"Show me your manhood, let me touch you."

She whispered, and he felt his control slipping away.

"I want you to mount me like a mountain lion. Come on show me what you have." He threw down the knife and checking to see his men were facing away, he placed his hand at the woman's nexus, and felt her sex. She was naturally moist, but the Prince wrongly thought that this indicated a woman was climaxing, and he wasn't ready, knowing he wasn't hard or ready, despite the two Viagra he had consumed in readiness for this moment. Usually it worked, but now all he could feel was a tremendously blocked nose, and a raging headache. He probed her with first one of his fingers, and as she bucked her hips to meet his thrust in simulated passion, he put two, then three fingers in her, with his thumb on her clitoris, half his hand was in her, thrusting in and out like a piston. But this was all wrong he thought, not caring for a fully mature woman using him for her sexual pleasure. But he had to admit she was like a magnificent wild animal as he watched her beautiful face contort in seeming sexual abandon, her powerful thighs crushing his hand into her wet softness as he licked and bit her erect nipples. She reached for his penis, but it was still too soft to be any use. But she was a grown woman with the knowledge that her survival might depend on the performance she put on for the next few minutes. This was about control and violent domination, not sex or sensual pleasure.

Alimah gripped his penis in such a way that he couldn't tell if she noticed his lack of hardness. She pumped him for all she was worth, panting and seemingly excited, it was enough for him that she panted with feigned excitement.

"You are magnificent, oh yes, and you are more of a man than any other!"

He felt he was harder now but before he could think of mounting her, she was bringing him to her mouth and she leaned forward to let him feel her wonderful breasts, as she did the one thing he loved above all others, and sucked and licked him until he could resist no more and he felt himself ejaculate, and she swallowed his jism.

No other woman except whores had ever done for him, even in London and the States. He shuddered as she forced every last ejaculation from him. He was unable to do anything but pant in release as she finally released him from her mouth.

She did this to drain his sexual appetite, to try and stop him raping her and it had worked. He smiled as he dressed. With almost gentlemanly restraint and courtesy, he helped her dress and clean up. Now they stood and faced each other. He kissed her demurely on the cheek and she pretended not to feel sick at his touch.

"You are simply magnificent, and from now I shall make you one of my future wives. You know how to make a man feel wonderful and it's a rare gift, I can tell you."

She smiled as if pleased by the compliment, just thinking of ways to end this nightmare. "That is so exciting for me, but you know I have to take care of the family I already have your Excellency."

He beamed with benign indifference.

"Well, of course, we will bring any children into our homes, and your first husband will be handsomely recompensed for losing you. Perhaps a nice new job for him with my government, something well paid. I am sure he shall be reasonable about it. He won't want to stop your advancement if he really cares about you."

Alimah nodded, thinking the nightmare was over, not realizing that this insane man meant every word. Her life now was his to order as he saw fit. He went over to the glass horizontal display case and pointed to a huge diamond ring.

"And take this for yourself. It's a little gift my lovely girl. My guard Nafti will arrange payment. You no longer work here."

He then told the big guard to help her close the shop and took her from her previous life as if it was of no consequence.

BOOK TWO
"Nice Guys finish Last..."

Chapter Twenty-Three

Grosvenor Square, London, England – 24th August 2020

The only moment Eddie remembered his adoptive father showing real emotion was the day he was knighted in the Queen's birthday honours list. It had been delivered as part of a deal promised to him by the Prime Minister when he moved his tax base to the United Kingdom. Now he had dual citizenship and his huge ego was even more inflated. Tears reluctantly welled from ice blue eyes and found their way down the handsome frown lines to be dabbed from the face by an immaculate linen handkerchief before the salty droppings could deface the symmetry of his perfectly-clipped salt and pepper moustache. Max had undergone extensive cosmetic surgery in his middle years to his teeth, now perfect, and liposuction had corrected his double chin and middle-aged tummy. His vanity had compelled his hair transplant, which had been successful. Now, thought Eddie, he looked like an older man who looked odd, rather than a handsome older man.

Eddie would never forget that day of the investiture of his adopted father at Buckingham Palace as he was transformed from the plain American Mister Roman to the almost mystic heights of being the now very British Sir Maxwell Roman, Knight Bachelor. The boy Eddie had been that sunny day in 2005 and the man standing in the office looking out onto the wet gloomy London scene almost a decade later, had at least one thing in common; the overwhelming wish that he had been blessed with Mr. Rupert Michaels as his father.

The night was going to be long and hard, thought Eddie Roman as he flung his copy of the *Wall Street Journal* onto the empty other half of his king size bed. He flopped back onto the soft, pink down pillows, and knew he should relish their comfort since this would be the last night he would own them, the bed and the spacious, gorgeously-appointed six bedroom house in Wilton Crescent, hard by London's Hyde Park. In his thirty-two years on this planet, Eddie had never been scared of anything or anyone but now he was scared of facing the meeting of his angry creditors at ten-thirty the next morning and even more scared of what the bank would do to ruin him at noon, he was afraid of being afraid.

His life partner, how he missed Barry, longed not for his decorative, receptive body or elegant haughty face but for an encouraging word, or comforting embrace that he'd forgotten or hadn't considered in his headlong, blind rush to make a property empire to rival even that of his hated father, Maxwell Roman. To better the old man had become his consuming obsession ever since that day ten years before, when Eddie had accidentally discovered how Maxwell was ruthlessly exploiting Rupert Michaels, his lifelong friend, who, like many others, was caught in the sudden overnight crash in the property market of 2018. Sir Maxwell was examining some papers on his rosewood desk as his son barged in without ceremony. Calmly, he looked up at Eddie while managing to ignore the other man.

"What is it, can't you see I'm busy?" Sir Maxwell asked of Eddie.

"Everything. Do you deny any of it?" Eddie responded.

Maxwell sat back in his comfortable antique chair considering his response carefully.

"No, I neither deny or apologize for what I did. I'm proud of it. I've told you before, boy, there are losers and winners in this world. I am a winner, while Rupert and, perhaps you are losers, don't you know that nice guys finish last?"

Eddie's anger welled within him, becoming a cold, hard, sharp-edged weapon, his eyes blazed with hate as he glared at his father who felt the power of this base emotion boring at his vitals like a scythe. "If that's how you go about winning, you can shove it father, right up your bank balance. We shan't be seeing each other again, ever, and I'll not speak to you as long as I draw breath!" Eddie stormed from the office without looking back to see the effect of his words on Sir Maxwell who for once in his life had badly misjudged the man he was dealing with.

He wished he could show the remorse he felt, but since his own time as the Jew boy bait for his young bullying class-mates, he'd never shown any genuine emotion to any person, because emotion to him equated with weakness, and that was to be despised. His whole life had, as its central theme, the search for cast iron safety and security, and it had cost him both his sons.

Oh God above, forgive me and help me find your strength, he thought, fighting back tears of self-pity, before he pulled himself together and resumed his analysis of a commercial property transaction he was looking at.

Mo went home and despised the wasted tears he spilt missing his family. He did what he always did when he was in a low mood, he exercised until the sweat poured from him and his muscles would simply not give him any more and they seized up with too much lactic acid. Only then, when he was totally drained, did he allow himself to think again, his mind now calm.

Chapter Twenty-Four

Allenby Road, Tel Aviv - Military G.H.Q., Israel
25 February 2020 – 03.00 hours

In the perennially twilight world of the central war room of Israel's military G.H.Q., stood Brigadier General Mordechai Zvi, commander of the Army. He felt his chest tighten as he considered the options open to him. He turned to Captain Bloch, a young, arrogant and handsome intelligence officer who had prepared the position papers and rushed them to the general, marked 'urgent'.

Zvi knew of this young man's hawkish reputation and of his steel trap, incisive mind. Some considered this a dangerous combination. The younger man thrived on conflict like Zvi himself. The General was a famous hawk, ever since he'd publicly repudiated the moribund Camp David and Oslo Peace Accords.

"Are you sure of these facts, Captain?"

Captain Bloch was tired of trying to convince old men of the dangers to their country with soft reasoning and calm argument.

"General, since the recent second wave of revolutions in Egypt, Tunisia, Libya, Yemen and the Gulf States we knew it was just a matter of time before the lunatics turned their weapons away from each other and back at us. In 1973 and Lebanon and Gaza, your predecessors waited so long to get the world onside it nearly cost us our country. The world still blames us whatever we do or don't do. We must not make the same mistake. They're coming for us, now!"

The general closed another button of his combat tunic in a futile attempt to keep warm in the freezing cold of the super efficient air conditioning in the deep subterranean structure. It might be great for the super computers but it didn't do much for him.

The General didn't reply as fast as he knew he should, or in accordance with standing orders. He had helped formulate plans for just such a national emergency.

Instead, he looked down from the raised dais to the young men and women staffing the cavernous room's flashing computer consoles and positional maps which plotted all military activity within a two thousand mile radius of Israel's frontiers. There, on the big board, he saw the electronic red dots symbolizing the Egyptian Second and Third armies moving at top speed eastwards across the Sinai towards Israel's exposed Negev Desert; its soft, lightly-populated underbelly. Egypt was once again an Islamic republic, like most of the other Arab states, its enmity towards its Jewish neighbour to the north had been expressed openly and the destruction of Israel was again on the country's agenda.

Since the eventual overthrow of the Assad dynasty in Syria, that country was also sworn to the destruction of Israel and now there were reported movements of their Lebanese forces of occupation crossing into the agreed 'no go' area south of the Litani River and preparing with Hezbollah and their concealed stockpile of more than 150,000 missiles and rockets for offensive action.

Other Syrian forces, estimated to be sixty-five percent of their total armed manpower, was pouring into Jordan linking up with the new King Hussein's Bedouin warriors and advancing towards the Jordan River's west bank. Their remaining units were already sending reconnaissance parties onto the Israeli occupied Golan Heights.

"Of course," said the general,

"They might just be posturing, showing the folks back home that they are tougher with the Jews than their predecessors, even the survivors of their revolutions want to show their big muscles. How do we know this is for real? The Americans and the Europeans, they're telling us to be reasonable, to be cautious."

The younger man was not to be easily deterred. He smiled and shrugged in that unique way that Israeli's adopt when faced with the impossibility of understanding the world,

"We live with these neighbours, it's our neighbourhood, not theirs, what do our Israeli eyes see sir?"

The general knew what his eyes told him, but since the Egyptian President's removal from office, his subsequent second re-trial and execution a few months before, no one in Israel's defence establishment had placed too much belief in the intelligence boys' analysis of the new Egyptian leader's raucous public calls for a Jihad, a Holy War. The Arab leadership had invariably said one thing in public and quite another in private meetings with the Israelis in Sharm El Sheikh or Eilat. "Surely," the Israeli Ministers said to their less-trusting military think tank, "President Mustapha Heikal of Egypt was just another pragmatist trying to be a populist politician by turning Egypt into a fundamentalist Muslim state, while privately he wouldn't say no to a Scotch or a curvaceous infidel woman like his less-hypocritical co-religionists."

The general's mind was pulled back from the past by Captain Bloch's insistence.

"With respect, Sir, do you want to be the commander of the Jewish people to face history as the man who allowed the third destruction of our beloved Jerusalem?"

Zvi felt the words sting. He stood ramrod straight to his full impressive height. He knew that he already faced court martial and charges of treason for failing to notify the elected government for his actions when he'd gone to Battle Condition Red without political approval, knowing that to wait for cabinet approval could mean Armageddon.

What else could he do? he thought. If I wait we're finished. Wiped from the map, destroyed forever.

Awaiting his signal to go were the cream of Israel's four hundred thousand fighting men and women, most of whom were reservists. Almost all of them wouldn't realize that this wasn't another sophisticated call up test or war game.

He turned to Bloch, his mind made up and grinned, exposing his many golden fillings to the surprised young man.

"Have I your permission to unleash the dogs, General?"
The general took one last moment to think about his own three sons; Don the brightest, in his F18 fighter bomber with his squadron waiting to follow him from their underground base in the Jordan Valley, Adam the calm, dour farmer from his Kibbutz in the Negev which he would unquestionably defend with his tank against any enemy, and lastly Jacob, the youngest, the dreamer, the idealist, who had the worst job of all, for it was he who would if all else failed deliver the first salvo of Israel's hydrogen bombs from his F16 onto Cairo while other such presents were simultaneously laying waste every major city in each Arab confrontation state. The irony remained for Mordechai that as long as Israel's existence was not threatened, Jacob and his friends would simply remain in a state of perpetual readiness.

The general closed his eyes and began to quietly chant the Hatikvah, Israel's national anthem. One-by-one, all the men and women present sang with him the stirring words that express the eternal dream of Israel to live as a free nation in the land of Zion. When they finished the beautiful, haunting tune, there was an embarrassed, shuffling silence.

The general, conscious of the historical importance of the moment, quoted the words attributed in the bible to God as he spoke to the ancient general Joseph, "Be strong and of good courage, be not scared, nor dismayed, for the Lord thy God is with you wherever you go."

As the sanctified words were uttered they heard the relayed sound of the Tel Aviv air raid sirens wailing their eerie warning of danger from the sky. The general spoke again. "Boys and girls of the Israel Defence Forces, we don't need dogs, we need young lions if we are to win this battle. Unleash our lions and tell them if they don't want their children to fight when they are grown, this time we don't stop for our politicians, or Arab armies, or the Russians or the Americans. This time I make an oath that no one will be able to sell out the gains they pay for with their blood, from the Nile to the Euphrates shall be ours or laid waste within ten days – go my lions of Israel, go and roar!"

Within twelve minutes of the order to attack going out, more than seven hundred Israeli warplanes were airborne in the purple sky en route to their targets. Three hundred thousand troops plus two thousand seven hundred and sixty-two tanks with full supporting equipment and personnel were rolling to wage war in Syria, Lebanon, Jordan and the great Egyptian deserts against four times their number.

This time it was the Arab world's turn to be caught unaware of an impending mighty hammer blow. They had never considered the possibility that the military would stage a coup and that their countries would pay the price. They were still labouring under the misconception that the lack of political will and purpose in Israel's cabinet would give their brave Arab armies the time needed to crush Israel once and for all; Palestine would rise from its ashes. It was time for what they passionately believed was their just cause to be served. They were wrong.

It would cost everyone dear.

Chapter Twenty-Five

C150 Air Transport Plane, An Aircraft Of The Royal Saudi Air Force
25 August 2020 – 03.38 hours

The mighty aircraft roared high in the empty desert sky as his Excellency Prince Mohammed surveyed the eighty men lined against the other side of the belly of the giant Hercules aircraft. He loved the fear he saw in their faces as they awaited their unknown punishment. The Royal Guard pointed their MI6 rifles unwaveringly at the prisoners, one of who prostrated himself at the Prince's feet babbling almost incoherent pleas for his life. The Prince kicked the man brutally in his upturned face.

"Stand up" snapped Mo.

The man leapt up, ignoring the broken teeth and blood in his ruined mouth.

"What's your name, worm?"

The man tried to answer through the blood he was swallowing. The Prince slammed his elbow into the soldier's solar plexus in feigned impatience.

The man vomited onto the hem of the Prince's traditional immaculate white Thobi robe. Prince Mo kicked the nearly unconscious man in the groin with all the power in his wiry six-foot body, sending his victim crashing down, screaming for mercy, writhing on the aircraft deck. Mo turned his savagely handsome face to see what extra effect, how much more fear, what hidden buttons of terror, he could toy with amongst the other prisoners.

His sadism was an addiction that needed a fix. With a measure of satisfaction, he saw that some of the men were near to breaking point, but this wasn't sufficient,, he pulled his razor sharp scimitar from its golden scabbard and held it aloft.

"Scum! You will all die for trying to mutiny against the Royal House and the state. Treason is punishable by death and I promise you it will be a death sufficiently terrible to strike terror in anyone's heart that may be thinking of such a foolish act in the future!"

He signaled to his personal guard, Nafti, the ever present and almost silent giant, seemingly carved from granite. The man grabbed a metal handle set into the fuselage with his huge right paw, while with his left hand, he pressed a green button, a large section at the rear of the aircraft slowly opened like some terrible, monstrous orchid revealing the black howling void; two of the prisoners were thrown out into the blackness by the Royal Guards before they realized what was happening, leaving their comrades to cling tenaciously to anything secure they could grab. Mo watched with growing pleasure as men somehow managed to embed their fingernails in the aircraft's metal structure, while others of their number were ripped from handholds, one-by-one, by the laughing guards.

Stories of the cruelty of the Royal Guard were legendary and they relished their unsavory reputation jealously; they vied with one another to commit barbarities on their screaming prisoners before throwing them from the aircraft to certain death. They joyfully hacked off limbs for they knew great rewards flowed from their royal patron when they managed to satisfy his almost insatiable appetite for inflicting pain. He stood watching the mayhem with mounting sexual pleasure, his eyes danced with madness as he urged the guards on to ever more savagery. One of his men was buggering a particularly handsome officer prisoner and the Prince, unable to contain himself from his own frenzy, rushed at them and shoved both the ejaculating guard and his victim into the abyss. He stood panting with laughter as he glimpsed the astonished face of the degenerate guard looking up at the receding aircraft.

Suddenly, a tremendous blow in his back stopped his maniacal good humour. He whirled just in time to see the prisoner he'd previously attacked, come at him again with a red mask of blood and hate where his face had once been, freezing the Prince in panic.

The man's hands tore at Mo's neck like talons, strangling his scream for help into a whisper lost in the madness and blood lost all around them; with one hand the Prince vainly tried to pry the terrible claws from his neck as the man tried to force them both out into the darkness beyond in a macabre ballet of death. Desperately the Prince fought to hack at his assailant with his sword but although he felt the blade repeatedly scythe into the man's back, it did nothing to stop their surge towards the void.

The Prince dropped the sword and used both hands to tear at the hands choking the life from him. He was aware that he was blacking out from lack of oxygen in his brain but seemed unable to coordinate his hands anymore, as inch by terrible inch he was dragged toward death, his will to live ebbed from him. Surprisingly he no longer felt the pain at his throat as he looked at his own situation as if through a misty cloud at someone else, the only emotion he was aware of was love for his killer. If Allah should only grant him one wish it would be to know the love and the body of a man such as this.

He felt one of his feet lose its grip and slide over the aircraft's edge into nothing. The hammering wind licked his body, inviting him to give in and join his ancestors, but strangely he then felt himself being propelled back into the safety of the airplane still locked together with the man whose whole frame seemed to be exploding in crimson.

At that moment Aziz's vision began to clear as he tasted something sticky and wet in his month, and he understood what was happening. His giant guard, Nafti was encircling both the Prince and his attacker, with one huge arm he was pulling them back further into the aircraft simultaneously stabbing furiously with his stiletto knife at the man's back. The awful pressure on the Prince's neck eased, almost imperceptibly at first, then more so with each sickening impact of the knife blade into the man's unprotected back, until Aziz was free as the treasonous officer's strength ebbed from his smashed body, the Prince found his resilient powers surging back as his blood was again free to pump into his brain.

Nafti held the attacker on the floor effortlessly with one of his enormous booted feet. Nafti looked for his master's approval and signaled for one of the other guards to pass him the Prince's sword. He took the weapon and handed it to Aziz who looked down at the man who had so nearly sent him to his maker. He lifted the sword as Nafti bent down and yanked the man by the hair to expose his neck to his Excellency's blade. Nafti however unexpectedly held up his hand as a signal for Aziz to stop the blow in mid-sweep. Reluctantly, the Prince managed to stay the coup de grace with only inches to spare. "What's wrong Nafti? The pig deserves death," he snarled at his savior.

Nafti replied with his usual mock servility.

"Lord, Excellency, Majesty, I have great apologies to make to your Highness for I, a mere foolish, miserable camel have already caused this carcass to feel your wrath. He is dead without ever having tasted your just revenge!"

Nafti prostrated his huge frame before the Prince, exposing his own neck.

"Take my poor head as my just punishment, my master".

Aziz cheerfully sheathed his sword and pulled his ever-faithful servant to his feet and kissed him on each cheek.

"Nafti, you are my brother. What is mine is yours. You can have anything you desire that's in my power to give. We are as one, men from the past, brothers of the desert, now let us rid ourselves of this vermin and go home, you all deserve great rewards for this night's work."

Nafti smiled in gratitude. Once again he had correctly measured his master's mood precisely and therefore he was still a man to be respected and feared by those one-step lower in Saudi Arabia's feudal class system. He picked up the dead man's corpse by gripping its head, and with an incredible display of brute strength, Nafti whirled the body into the air above his head and out of the aircraft like an athlete hurling the discus. Prince Mo looked at his men in satisfaction. They were cheerfully cleaning up the mess left by their carnage and elaborating to one another with stories of their daring and courage against the defenceless traitors they had massacred. How their friends would have relished stories of their heroic actions, thought Nafti, as he pressed the trigger of his new American sub machine gun, spraying thirty rounds of lead into his men. Within seconds the bullets hit all of them in the confined space. The Prince rushed at the writhing mass, hacking at any movement with his gory sword until even their death reflexes were finally stilled.

The Prince breathlessly looked up from the pile of bodies to Nafti whose gun was aimed straight at him. For one moment the Prince tasted fear, but as the gun was lowered, he knew he could trust this one man in the world totally.

"Nafti, are you sure the traitor is amongst this pile of rubbish, that we are now safe?"

Nafti calmly surveyed the dead bodies of Saudi Arabia's elite Praetorian Royal Guard before replying,

"Your Excellency will always be safe as long as Allah allows me to draw breath so that I may guard your Majesty."

"But the traitor... Are you certain, Nafti, that the danger is past?"

Repeated the Prince.

"Your Excellency received the intelligence report from our brothers in Beirut. Did it not warn us that the danger to our royal family would come from a Jew Zionist spy in the Royal Guard, and now are they not all dead?"

The Prince nodded but still felt uncomfortably aware of an invisible threat lurking in his shadows waiting to devour him.

"Yes, you're right as ever, faithful one. We did as we must do. Now, clean up this mess. We return to Jeddah for our rewards and there must be no evidence of tonight's work, not a single trace can point to us, understand... our story is of a terrible fight between the prisoners and the guards should anyone ask, the aircraft out of control, bullets indiscriminately killing friend and foe, O.K.?"

Nafti grunted agreement.

"Now clean this mess up, will you. I'm going to take a drink with the pilot. I need a whisky. I'll tell him the night parachute landing exercise went well, eh!"

The Prince walked towards the flight deck, leaving Nafti the messy task of flinging body after body from the airplane to the desert below. The giant inaudibly whispered an ancient prayer as he did this gruesome work.

"Hear, oh Israel, the Lord our God, the Lord is one. Yeah, though I walk through the valley of the shadow of death, I shall fear no evil, for you comfort me."

Nafti thought of the home in Israel he hadn't seen since the Lebanon war when he'd been infiltrated into the enormous numbers of released Palestinian prisoners of that conflict. Initially it had been simple enough to substitute him for a genuine dead Arab peasant soldier. But after many years living as Nafti the unthinking guard, the man born Benjamin Mizrahi, was finally nearing the end of the terrible task his masters in Tel Aviv had set for him so long ago to which he had dedicated all the strength in his mighty body and every atom of his incredibly patient, analytical and methodical mind.

How he missed his wife and child in Basra. It was so many years since he had any contact with them, having paid such a price for his country.

Nafti dare not allow himself to dwell on his past for he knew the terrible price of torture he would pay if he were even suspected of being the spy. He knew without doubt that the revolution, which had spread across Islam's many countries, had huge implications for the situation here in Saudi Arabia. If she were to collapse, so might the hated and envied organization of petroleum-exporting countries, and should that happen, anything was possible in a new Middle East order, even peace. He was aware that the leadership of Saudi Arabia was covertly working together with the Israelis because their fear of Iran was greater than their hatred of the Jewish state. They followed the maxim that the enemy of my enemy is my friend.

It was a badly kept secret in royal circles near to the Royal Palace that there were those closer to Prince Mohammed who would do anything to stop any rapprochement with Israel.

تحت الآلهة الجدول

Chapter Twenty-Six

The Conference Room Of Applecrombie Bros. Merchant Bank, London, England
25 August 2020 –12.00 hours

Seated along the left side of the long teak conference table were six representatives of the Merchant bank, Applecrombie Brothers. Each had an untouched glass of water and a blank lined yellow legal foolscap notepad with pencil neatly arranged before him. The chair at the table's head was still vacant as were all the chairs facing the impatient bank personnel in their claustrophobic lair. None of the men present knew who had designed this room without windows but everybody cursed the unknown person for depriving them of fresh air and a wonderful view down onto the centre of London's West End from this office perched near the summit of Colossus, the Bank's sixty-five floor world headquarters.

One of the group, a young American called Dean Bedlow from the bank's burgeoning foreign industrial investments division, voiced everyone's thoughts in his usual Boston accented search for equality with his older English colleagues. They had politely but firmly kept their distance from him because he was young, American and he had a speech impediment. This was considered an unforgivable triple transgression.

Bedlow's new department also caused concern since it crossed into areas some of the men at the table had considered there private preserve.

"I make it tttt…ten after ttttt….welve," he stuttered as he examined his watch to emphasize the tardiness of the occupants of the empty chairs.

"Perhaps they're not overly concerned that you and we are waiting, Mr. Bedlow," said George Sylvester, the bank's venerable and caustic chief of legal affairs. He arched his eyes in his quizzically assumed paternal way that said to most people,

"Shut your stupid mouth!"

But any such subtlety failed with Dean Bedlow whose mind only measured facts, not looks or opinions.

"I have a lllll...lunch appointment at one in the cccc...city," he explained to the uncaring group.

"Oh, most interesting, young Mr. Bedlow, and who are you eating today?"

Asked George Sylvester, obtaining chuckles and smiles from all the men except the mirthless Bedlow.

At that moment the bank's chairman Lord Radling entered the room arm-in-arm with the object of their meeting, Eddie Roman, who looked as if he'd been on a diet of many such unpleasant encounters. Lord Radling led Roman to the seat at the right of his own at the table's head.

As was his habit, Radling began the discussion without preamble. He assumed that every executive he'd selected to be at this table was intelligent enough to be fully briefed on the background of the subject in hand.

"Gentlemen, you all know Mr. Roman, whose business interests we are about to debate."

Radling's clipped speech perfectly complemented his neat unfussy features, clothes and manner, all of which seemed ideally designed for a banker, which indeed was the case. Radling had metamorphosed from his humble origins as an insignificant, uncouth, ill-kempt Applecrombie book-keeper who left the Army at the end of the Malayan Emergency. After ending his service as a dashing Captain after having risen in active service from his humble enlistment. After he was demobilized he again transformed himself, this time into a graduate of economics and business studies on the ex-army officer's state funded Higher education scholarship in late 1947.

His return to the bank on January 3rd 1948 had been a momentous day for Radling and for old Mr. Applecrombie, the bank's founder, whose own son had been killed while evacuating with the Royal Scots Guards from Dunkirk. Applecrombie had assumed and planned for his son would take over the business after hostilities had ceased, but now his boy would never come home, and here was young Radling who'd gone from the bank a humble clerk and who had come back not only alive but as a first class honours graduate after a distinguished war serving his country. He was an officer and a single gentleman, these last two descriptions being a consideration of prime importance because the old banker had an almost unmarriageable daughter to be rid of named Letty. She had contrived to keep most of the American G.I.s in England sexually fulfilled. She was known in her racy circles as a bit of a girl!

As an astute young man, Radling could see how he was being manoeuvred and subtly encouraged the old banker's plans. After all, a soiled woman giving you a solid bank was, he considered, a very reasonable and solid dowry exchange. The marriage duly took place despite Letty's reluctance and then the most bizarre thing had happened. During the honeymoon of Mr. and Mrs. Herbert Radling, they had fallen irretrievably in love, to their own astonishment and her father's deep gratification. With immense happiness and gratitude, he allowed his son-in-law to have the chairman's seat for his own as his fifth wedding anniversary present and since that day in 1953, the bank and young Mr. & Mrs. Radling had never looked back.

The loving marriage had mellowed the young man's abrasive edge until the day came when he, his wife and his bank, had become part of the establishment they had so yearned to join. Success followed success until the present, which found Radling a life peer of the realm at the helm of an institution that he'd safely, sometimes brilliantly, steered through all the hazards of boom, bust, recession, wars, conflicts, stagnation, too little regulation and too much, inflation and stagflation.

He looked at his men as they, in turn, waited for him to continue. Somehow, the God he so passionately believed in contrived some universal measuring scales, which dictated that no individual could have everything they wanted.

He had it all bar a child, and now looking around the prospective leaders of his empire he wished Eddie Roman, who was today's offering on the bank's altar of failure, could be told of his deep felt wish to be of help and encouragement.

"George," he said to the bank's chief legal officer, "Where do we stand legally?"

George Sylvester carefully put on the half glasses he used for reading and peering over at clients of the bank who hadn't measured up to his codes. He slowly reached into his bulging briefcase and drew out a large cherry-red leather folder stencil-marked 'Roman Files 1991-2018'. He opened it and quietly to himself, read from papers in it for a full minute as a theatrical hush fell over the room. They were all aware of Sylvester's technique, but you had to admit the old codger had style, even if it was a bit operatic and pedantic. He closed the file and placed it before him on the desk as if to distance him from the distasteful contents.

"Mr. Chairman, gentlemen... Mr. Roman."

He pointedly divorced Roman from the gentlemen's category.

"Unfortunately it is my duty to bring to the notice of this meeting that our client Eddie Roman Properties Ltd and its affiliated companies is in default of clauses 9, 13, 14A, B, C, sub Para (i), (ii), (iii) and (iv) plus clause 16, 18, 19, 20A..."

Before the punctilious lawyer could elaborate on Roman's legal breaches of contract further, Lord Radling held up his hand as if he were a traffic policeman halting traffic at an over-busy intersection.

"Yes, I'm sure George, it's all as you say it is, but can you just hop along to the bottom line."

George was rattled when not allowed to unfold a case piece by logical piece, but orders were to be obeyed, especially when one's pension beckoned within the year. He barely looked at the downcast businessman whose professional obligation it was his duty to crucify, after certifying the nails were of uniform length.

"I'm sorry. Mr Chairman. Put in brief form, I would state that, legally, the bank has Eddie by the short and curlies. He owes more than was allowed for, he's overdue on his notes, we have his personal guarantees against his personal holdings and properties which we now find are either charged to other lending institutions or perhaps even worse, sold to pay us our interest charges on established debts without our approval or consent, which of course we couldn't give because we didn't know what he was up to, and were misled to boot."

Lord Radling noticed that Eddie Roman never showed any telltale flicker of emotion as Sylvester remorselessly and systematically, tore him to shreds.

"Further to which, we discovered, entirely by chance, that the companies to which we were making a facility available were trading when insolvent, which apart from breaking explicit contract terms, is also a criminal breach of law for fraud, malfeasance and theft. Nothing personal of course Mr. Roman... Need I go on, Mr. Chairman?"

Radling watched Roman for some look of remorse or defiance, a gesture perhaps, something for the older man to latch onto, but the face of the young business entrepreneur was blank, giving nothing away.

Knowing only the deepest of sorrows, the bank chairman turned from Eddie to address his junior colleagues in the formalized ritual of clawing back money used by a bank when the veneer of public attitudes is dropped and the raw meat of avarice, cloaked in commercial sense, is exposed.

"Yes, we've heard enough, George. Before I continue, have you anything you wish to say to this Board, Eddie?"

He didn't expect a reply but Eddie looked up and to everyone's amazement the only thing on his face was joy.

"Yes, I would like to say a few words before I'm discharged as if I were a piece of smelly crap on the bank's shoes!"

Radling was starting to enjoy himself; perhaps the boy was going to fight after all. "No need to be offensive, old boy. We're all civilized, I hope!"

Sylvester interposed to muted "Hear Hear" noises from all his colleagues, apart from the Chairman and Bedlow who hadn't ever seen his first bank in Detroit employ such methods, which seemed to him a waste of his valuable time.

"Stuff it up your ass, you old humbug!" Eddie snapped to the horrified, now-huffily angry Sylvester.

"I came here because I had to try and straighten up our business together. I don't have to listen to your stupidity and duplicity. In fact, apart from his Lordship and the young guy there." Eddie indicated Bedlow with a jab of his forefinger towards his position. "You're all a bunch of fucking hypocrites, and whatever happens now, I want you to all know that I hate your rotten guts. The reason I came here was so we could do a deal instead of me taking the first jet out of the country with a big bundle of cash. You'd have liked that, so you could close the book on me as if I'm the criminal when we all know the big criminals here are all wearing pin-striped suits. I couldn't give a damn about the bank or any of the rest of you but I do have respect for your boss, Lord Radling here. He's the only one of you with an ounce of humanity. He, at least, helped me, and that isn't crawling. To prove it, I'll now expose your little corrupt games to him and damn the consequences to me; you've just proved that they don't matter anymore, do they?"

Anxious glances were flashing danger signs from face to corrupt face amongst the bank's executives. Members of the board reacted in singular, different ways that added together spelt 'guilty'.

Lord Radling, who knew more than his over-clever staff thought possible, was hugely enjoying young Eddie's blitzkrieg counter ploy.

"Steady, Eddie. Think about what you're saying!" he said for all to hear, only Eddie could see his conspiratorial mischievous and encouraging wink that both mystified and pleased him.

"Now, which one of you should I start with?"

Eddie looked from one squirming man to another, and gratefully remembered why he'd kept such a careful and detailed log book of every single piece of graft and corruption he came into contact with, thanks to advice he'd received many years ago from Max Roman to trust no one and keep himself always protected.

"Don't sssss..stop now, Mr. Roman. This is real ddddd...drama, kinda like *Dallas* with hatchets and bbbb....blood instead of bbbbb..broads and oil!" said Dean Bedlow, grasping at a chance to leapfrog over soon-to-be-dead executive lepers on the corporate ladder. His Chairman noticed the youthful, bright, sharp eagerness in Bedlow but also the callow, see-through opportunism which could lead to his own exposure, for any well-aimed kicks below his own belt by those present that Roman didn't bring down with him in his final business death throes.

Eddie was about to speak when a middle-aged lady rushed into the room without knocking. Her name was Miss Jean Docker and she had been Radling's ultra correct and old-fashioned personal secretary for more than thirty years. What came next was even more out of character.

"Oh Bertie, have you heard what's just happened?"

Everyone, especially Lord Radling was dumbfounded by her entry and now this. Must be her change of life, he thought, send her for a nice long holiday. She wasn't put off by the frosty silence.

"You haven't heard? It's total war in the Middle East, a big all-out war this time!"

Eddie would remember the next few minutes for the rest of his life as these men he'd written off as nothing more than merchants of misery, came alive. "What? Whereabouts exactly, Jean? Any of our people hurt?" asked Radling,

"I'm not sure but I think the Syrians have retaken Beirut, and we've lost contact with our bank there after it tweeting us earlier to say they'd been hit by Israeli bombing."

"Much damage to the building?" Dean Bedlow asked, suddenly not stuttering.

"Fuck the building!" bellowed the Chairman. "How about our people? Get our people out of the affected area, Paul. That's your top priority, do it right now!"

Paul Glassner, head of personnel, rushed from the room to do his bidding. "George," the Chairman continued, "get onto the Foreign Office and see what the official attitude is. That could well affect us medium and long term, but we need to know how it's likely to go." George Sylvester was out of his chair and gone from the room quicker than the forgotten Eddie would have thought possible.

"Next, Bedlow!" barked Radling to the young, now-nervous American. "You went to school with half of the whiz kids at the State Department in DC. Get some solid information from them how long this is going to last, who'll win, who'll lose, and for Christ's sake, will the world still have oil-power next month or do we all just get our bloody candles out? Go!"

Without waiting for Bedlow's scurry out of the room, the bank's helmsman turned to the remaining three executives. "Tappis, you get onto the Treasury. Find out what's going to happen. We'll need to know, for instance, if the Arabs are going to keep up supplies of crude. If so, will it… no, can it continue to be paid for in dollars. If not, what the bloody hell apart from camels or blondes do they think it'll be, got it?" Tappis, in charge of the bank's activities in currency movements, was out of the room like an Olympic athlete.

"Chapman," said the Chairman to a timid, mousy little man sitting on one of the last two chairs still occupied. "How much have we invested in oil, petrochemicals, plastics? You know what I'm getting at; any companies likely to be hit hard by a big shooting war."

Chapman's brain, his boss knew, belied his humble looks. He had by far the highest I.Q. on the board, but his character lacked any authority and not even his children gave him the respect he received, and greedily cherished, from his beloved chief. His giant intellect started to collate the bank's enormous and varied international investment portfolio, one of the biggest of its kind in the world, and was Ben's proud boast to his patronizing golfing partners. In more relaxed moments, he tested his photographic memory and lightning-speed mental facility with numbers against the bank's computer to see which could give a true value to the bank's world portfolio at the close of the world's major markets for business on Friday nights. That was easier than this; middle of the day, middle of the week, only part of the portfolio, that notoriously volatile when there was tension as there had been for the last several weeks. He sighed.

"What is it, Chapman?" Lord Radling asked. "You need the computer? I only need a rough estimate."

Chapman was torn, as usual, by self-doubt and fearful as ever of letting down his revered Chairman.

"C'mon tell us. What could be the damage?"

"Well Sir, I can't be more accurate than plus or minus approximately three per cent for a multiplicity of variables which include fluctuations in–"

Radling cut him short. "The figures, I'm sure you have it quicker and better than any other man in any other bank."

Chapman, his slight ego pumped up almost beyond his ability to endure, made him certain his figures were accurate to within one per cent. "Sir, we have world assets with a total face value of two hundred and twenty-two point four-five billions of pounds sterling, assuming last night's rate of exchange holds true at present, and that a panic sale of such commodities has not yet sent their value down drastically. Plus of course today's traffic, such as it is, in foreign currency exchanges, which as you know can be many times that number, although our exposure will not be."

Eddie Roman was quietly awed at what he was hearing. He'd seen large money being moved and used to buy and sell, but nothing like the extravaganza he was now witnessing.

"Chapman, Maxwell," he indicated the tall cadaverous man, who Eddie remembered as a highly-qualified auditor who'd turned this considerable acumen, and his talent for problems analyzing and evaluating assets against liabilities, into the 'new investments' branch of the bank. Chapman and Maxwell were known by their less charitable competitors as the banking world's new Burke and Hare; the take-over cradle-snatchers, for always making it appear so easy to get just what they wanted, and making those lame ducks fit to fly again, which was why Eddie had presumed they'd carved his little company into such neat, palatable morsels, ready to be eaten whole by this gruesome twosome.

They avidly listened to their marching orders from Lord Radling, who Eddie now realized was another man entirely when push came to shove, a man never to be underestimated, unless of course you liked failure. "Sell all our holdings in anything vaguely oil-based immediately, right?" They nodded, and Eddie thought they looked more like eager foxhounds after prey than city high flyers in mid-crisis.

"What losses can we afford to take before we stop, sir?" asked Maxwell in his flat north country accent which many caricatured, but never to his face, which held no hint of anything other than hardness on its craggy, perpetually scowling, pitted surface. This hid the man inside who was just as tough and nasty, which didn't worry Maxwell in the least because he knew he wouldn't have been in line for his Lordship's chair if he were soft.

"Any loss we take today," said their Chairman, "will be less than tomorrow or any subsequent day in the near future,".

"Can I ask you for clarification, Sir, something in writing?" asked Maxwell in what was for him an amazing outburst.

"The world's falling apart and you want a bloody memo!" exclaimed the Chairman, before he paused for theatrical effect. "You take your losses, whatever they are and buy into Lockheed, General Motors and Vickers, get my drift". The two men obviously did but Radling decided to think out loud anyway. "Keep a cash liquidity buffer of five hundred million and keep your portfolio buys secret. We've probably got an hour or so advantage on the Yanks. It's still not dawn in New York so get our men there moving straight away. Now Chapman, before you go, what do you think will be the effect on the Seven Sisters of this war?"

Chapman had already been thinking how he would answer such a question, so his answer was sure and quick. "The big oil companies will hold up for a day or two while everyone verifies that the war's as bad as it sounds. Then they will, as usual, panic to get out of oil. Their price will then drop like a stone, probably a fifty percent markdown in five days, then they'll stick at around that while they make soothing noises about worldwide assets and the rest of their nonsense. After that it depends." He fell silent under his Chairman's inquisitive gaze.

"On what precisely does it depend?" he asked.

"Prices could rocket if hostilities cease after a week, to buy back in could be extremely punishing, but should they keep fighting into a second or third week ir will be an entirely different matter. If the Israelis had a crack at the odd oil installation then who knows how low those shares could drop. I'd guess below a third of their present value."

The bank's chief whistled a low-pitched note of appreciation.

Eddie watched and listened. He'd already decided to copy whatever moves this man made in the market and he didn't give a damn how he'd got hold of the money to do so. Lord Radling stood up and paced the room in a frenzy of mental calculations, his brain sifting options, rejecting, probing, measuring until his decision was reached. "We go for it, gentlemen. We sell short now and we buy in with everything we have the moment those prices have gone below forty percent of their cost today!"

Chapman got up from his chair to do Radling's bidding, but Maxwell was made of sterner stuff. "I must register my reservations, sir. What happens if we take a caning, if the war stops before the shares tumble, if we take a loss transferring funds from one area to another? It could be well in excess of twenty percent. That's billions of pounds of other people's money."

Radling didn't even pause before replying. "Any other course is just as risky and probably more so. If we leave money in oil shares when we know there's a war right on their doorstep, we could easily be accused of being caught with our pants down, of being another group of fussy old English gentlemen, and quite likely poor, bankrupt Englishmen at that. We made our reputation as a country, not with preachers and shopkeepers but as pirates and fighters. No, we'll do things my way and we'll aim at winning this particular battle by attacking rather than sheltering for cover, hoping we don't get raped. We're a bit like the Israelis. Don't you see? We can only attack when and how suits us best, because to defend a bank our size in with the big boys on their terms would be suicide. They can take losses of billions and survive because the fucking governments will bail them out yet again despite whatever they say to the contrary. They're still too big to be allowed to fail. It doesn't matter what any minister says, so let them, and perhaps we'll come out of this ahead of the game."

Maxwell considered another verbal parry but thought discretionary caution was his safest exit when he saw the frosty look on his lordship's face that eloquently said, "Get on with it!"

Maxwell and Chapman left the room for their appointed works, leaving Radling and Eddie alone together.

"What happens to me now?" asked Eddie, his expression giving the older man the feeling that he didn't care much whatever happened. He couldn't have been more wrong. Eddie desperately craved success but no longer judged his life by commercial criteria. If you make a few million profit by the age of thirty, you are a success, pass go, collect a wife, a house in Chelsea or Kensington and two mistresses. Another million by thirty-five, pass go again, divorce wife, smile fading, hips bulging, change mistresses for friends of your daughters. No, all the bullshit status symbol race had vanished from Eddie's mind since he'd had pause to re-evaluate what life for him was about, and it wasn't things that mattered, not cars, houses or what other people thought about him, it was what he thought about himself, the pleasure of sleeping peacefully without the aid of drugs or booze and waking up pleased to be alive. In future, he thought, that's the way I'll be then none of the bastards can hurt me again.

"I won't offer you money for them, but tell me what are you brooding about so deeply. My problems and yours could be mutually self-effacing, if you understand a humble banker's opening gambit, that's a form of invitation from me to you," said Radling.

Eddie understood the game well enough, but considering how the banker liked to demonstrate his brilliance, he wasn't going to be a killjoy. "No, I can't see that our problems are mutually self whatever. I have creditors of a couple of million, I owe you bunch a bloody fortune which wasn't due yet and because of some fancy footwork now is, while you're juggling zillions around the place like there's no tomorrow. I can't see anything mutual at all."

Radling was clever enough to recognize the feeling of being towed around by the nose, but as he'd made certain that the bank compromised itself before young Roman so that he'd have some justification to help the young whelp, he didn't mind overmuch. "What I'm so inadequately saying, Eddie, is that you know the bank's most intimate and urgent business which must always remain confidential. Anything other could be disastrous for us. Now do you follow?"

"Yes," Eddie said. "You have a problem other than me."

Lord Radling smiled to hide his growing impatience. "Eddie, I do believe you're being intentionally obtuse. You understand my offer well enough; we'll scratch your back if you - in - return, scratch ours."

For the first time in a long while, Eddie Roman smiled. He knew he'd only got a reprieve rather than a pardon, but if he now had some time to breathe, a chance to take stock and explore new, unexplored territory, anything was possible, even the resurrection of his self-belief that had been so relentlessly stripped from him in the last months. "Yes," he said. "We can work something out, Lord Radling. But I should tell you before we start that I've got an uncommonly-itchy back."

Both men smiled in anticipation of an interesting little transaction that was to mean very much more to many people than either of them would have dreamed possible.

Chapter Twenty-Seven

G.H.Q. Of The Palestine Unified Army Of The Liberation, Beirut, Lebanon
27 August 2020 – 14.30 hours

The brown two-story building looked nothing like a military headquarters should look, thought Prince Mo as his man Nafti drove their jeep close behind the Range Rover driven by the accursed Palestinian terrorist into the sand-blown unkempt courtyard. The Prince missed none of the bristling gun emplacements or the tell tale watchfulness of the ten uniformed Palestinians who were obviously extra security in case he had led the enemy to their lair. As if he would betray them, he thought. As much as he might like to, he could not.

Nafti opened his door and the Prince followed the giant to the entrance, which was guarded by two more Fedayeen with their guns cocked and aimed at their prospective guests. Much to the Prince's displeasure, one of the guards asked to see their official passes issued with today's date embossed on the digitized photos taken by their first contact beside their hotel pool earlier still in the already-boiling sun. Nafti gave the man the passes and he examined them closely for what seemed to the Prince an unwarranted period.

"Do you know who I am?" he barked at the Palestinian who was now casually picking his teeth with a corner of the Prince's identity photography.

"Why, don't you know who you are, camel fucker?" the guard responded.

Before the Prince could act, there was an enormous bang as if the biggest paper bag in the world had exploded above their heads, leaving the Prince and the Palestinians momentarily too stunned to react. Nafti seemed unaffected as he sunk his razor sharp knife into the guard's heart leaving the man to choke bloodily on his last words as he collapsed against the double doors he'd been guarding. The shelling sent the Palestinian security men scurrying for cover. All except the Prince, Nafti and the remaining guard vanished into shelters. The guard rested his Armalite on Nafti's lower lip, forcing his jaw open with the barrel pointed down his throat. Nafti, the

Prince noted with approval, had in turn manoeuvred his deadly knife so that its razor sharp point was dangerously circling the guard's nervously bobbing adam's apple.

"I have no argument with you. Your friend here," Nafti spat towards the corpse on the floor by his feet, "Insulted his Excellency Prince Mo and therefore paid the price. You do not wish to die, do you?"

Nafti spoke so quietly and sincerely that the guard became far more nervous of the wicked blade at his throat than of the increasingly-accurate shells that were exploding ever nearer. He turned slowly to the door and knocked on it with the butt of his gun several times before it opened slightly.

Nafti yanked Mo behind him and crashed into the door with all his massive strength, and rushed into the darkness beyond, scattering the two guards who supposedly guaranteed security behind the first line of defence. Nafti viciously chopped at the throat of the man to his right who bounced off the grimy whitewashed wall as if he'd been shot from a cannon. The Prince had now squeezed into the dark corridor behind Nafti and - realizing the danger from the guard still outside - instinctively swung the heavy door closed, just as the man was trying to creep in. He took the door's full weight on his left cheekbone, which broke inwards, as did the rest of his surprised, wrecked face. Nafti had meanwhile grabbed the fourth and last guard, lifting him up into a backbreaking bear-hug and was rushing with the man at some further soldiers who had entered the hall to see what the noise as all about.

The Prince screamed, "Nafti! Stop! I command you!"

Nafti stopped within a few feet of his next victims who looked on with mouths agape as the man mountain carelessly squeezed the guard's back one last time. They all heard the crack as the column snapped immediately prior to Nafti dropping the dead man before his comrades. Nafti and the Prince turned towards the sudden sound of a gun's safety catch being removed somewhere on the ill-lit shadowy stairs to their left.

A man with the face of an Arab, but the near white blonde hair of a north European, came into the light. His one blue eye and his khaki eye patch where the other eye had been supposedly shot out fighting the Israelis, identified him at once to the Prince and his guard as General Yasser Nabul, leader of all the now-united Palestinian factions, splinter groups and armies; the undisputed premier designate for the embryonic Palestinian state.

"Your entry is that of an enemy not a brother, your Excellency," he said to Prince Mo in that hushed way he always talked in any of the seven languages he'd mastered.

"Your hospitality and greeting were also most novel, General," replied Mo, adding the man's courtesy title more from fear of reprisal than respect. He saw Nafti edge towards the stairs, but so did Nabul who now aimed his gun at the giant.

"You are clearly an excellent guard, if a little over-eager, but this gun would still kill you before you took another step. Shall we start again, this time as brothers?"

He holstered his revolver and walked down the few remaining steps with his arms outstretched to the Prince who responded in kind. The two men embraced, kissing each other on the cheek in the prescribed manner, using the opportunity to look the other in the eye.

"Now you are in my house, anything in it is yours to take and to keep. Let's go and take tea while entertainment is arranged for your companion," offered the Palestinian.

"You are most kind, General, and I hope some way for me to repay such kindness becomes possible since otherwise I should be eternally miserable. But Nafti, my guard, is also my right arm and trusted advisor therefore much as I'm sure he appreciates your offer to let your men entertain him, he must also take part in our discussions, if you would be so kind as to allow such an unworthy imposition."

Both the Prince and the general had spent their adult lives learning well the Arabic code of manners which to a western ear was confusing since you said one thing and meant another; furthermore when men of the Middle East discussed a single issue of importance, it was bad-mannered for either party to raise the matter at hand until all the niceties had been systematically observed.

Even then, thought Benjamin, formerly of Iraq and Israel, but now known as the Saudi bodyguard Nafti, who silently sat with the two men as they drank yet more Turkish coffee, they sometimes even then don't get to the point because of some fault in etiquette or an unwillingness to ever decide anything. These two men, the Prince and the general; only in Arabia could an alliance of convenience between a feudal monarchy and a Marxist revolutionary be considered.

As he listened to the men gradually edge closer to the subject at hand, he thought, 'not bad, only two hours and they'd nearly got it together'. If he ever made it home to Israel, he would never again complain about his government's slowness to act; comparatively they worked at the speed of light.

The Prince put down his coffee cup and sadly shook his head. "It is indeed unfortunate that we did not meet previously. Perhaps it is the will of Allah that we waited for this propitious day."

The one-eyed general knew enough about politics to realize when a deal was on offer, but could this fat, wild-eyed royal emissary deliver anything other than more dead bodies of which he already had a surplus courtesy of the war-mongering Israelis.

"Your Excellency intrigues this humble soldier. We brothers in Islam are however from far distant lands so you must excuse my ignorance and lead me by the hand to your innermost thoughts."

Like most Arabs, the Prince always disliked the Palestinians in much the same way many westerners hated the Jews; borne out of unreasoning fear and envy. He swallowed the rising bile in his throat and maintained his smiling countenance.

"You flatter me too greatly, for it is you who has welded the Palestinian nation into one force for its holy purpose of reclaiming for Allah your homeland."

The Prince enjoyed the subtlety of his speech, for didn't both men know only too well that the Palestinians, like all their Arab brothers, were again being swept aside by the rampaging Israelis, But now some sugar for this bitter pill.

"I understand your soldiers have been heroic in their attacks on the invaders and have inflicted enormous casualties. This morning on your Free Palestine radio broadcast I heard myself how you had shot down over one hundred Israeli jets in the first two days. Why, if you should continue for another week like that they will have no air force at all!"

Although Mo said this with seeming sincerity, Nafti couldn't conceal the smile on his face from the bitter general who finally started to lose some of his famed patience. Now it was Nabul's turn to speak some home truths,

"Your Excellency also heard, I'm sure, the Syrians' claim that they had shot down one hundred and thirty-five Israeli aircraft, the Egyptians more still and yet only the Jordanians are gifted with good eyesight; they claim to have brought down thirteen aircraft for a loss of sixty-seven of their own ancient heaps, and before we go any further it is also not entirely accurate to say that all the Jews are running into the sea. In fact if our allies continue to advance backwards at their present rate, the new capital of Israel could well be Cairo or Damascus!"

The Saudi Prince had known things were not good, but like most people in Arabia, he listened to the broadcast propaganda and divided claims of success by four which still wouldn't have been as bad a picture as the terrible story of defeat the Palestinian was drawing for him.

"What of all the weapons and money we have poured in over the years? What happened to all the aircraft we shipped here? The tanks, the guns, the missiles, the air defence systems? Why aren't they stopping the Jews with them?"

The Palestinian walked over to the map of the region that covered most of the wall in the otherwise-undecorated Spartan room which served him as both office and living quarters. He pointed to each country as he lectured the Prince.

"Your Excellency forgets that an Arab is a mythical creature. Here are Syrians, Jordanians, Egyptians, Iraqis, Lebanese, Saudis and lastly, spread throughout the map, my people, the Jews of Arabia, the Palestinians. You ask what happened. I'll tell you. As usual, every group is looking towards it own salvation and benefit, the Iraqis would like to use their weapons on Israel for itself, Hussein wants the same for himself, and we the Palestinians once more get put, as the Americans say, 'on the back burner'. Your guard, Nafti, showed you downstairs what one determined man could do against a disorganized rabble. That is again what's happening; the Israelis are organized, intelligent, capable and above all, united by their battle for national survival. A battle we understand only too well. Once again, they enjoy support from America and Europe because we used oil sanctions as a political weapon too often, and now Israel is once more their heroic proxy warrior at the same time we huff and puff, unsure, uncoordinated, and with no central command structure worthy of the name. When the west did what the Arab League asked of them in Libya against the lunatic, they turned on them within one day. They just don't trust us. We had it in our hands with Obama hating their leadership for a time. He was a potential friend, but we lost that chance to the Jewish vote in the last American election!"

The Prince knew the truth in what the Palestinian had said, but it didn't make it any easier to swallow.

"You sound almost as if you admire the Zionist swine, my brother."

The general once more sat down. "As a soldier, I envy them their generals. As a Palestinian, I envy them our country. Admire is not the word I would use, but it doesn't matter now for our world once again is in despair."

Nafti looked at the tormented Palestinian leader and made a mental note to report to his masters in Tel Aviv that, in his opinion here, was the new, most dangerous Arab leader Israel would face since being politically outflanked by Anwar Sadat in the late seventies, but inside, he wished the man a long life because surely a man like this, of genuine intelligence and feeling must eventually understand that the Jews also deserved somewhere to call home.

Prince Mo thought Nabul was a gullible but necessary fool, a man who obviously could sway the masses, a man who had somehow undermined and destroyed both Hamas in Gaza and the Palestinian Authority as self deluded failures and then systematically crushed all splinter groups, or incorporated them, impressive if incomprehensible to Mo as he pondered his next ploy to the young general.

"As you say, General, every group is after its own ends and no one, not even you with your holy cause of reclaiming Jerusalem, can unite them, but I believe there is an alternative for you and we, because when the whole cake is not possible, then half the cake is at least comforting. Who knows what can happen once we have full bellies from our cake? We may then be able to take the rest."

The general began to see the devious Saudi Prince's logic and was more than willing to listen, although he wondered what this piece of cake might cost his people. The answer to all his questioning thoughts was not long in coming from the Prince. "Many people make guesses about my country's wealth. What do you think we're worth?"

The general shrugged.

"It is important you understand our financial power because should you and we become bed-mates, we must both bring the wedding price; you your military prowess, ourselves our money. No marriage can be properly consummated if we are not mutually attractive. So I ask you again, what do you think Saudi has?"

The general was bored by his guest's Levantine manner but knew he had to listen to any proposition that could lead his people to their Palestine.

"I am not a man who knows too much about capitalism or imperialist banks or Swiss deposits, but I would guess your country has reserves of several hundred billions of dollars, apart from your oil."

The Prince turned to Nafti with a triumphant smile on his satanic face. "You see how well we have hidden our light, no one but the inner circle of my family and now you two know."

He looked back at the impatient Palestinian who was pointedly examining his watch. "We sell every barrel of our oil on the spot market these days. You are aware we unilaterally withdrew from all our prior long-term contracts. We also cut our production by half when we realized the west was drowning in our petro-dollars; our price for one barrel of oil is now two hundred and seventy-five dollars. It was two dollars fifty-nine in 1973. Our oil income last year alone was over four trillion dollars, that is four thousand billion. We are the world's biggest oil producer, biggest earner and biggest investor. We could buy the world's ten biggest corporations with just twenty-two weeks of our revenue at the new levels of production. We have current foreign investments that exceed five trillion dollars, that's a five with so many zeros behind that the mind cannot imagine so much money exists. Amongst just three of our biggest American bankers, we are openly holding deposits that are fifty times greater in value than all the gold reserves their government has. We control whether the world stops or goes, lives or dies!"

The general's one good eye stared unblinking at his lecturer. Laconically he said, "You have told me you are wealthy beyond measure, but soon the Zionist entity will be as rich as you. Are you not aware that they have now stolen the gas fields from the sea which we believe should rightfully belong to Lebanon. Soon they will be supplying between three per cent of the world's needs via their new processing plant in Cyprus, and they have somehow also robbed and plotted so that they have a stranglehold on more high tech infrastructure than anyone other than the #Americans. So how does your money stop Israel's tanks?"

The Saudi Prince bristled at this flagrant taunting of his country's military impotence compared to Israel's much-vaunted leap into the forefront of the developed industrial nations which had been suddenly and shockingly assisted by their finding the biggest new gas fields in the world. Nevertheless, the Prince well remembered the precise orders of his uncle, the King, were not to be disobeyed in any way, so he kept his temper and continued,

"We underestimated America's anger at our OPEC agreement to cut production. We'd become used to raising prices as and when we saw fit, we assumed that we could equally well reduce their supply of oil. Hadn't we warned them for years that it was a finite resource and had to be carefully guarded since it was, and is, our only natural asset? But they didn't hear us... we knew they would scream. We'd even carefully invested trillions of dollars in America and elsewhere through not only our visible sovereign funds but also a carefully-planned labyrinth of nominees and dummy companies which no one could touch, should the US and Europeans decide to freeze our openly held deposits as the Americans did with Iran's holdings during Khomeini's madness.

We thought... no, we were certain, that our decision of yesterday to refuse dollars in payment for oil, plus exchanging all our dollars into Euros would kill off America's ridiculous support to Israel overnight. Do you know what's happened on the exchanges today? The dollar had lost fifty percent of its true value within the thirty minutes it took for their President to declare a state of national emergency and order all banking and share trading closed till further notice. Their Federal Reserve had spent about four or five hundred billion dollars in half an hour of buying back their own worthless money to stop it going even lower. This is purely an indication of how we Saudis intend to fight with you against our enemies."

The general's Marxist soul crawled with discomfort at his hearing of this huge waste of money, one millionth of which could have alleviated his people's long suffering in those terrible refugee camps into which he'd been born and bred in squalor and hate.

"Forgive me, Excellency," he said. "But if every one of your dollars was transformed into a man with a gun, it would help us far more than your economically crippling the imperialist running dogs and their lackeys. What precisely are you offering and what do you want in return?"

Prince Mo's reluctance to hurry his monologue ended when he heard low-flying enemy fighter-bombers swoop overhead. Nafti looked from the window at the jet's cannons blazing ferociously into the Fedayeen who were caught unprotected in the open courtyard transforming them into yet more carrion for the region's ever-growing mountain of the dead. Neither Mo nor his Palestinian host looked out. The Prince's cell phone rang. He held up his hand to the Palestinian leader, pressed his telephone to his ear and listened for a moment, then said, "Understood,"

Before he disconnected, then resumed their conversation. "The Americans just publicly pledged their total and unconditional support to Israel in the war as long as they don't seek new territory. They have also told the Russians that any attack or military moves by them in the region will be considered an act of war on America itself. They have openly stated they would declare total war on the Russians should the warning be ignored. Russia has said nothing yet in reply.

America's entire Seventh Fleet has been sighted steaming towards the Gulf of Oman. We believe it is their intention to land their marines in our country and possibly in Iran also. Our intelligence people estimate they will parachute seventy thousand men and equipment within two to four weeks and seek to take our oil installations within hours of that. We haven't got the capability to stop such an attack; it would be national suicide. Also they have more fighter aircraft on their three aircraft carriers than we have altogether, and once you realize that most of the planes we have are fighting the Jews, do you fully understand Saudi and the Gulf are almost defenceless?"

The Prince paused so that the Palestinian could digest what he'd been told.

"We can't yet beat Israel Your Excellency. How can we help you against

America? As you say, it's suicidal. We also must adjust ourselves to half the cake, my friend Yasser, for as I said to you earlier, at least that way a society survives. We want you to help us so that we may help you. Our plan is simple; you get Jordan, or what's left of it when the Israeli's are through, we get the Yemen, Oman, Bahrain, Qatar and the Emirates. We have no alternative but to abandon our homelands to the enemy."

The general stood up. The air left his lungs, his normally immobile features registering a mixture of shock and incredulity. "If your uncle the King hadn't sent you as his personal emissary, I would have thought you mad. As it is, I think you must have stood far too long under your desert sun. What you're suggesting is neither practical nor sensible."

The Prince enjoyed the effect of his words on the arrogant general who so obviously regarded himself both intellectually and morally superior. How he'd love to put out that remaining ice blue eye with his own bare hands.

"Why is it so impractical? You have men with guns, we have money."

"Because Jordan is not Palestine for a start!" retorted the angry general.

"None of the countries I listed are my beloved Saudi Arabia, but something is still better than nothing," said Mo, now calm and feeling himself to be in control of the situation. "Besides which, when you give your people Jordan, they will correctly regard you as their first leader who gave them anything. You'll be like God to them. You'll also be just one step from all the rest of Palestine. You'll be able to build yourself a mighty army from the ashes of defeat, You'll never need to rely on anyone for help again. When you feel ready to wipe out the Jews, you'll have it in your own power to do so. Come on my brother, your people never had a country called Palestine anyway, and we never came from Saudi Arabia. We've had to adjust our visions in the past, so we must do so again. We're Arabs and Muslims, we play the long game.

Let the Jews and the west think of today. We can wait a year, or a hundred years, but in the end we will win. We will have more money, more people and right on our side. How can we lose?"

The Palestinian leader listened with rising interest. Nafti also carefully weighed every word, for he had known nothing of this audacious plan, which he was certain could not have originated with the dangerously unbalanced and unpredictable Prince, but must have emanated from his father, that wily old survivor, the King of Saudi Arabia. No, he was telling the truth for once. He had surely been used as an envoy to the Palestinian terrorist leader, because he was far more expendable than his senior, more exalted, royal cousins, should the infamous blood lust of Nabul, against any he considered the enemy of his people, show itself.

"What about the new King Hussein, his army. Are they all to evaporate when you wave your cheque book at them?" Nabul asked.

Mo answered as if he were teaching a simple child.

"The Hashemite goes to Riyadh, to meet with our King tomorrow. He is coming to beg for more of our money so that he can carry on fighting the Jews. He has offered our royal family sanctuary in Amman as a fair exchange, should the Americans drive us from our country. He and his family will not live to see our shame; they will all die in a mysterious explosion aboard the Lear jet he so loves to pilot.

Halfway home approximately there will be a loud noise, and the Jordanians will be leaderless easy prey. Naturally we will issue a statement condemning Israel's barbaric attack on the defenceless and noble King. You will simultaneously be marching into Jordan and will issue a press release barrage explaining that you are coming to the aid of your Jordanian brothers in their hour of need against the Zionist aggressors, as this had been requested and pleaded for by their government and people. You see, General, even we bloated plutocrats have learned something from your Russian masters."

His smile was not answered in kind by Nabul who again walked over to the map and examined it as he spoke.

"What about their army? What about the Syrian's army? What about the Iraqi brigades? For the mercy of Allah, what will the Israelis do? Dance the fucking Hora?"

The Prince rose stiffly from his seat and joined his host by the map. "The Jordanians are, I understand, almost out of aircraft, ammunition, oil, spares and supplies. You have no worries with them, one prod from your battle-hardened warriors and they'll evaporate; the Iraqis. Despite all their training by the Americans and the British, were yesterday encircled by the Israeli third army at Damiya. They either surrender within the day or shall be but a memory tomorrow. Our Syrian brothers have already started withdrawing their forces to a more defensible position. This will take them only another day or so, but their priority now is national pride, and they can't allow Syria to become part of greater Israel. Our people calculate that even the Zionist entity doesn't want more Arabs within its borders."

The Palestinian interjected in surprise.

"Those are their crack troops. I don't believe they'd withdraw before they had to. The Israelis haven't even gone onto the offensive yet from the Golan Heights.

Damascus isn't under any threat."

The Prince pointed his finger to Syria's west on the large-scale map.

"Who said anything about Damascus, my brother? No, our Syrian friends are coming here again, to Lebanon. They'll take it and keep it for its own protection against the marauding Zionists who will be allowed to nudge up to the Litani River into which we'll dump all their Lebanese Christian friends whom they seem so concerned over. So you see, I am right; there is nothing to stop you, is there?"

The general looked with new respect at Mo, but before he could ask any further questions, the Prince continued.

"You now want to know if the Israelis will dance or fight. You, as the new President of Palestine, will call for a special session of the Security Council to arrange an immediate ceasefire. Privately, at the same time, you will meet the Jew leaders in Paris or Zurich and guarantee them an armistice, with agreed borders on the line of the Jordan River. They will be delighted. You'll even reassure them that you have no designs on Jerusalem, they will then be elated. You will sign nothing but verbally agree anything. You'll even recognize Israel as a Jewish state. They will joyfully take out their reserve and use it against those pumped-up fools from the Muslim Brotherhood who now run Egypt, which I'm sure you won't lose sleep over.

When the shooting's over, you can then allow your negotiators to get bogged down in technical problems for a year or so when they can respectably be withdrawn and hand on heart, you will face the world, declaring the Jews are impossible people who have lied to, and cheated, your people, and you can reassert your claims to the West Bank, Gaza, Jerusalem and the places between... or put another way, Israel!"

The general's face wreathed in smiles. Laughing, he clasped Mo to him in an affectionate embrace. "You, my Prince are Arabia's answer to Kissinger. Your plans are ridiculous and brilliant. Now tell me the rest for only now do I realize that I am listening to a prophet."

The Prince glowed at the tribute. As he resumed his seat, he began to think that he'd misjudged the general, who was obviously more intelligent and worthwhile than he at first appeared. The general and the Prince both thought themselves the superior of the other.

"First I must ask you a question," the Prince told the general.

"Anything, Prince Mo, for as you say, we have a brotherhood made of need," replied Nabul.

"How many men have you of first class in your army?"

The general answered as if by rote. "All my men are first class. There are over one hundred and seventy-five thousand at present under arms."

The Saudi smiled, he had thought there were far fewer. "How many could you spare us for our small adventure?"

The general still didn't like this part of his involvement. Hadn't enough of Palestine's children died without fighting strangers' wars also?

"We agreed that we are not going to fight the Americans."

The Prince answered, with the hard edge returning to his normally cultured voice, "Yes, that is our agreement, but once they control the oil of Kuwait, Iraq, Iran and Saudi, do you seriously believe they'll be anxious or willing to fight over a few sandblasted tiny Kingdoms?"

"No," Whispered Nabul,

"But are you saying you're not even going to try and defend your country against the Americans?"

"That's exactly what I'm saying Nabul, because no one could, even the

Russians couldn't in this part of the world. Since the east European troubles, they have other worries, especially when the whole world knows America trebled its defence spending over just three years and reinstated their draft when they elected their ridiculous reactionary woman President after that weak fool Obama. Even the Chinese can't begin to take them on yet in this part of the world. No, we can only fight when we are strong again, not yet. We want you to lend us, yes, lend us as much firepower as you can. You'll send them under our selected officers across Saudi by our transport and you will land with us at exactly the same moment as the Americans invade my country. Furthermore, your commandos and sappers will help us destroy every oil installation in the country. When the Yankee swine arrive, they will find only sand and fire. We will take everything that is not bolted down and destroy all that is – every car, every bauble, every reliable person will come with us to their new home. It should be simple for you to disarm our new hosts who will naturally ask our noble King to be their leader also. Anyone who shows an unsatisfactory attitude and resists our protection from the American aggressors is obviously a traitor and you'll execute the unwise ones as a warning to others.

General, you see everything as a matter of principle because you are tainted by Marxist ideology and dogma. Your clothes have become westernized, as is your mind. We are still fundamentally men of the desert, nomads. We may change from a camel to a Rolls Royce, but we learned long ago that when a tribe with new, better weapons came too close when we were in the oasis, we would fold our tents and creep into the night and wait for the day we could march back to re-claim what was rightfully ours. We can still do this because we are not contaminated by false and foreign values.

The world will go round, the tides will rise and fall, our women will give us many sons and one day, Allah the merciful will listen to our prayers and we will march back to destroy our enemies. Perhaps we have had too much wealth too quickly, and we are being reminded that possessions are nothing but a weight around our vain necks. But I speak of philosophy when I should speak of our plans. Yasser, do we draw a new map of our world or do you and I wait to become footnotes in history written in sand, to vanish when the wind blows?"

Nafti watched the strange partners embrace once more to seal their bargain. His head was spinning with the enormous ramifications of what he'd heard and he didn't envy the Mossad their task in evaluating the data he was to transmit that evening to an unknown contact code named Thunder Thighs by an obscure wit at headquarters. Well, at least no one would accidentally identify themselves by such a name in Beirut.

The Prince turned from Nabul to his guard and beckoned him forward.

"Nafti, I believe we should allow ourselves a toast to our new alliance with the general. Have you got the provisions with you?"

Nafti withdrew a drinking flask from his loose-fitting combat fatigues and looked enquiringly to their host who loped to the utilitarian book case and returned bearing the three chipped, unwashed coffee cups they had previously drunk from. Nafti unscrewed the top from the flask and poured each of the other men a generous measure and an enormous portion for himself. The Prince smiled benevolently, for Nafti's appetites and capacity were the stuff of legends amongst the men who saw him eat and drink and the women whose bodies he had satiated.

"To our eternal brotherhood,"

Toasted the Prince. They drank, the whisky sipped slowly by Mo and his newly found ally Nabul while their gigantic provider knocked his cupful down in one gulp.

"This whisky, Nafti, what is it?"

Asked the general, having little familiarity with alcohol borne out of self-discipline rather than observation of religious prohibition.

"It's Scottish, sir. Lovelace whisky, the best in the world," answered Nafti already pouring himself another generous measure.

"Your man Nafti is full of surprises, Excellency, whoever heard of a Muslim soldier carrying a flask full of the best whisky. I'll have to keep my eyes on such an unusual man. I might want him for myself."

Although said in jest, Nafti detected the veiled threat in the Palestinian's words, but Mo - as ever without any peripheral emotional intelligence - failed to see anything untoward and laughingly revealed another flask from the folds of his own dhjiba.

"Allah is bountiful my friend, but sometimes needs a little help."

They all laughed but both the Israeli spy and the Palestinian commander somehow knew that only one of them could survive their relationship, though both would certainly be much surprised at exactly how and why they would eventually come into open conflict.

Chapter Twenty–eight

The Empress Restaurant, London, England
28th. August 2020 – 21.15 hours

Eddie Roman leaned back in his comfortable red velvet chair and watched Chip Malone, his dinner companion, wolfing down his second helping of chocolate mousse. Rather than concentrate on the piggish sights and sounds of Malone eating, Eddie glanced around the high-domed and luxuriously-appointed dining room, one of the few imperial havens left to London's elite after the naughty and ultimately ruinous first decade after the millennium. His eye took in the quiet opulence of the establishment's diners who, as usual, were mainly businessmen entertaining other businessmen on company expense accounts. There were also a few glamorous young women sprinkled around two or three of the corner, more dimly-lit tables, accompanying portly elderly gentlemen. The recession of the last few years didn't seem to affect this group.

Malone interrupted Eddie's perusal in his assumed broad cockney dialect, assumed, Eddie knew, because he was one of a select band who had accidentally learned the man was, in reality, a middle class grammar school product of a middle class home in the very unfashionable suburban town of Surbiton, but - as being streetwise and Cockney was again in vogue - Chip Malone had come to mold his speech and style as if he were one of the chaps. Even his first name had been borrowed from the up market golf course where his chipping skill was legendary. "Here listen, Eddie," he said between gulps from his second double brandy. "What's all the crap I've been hearing that you've gone and done a wobble?"

Eddie smiled phlegmatically in response to Malone's suggestion regarding his near bankruptcy.

"You can tell me, mate. I know how to keep quiet. I might even be able to help if you level with me, give me something good and juicy for the rag and you can rely on me not to reveal my source. Come on, you know the kind of stuff my readers love; Arabs on the run from defeat buying up London! That kind of stuff sells papers and makes me look good, which means I can make my friends look good. So, come on friend, give me some old fashioned dirt and I'll even pay for the supper."

Eddie had never liked the overbearing newsman and the man's insistence that they were good friends of long standing actually meant that historically *both* men had once or twice done favours for each other for their own purely selfish reasons.

No, Eddie didn't like Malone, but regarded him as a tool to be used and discarded when its purpose was served. He wished that he had no present need, but recognized his own total vulnerability to any press suggestions that he was trading while insolvent. That would be a punishable crime which Malone was, out of pique, more than capable of using to ruin Eddie. One damning paragraph in the man's money column read by five million people daily, and all those creditors Roman had just persuaded to allow him a period of six months' grace, would forget their promises and pull down the shaky house of cards his facade of a company had become. He decided to cautiously help the journalist if he, in turn, would help in his last throw of the dice.

"O.K. Chip, we've always understood each other well enough. Can I be entirely frank as a friend to a friend?"

The newsman nodded so emphatically that he had to adjust his ill-fitting sable coloured wig; he nodded to encourage Eddie to continue, unable to speak because yet another drink was entering his avaricious, thin-lipped, mean mouth.

"I'm sure you know all the usual stuff which has been milked to death for years; Arabs buy the Dorchester, the end of Little England is nigh, it's old hat, but I have heard an interesting whisper or two that could well make a good two page exposé for you Chip."

He paused to see if the hook had sunk into the journalist's maw.

It had.

"But I'd like you to be a touch more specific on what this might be worth, how far you could go if you had to?"

The newsman put down his drink on the crisp white tablecloth. This was serious. Money was - he felt - about to join mousse on the menu. It always spoilt his digestion, because although he always claimed expenses from the newspaper's ample slush fund to pay for information received, he hardly ever actually passed more than a small percentage of the bribes onto their stated destination, and he still had enough of a conscience to worry about being found out. But the money always fitted snugly in his bank deposit box. The best thing about this, his favourite scam, was his belief that no one could ever tell because they were all acting illegally. Malone's take was additionally boosted by extra payments from grateful businessmen whose scandalous exploits he had a healthy knack of discovering, but he'd never rush into print without checking back on his facts, and being a man of impeccable honour, he'd always meet the alleged offenders so that they could answer the charges in person... or ask good old Chip if he couldn't lose the story in his wastebasket for a friend who'd be so grateful, he'd see that Chip's moneybox be kept well stocked. No, thought Malone, Eddie Bloody Roman always was a fucker, a bloody spoiler. Didn't he know the name of the bloody game. Cheeky sod should realize I've got a fat assed ex-wife with two snot-nosed kids to support and a bloody model to keep in suntan oil and tiny, but ultra expensive, bikinis.

"Now Eddie," he said,

"Let's keep it in perspective, shall we? I admit a two-page spread is appealing, very appealing, but on the other hand, how would it be if there was a two-page spread crucifying the reckless, possibly criminal son of our country's most respected businessman knight, Lord of the Construction World? Remember I gave him that moniker, I can turn it around."

Eddie laughed, startling Malone who'd anticipated the usual groveling climb-down he was used to extracting from the vulnerable entrepreneurs who peopled his columns. "You don't even scare me, Malone, but my father, that's priceless, it really is!" Eddie laughed again, tormenting Chip beyond endurance.

"Listen, you stuck-up sod. If I say I'll print a story, I'll bloody well do it!"

He hissed at the handsome young man, still-chuckling opposite him.

"Oh Chip, I don't think so. Don't be a silly boy, unless you want *real* trouble. Firstly, we both know that my esteemed father is so high and mighty that if you even pointed your nasty little pen in his direction, he'd have your shriveled little balls hung up on a pole at the end of Fleet Street within the hour, as an example to others of your ilk, and as for me… well, I guess you realize I don't have my father's undying love or protection, but I don't care anymore. You see, when someone's not got a pot to piss in, and I can tell you, as a friend, as a mate, that said pot is not in my keeping, then you can publish and be damned, but before you do, I want to know what's got you so excited. I've not seen you like this since your divorce judge awarded your ex-wife your old house because you hadn't kept up your agreed maintenance payments."

Malone, red faced and furious, tried to stand up, but Eddie leant forward and pressed down hard with his two powerful hands onto the journalist's, who found himself unable to move.

"Let go, you shit. I'll have you for this. Let go. You're bloody well hurting me. C'mon, let's just forget the whole thing!"

Although they both spoke urgently, neither raised their voice to attract attention. This was still a private war of attrition they were waging, this drunken pressman and desperate businessman.

"You know how I got so strong?" Eddie asked. Chip hissed his response.

"You did a bloody Charles Atlas course for all I care. Let me go or I'll kick you where it hurts!"

Almost before Malone finished his threat, he regretted it as Eddie kicked him in the balls instead… once, twice and a third time just for luck. The journalist nearly passed out in agony, but Eddie calmly released his hands and threw a carafe of iced water over him, bringing him to with amazing speed and also bringing over the tail-suited Maitre D, all French concern and charm.

"Is everything quite alright messieurs?"

He asked them, discreetly managing to avoid looking toward the moaning and drenched Malone, but nevertheless making certain by his tone of voice that his two customers understood that any more nonsense and out they would go.

"No," Eddie replied, his manner as ever calm.

"My friend here didn't feel quite himself for a moment so I thought a quick, sharp, shock was needed. You see he's much better now, aren't you my old friend?"

Malone forced himself to smile through the pain and even suffered quietly as the waiter fussed over him with a napkin, drying him down and cooing at him about sitting till he felt better.

No one at the other tables seemed to pay any attention to the entire interlude, although they had all covertly seen some of what happened and drawn their own conclusions - naturally colourful and erroneous - ranging from the majority view that it had been a lover's tiff between homosexuals or a drunken brawl between people more suited to an East End pub than their favourite restaurant.

"I got muscles working on my own building sites," Eddie continued,

"After my old man and I fell out. I didn't get all the way up spending my own sweat and blood for a prick like you to send me all the way back down again. I was prepared to go along with you if you were going to play fair, but you want it all your own way so now we're going to change places."

The pain had more or less died in Malone's groin but the anger still burned bright in the man's eyes.

"You can do what you bloody like here, Roman, but I'm going to get you for this. Mark my words. I'll have you. It's a promise!"

Eddie leant forward as if to launch another attack and Malone looked more like a transfixed rabbit to Roman than a threat to be worried about. "Now, Mr Malone, here's your story for nothing."

"For nothing?" exclaimed Malone, perking up.

"Why all the aggravation if you weren't going to charge me anything?"

Eddie smiled in a manner so obviously ironic that even the non-sensitive soul of Malone knew he was being led to the slaughter. "I said the story wasn't going to cost you anything, and unlike you, I mean approximately what I say, but you will have to spend some money," he said to Malone who was nearing uncontrollable rage at being bullied and manipulated by this bastard.

"Listen, Roman, right now you have the upper hand but if you think you can blackmail me with your clever Yid con-tricks, you've got another think coming!"

The smile vanished from Eddie's face. He didn't speak for a moment, but when he did his face had become a mask of stone.

"That's your last allowed mistake, Malone. Now I'm not even going to be nice anymore. You want it tough, then you'll have it tough. I was going to be nice and give you a genuine chance to make a few grand but a blackmailing shit like you pigeon-holing me with you in your slot, that's enough to make me vomit. Next, you insect, you called me a Yid as if being a Jew was an insult, but if I hear you use the word Yid again, I'll forget I'm a gentleman and I'll show just how nasty I can be when I try."

But Malone had only heard the words "make a few grand," and he was a very greedy man with a one track mind. "I didn't mean you're that bad, you personally, but Jews generally. You know what I mean; money, money, already, so soon. You know what they're like? But I admit there are some very nice ones I count as my friends. Listen, my old lady had a bit of Jew in her, didn't she, so it shows you I'm not anti, doesn't it? But I'll say one thing you people are good with money, bloody clever with money. I always say you can't take that from 'em. Not much good at anything else except for those bloody Israeli lunatics who only know how to fight. They're gonna' send us all back to the Stone Age. But let's get down to cases. You said we could make some money together. If I'd have known that before, we'd have had no misunderstandings. You know how I love a good deal."

Malone tried so hard to inject some sincerity into his bullshit speech, Eddie was sorely tempted to inflict a bit more punishment on the man, but decided not to. Mentally, Chip Malone, the object of his deep-felt loathing, was so insulated by his overpowering greed that any point-scoring by Eddie would be a waste of his incomparably more able mind.

"I've heard on the grapevine that there are a whole new bunch of Arabs on their way to buy up London..."

Before he could continue Malone interjected. "I've heard all that before, Eddie. Look, we'll get back to that later, but I didn't get kicked in the balls for that. What about the bloody deal?" Eddie stopped this interruption with one of his own.

"Shut up and you'll hear. One would take you as Jewish you're so obsessed with money."

He enjoyed Malone's discomfort but didn't indulge his desire to belittle the man. "There is one major difference between these Arabs and their predecessors, they're almost one hundred percent from one country, Saudi Arabia. From my information, it seems like everyone who can is getting out. You're talking about something between fifty and a hundred thousand Saudi Arabians landing in Europe within the next two or so weeks!

Malone went silent. This was some story; he'd not even heard a whisper that something like this was on the cards. An exclusive story about oil-rich Arab refugees buying all Europe up had to be worth more than a hundred grand if he went freelance or got someone to ghost it for him.

"Where did you hear this from? The sugar fairy?"

Eddie ignored Malone's clumsy sarcasm.

"I know I'm right, Malone. Near enough the entire Saudi middle and upper class is on their way by ship, plane, anything that moves out of Saudi. Why? I couldn't tell you, unless there's something for real in those reports about America and NATO invading the place, but who cares why, they're coming and that's what counts."

Malone was calculating what piece of the action he'd be able to get away paying Eddie, figuring that Eddie would probably be happy with ten thousand pounds ceased with Eddie's next words.

"Of course you won't print a word of what I've just told you. You'll do a nice bold story emphatically saying that unconfirmed scare-mongering rumors by devious self-serving property manipulators that Arabs were coming by the boatload out of their nice safe oilfields is a total fabrication to your certain knowledge. Also such property men are evil and scheming bastards who are trying to increase their badly-sagging property market. You believe available residential is mostly rubbish and if any interest is shown in their lousy overpriced houses by the great British public, it will be when the day comes for them to sell to good old Anglo Saxons at the correct low price when their stupid conniving rumors of rich Arabs inflating the market come unstuck when none arrive. You'll even call it your patriotic duty to fearlessly tell the truth without fear of the consequences. You'll be a bloody hero!"

"Are you bloody mad?" roared Malone, momentarily forgetting the restaurant's hushed ambience. His voice went down a couple of decibels but still loud enough for a few inquisitive heads to turn.

"You give me one of the hottest stories ever and you not only want to kill it, you want to turn it around so that it comes out and depresses an already-crappy residential market, and you..."

Malone stopped so suddenly with his mouth still half open that it would have seemed to a casual observer that he'd been turned to stone, but he hadn't seen Sodom and Gomorrah, he'd seen the Promised Land, and like they said it, flowed with milk and honey.

"You are a fucking genius, Eddie fucking Roman. You are the Lord's gift to brilliance. I take off my hat to a master. You're so bloody devious you make me look like the Archangel Gabriel. Who'd credit a public school type like you pulling a stunt like this?"

Eddie merely smiled in acknowledgement because he knew trying to stop Malone speaking at that moment would rank with making apples fall upwards.

"You're going to create, no, we're going to create an instant buyers market. It's already bad but when I spread the word there'll be such a panic to unload for anything, they can get that someone with a few bob in his pocket and a bit of common sense will own or control a healthy chunk of the available desirable homes in London, namely us, am I right or am I right?"

Eddie's face, which looked happy, wasn't reflected in his voice, which came from the icy wastes of a soul twisted, pulled, dragged bleeding from its protesting bedrock of goodness and honest intentions.

"You're right," he said to Malone's obvious delight,

"And because you're such a lousy, obnoxious, negative piece of rubbish, I'll allow you to put up all your money as an investor in our venture. Everything, you understand. Your flat is good collateral, plus your car, plus your bank will lend you about one hundred thousand, everything you have or can get goes into this starting now, understood?"

Malone's Adam apple bobbed up and down. He couldn't bring himself to talk, such was his shock at Roman's proposal. Eventually after a full minute, he managed to answer.

"Look, can't I put in, let's say, well about, roughly fifty thousand pounds to start with and see how it goes, then see if I want to put in some more?"

Eddie had that dangerous mask-like set to his face again, but now Malone was quick to recognize it as a warning in this abrasive, but obviously very underrated, young man.

Malone now knew that Eddie's face was his one sure give away. When the younger man's hooded eyes went ominously gun metal grey as if a light somewhere behind them was extinguished, when his jaw muscles bunched so that he seemed to be gnawing at his cheeks, you knew you'd better be ready to fight Eddie Roman or run for your life. Malone didn't want to fight this fearsome and determined young man. He knew he'd lose to Eddie in any battle because he understood his own fears, but also knew Roman didn't have any real idea what fear was, and a man you couldn't frighten could be deadly, but a very clever, confident man full of brilliant schemes who was not aware of his fears could be dangerous to himself as well as others.

Malone considered running away, say yes now, tomorrow go on the missing list, take his new bird down to Marbella till the man here pisses up his own trouser leg or... and in the moment Malone started to consider or, he knew he was in because there could be no or. Or didn't exist when Eddie Roman was dealing the cards. It was his way or not at all.

"O.K.. I'm in for my bit, but I don't reckon I can raise more than thirty-five thousand pounds within a day or two."

He said it with seeming sincerity but Eddie had the man running scared and knew it. Perhaps another shot across the journalist's creaking bows might bring him further booty.

"What about all that cash you've got stashed? How about that money? Or do you really want to test me and see if I'd send an anonymous letter to the Inland Revenue about this corrupt well-known press bloke?"

Malone went about as white as a cold albino who'd not been in enough sun lately. Eddie was certain that he'd struck pay dirt, and loathed himself for having to demean Malone. He was denying all he'd ever cared about, ever valued as true barometer of himself as a man, but Malone had been wrong about Eddie for the latter man did know fear. It was fear of fear itself which consumed him, his inability to accept public failure that had brought Eddie to this moment in this place, and Eddie needed to win in business, the only arena he knew that those shadowy snakes of self-doubt would be either wiped out or strangle him, for only by being more successful than his father... But Eddie stopped the wicked sibilant inner voice that taunted him. Somehow, he wasn't surprised that when he spoke out loud to Malone it was that same voice, his own, which he heard.

"Malone, you'll bring me seventy-five thousand pounds cash plus any paper collateral you've got on top of that by lunchtime tomorrow. You'll get one percent of any profit I make. After tomorrow, until I say different, we won't meet, you get the story in your rag, and if I hear one whisper, one suggestion that you're playing a double game, you know I'd kill you without even thinking about it, just like I'd be stepping on a spider. Do you believe me?"

Chip Malone was all the damning things said he was but he was no idiot. He had come to know Eddie Roman better in one hour than he'd known anyone else in his whole life, and he believed the man's threat.

"Look Eddie, I do believe you, but why me with my lousy seventy-five grand? You could have got more from loads of blokes."

Eddie was looking past Malone to the bar because for a fleeting moment he thought he'd seen his father passing through the restaurant's remote foyer, with a gaggle of elegant men and coiffured women in tow, towards the bar, which was shielded from his view by three immense potted palms.

"I didn't choose you, Malone," said Eddie, "You chose yourself. We are ideal partners. We both don't care about anyone except ourselves, and - don't worry - I *do* intend to collect money from *all* the Malones, and all those greedy people are just the same. They'll all pay the piper one way or another.

I'll convince them that Eddie Roman is a sound investment."

Eddie stood up, leaving Malone to his thoughts and the remaining dregs of his last brandy. "I'll expect you at one at my office. Don't be late there's a good boy. Good night."

Eddie started to walk away but Malone caught him by the elbow. "Will there be a contract ready for me to sign?"

Eddie shrugged off Malone's hand as if it might contaminate him. "Malone you have to be joking, there'll be nothing in writing, you'll just have to trust me..."

He paused, as ever amused with Malone's slack-jawed expressions of astonished and injured innocence.

"Like I trust you to pay the bill for our dinner because you said you would. Good night."

He walked out on Malone, whose quiet prayer for a lethal bolt of lightning to strike Eddie Roman down went unanswered. Eddie strode towards the bar, his long-legged athletic stride somehow seemed at odds with his conservatively-cut suit. He skirted the palms and came face-to-face with Barry, his estranged civil partner. They silently examined one another, lost in a whirlpool of emotional confusion and exposed raw nerves.

"Hello, Eddie. You look well. Don't you say hello to your father any more?" Barry said it rhetorically, with that husky chuckle of his that Eddie knew was his lover's way of papering over the cracks in any public crisis, big or small. Barry was still gorgeous and desirable, but Eddie obediently followed Barry's eyes towards his father who stood amongst his dinner guests who, as ever, he dominated by dint of his sheer size and bulk, animal magnetism and that special aura men of awesome power exude.

"Hello, Eddie. It's good to see you, son."

Max extended his hand and there was an embarrassed moment for the people around this small confrontation between father and son whose battles were legendary.

"You too, sir."

Eddie shook his father's hand, which clasped Eddie's hand longer than the younger man found comfortable. It was the first time the two had touched each other in more than a decade. They had never spoken, or acknowledged one another when accidentally their paths had crossed at oddly hurtful moments to both.

Eddie returned his father's stare and it was this trial of wills, which was finally broken by Barry.

"Isn't one of you going to buy everyone a drink?"

Eddie followed him to an alcove while Maxwell gave his apologies to understanding guests who were only too anxious to gossip about their witnessing of a possible reconciliation between father and son, and the two handsome young men. This evening which had promised to be a formal bore had all the ingredients necessary for these lucky ladies to be socially lionized for months regarding their observations on the Roman family's every word and gesture, while their men pondered many a share deal which could well be affected by the possibility of Eddie returning to claim his inheritance. Therefore, Sir Maxwell encountered no difficulties arranging for them to eat as his guests without his presence.

Maxwell rejoined his son and his estranged partner. Eddie was smiling with unconcealed pleasure which Maxwell wished was for his presence but knew it was too early for him to harbor any such hope. No, Eddie was entranced with Barry and he with him; the handsome pair knew even without exchanging words that the flames of their lost love were rekindled in eyes which spoke eloquently of loneliness, despair and now, hope.

"What can I buy you two?" Maxwell asked. Eddie turned his head reluctantly from Barry.

"You can't buy us a thing, my hello to you was purely cosmetic, father, but I'll show you the same generosity you always display to old friends."

Eddie stood up and peeled two five-pound notes from his wallet and placed them on the table before Maxwell, who was too shocked and hurt to respond. Eddie held his hand out to Barry, who paused, his brain telling him that life with Eddie would always be hurtful, but his heart dictating he leave with him because he had now realized that his love for Eddie was forever, and Barry's heart won.

Barry took Eddie's hand and stood up to leave, "I'm sorry, father-in-law,"

He said to Sir Maxwell and he bent to kiss his cheek, which tasted faintly of salt where a solitary tear was the only evidence of how deeply he'd been hurt.

Eddie didn't look back as he led his wife from the restaurant. If he had, he would have seen his father's shoulders sag as if all his world's troubles had now become too heavy even for him, an unlikely, reluctant Atlas.

Chapter Twenty-nine

Outside The Empress Restaurant & Barry's Apartment, Hollywood Road, Fulham, London, 29 August 2020 – 01.00 hours

Barry had refused to go with Eddie into his Rolls Royce as they left the Empress. Instead he had insisted that he wait with him for the doorman to bring his small, black Japanese hybrid Lexus.

"Join me?" he asked Barry; they climbed into his car and steered into the late West End traffic. " I'm going to invite you in for coffee, at which point I shall ravage you!"

They laughed, but Eddie didn't understand. "But you could ravage me in comfort."

He momentarily shut his eyes in terror as Barry overtook a bus in the King's Road and went the wrong side of a traffic island towards an oncoming taxi. At the last possible moment, he swerved back in front of the bus missing the cab by inches. Barry turned to Eddie unconcerned by the near miss.

"Don't you understand anything, you great lunkhead? I want you to see what I can do, what I've done for myself, without your help." Barry returned his eyes to the road ahead and just managed to stop at a red traffic light on a busy junction.

"I'm sure you've managed brilliantly, Barry, but you still can't bloody well drive. Let's swap." With feigned indignity, he changed places with his man by hopping out of the car and going round to the passenger door as Eddie shuffled over the gear lever to the driver's seat.

They drove to Barry's flat without further incident, parking in the narrow, newly- fashionable Fulham street where he lived. They walked hand-in-hand to his door as if nervous new lovers, scared to let go for fear of losing one another. Awkwardly, Barry used his free hand to search for the door key before he eventually found it. Eddie pulled Barry towards him and crushed his willing lips with his own probing mouth. Their bodies melted together, their equal male hardness finding each other's secret soft places, and their kisses became deeper and more passionate, somehow without knowing how they found themselves in the bedroom, on the huge soft bed.

Hungrily, Eddie ripped off his clothes then wildly stripped Barry who was lost in passion. They took each other like animals, without any thought but of gratification, every lunge met by an upwards thrust of taut buttocks that soon wrapped his trunk, one of Eddie's hands cupped Barry's buttocks as with the other his fingers scratched at Barry's muscular shoulders in an uncontrollable frenzy. He flipped over his willing, but lighter partner, and his mouth moved from Barry's and found his chest, sucking and licking his deep brown distended nipples with a ferocity that hurt and excited Barry until neither could soar any higher. They orgasmed as one, their love juices gushing as their sex found expression in its own ecstatic harmony of carnal knowledge.

Eddie looked down at his husband, his lover; Barry's eyes were still closed in private joy. His pale face he'd always thought regal, looked so beautiful in the moonlight coming from the open window that, for a short moment, he held his breath. How could he have let anything come between this wonderful man and himself? Barry's full lips curved upwards in a cat-like smile of pleasure. His pale blue eyes opened and searched Eddie's face to look for a sign there that he wouldn't be hurt again, that he wasn't exposing his freshly healed wounds to new injury. Eddie gently stroked away some of Barry's thick, black hair from his prominent cheekbones, and kissed the tip of his straight perfect nose then caressed each small ear with his tongue, a bee with flower petals, tasting Barry, smelling his good clean smell. Eddie nuzzled Barry's throat with his lips and kissed his dimpled slightly-pointed chin.

Barry moaned with relaxed pleasure; slowly he felt Eddie grow hard again, still thrust deep inside him, gradually his hips circled below his, lovingly he moved his hands down to his full, finely-muscled chest, his large hands just spanning him, his penis began to move in his lover with long, slow thrusts, his thumbs brushed at his nipples which became hard as he felt himself rise to meet his powerful plunges.

Eddie massaged Barry's chest, kissing and nibbling at the nipples. Barry caressed Eddie's firm buttocks, his lithe long fingers alternately pulling him further within him and teasing him with feather light tickles of his scrotum. He cupped his testicles as once more, he ejaculated and Barry felt his inner muscles contracting with intensity more gratifying because it was less urgent than their first coupling.

Languidly he rolled them both onto their sides but kept him in his embrace. Barry let himself be cuddled like this for an endless moment as Eddie held his man tight to his chest as if scared to ever let him go, in case once again he might lose him. He began to say something but Barry hushed him with a finger to his lips. "Eddie, don't spoil the moment with a speech. Let's enjoy now, and worry about tomorrow when it comes." He smiled and slowly shook his tousled head.

Eddie put his hand over Barry's mouth to stop him talking, and he said what he thought he'd forgotten how to say, what he now realized he should have said a long time ago to this wonderful man. Without Barry, he existed, with him, he lived. He desperately wanted to start living again. "I love you, Barry. I want you to be with me, and I don't care how, and I don't care about anything else as long as we're together, always." Barry smiled radiantly as he took Eddie's hand from his mouth, his arms circled Eddie's neck, and they both cried from sheer joy until sleep overcame them.

"I've got to tell you something," Barry whispered. Eddie dreaded hearing that his partner might have been with someone else while they'd been apart, but he was a grown up, he could take it, but it wouldn't be easy.

"I understand," he said. "It must have been lonely."

Barry looked hard into his eyes, and then shook his head and smiled. "No, not that. There's been no one else. How about you?" Barry stared hard back into Eddie's eyes, checking to see if he was about to tell the truth.

"No one."

"Promise me!" Barry insisted.

"I promise. Hand on heart." Eddie put his hand on Barry's chest, which he laughingly pushed away.

He smiled again. "I would be the proudest man in the world." They kissed and hugged again.

Barry went to sleep happy. Eddie considered he had been honest enough.

Eddie woke first and spent self-indulgent minutes just examining Barry's beautiful face in repose. He had meant what he'd said the previous night, and he silently repeated his pledge to him as the day's early golden haze spilled through the frilly lace curtains and dappled the pastel green and yellow painted room. He did love this man, and truly wanted a life with him, but he couldn't simply turn off who he was all the time.

Eddie looked around for the first time and was surprised and delighted to see his picture smiling back at him from its perch on Barry's antique Louis XIV dressing table.

The bedroom wasn't big but it had an extremely high ceiling, the kind builders didn't build anymore, not for nearly a hundred years. There were no wardrobes which meant Barry probably used a spare space as a dressing room; his one vanity was the way his superb body dressed in what he wanted rather than in what others considered fashionable.

Barry's eyes opened reluctantly, fighting a battle between sleep and duty, Eddie thanked his good luck as he again studied his partner's face.

Barry smiled dreamily and stretched when Eddie released his embrace, the sheet came away from his bare torso but he made no move to cover his nakedness from Eddie's lingering gaze. Barry had changed, thought Eddie, when they'd been living as a couple he had never wanted to make love more than once a night and never on more than two or three nights in a week, in darkness and more as a duty than as the pleasure of their previous night's lovemaking. The Barry of old would never have let him luxuriate in the sight of his nakedness, fearful of reviving his lust, but this man, five years older than when they'd parted, was not only seemingly unembarrassed but appeared to relish his appreciative caressing look. To Eddie's surprise Barry pulled the sheets off them both and frankly looked at his body. Barry saw his deep, broad chest and let his fingers stroke him on its nearly hairless expanse.

"That tickles," Eddie protested, pulling Barry's fingers away.

"I just wanted to count the trees in your little forest,"

Barry whispered, letting his hand glide down Eddie's taut abdomen as he rested his head on Barry's free hand, affording him a better view as his lower stomach muscles jumped involuntarily to his partner's touch.

Eddie wasn't used to a passive sex role with other men and although his member's increasing stiffness was testimony to his pleasure, he felt he should be more active, so he inched his hands down from Barry's shoulder and traced a line with one finger towards his navel, where he paused. Eddie hadn't usually allowed him to touch his lower half with his hands, except when in the act of lovemaking, but now Barry had him by his rod and was expertly toying with it, using his hand to give Eddie maximum excitement.

Once Eddie was happy, Barry placed his hands on him again; bringing him to the brink of orgasm repeatedly but each time increased his pleasure by holding back his release until Eddie thought he could stand no more, Barry's two hands exploring, playing, with his trim, well muscled ass. His mind could hardly equate this super-sexy confident man with the prudish boy who'd left him, but all such thoughts went from his head as this now-mature and hungry man began French-kissing him aggressively with Barry's head above his in his usual dominant male position. Barry moved down him, kissing his nipples forcing him to an even higher plateau of pleasure.

"What are you doing?" Eddie grunted, his own prudery showing itself.

Barry looked up. "I'm just going into the forest to chop down the tall trees," he answered, astounding and pleasing Eddie by taking him into his mouth. Barry turned around onto him so that Eddie found himself similarly occupied, licking, sucking and nibbling as Barry's clever mouth made him even bigger and harder until he thought his head might explode if he didn't let him orgasm soon.

Barry surprised him again by sitting up and holding his member hard in his hand and guiding it achingly slowly into his inner recess. He gripped Eddie vice-like and lay still, letting himself be dominated. When Barry was fully impaled, he sat astride his legs and threw his head back in abandon and yet another orgasm racked his body, sending muscle quivers into every part of him.

When this passed, he brought his head upright and looked at his man's face. His lips were moist and slightly parted as he licked them, his eyes were slits of pleasure, his breath coming in spasms. "Do me, go on, and do me now, hard!" Barry began to buck on him as he watched his sexual fantasy come to life, pumping him so fast and so hard that the only thing he could do was feast his eyes and hands. He felt his orgasm begin just as Barry began screaming in fulfillment until his body seemed to collapse into a long quivering orgasmic explosion which had no sooner ended than Eddie, still hard, lifted and turned Barry over, he manoeuvering him to the edge of the bed and entered him from behind, with demonic thrusts. He lifted the lighter man's torso from the bed and held him in place as his pumping caused both men to moan in ecstasy, each meeting the other's every movement until they both came together in a gasping pleasure-riddled heap.

Afterwards, when they were dressed, it was Eddie who was shy and reserved, whereas Barry munched his breakfast toast as if nothing had happened. Eddie wanted to know when, where and with whom Barry had liberated himself from his previous hang-ups, but thoughtfully he didn't. After all, he'd been no monk over the period of the long separation.

"I never asked you, Barry, why didn't you let our separation go through smoothly?"

Barry smiled as if to a foolish child. "Because I knew you'd come back and we'd be together!"

Eddie looked at Barry, unsure how to react. He'd become his own man, self-reliant and self-aware, but like him, Barry needed a partner to share with, someone to be cared for, someone who cares about you. Their love was equally evident over coffee and toast as it had been in bed, their search for themselves and each other was over, and they could live together.

"Do you still have the key to our place?" Eddie asked. Barry walked to a small kitchen cupboard and opened it.

"Come here and see, lover."

He did so and saw Barry's old key to their home encased in a small glass case bolted to the wall, underneath were printed the words. "In case of Eddie Roman's stubbornness, break glass and enter house."

Eddie laughed at Barry's quirky sense of fun. They kissed briefly as he made for Barry's front door. "By Christ, I didn't ask you one word about how you've been making out since you haven't been taking my money, or what you've been working at, or where. I'm sorry.

What have you been up to? I'm so wrapped up in myself, I didn't ask."

"You won't like it," Barry replied.

"Try me," Eddie answered.

"As long as you didn't learn last night's stuff hustling, I'm sure it can't be too bad. "Barry paused then hurried his words in an effort to mitigate their effect on him.

"I've been working with your father as his personal assistant."

Eddie's face went white. He managed to choke back the hurtful words that jumped unbidden to his mouth. Instead he calmly spoke with such low-pitched intensity, Barry was left in no doubt about his deadly earnest.

"You mean you worked for my father. If you and I are to be together you'll have to choose: him or me. You know how much I want you back, but nothing anyone can say or do will change my mind. If you want him as your boss, forget me as your husband."

He walked towards the door, but Barry's voice stopped his departure.

"It's too easy for one of us to walk out, isn't it? After all, I started it didn't I? Well, I'll quit your father, although I have to tell you he's been absolutely marvelous, but I still want to work, I'm not going to vegetate. But next time you walk out on me I'll cut your bloody cock off, understood?"

They hugged, but Eddie looked at his watch and pulled away.

"I must go, I'll be home about seven; and if you really want to work you can start tomorrow, there's a position going as my executive assistant. How's that sound?"

"Very confident," Barry said doubtfully.

"I heard stories about your business being in trouble, but here you are, still with the home, a new Rolls Royce, eating at the best places and running around without a care in the world, now you're offering me a job. Are things really that good or are you bullshitting me? I'm with you whichever way it is, but you don't have to bullshit me. I'm on your side."

Eddie considered his reply and decided to level with his rediscovered partner. "You've been straight so I'll be the same way. The Roller's leased and I'm two months behind on the payments, the house has three mortgages charged on it and I'm on the edge of late on those payments, the restaurant check the other guy paid, which all means I really need some help from a good assistant. A great assistant, more like another half. As from last night my luck changed, and it's all going to work out fine because I found you again. Are you still interested? Do you still believe in me?"

He asked anxiously, his eyes narrowed as he stared at Barry, knowing he needed this man who he really cared about. They exchanged a serious and loving tender look. Despite the banter there was a deep fondness underlying their relationship, Barry traced Eddie's face with his fingers.

"Eddie, there's more of your father in you than you'd care to admit. I knew you're in trouble and you're too bloody good at everything you do not to bounce back. I always believed what you told me. It was what you didn't say that used to worry me, but now we'll both stick it out, for better or worse."

They smiled warmly at one another.

"For better or worse." Eddie repeated as he kissed his lover on the cheek, stood and moved to the door and turned as Barry responded, "And I love you! I always loved you!"

"Ditto!" called Eddie over his shoulder as he gently closed the door as he left. They both knew he'd once again not expressed his love. Barry breathed deeply in resignation as he reconciled himself to the present and hoped the time would come for their expressions of love to be mutual and genuine. Eddie was already thinking about other things.

Chapter Thirty

Suite 1782, The Washington Hilton Hotel, K. Street, Washington, U.S.A.
4th. September 2020 – 14.20 hours

In the elegant hotel suite high above the hot Washington streets sat the two perspiring men, the Israeli and the American, as they ate the last of their sandwich lunch. Yehuda was unusual for an Israeli politician, thought Peter O'Leary, America's Secretary of State, perusing the impeccably-suited Israeli Minister of Defence who was more the formal well trained and polished international diplomat than his many famous and dashing predecessors. O'Leary, himself a career diplomat, preferred dealing with this kind of fellow professional and it showed in his under stated, small smile.

O'Leary had spent over four hours trying to cut through the man's diplomatic hedging and get to the truth, but much though he enjoyed this thrust and parry he now needed an answer.

"Yehuda, I'm confident we can agree that two days ago, your government said they were ordering a ceasefire, yet your armies are still advancing?"

"Mr. Secretary…"

The formal, perfectly-enunciated Oxford English of Yehuda surprised everyone until they knew he'd been born and educated in London and had only gone to Israel to fight in the Yom Kippur War of 1973, changing his very English name from Ben Gibson when he'd become an Israeli citizen and moving on to a dazzlingly-successful political and military career. What was considered even more bizarre in Britain's upper classes, was the fact that Yehuda was in fact a devout Christian, who also happened to be an unshakeable Zionist, believing that the world could never achieve its spiritual ends unless, and until, all the Jewish people were reunited in the Jewish state.

"Do you agree that to be effective, a ceasefire has to be a two-sided affair?"

"Alright," acknowledged O'Leary,

"You blame the Arabs for continuing the war and they blame you, but this thing is getting out of hand. The whole Middle East is exploding"!"

The Israeli retorted angrily. "Oh, and it's only acceptable when Israel is being attacked, but when your oil is at risk instead of our children's *lives*, we should take notice. My God, don't the Israelis know America's air conditioning's been switched off to save fuel, when all we're sacrificing is our blood? Isn't this the question you're really asking? Why don't we realize American sweat is far more important than our children's blood? No, Mr. Secretary. Israel will not apologize for America's small inconvenience. If you want to solve your problems, send your mighty armies and take the oil from your Arab blackmailers. You should have done it years ago!"

The American was surprised by the Minister's vehement attack, but he thought he could understand the pressures the man had been under, so he kept his response cool and low key. Not giving vent to his fiery Irish temperament, he carefully kept to his instructions from the President to try defusing this dangerous war. "You know the U.S. government and its people are pledged to ensure Israel's survival within secure, defensible borders. Nothing has changed, but your actions have been aggressive not defensive. How can we, your only real ally, justify them in the world's forum?"

Yehuda stood up from his chair to stretch his back, his poker face giving no clue to his thought process or mood. His Irish American counterpart, O'Leary, was, in his opinion, a basically decent man with little or no sophisticated understanding of international affairs, much like the rest of the newly-elected administration. "We don't care, Mr Secretary, for you to be able to justify our actions. We only care about winning this war so that we can survive. What would America do if Canada, Cuba, Mexico and South America marched together on your borders and stated that their collective aim was your destruction?"

O'Leary kept his reply to himself, knowing that Israel had done only what anyone else would do in the same situation, and he - as an Afghanistan combat veteran - greatly admired the brilliance of the small nation's achievements. Nevertheless, he had a duty to his country, not to some fly-blown troublesome speck in the desert, and O'Leary was a man who took his duty seriously.

He spoke again in his heavy Bostonian accent. "Yehuda, it will be with the greatest possible reluctance that we shall be forced to issue Israel with a stern ultimatum from the President unless your government reconsiders its actions by midnight, Washington time, tonight."

The Israeli met his stare head on. O'Leary admired the man's dignity and courage but knew the Israelis would have no option other than to cave in to America's demands. "Unless by midnight your Prime Minister unilaterally and unconditionally ceases all military activities, the United States government reserves all its rights including, but not limited to, withdrawal of all aid, whether political, financial or military, immediate cessation of all arms, supplies and spares, and naturally we will therefore be forced to call in all your country's outstanding loans... Do you get our message?"

Yehuda had turned his back on the Secretary of State and was looking out onto Washington as the American finished his dire warning. The Isrseli then turned back to face the man. "Mr. Secretary, I couldn't previously understand why we should meet here in so much secrecy, but obviously your administration didn't want to allow your public to see its election pledges of total support for Israel's secure borders being broken. You don't want witnesses when you promote our genocide!"

O'Leary also stood and shouted back at the outraged Israeli. "Where the fuck do you guys get off? We've been keeping you alive! We didn't need you, you need us, and you'll do what you're told or pay the consequences!"

The Israeli stood toe-to-toe with O'Leary, forcing the tough American to avert his eyes. "Do you believe we can be threatened by the United States of America?" he said incredulously. "The Jewish people have been threatened and massacred by experts from Rome, from the Inquisitors, from the Tsars to the Communists, the Arabs, the Crusaders, even Hitler, the master himself, couldn't crush the Jews and all those monsters have vanished into the shadows of history but the Jews are still here..

If murdering maniacs like those couldn't wipe the Jews out, why should they be scared by such threats from a friend? Before you carry on with this outrageous bullying, let me warn you that Israel gives America until midnight to reconsider, or Israel reserves its rights to take whatever actions it sees fit against America to protect its interests."

O'Leary would have laughed out loud at little Israel threatening counter measures against America's giant powers had he not seen the graven seriousness on Yehuda's face. "You can't expect me to believe Israel is threatening the U.S.A.?"

Yehuda's expression didn't change as he answered. "Of course we wouldn't threaten our ally. We, like you, are merely reserving our rights. This war was not our creation, but we do intend to finish it exactly when and how it suits us, and nothing, I repeat nothing, will stand in our way. We have carefully planned for many years for any contingency. Your country's present posture is such a contingency.

I beg you to treat what I have said as a statement of fact; it is no bluff on my part. If we are hurt, we will not hesitate to retaliate, and when and if we did, the world will tremble in memory. I beg you to believe what I say, Mr. Secretary. We are desperate men and if you push us too far, we will take desperate action. Withdraw your ultimatum and we can forget the whole sad interlude in our countries' happy friendship."

"I don't believe this. It's like an elephant being threatened with rape by a flea. Do you know what you're saying? How crazy it sounds?"

But the Israeli stood his ground.

"You're so used to your threats working that you forget it only takes a small infection to kill the biggest giant."

The American diplomat didn't trust himself to speak; he was so angry that it took him minutes of silence before he began to *consider* whether or not he was simply being out-bluffed by a master card-shark What can Israel do to America that America can't deal with? It doesn't make sense But on the *other* hand it's important to question the Israeli to see if there's more to this than bluster and tough talk.

"I have enumerated some of America's options to you, will you be more specific regarding Israel's?"

The reply was emphatic and swift.

"No."

O'Leary knew he'd have answered in the same way given the same situation in reverse, but he tried one last time; a desperate appeal on a man-to-man basis.

"Let's forget you're a Minister representing Israel and I'm America's Secretary of State. We're just two guys. Can't you and I sort this mess out quietly, without a fuss? Who needs trouble like this between such good friends? Just think how the Arabs and the Russians would love it if they could hear this conversation."

The Israeli who had sat on the edge of one of the room's two double beds nodded. "If it were up to just you and I, things would be very simple, but it isn't. It's about history, emotions and blood. Do you seriously believe we want to be branded international criminals? The answer is simple; just get off our backs for a few days. I promise you that will be enough for us to deliver guaranteed peace in our region for a generation, perhaps more. I can't tell you how I know this, but rest assured our intelligence is correct. Is a few days of your embarrassed silence too big a price for you to pay?"

O'Leary who had already removed his navy-blue lightweight suit jacket, took off his burgundy silk tie and undid the collar on his white Bloomingdales shirt. The room's windows were sealed to accommodate the air-conditioners, which were shut down as instructed by the government's emergency fuel conservation legislation. The result was a room with a temperature of over one hundred degrees Fahrenheit which taken together with the seasonal humidity made the room claustrophobic and unbearable. O'Leary wiped the heavy perspiration from his face with his already damp silk handkerchief. "Yehuda, I sure wish that if we *have* to talk like this to each other we could do it in a cool place and you'd call me Pete, and we'd down a couple of long iced drinks. It may not improve things a damn, but we're not kids anymore and I'd sure as hell feel better."

Yehuda removed his jacket and tie, his face wreathed in smiles. "Pete, you know in better circumstances we would be good friends, but talking over a cold drink is a better move than *anything* else I could suggest."

"How about I order us two lagers served in a bucket of ice?"

Asked the Secretary, picking up the phone and pressing for room service. Yehuda nodded as O'Leary ordered two iced lagers.

As he replaced the receiver, Yehuda spoke again.

"Have your Pentagon boys been keeping you posted on our progress?"

O'Leary chuckled, "You bet, they're convinced it's about fifty-fifty."

The Israeli interjected,

"What do they mean fifty-fifty ? We're winning along the entire front. If we wanted an empire, it's within our grasp."

O'Leary shook his head and laughed.

"No, I don't mean that. My generals reckon their weapons are fifty percent responsible for your victories and your troops the other half. I have combat experience though. I know it isn't like that. I know it's the men, the training and the motivation. The weapons sure help, but never fifty per cent if two sides are pretty evenly matched in the first place. But tell me something off the record. We heard a whisper from our sources that your general Zvi is holed up in your G.H.Q., directing the war like some kind of Jewish Napoleon. We heard a story that no one even gets to speak to this guy unless he says so. We also learnt that it was this man and a few of his friends high up in the military who *really* call the shots. That would mean you couldn't stop this war even if you wanted to. Is that right, Yehuda? Is that how it is?"

Yehuda had played a lot of poker over the years, and was a consummate bluffer. He kept his face impassive although he was astounded that Israel's awful secret was known; that her war leaders had assumed almost total power and that the government was relegated to pawns at the mercy of the generals. They had conducted a clandestine military coup immediately before the war. The politicians maintained the public pretence that they still had control in their country's normal democratic manner, but it was the military high command that conducted the successful war and who had so brilliantly prepared for it, bearing in mind all the lessons from previous conflicts that the politicians had forgotten.

Yehuda was a democrat who hated the situation, but above all he was a patriot who had to defend the interests of his country even if it left a bad taste in his mouth. The generals had planned for all these contingencies and they'd issued explicit instructions to government ministers on political matters including their very real threat that he, Yehuda, had been forced to relay to O'Leary. The Foreign Minister was a man of the world, and he understood the implicit and ominous threat that his security guards had, in reality become his prison warders. He'd also had a telephone call from Rachel, his precious wife, who told him in a fraught telephone call that she was effectively under house arrest in their modest Jerusalem apartment. The military had not understood their man, because above all he was a diplomat and peacemaker. If they hadn't sought to force his hand he would have 'played ball', but now he was tempted to spill the beans to the American.

Yehuda's face didn't betray his inner torment; his life was now a nightmare. He wrestled whether he should play it the general's way. They were, he believed and hoped, honourable - if misguided - men who would return power to the country's government as they had promised. But that could only happen if and when the government kept their part of a private agreement to write an official pardon for the men, and honoured all the arrangements reached in this period. Public disclosure could lead to open civil war between those supporting the generals and those democrats who stood with their elected representatives.

The democratically elected cabinet had unanimously decided that any price was worth paying to avoid such a tragedy. In public, the politicians said what they were told to say in curiously quiet, subdued speeches for a group known to be so aggressive and fractious.

This transformation had alerted America's C.I.A. to check with their Israeli contacts who were normally amongst the best informed of their ilk in the world, largely because of the constant flow of intentionally-leaked cabinet secrets by divisive, bickering ministers. The contacts came up blank, not only blank but scared; someone had warned them to keep their heads well down.

Next the C.I.A. had mysteriously lost three of their best operatives on the first day of the war. They had been dispatched by the chief to observe; the Israeli military intelligence politely reported finding three mutilated corpses, believed to be Americans, on the West Bank, miles from any fighting. The Israelis led the Americans to believe that these operatives had been killed by a radical West Bank section of Hamas, the Palestinian group in control of Gaza. If the Americans had been able to check the facts, they would have eventually discovered that the Israelis had leaked the location and identity of the three Americans to the Palestinian hit team through back channels.

The upper echelons of the C.I.A. knew something very unusual was happening, but only discovered how unusual via a regular clandestine meeting between a Russian SVR man and his American C.I.A. counterpart in Beirut. These strange bedfellows often swapped information about their client states in the area, nothing too sensitive, approved chit chat, jig-saw problems, puzzles being solved with mutual ease. However for this particular rendezvous, the American had been ordered to forewarn the Russians that the U.S. was going to exercise its military option in Saudi Arabia and he dropped the none-too-subtle hint that Russia should stay well clear unless they wanted some American interference in their defined sphere of influence, say in Iran, Russia's energy-rich faithful new ally and essential supplier. By way of a return of information, the Russian had told the disbelieving American of Israel's increasing instability and covert military takeover. Curiously, the Russians wanted America to calm Israel down. They knew of the little state's nuclear capacity and didn't want any excuse for the holocaust to start by accident. The Russian explained how they had obtained their Israeli intelligence reports by having planted numerous K.G.B. long-term sleeper agents amongst the million or so legitimate Jewish emigrants to Israel of the sixties, seventies and eighties. The Russian sleeper agents had been almost totally weeded out by Israel's ruthlessly-efficient counter intelligence bureau but the few survivors who had infiltrated the little Middle-Eastern country successfully were unanimous; the generals had wrested power from the politicians in all but name. Russia wanted this reversed and their sane pragmatic predecessors re-instated before it was too late. If America didn't do this, Russia wouldn't pledge herself to non-interference in America's Saudi Arabian adventure which the Russian said the Kremlin had known about since the initial task force of U.S Paratroopers had started their seemingly-clandestine mass airlift out of their Georgia base.

Armed with this knowledge, the American Secretary of State pressed the Israeli. "Yehuda, we want to be of assistance, we're the good guys here, we know all about it, we want to help you and the guys who were democratically elected to represent your people, but you have to level with me, please."

Yehuda was not surprised that O'Leary had become a successful politician. But he valued his own inner-core moral strength, the durability of his faith, but most of all, he was an old-fashioned, almost Old Testament, believer in God and the chosen people's destiny in Zion. However much he might regret Israel's flirtation with military dictatorship, for him it was still infinitely preferable to outside, non-Israeli control. His face remained blank as he spoke.

"Forgive my silence, Mister Secretary, but I'm stunned by these unfounded allegations. I've never heard a more preposterous fabrication in my whole career. Not even the Palestinian propaganda merchants could dream up such falsehoods, distortions and malicious lies. With respect, if you honestly, even for one minute, give the rubbish credibility, I'll have no alternative but to personally request of your President that he appoints another, saner, negotiator. You are either deliberately being fed false intelligence by fanatic pro Arabists in your State Department or you, Peter O'Leary, are engaging in your favourite pastime, fishing!"

"Oh Christ," Said O'Leary, "The Russians were right, you've been taken over by the military."

"I most strongly protest," the Israeli Minister retorted.

"You can protest all you like, Yehuda. I may be an ignorant Irishman, but I can smell a rat, and you're a mite too angry for someone with nothing to answer. Methinks you do protest too much!"

As O'Leary finished there was a polite knock on the connecting door to the left of their room.

"The drinks," said O'Leary, going to the door behind which were his F.B.I. guards. As he turned the handle, the door crashed open, slamming into O'Leary who flew backwards, tripping over the bed. The Israeli Minister ran for cover but both men were hit by the first murderous spray of machine gun bullets fired by the swarthy, lean man who emptied his entire clip into the two already-dead bodies. As he turned to hurry away, the other interconnecting door opposite burst open and the two Israeli security men each shot the assassin with two pistol rounds, accurately pinpointing his brain and heart, killing him before he fell to the carpet. The two men from Mossad efficiently went about their business, their gimlet, restless eyes taking in the scene. Both had seen much death and instantly recognized its stench. Their Minister and the American were dead and were therefore not the main priority because only seconds would elapse before someone came to investigate the noise of the gunfire.

The Israeli security men quickly and methodically took photographs of the scene on their camera phones that were almost instantaneously encoded and accompanied their brief texts to their military masters in Tel Aviv, as one of them compose the message. "Aleph 2 + Eagle 2 + Hamed + Goofy, en route to nest." The other man also recorded the scene while he quietly muttered the Kaddish, the ancient Jewish prayer for the dead.

In Israel, Colonel Raviv, the Deputy Controller of the Border Guards, the group responsible for Israel's diplomatic security around the world, read the message and grimaced before putting in a call to the military HQ just a couple of streets away.

The Israeli security men walked over to the assassin's body and one photographed and fingerprinted him with their portable, miniaturized equipment they always kept near. The other man systematically searched the corpse and its clothing for any clues to his identity or origins; there were none to find. The men didn't like the result but did have professional respect for the process. They hadn't expected anything less, but specialists were methodical and observed procedures.

Carefully, with pistols cocked, the two young, tough wiry men crept into the room from which the assassin had attacked. The picture was simple to comprehend for the Israelis, and the carnage they found was total. The F.B.I. special agent who'd answered this room's front door was stretched flat on his back, the look of shock still comically present on his face. The Assassin had merely sprayed him with deadly K5 poison. It had originated with the Russian FSB, the successors to the famed KGB, but the poison had since been widely-distributed to most of the former Eastern European allies intelligence service for their operatives use and it soon found its way from these to various illicit organizations around the world. Once in the victim's system, the heart and brain ceased functioning, almost instantaneously. The other F.B.I. man had been murdered while he'd been snoozing on one of the beds. The assassin's combat knife had nearly severed through the now-perpetually sleeping man's neck.

The Americans should have agreed to the Israeli's suggestion of shared guard duty; one Israeli with one American in each adjoining room. They'd tried to insist but those damned politicians with their stupid, clandestine meetings, and low profiles, they made targets of themselves and everyone unlucky enough to be guarding them.

The young men checked for, and found, the three tiny limpet microphone bugs stuck one to each part of the wall connecting this room with the dead politicians' suite next door. They wrapped this specialist equipment in a plastic laundry bag, together with the encoder they found in the shirt pocket of the corpse on the bed. This magical instrument, measuring just three-and-a-half inches long and two high, was wafer thin; both recorded and scrambled any conversation relayed by the limpet bugs. Its tiny microchip brain instructed it to only record speech, automatically eliminating pauses, even the breath between words. Its amazing capacity allowed it to filter out any and all extraneous sounds. On its tiny wire, you could record in excess of twenty-four hours. This was then played to a computer that would descramble its content for the geeks back in Tel Aviv to print and interpret as necessary.

The Israelis left the room with their booty in less than one minute and were far away from the hotel by the time ten minutes had elapsed when two nervous police patrolmen burst into the room too late to do anything but call for help.

Chapter Thirty-one

Eddie Roman's Office, Chesterfield Street, London, England
10 September – 8.30 a.m.

The last couple of weeks had been the best Eddie could remember. The world might be going crazy but he couldn't keep the smile from his face as he thought of the joy he felt. Barry and he were together again, better than before. In addition business was great and he'd raised over twenty-two million pounds cash through both fair means and foul, and had arranged for a big loan against these funds as a deposit. He'd persuaded - some might call it bribed - Andy Skouras, an acquisitive young Greek American vice president at the London branch of one of America's biggest banks, First Central of Boston. They had advanced him a further eighteen million dollars revolving line of credit using Eddie's property portfolio collateral and conveniently losing their encumbrances and charges. As Eddie had wined and dined the shrewd graduate of Harvard's School of Business, the tall, thin, black-eyed Greek had discreetly let it be known that although honour might have no price, he did; a cool two million dollars banked in Basel, Switzerland at the small, very private Graffman Bank; and the deal idea became a reality, everything smoothly arranged and in place.

Eddie didn't want to take any risks, so he paid the money into the bank himself after flying in and out of Switzerland the next day.

Now he had his bank loan, nearly thirty-six million pounds, or in excess of fifty million dollars after all bank charges, plus legal fees for drawing up the lengthy meaningless contact between his new company Arab-Roman Property Ltd and First Central Bank of Boston.

His raid on London's depressed residential market was swift and silent. Even the shrewd, tough men in the city's property world didn't have time to counter Eddie's well-mounted assault.

Within one week, he'd invested thirty million simply as deposits of between five and ten per cent on a cross-section of more than two hundred and sixty of the available, most desirable, stylish and exclusive properties in central London, purchasing either the freehold or long leases.

Almost without exception he bought from people desperately needing cash or about to go bankrupt. The sellers were glad to sell at any price to anyone stupid enough to part with real money when the banks had cut off the supply to almost everyone, except those that were so rich that they didn't need it.

Eddie, because of his very special banking connections, was able to mortgage these properties with many different banks all of whom were rich in liquidity but starved of solid, good borrowers with interest rates static at an astronomical eighteen percent after they had been stuck in the basement for years previously at virtually zero per cent.

Eddie then managed to raise another thirty million pounds in cash by then inflating the value of his new property portfolio with the corrupt and greedy young banker, Andy Skouras, and used it all, plus five-and-a-half million of his original money in his second week of feverish buying which had just ended.

Eddie added it all up, his property portfolio made him grunt with satisfaction. He now owned nearly four hundred luxury properties, purchased at rock-bottom prices. He had been almost the only buyer in a market that was still crashing to its lowest levels for more than thirty years. Eddie managed to grab a progression of ever-more desirable properties for ever-lower price, and more than half of these new purchases weren't even mortgaged or encumbered in any way. Because he'd then been able to pump some of this activity through his publicly traded company he created more asset value resulting in even more collateral under his control to use. He still had a considerable pile of cash to fall back on. All things considered, he was a contented man. He was ready. All he needed now were a great many rich customers!

There was a light tap on his office door and Barry, looking secretarial and prim in a smart black suit, led in Robert Falcon, the lawyer he'd employed to represent the new company, based on glowing references from Lord Radling, the chairman of his main bank, Applecrombie's. Falcon had another self-evident recommendation; he was an Arab and would understand his people's ways. Eddie thought the nervous brown-skinned little man had the wrong Anglicized name; he seemed more sparrow than falcon as he sat down opposite Eddie.

Eddie had never invited the man to his office before and realized Falcon didn't know that Barry was his partner; who turned at the door and pretended not to notice that Falcon ignored him as if he was just the hired help. "Will that be all, Mr. Roman?" Barry asked Eddie.

"Mr. Falcon, would you like any tea or coffee?"

Falcon said yes to tea in his high- pitched, almost childish voice.

"Anything with it, sir?" asked Barry.

"No, thank you."

Barry returned with their coffee and tea. "Have you two been introduced?"

"No," said Falcon, not interested, but being polite to his important new client. He stood up to his full five feet four, which brought him roughly parallel to Barry's chest.

"Mr. Falcon, legal adviser, meet Barry, my personal executive associate and civil partner." Falcon was shaking Barry's hand over enthusiastically when the words civil partner sank in. He dropped Barry's hand as if he'd been electrocuted.

"Oh, you two are playing games with me," he said to the laughing Barry and Eddie, their fun so spontaneous and endearingly innocent that the lawyer's attempt to appear insulted collapsed into paroxysms of high-pitched laughter aimed at his own stuffiness. "You two devils would be whipped for saying such things in a proper Muslim country, exciting evil thoughts in my poor brain." He sat down once more.

"It's a pleasure meeting you Mr. Falcon,"

"Yes, me too, Mr. Barry, or is it Mrs. Roman. Oh, you two are joking me, yes?" the lawyer said to Barry as he left the two men to their business.

"Let us always understand each other with perfect clarity," Eddie said in perfect Arabic.

Falcon was now nonplussed. "Where did you learn to speak Arabic like that? You're fluent."

Eddie smiled. "I come from Iraq, my brother. All that separates us is our faith, but I grew up an Arab, albeit a Jewish Arab!"

Falcon smiled at this surprising turn of events. " We should both fight in the way of Allah with those who fight with you, but aggress not: God loves not the aggressors."

"Ah our bibles," responded Eddie. "The race is not to the swift nor the battle to the strong. You know your Koran and I my Old Testament. I'm sorry, Robert, I couldn't resist teasing you, I hope you don't mind."

Falcon raised his hand to stop his client. "Never apologize for making a person laugh. It's the best gift in the world, but do you mind if I told you something personal?"

"No, go ahead. We should be frank with each other if we're going to work together." Falcon paused, searching for a polite way to say what he felt needed saying.

"Mr. Roman, I am a westernized Arab, my culture, my upbringing, even my clothes would tell you that. I went to Oxford University and before that to Gordonstoun School in Scotland. I was articled with a firm of London solicitors, curiously enough for a Syrian businessman's son, they are a Jewish firm, but despite my outward Englishness, I am still an Arab, inside, where it counts. I must tell you with all respect that should you want me to represent you with Arab clients you will have to learn to adapt to their ways, or fail."

Eddie answered quickly. "No one can tell me about the sensibilities of Arabic culture, and while you were growing up here, I spent some of my best years as a street kid in Basra."

Falcon shook his head and smiled. "No, no, Mr. Roman, you don't understand me."

"Eddie. Call me Eddie," said Roman.

"Yes Eddie, it will be an honour to call you by your given name. No offence was intended by you or taken by me, honestly."

He paused before continuing.

"But most Arabs that you will be dealing with have two sets of behaviour, one very puritan, almost aesthetic at home with their own families, eating sparingly, never drinking alcohol, never fornicating, yet when they come here they are like prisoners released from jail, they undergo a complete change; they do not rise from bed until noon to eat and chat with friends for a few hours. By four or five o'clock they go back to bed with the hooker or good time girl from the night before, screw themselves silly, have a siesta, get up at nine or so, fresh and raring to go, get rid of yesterday's woman and out they go to sample London's pleasures yet again. It's an endless circle of booze, gambling and women, not much time is dedicated to business so you will have to spend time with them in their schedule, otherwise you'll never do a single deal. Don't expect them to come here even if you have what they want. They would feel it to be a loss of face, and most of all, don't let them misunderstand your humour about your civil partner, it could be a grave embarrassment to you if they thought he might be available, if you understand my line of thought."

Eddie did, and furthermore was pleased to hear the lawyer talk about the do's and don'ts on how to work with the Arabs. He admitted to himself that his knowledge of Arabic society stopped as a small boy and he knew almost nothing of the ways of the elite sections of mature Arabs when they were away from home and free of constraints and the way they operated their business investments once they were in places like London. He smiled.

"Kind of like what happens in Vegas stay in Vegas?"

Falcon matched his smile. "That's it, almost exactly what I'm saying, but that's why, as they say, you will be paying me the big bucks. I shall be here, by your side to advise you. We're both in it to win it!"

Eddie was aware that, in their brief period as client and counsel, they hadn't spoken about anything other than the mountain of paperwork and conveyance of properties Eddie had been pouring into Falcon's office.

"Robert, I hear what you're saying and to be honest with you any more pointers you think of along the way would be very much appreciated. I've got a lot at stake in this. I don't want to blow it. It goes without saying as far as you're concerned that any help you give me personally, let's say not within your purview as my lawyer, will be rewarded with my tangible gratitude. You understand?"

Falcon's perpetual smile broadened still further.

"Eddie, we understand each other absolutely it appears. I have the feeling you will do very well with my Arab friends."

It was Eddie this time who held up his hand to halt the other man's speech. "We will do extremely well, not just me. I'm not greedy; if I can make a few hundred million I'd be happy."

He laughed with Falcon. "Now Robert, down to cases. How are you doing?"

The lawyer extracted a thick sheaf of yellow legal notepads from his soft leather briefcase but Eddie stopped him before he could say anything. "I haven't the time or inclination to deal in the minutiae, Robert. That's what I'm paying you guys for. I trust you'll tie up the ends, and do it properly. No, all I want to know is the broad picture, are we completing the bulk of our buys according to my schedule? Has there been any sudden increase in failures to complete? You know the kind of thing I want, so tell me."

Falcon scanned his notes, making penciled margin notes by some of the items. He looked at Eddie as he finished this chore. "Broadly speaking, Eddie, your acquisitions are going almost entirely to schedule. I trust you realize to achieve your objective we've had four senior partners, plus six juniors, plus God alone knows how many articled clerks, typists, computers and telephone lines tied up solely on your business for two solid weeks."

He paused significantly... "Your account with my firm will not be modest."

Eddie smiled indulgently. He enjoyed having money behind him in this kind of conversation. "I didn't imagine for a second you'd undertake my task for a low figure, Robert. I can't pretend that I ever relish waste, but I have long since learnt that if you pay peanuts you get monkeys. If right now I paid your firm a retainer of let's say three hundred thousand, would that keep you and your partners happily beavering away? I like to keep my friends happy if they keep me the same way."

Falcon's smile became even more radiant, his large white teeth looking like a row of enamel pots set in the wood cabinet of his teak brown face.

"Three hundred thousand, Eddie, would make us very happy, for a short time, however. I should imagine enthusiasm would be unlimited for, say, half a million. There would be no night or day for that."

Eddie's smile was almost as broad. "No, let's say three hundred and fifty thousand and settle for us both being very happy, and I expect your people to work without knowing what a clock is, O.K.?"

Falcon cheerfully nodded his full head of black hair. "Most agreeable, but all we lawyers are itching to understand why you need us to work with such dispatch to complete purchases of properties that have lain fallow without any sign of being sold for ages. Why the urgency? You know of course that you can rely on our absolute discretion."

Eddie shook his head.

"I'm sure I could, Robert, but I was told what I know in confidence, and you're too astute to hear part of my story without being easily able to tie in the missing pieces, so I'm afraid you'll just have to wait and see whether I'm either a raving lunatic or simply a well-informed businessman."

Falcon shrugged his narrow shoulders. "I quite understand Eddie, you're a man of honour. You gave your word and you don't do it lightly, I respect that, and I should add I for one, don't believe you're a lunatic."

Eddie indicated the Anglo-Arab's briefcase. "You're in good shape then?"

"Yes, as I told you, we have worked with exceptional speed. In the words of your American cousins, we've been kicking ass. We have made the vendors' solicitors work as they never worked before, assisted, no doubt, but your insistence to the clients that non-completion of all paperwork within seven days and you would withdraw, deals that normally take seven weeks or more are going through in hours. It's quite amazing. We have firm agreements, signed and sealed on all but... let me be specific... " He consulted his notes. "On all but twelve transactions, and some of those are being handled by my junior even now. We'll have everything done by Monday at close of business, exactly as you demanded when you engaged us. I trust this is satisfactory?"

Eddie opened a drawer in his desk and drew out a fat manila envelope, which he casually tossed onto his surprised lawyer's lap.

"What is this? Another joke?"

He asked Eddie.

"Open it. If it makes you laugh then it must be. I call it a personal gratuity, between just you and me, you don't have to bother your bosses about this one."

Robert Falcon's nimble, surprisingly-long fingers opened the bulging envelope and discovered the contents, one thousand crisp fifty-pound notes. His bulging eyes rolled in pleasure. His smile would have shamed Liberace's dentist.

"Eddie, you are truly a brother. My brother, what can I say in reply to such magnanimity, an additional fifty thousand pounds?"

"It's just a gratuity. How about a simple 'thank you'?" Eddie said, deadpan.

"Thank you a thousandfold my brother, for placing your trust in me, and in favouring me with payment before I have even sent you a bill. Many good things shall come of this, I swear it."

Eddie wasn't sure how to react to such effusive emotions from a man who was still a relative stranger. "I'm happy, you're happy. Well, if there's nothing else." Eddie stood up, as did his guest who extended his hand, which was surprisingly strong when Eddie shook it.

"One thing about Arabs you should always remember, Eddie."

"Oh, what's that?" asked Eddie.

"Be on your guard the second they call you their brother. It's a code for them wanting something from you. O.K. my brother, until next week." The wily little Arab pirouetted and left his amused host who had already decided that Robert Falcon was an associate not to be abused, possibly a future good friend. He would probably be a terrible, unrelenting enemy.

Chapter Thirty-two

The Jeddah Road, Saudi Arabia
12 September 2020 – 06.45 hours.

Nafti drove Prince Mo fast on Jeddah's main highway road across the desolate distant sprawl of the town's suburbs. They had been travelling for three days in a curious convoy composed of two jeeps full of Palestinian commandos bracketing their bullet-proof, armor-plated Rolls Royce Phantom. They had left Beirut on the ninth, which seemed like an eternity ago to both men. An air journey had been considered certain suicide; the Israeli Air Force would use the Saudi's royal Lear jet for target practice. They had no alternative when King Ibin Saud summoned them home from Beirut's lush enjoyments, they would travel the two thousand miles by road.

They had secured their Palestinian guards from their new ally, General Nabul, who had insisted on the two Saudis travelling under his protection; but they all knew this was a transparent subterfuge to keep the devious Prince under the Palestinian's constantly-mistrusting observation.

"Nevertheless," confided Mo,

"It is a long and dangerous road, Nafti, and these Palestinian pigs need us alive and well. What wonderful irony that such enemies should have to keep us protected!"

Nafti had grunted in a non-committed way. "You trust no one Nafti, not even me, your Prince."

Nafti had looked horror-stricken at this outrageous suggestion. "My Prince, you are the one constant factor in my life,

"He said truly, for the Prince was constantly insane, the only variable was how much insanity showed itself.

The Prince smiled, "I will lead all our people, the Sunnis and the Shia, everyone from the Danube to the Euphrates and beyond, and one day our black flag will fly over the White House and I will lead those that are with us in prayer and they will all bend at the knee."

He sighed and fell asleep as the convoy left the once-again-ravaged, formerly- beautiful Lebanese capital and joined the main Beirut to Damascus highway.

Syrian soldiers were everywhere; they had moved back from contesting the Golan Heights with the Israelis, and now formed a defensive perimeter running from Tyre at the western extremity.

North of the Litani River they had annexed Lebanon into an embryonic Greater Syria, that was however, diminished by the Israeli's recapture of Mount Hermon. Their heavy guns threatened Damascus itself, only a few kilometres distant from their forward position. Nafti had carefully memorized the Syrians' dispositions as they neared the capital and could see Russian officers ordering the harassed Arabs where to dig their trenches, foxholes and tank traps. The scene was utter devastation where the battles for control over this haunted part of the Middle East had raged for decades killing millions of people and displacing countless others.

Nafti and the Prince saw battered T80 and T90 main battle tanks camouflaged by the roadside and as they neared Damascus itself, they witnessed the wreckage of many old Soviet-supplied SAM ground to air missile sites, obviously hit by Israeli jets several weeks before and still not serviceable or replaced.

The Palestinian jeep riding point had swerved off the road, careering into a dense clump of trees. Nafti's battle-tested reflexes sensed danger and he followed the guards, his immensely heavy vehicle carving deep twin furrows in the loosely-packed sandy soil. As he fought to stop the Rolls crashing into the trees ahead, he had seen the trailing jeep following in his mirrors, the commandos firing their weapons wildly into the sky at some unseen enemy. Nafti pulled up inches from the trunk of an enormous tree, but was then rammed viciously into it by the chasing jeep, the driver's head crashed through the front window, a puppet with the strings cut, his face disintegrated as the jagged shards of glass ripped and plundered his every feature of its human form.

Nafti and the Prince jumped from their car and as they did, they heard the fearful whooshing sound of fast combat jets flying overhead. The two men joined their guards who were running towards the shelter of a steeply-cut railway embankment through the dense trees and bushes which scratched and clawed at their exposed faces and hands as they fell and slithered down the gravel slope of the well-concealed cutting which framed the railway tracks. They heard the clump sound of bomb clusters exploding down onto unseen, nearby targets, then even closer, more insistent, the regulated noise of anti- aircraft batteries replying.

Nafti realized that they must have wandered into a target-rich environment as the incoming attack appeared to have been launched over the horizon by long-range 'fire and forget' systems from aircraft they couldn't even see.

The Prince screamed to Nafti but couldn't be heard above the crescendo of battle. He pointed wildly across the tracks at an enormous round mushroom-coloured building a hundred metres beyond an electrified barbed wire fence. Nafti understood; it was a nuclear reactor. They had stumbled into a veritable hornet's nest for, as they watched in spellbound horror, eight F18's flashed overhead racing to this target. The jets flew in a tight- shaped formation at about one hundred feet, launching their air-to-ground rockets at the reactor from near point-blank range. The aircraft peeled off into two groups of four and zoomed straight up as the nuclear power plant seemed to tremble and sway under the deafening impact. Nafti pulled the Prince to his feet and screamed above an ominous rumble coming out of the earth itself.

"The tunnel, Your Excellency, quickly, the tunnel!"

The Prince followed him at a dead run towards the tunnel, cut into the sheer grey rock face. They had nearly entered its welcoming blackness when the ground underfoot betrayed them; it bucked and heaved, its solidity gone, now a sea of crazy, dancing, molten movement. Nafti recognized the threat as a bunker-busting bomb, designed to enter a deep underground target and to blow up once inside and suck all the air out, both destroying the targets and killing everyone inside.

Prince Mo was thrown into the air as if weightless. Somersaulting uncontrollably, he landed head first between the rail lines. The shock waves from the exploding building roared at them. As Nafti uncertainly recovered his footing and made his way to the Prince's inert form, the giant Israeli agent was hurled forwards like a leaf by the hurricane-force wind. As he saw the ground rush at him, Nafti balled his legs into his torso and bent his head inwards, covering his face with both arms. He rolled onto his back as he landed, the impact expelling all the air from already-tortured lungs. He tried to gather his wits, his eyes battling with sand and grit to see a nightmare apparition. The reactor's shell was ablaze in a haloed inferno. Nearby was a Palestinian draped lifelessly on the electrified fence, his blackened, charred face frozen in an everlasting grimace of surprise and terror.

Nafti stood and felt sharp pain shoot up from his feet. He looked down and saw the cause, his tightly laced army boots had been sucked clean off by the blast wave, and he was standing with his bare feet on the sharp pointed little stones between the wooden sleepers of the track. To his left, lay the Prince as he'd last seen him, and a metre or so further along from him was another commando, pinned hopelessly, butterfly like, under a big boulder which must have popped out of the rock face above the tunnel and with malicious cruelty snared the moaning man. Nafti rushed towards him, forgetting his own pain as his feet were shredded with each pace. He reached the young man, and guessed him to be no older than sixteen, or seventeen at the most, his dark handsome face was contorted in agony as Nafti put his massive back against the boulder and anchored his bleeding feet on the railway lines seeking purchase. He slowly bunched his corded muscles as he consciously tried to raise his adrenalin level for one superhuman effort, his huge bulk strained backwards against the monster rock, every sinew of his being pushed, every vein stood out, every pore seeped with sweat – either the rock would move or his back would break.

The boulder moved, infinitesimally at first, but Nafti felt it move, and knew he could do it. The Palestinian's screams redoubled the Jew's effort, and with a scream of his own, he smashed his back into the pitiless stone. It lifted again, a few inches, but this time Nafti's pressure was unrelenting. He kept the movement's momentum and inch by terrible inch, levered the boulder up until finally it rolled and crashed clear of its victim. Nafti examined the boy whose grateful eyes followed and understood his rescuer's sad examination of his paralyzed body. He tried to express his gratitude to the big man but no words, only dark blood would come from his mouth. He begged in mime for his misery to be ended, for Nafti to take out his gun and blow out his brains. The giant pulled out his own pearl-handled revolver and aimed at the boy who smiled in encouragement. A shot rang out to end the boy's tragedy but not from Nafti's gun, Prince Aziz had revived and held his still smoking pistol near the dead boy's head.

"How long was I out?" Aziz asked his bodyguard.

"A few minutes, your Excellency," said Nafti, instinctively reverting to his role of loyal servant.

The Prince looked in awe at the flaming reactor, now a fireball. The remaining Palestinians sheepishly appeared from the tunnel and they also stared, transfixed by the vast flames seemingly licking the heavens themselves. Also out of the tunnel came the low-pitched hum of a still-distant, approaching train. All the men scampered off the rails as the rumbling drew nearer.

"The reactor could explode. We should go quickly, Your Excellency!" Nafti urged. Once the Prince realized the danger of a nuclear leak, he was very quick to comply. It seemed certain to everyone that in only a few more minutes, the reactor's core would become the centre of a nuclear explosion. As the men scrambled up the banking, the train came slowly out of the tunnel's blackness. It was no ordinary train; pulled by a standard diesel locomotive but tied behind it on a specially rigged flat bed, was a unique piece of weaponry, a mobile, computerized SA-17 missile base.

The train stopped below the Palestinians. Twenty well-armed Syrian soldiers jumped from the train and charged after them, screaming for their surrender. Thankfully no one panicked and consequently no one was hurt. The Prince and his men surrendered their weapons while walking back down the hill towards the missile launching train.

Standing casually by the locomotive was a smiling Russian officer. He wiped his bald, perspiring head with a filthy oil-stained rag, formerly a handkerchief, and put his dark-brown cap back on at a jaunty angle. The cap had a red star badge stamped into its centre.

"What have we got here?" he asked, almost jovially.

Mo stepped forward and saluted. "I am his Excellency Prince Mo Aziz Ibin

Saud of the Royal Saudi family. And what have you got here?" he demanded with imperial bluster in the direction of his Russian captor, whose broad flat Slavic features beamed in mockery and derision. He executed a Germanic-style heel click and salute for the benefit of the laughing Syrians in his troop.

"In Mother Russia, we know how to treat royalty, perhaps you have you heard about what we did with the last Czar?"

He was clearly baiting the Prince, and Nafti knew his manic mind had no concept of fear and that he was likely to get them all killed; so Nafti intervened. He interposed his bulk between the Prince and the Russian who stepped back a pace, feeling intimidated.

"You will address the Prince as His Excellency or Sir!"

"Who asked you anything, Mr. big shit?" The Russian laughed hugely at his own feeble joke.

Nafti responded, "Sir, aren't the Palestinian Freedom Armies your comrades? Why don't you ask them why we travel together?"

The Russian nodded thoughtfully, it had seemed to him an odd marriage, a Royal Saudi Arabian and Palestinian commandos, if their uniforms were genuine.

His next question was cut off by his assistant's shouted warning from his tiny enclosed control and communications room perched the other side of the train on a retractable hydraulic platform.

"We've got company!" he shouted, scuttling for the control cabin across the flat car, kissing the rocket housing en route. Everyone else ran for cover as they heard the warplanes coming in low and fast. It took only seconds, but - for those watching the screaming formation of Israeli F- 35's remorselessly arrow towards the nuclear reactor - the moment seemed to linger in slow motion. The first jet fired a red beam of light at the fiercely-burning structure and peeled off to the right, as his comrades fired their laser guided 'smart' bombs down the path of the constant but invisible to the naked eye red light; every bomb hit its target as the formation peeled into two groups both going higher and circling for another run, but as the formation leader completed a high confident turn, two SA-17 missiles snaked after him from their launch train, rocketing towards the heat of the hot jet engines as he twisted and turned, trying to shake off the missiles. One whistled past his port wing and exploded harmlessly in mid-air, but the hunted pilot had seemingly given up avoiding the other inexorable rocket. He had aimed his plane straight at the reactor and ejected almost directly above the train, his parachute forming a silhouette against the spectacularly-explosive collision of his jet and the missile into the now-smashed reactor, which dramatically collapsed into itself, although it still didn't explode.

Nafti pulled the Prince towards the tunnel. "Hurry! We need cover!"

Mo didn't move easily, instead he protested. "Don't pull me around like a camel. Can't you see we're safe. The reactor's not going to explode and besides, I want to personally greet our Israeli friend."

The Prince began to walk around the train in the direction of the field the pilot had landed. Nafti followed and pointed his revolver at Mo's back.

"It is my duty to our King to protect you, your Excellency. Now get into the tunnel Excellency or I'll carry you!"

The Prince reluctantly made for it as ordered, surrounded by equally-bemused Palestinians. As they entered the tunnel, Nafti ordered them flat against the wall, which they did, despite the Saudi Prince's dire threats. Nafti warned the others.

"I moved us under cover because the Israelis will bomb the shit out of that Russian unless he moves his train here now!"

Instants later his words bore fruit. They couldn't see much more than the flash of gunfire and the orange afterglow of explosion, but the sounds and images were unforgettable. Jets flying at near maximum speed, their cannon spitting venomously at the train which was ponderously trundling for cover away from the tunnel, its defenders blasting fusillades of automatic gunfire back at the sky in a gallant if impotent gesture of defiance. As abruptly as the dreadful sounds had started, they ceased. The Prince turned to his guard and embraced him.

"Allah was merciful to send a man like you to me. Again you must accept my thanks and treat anything I own as yours. What can I give you? What do you want, name anything and it's yours?"

Nafti smiled and holstered his gun. He led the small group out into the burning sunlight. "Just allow me to continue in the service of your Excellency,"

He said as they walked cautiously to the twisted wreckage of the missile train in the eerie silence. The Syrians were dead, the two Russians were injured but they had survived more serious wounds by clambering under the locomotive for cover. The senior officer who had previously taunted Mo came out of his hiding place. The Prince smiled warmly at the shell-shocked Russian and walked to within a pace. With the calm serenity of a true psychopath, he picked up a discarded rifle and pushed the barrel into the officer's mouth.

"My Russian friend, you know we do the same things to republican dogs in my country that you do to royalty in yours. Goodbye."

The Prince squeezed the trigger and watched the Russian's death with pleasure. The more junior Russian officer crabbed awkwardly backwards as the Prince bent to watch his retreat, the snake and the rabbit. "What shall we do with this one? Eat him or throw him back?" he asked the ever reliable Nafti..

"He's only a small fish, your Excellency. Let him stand as living proof to Russian excellence in battle."

One of their Palestinian escorts pointed excitedly towards the fields where they saw the Israeli pilot limping towards them, both his hands raised in the internationally recognized symbol of unarmed surrender. He approached a hole in the electrified fence created minutes earlier by his comrades seeking vengeance. The Palestinian commandos rushed at the wounded airman who attempted to mollify their screaming anger by repeatedly saying,

"Shalom, shalom, peace, peace." The Prince led Nafti towards the prisoner; Mo surprised his men by walking between them and the flyer.

"This man is a prisoner of war, you scum, haven't you heard of the Geneva Convention?"

The men muttered menacingly but lowered their weapons. It was at this moment Nafti recognized the prisoner, Shlomo Glickstein, his first cousin. Without hesitation Nafti circled well behind the man, carefully concealing himself until he pounced, locking his arm around Shlomo's neck before he could turn and see his attacker. Mo turned hearing the prisoner's strangled cry.

"What are you doing, Nafti? Didn't you hear what I just said?" he asked the stern giant, who appeared to be choking the captive to death."You asked me to accept a gift, your Excellency. I want his man's life as that gift if you would grant it to me."

The Prince inclined his head. "Of course. Your Prince always honours his word. Do what you want with him."

Nafti dragged the Israeli prisoner backwards towards the dark tunnel. "I have a personal desire to experiment with this camel shit eater in private, your Excellency. I will not be gone long."

The Prince shivered. Like everyone who met Nafti he was scared of his own guard. Although he'd never let it be known, he thought the giant was mad, regarding him as a sadist. As he and the Palestinians heard screams from the cavernous darkness they all imagined different, hideous tortures being inflicted and hurried up the embankment to escape the terrible sound of screaming.

In the tunnel, Nafti was shielded from his cousin's eyes by the darkness. He talked in Hebrew as he turned the astounded airman around, but he took the precaution of disguising his voice. "Don't he scared, I'm on your side."

"Who are you? What's going on?"

"Scream,"

"What?" asked the airman.

"Scream, like I'm torturing you, like your life depended on it!"

The airman screamed loudly twice.

"That'll do for the moment. Now I can't tell you anything in case you're re-captured, but keep your uniform on, or they'll shoot you as a spy if you're lucky enough not to be torn limb from limb. Make for the west, you'll never make it through to Mt. Hermon but you could just get through to South Lebanon, the Christian militia there will help you. Here's a gun and some iron tablets and a bar of chocolate. Another scream."

Nafti insisted and the airman screamed and wailed. Shlomo had clearly grown up to be a frustrated actor. Nafti longed for news, not about wars, or oil, or politics, but how he wished his cousin could tell him if his mother was well, how had his sister Zeporah fared. Was she married, to whom, did she have children? How was his boy, Ehud? Where was he? Oh God, how he yearned for home. No one should be asked to give more than his life for his country; a man's soul was too high a price! But all he said as he glided towards the sunlight was.

"Airman, you get home safe, you hear me, wait for nightfall."

He paused, "and airman, do me one favour, if you make it, light a candle for me, you know what I mean? Say a prayer."

Glickstein called out, "You don't light candles for people who are still alive!"

But his savior had already gone. The pilot pledged himself to get home safely. He had to say an important prayer for a very brave man, and he would light that candle for this unknown, lonely soldier of Zion.

Chapter Thirty-three

The Scheherazade Club, Mayfair, London, England
14 September 2020 – 02.00 hrs.

One thing Eddie Roman had discovered in his recent brief flurry with Arab businessmen was the fact that they loved to be lavishly entertained and, in turn, were themselves magnificent hosts given any excuse whatsoever. Tonight's junket was by courtesy of Robert Falcon.

"A celebration of our mutual brilliance in finding each other,"

The Anglo-Arab lawyer had said that morning, when he had seen how well Eddie's plans were maturing.

America had issued a stern last warning to Saudi Arabia, step up oil production or else. There had been no immediate reply but news reports indicated an ominous string of events. Firstly Israel had openly invited America to use her air bases and facilities, "for any policing action in the region not directly concerned with Israel's present conflict."

The American air force was taking part in massive exercises around the world to remind everyone that might want to get involved of their tremendous military resources.

The American Navy had also been active; the Mediterranean fleet was sighted steaming up the Red Sea on Saudi's western flank while their Indian Ocean counterparts simultaneously rounded the Straits of Hormuz and appeared to be heading for a point between the two tiny Kingdoms of Kuwait and Qatar on Saudi's eastern coast. Another aircraft carrier group was already blocking any Russian interference that might appear from the Northern flank. Each of these groups of ships had more aerial firepower than the entire Royal Air Force of the United Kingdom.

However, the news item that had most excited Falcon's imagination was a footnote tucked obscurely at the end of the B.B.C. World Service radio broadcast. A plummy voiced British announcer intoned;

"It has also been reported by a reliable source that units of the Palestinian Army were seen pulling back from Jordan, in what the Palestinian High Command described as an orderly retreat to a more southerly defence line."

'Southerly' was the word that made Falcon sit up and take notice, and it suddenly all began to fall into place in his capacious mind.

The Americans take Saudi, so the Saudis have to take somewhere else, not by themselves - of course - but courtesy of grateful beneficiaries; the Palestinians. Whichever way it worked out, there was going to be a mass exodus of the richest refugees the world had ever seen. The Arab Princes would be stampeding to anything that would fly and Roman could safely wait at London airport collecting their bulging wallets as they stepped off their transport looking for a suitable temporary residence. Falcon, who had begun to doubt and lose faith in his client's scheme, now saw his own opportunity to feather his own rather modest Putney nest.

He sat with Eddie, who seemed far more interested in his champagne than in the undulating and amply proportioned charms of the Turkish bellydancer who was doing her best to shake out of her scanty costume. The wailing music from Cairo's favourite daughter, the singer Soraya, blared over the sound system, drowning out all the other sounds in the busy Arabic nightclub. As usual it was packed with a Who's Who of Arab dignitaries who were only interested in fun while their western companions were interested only in business.

The latter group ranged from English corporate chiefs to the busty blonde Slavic girl Falcon had signaled over from the bar. She smiled vacuously at Falcon every time he stroked her firm, smooth and stockinged thigh under the table. He shouted to Roman, "You want this one?"

Falcon nodded in the direction of the blonde.

Eddie shook his head emphatically. "No, that's OK. You have her for yourself."

Falcon shrugged, his plan was not quite working out. He understood that his client had somewhat exotic tastes, but his own understanding was that any port would do in a storm, and some ports were much more attractive than others!

The dancer finished her routine and took a bow to enthusiastic applause. As she walked past the table towards her dressing room, Falcon grabbed her hand and pulled her onto his lap. She laughed as he shoved a handful of fifty pound notes into each cup of her bikini, which was already more than full with her bountiful chest. He half-playfully tried to wrap the notes around her nipples.

Eddie was amazed with Falcon's metamorphosis from Anglophile solicitor into this leering wild man. The dancer whispered into Falcon's ear, but all the time kept her eyes on Eddie.

"She says that if I put enough notes to fill her up she'll be yours free of all charges," laughed the lawyer. Falcon felt inside the woman's pants and shook his head playfully as she also laughed.

"That's going to be quite expensive!"

He cheerfully rolled another bunch of fifty pound notes and reached into the woman's briefs and put the money there. She giggled and laughed, revealing two rows of gold fillings. Unabashed by Falcon's still groping hands, she slid off his lap and unceremoniously pushed past the vapid blonde from eastern Europe, and sat her large posterior down close to Eddie on the curved bench seat. Roman couldn't help smile at the woman's forthright attempts to encourage his interest.

"You're gorgeous," he whispered and leaned forward so that his mouth was almost touching her ear. She purred with pleasure as he spoke softly to her.

"But I have crabs."

She jolted her head away and stared at Eddie who continued,

"I'm sure this form of sexually transmitted disease probably isn't that contagious!" He reached for the now-reluctant dancer as she scampered away without a backward glance. Eddie smiled as Robert leaned forward, resting his elbows on the table, and wagged his right forefinger in admonition.

"You are a hard man to please, Eddie."

"Why should I eat fatty pork out, when I've got prime steak at home?"

Roman answered, pointing his own finger at the lawyer.

"Would you be interested in business other than property, my friend?"

Eddie was about to reply when the loud music resumed, drowning out all thought of conversation. Robert indicated to Eddie that he should follow him as he led the way through the club to a door opposite the dressing room simply marked 'private'. As the lean young man knocked on the door, he turned to the blonde girl who seemed unable to do anything other than smile, and whispered something to her that sent her away in a hurry. The door opened with a metallic click and Eddie found himself confronted by a room straight out of some Arab potentate's wet dreams; a crazy mosaic of red velvets, mirrors, patterned cushions, brocade drapes and golden tassels.

Dominating this bizarre setting was Abbas Rashid, a huge, frog-like figure who squatted cross-legged on a gigantic cushion and grinned enthusiastically to his guests.

"Come in, please come in Mr. Roman. My nephew Gamal has told me so much about you. I feel we are already friends."

Eddie let Robert seat him on a smaller cushion next to their host.

"Gamal, Is that your real name, Robert?"

Robert, also now sitting on a cushion, nodded. "Yes, that's right. Now, may I present to you my uncle, Abbas Rashid, and this, as you know is my honoured friend and client, Eddie Roman."

Eddie was amused by Robert's sudden deep friendship but he couldn't help liking his quick enthusiasm and agile mind. Abbas's bloated body hid a youthful spirit every bit as playful as his nephew's. His voice, curiously sing song, always seemed on the verge of laughter but Eddie was soon to learn that the man had an uncannily perceptive business brain.

"Could we get you anything to drink?" he asked Eddie, who shook his head.

"I didn't know you were involved in this place, Robert?"

Eddie asked the lawyer, but it was Rashid who answered for him. "Robert is involved through me, Mr. Roman. I own fifty-one percent of this place."

Eddie stopped the man. "Call me Eddie'. I'd prefer it."

"Okay, Eddie, and I'm Abbas."

Eddie was well aware that there were two distinct ways that business with Arabs could go; either you could spend months trying and get nowhere, or you met someone and within a very short time form the basis for a long and fruitful relationship. Abbas Rashid placed himself in the second category.

"My nephew speaks very highly of you. He is most flattering." Eddie turned to Robert who returned his smile.

"We are keen to discover trustworthy associates in the west during these difficult and unsettling times. Would you be interested in working with us?"

Eddie tried to keep the astonishment from his face.

"Why me? You don't know anything about me, or vice versa. What kind of business are we talking about? I'm used to quick deals but not as quick as this, don't you think we'd be better off giving ourselves some time to get to know each other?"

Abbas sighed, the sound was at once sad and wistful. "I agree, Eddie. Normally I am very careful about hasty decisions that might later be regretted at leisure, but these are dangerous and unique times, one moves swiftly or not at all. This is going to go down in history as either the Arab summer naturally following the Arab spring or the beginning of the Arab winter; either way there will be those who will soon be making vast fortunes and those who lose perhaps even greater fortunes in the Middle East. I don't wish to be among the latter when we could so easily find a place in heaven with the former. I'm a businessman, as are you. We both have the contacts and trust of many people of great influence. You are rapidly accumulating a reputation for cleverness and perception with the same people. We both have much money coming in but only as long as the status quo remains. My nephew tells me you are honest and do not cheat your new Arab clients, although the temptation must have been great. I understand once you have given your word, you honour it. I like to think of myself behaving in the same way.

My honour is everything to me. Unless it concerns an enemy, then I don't give a fuck!"

He burst out laughing in self-mockery.

"I cannot speak on my own behalf except to tell you about myself. I am fifty-seven years old. I was born in the Lebanon but I'm a Palestinian. I have one wife, four sons and a wonderful daughter. My London office is in Chesterfield Street, Mayfair, and in the Gulf, I have my main business in Abu Dhabi trading in imports from this country that covers anything from fertilizers to civil aircraft spares. What more can I tell you, Eddie?"

The young Anglo-American was surprised and flattered by the corpulent Arab's frankness. He replied in kind.

"Abbas, you've told me a whole pile of reasons I should want you as my partner, but I still don't understand why you want me as your associate, and until we understand each other's motivation, we'll both feel uncomfortable, so level with me, what do you want from me?"

Robert smiled at his uncle.

"You see uncle he thinks like us. He is fluent in our tongue, but talks like them. He's even Jewish, but looks like a handsome Gentile. He couldn't be better designed for our purpose. He is perfect, like I told you?" Robert said to Abbas who lit an evil-smelling Turkish cigarette before replying to Eddie.

"Yes, you are of course correct. I do want you for something more than your expertise. Just as you need an Arab partner in my world, I need an American here in yours. The whole Gulf eruption could turn into a total collapse at any second, no one knows where the pieces will fall. If I am lucky, I'll be safer and richer than before. If I'm not so fortunate, *everything* I have created will disappear overnight, contracts will be invalid, regimes overthrown, who has any idea how things might change. All I can safely predict is that under some sand will still sit much oil, and whoever owns the sand will want to spend a lot of money building or re-building everything from cities to armies. If I'm only half correct, the boom will be gigantic, and we'll need each other much like my nephew now needs a woman."

Eddie and Abbas laughed easily at Robert's embarrassment.

"Okay, hypothetically let's say I agreed. What happens next?"

"My nephew will tear himself away from women long enough to form a trading company owned equally by you and I. Its business purpose is simply to exploit any new opportunities in trade and construction between the Gulf and the west. We'll share any profits, and of course, we'll also share any losses. How does this appeal?"

Eddie ruminated for a while. If he agreed too quickly, he thought the man might well regard him as over-eager, except it was Abbas and his nephew who'd made all the running. More pressing still was the feeling that this was a golden opportunity.

"You've obviously done your homework, Abbas, and already know that I've got only limited experience in construction or trade in anything but bricks and mortar, but it looks like you've got yourself an associate."

He put his hand out towards Abbas who gripped it firmly in his own, small, podgy, well-manicured paw.

"To a good partnership!" added Robert, toasting the deal with a bottle of champagne he had mysteriously conjured from a secret drinks container set into the floor at the corner of the room.

"To our friendship, Eddie, friendship is far more important than any partnership." said Abbas sipping from the crystal goblet, which his nephew had somehow materialized from thin air.

"To both our friendship and our partnership," Eddie responded, raising his glass to both uncle and nephew.

"Forgive me, but aren't you prohibited from alcohol?"

Robert and Abbas glanced at one another sheepishly. Robert answered. "Eddie twice over, we never drink, in the Gulf or Saudi Arabia we never ever drink. Everywhere else we never ever stop drinking!"

They all laughed and so an unusual marriage of convenience was born.

"Buying and selling some London properties will become just a little sideline in the scope of what we can achieve in our team. We will need just a little bit more help of course, to really cope with the enormity of our possibilities. Now, who do we know who has connections to the money in London, the top financial muscle in America and who already has the one precious, we could say, vital missing ingredient?" said Abbas with eminent satisfaction, wanting to be asked more questions, to tease out the responses.

"What do you mean?" Eddie asked.

Abbas smiled and crossed his pudgy hands in his lap.

"In the new, improved Royal Kingdom of Saudi Arabia there will be a continuing need for licenced companies to be able to bid for all new major capital projects for the government. These licences will follow the pattern of the old Kingdom and only be given to less than a dozen firms in civil engineering, a few more for construction and even less for defence projects. Such licences will allow those companies that have them to bid for the big jobs. Without a licence and you won't even be allowed to bid. Like the joke says, if you're not on the list you're not coming in! Allah has blessed me, no us, and through an intermediary, I managed to secure such a company with such a licence from an expatriate British gentleman who is, rather was, a civil engineer, but who sadly is now a little too unwell to work all the time. In exchange for some of our investment he is now still a small shareholder, and our consultant."

"How do I fit in?" asked Eddie, "I don't know anything about civil engineering or construction or defence."

Abbas smiled.

"This is where my nephew comes in. Robert, explain to Eddie how this works."

Robert Falcon smiled, stood up and started to pace. He spoke with intensity. "There is a particular beauty to this first transaction, and it is that we don't want to win. In fact it is imperative that we lose this bid in a particular manner or our competitors will be very upset."

Eddie looked quizzical as Robert continued.

"There is an extremely large tender process about to take place. We are talking trillions of US dollars, not billions. It is to build the biggest new military airbase in the world, and involves the biggest single contract ever in the Middle East. Five companies from around the world are invited to bid, and we are one of them. We get the chance because our company's original owner had built an international consortium that has credibility because one of the relatives of the King, someone in his inner circle is also a shareholder. But the difference between ourselves and the other companies is that we are only eligible on paper, whereas the others are actually huge international conglomerates who could do the job. We want you to go to the U.S., to Los Angeles, meet with the other companies, and arrangements will be made for the process to begin. How does this appeal to you, my friend?"

Eddie stood up and shook his head.

"To be honest it doesn't. Why should I put my head in the lion's mouth for you guys, nice as you are?"

Abbas smiled and indicated that Eddie should resume his seat. "We need someone like you and we are prepared to pay well for the service. How many Englishmen with an American passport who speak fluent Arabic and trusted by many Arab businessmen do you think there are, Eddie?"

Robert smiled and continued for his uncle. "You're just what the doctor ordered my friend. We need you and you asked a very reasonable question, and the answer is because we are going to make you so rich if you do this that you will never have to worry about money again."

Eddie sat down again. "I'm beginning to get interested. What kind of share and how much?" Eddie asked in Arabic.

"Good, I was beginning to think you might have been living too long in the West." Abbas said without malice, lighting a French Gitane cigarette and wheezing as he inhaled the acrid fumes.

Eddie responded in the same language. "A wise man learns from every culture."

For a few wonderful weeks after they agreed the deal terms, everything in Eddie's life became a gourmet feast of delightful dishes, fulfilling his old hunger for success, every property he'd recently purchased in a storm of withering scorn and derision became his barbed symbols of victory as one-by-one the fast-arriving Arab exiles forced enormous profits on him, which in turn he ploughed back into yet more properties which again were sold to the ever-willing, super-rich refugees.

Eddie became progressively more popular with his customers despite the hard deals he did with them. Eddie was, without fail, transparently honest with every buyer and when he believed someone's hard luck story, he would extend his personal credit to tide them over. What none of his clients knew was the thoroughness of Robert Falcon's checks into their true long-term credit worthiness. In this way he convinced

Eddie to cloak convenience in magnanimity. Who knew which of these people might find themselves in power one day, and favours costing Eddie little or nothing now, would then be repaid a thousand times over.

Abbas soon proved to be both a good partner and trustworthy friend. Uniquely in Eddie's experience, he'd found the man not just as good as his word but far better. Eddie had anticipated a long hiatus between every step of their relationship, with the continual probability in his mind that the Arab would terminate the agreement if it didn't work to his own advantage. Roman soon realized he couldn't have been more wrong.

Their contract had been drawn up and signed one day after their first meeting and unlike many contracts, it was exactly as agreed, with neither side of the deal trying to take advantage of the other. Robert had opened the company's bank account at Lloyds Central Branch in Lombard Street with a deposit by Abbas of ten million pounds. The bank manager was very polite after that.

Eddie hadn't even had time to gather his wits and deposit an equal amount of his own before the new company's first transaction was underway, a lucrative contract to send ten thousand state of the art British army surplus gas masks by air express freight to Oman. The company's profit was an astronomical and easy two-and-a-half million dollars. Deal followed deal, as the Gulf area became embroiled in the ever-spreading war between Arab and Jew, with the costly, but lucrative, addition of the 'Great' powers becoming progressively more embroiled.

Communications with Abbas, who had returned to the Middle East, were already difficult and became progressively worse until they were almost impossible.

Robert made it his mission to discover if his uncle was still safe, since the news from the area had degenerated into a series of baffling claims and counter claims. Saudi Arabia announced it was under attack from Israel, which Israel denounced as pure fabrication.

America had again warned Russia not to become involved in the dispute and Russia was rumored to be attacking Iran in order to grab her oil and gas deposits for itself.

All in all, it seemed as if the entire Middle East was exploding in a series of uncontrollable cataclysmic events. Even the satellite broadcasters with their rolling twenty-four-hour news services and social media, including Facebook and Twitter, were caught off guard as the secret cyberwarriors from the warring countries fed endless fake stories and leaks of misinformation which clouded further the already-dense fog of war.

Eddie had once more, on paper, become a wealthy man, now richer than ever before. He repaid all his debts and was feverishly busy amassing a huge mountain of capital which he ploughed into the new company he shared with Robert and his Uncle Abbas. The only cloud on his personal horizon was his increasing anxiety about the older man.

Barry was - as ever - supportive, but he understandably centreed his thoughts on the baby that he and Eddie had agreed to adopt. Eddie slept soundly again, secure in the knowledge that although he wasn't yet at the top of the heap, he was climbing fast.

It was three a.m. when the telephone rang. Eddie brought it angrily to his face. "Who the hell is it, don't you know it's three a.m.?"

When he heard Abbas's plaintive response he felt contrite for his testy words. "I am sorry, Mr. Eddie. It is very late."

"No, don't worry. I didn't know it was you, Abbas. I'm really glad to hear from you. We've been trying to get hold of you. Is everything all right; Are you well?"

"Yes, I am well. Tell Robert everyone is well. We are all safe amongst our people," said Abbas enigmatically.

"Are you in Lebanon, Abbas; Your people come from Lebanon?" Eddie asked, then wished he hadn't, his friend was giving him veiled news. He was Palestinian, if he was amongst his people in Saudi Arabia it meant that the country could already be under Palestinian control.

"I meant amongst the bosom of my kinfolk, you understand, Mr Eddie?"

"Yes, of course I do, Abbas. I'll pass your message to Robert. What's happening, Anything new from a business angle?" Eddie asked, careful to avoid any mention of the war over an open telephone line.

"No things have become silent. No one is planning long term at the moment, but from an old man's tired eyes and ears, I feel that our ideas and location might turn out satisfactory. Can you meet me at our place? I promise you that the great possibilities we talked about exist as the circumstances change and mature."

Eddie was surprised and confused in equal measure; did Abbas mean that the plan for meeting in Los Angeles was now for real or had it been replaced by a new meeting in the new Saudi Arabian Kingdom?

For them to meet in Saudi Arabia could be the next best thing to a suicide pact in these dangerous times. He must be talking about good prospects in Abu Dhabi, where the office was located, but how could that tie together with the Palestinian forces secretly in Saudi Arabia? Why was Abbas there, in the hornet's nest? What was happening?

"It's extremely busy right, I'm tied up with your other business and selling the properties to turn the money over as we agreed, as quickly as possible. Could our meeting wait?"

He asked his partner and friend, hoping to draw out of Abbas some more helpful information.

"No, it cannot wait, my friend. This is what you would call a first-come first-served situation. Trust me, everything you ever dreamed about is possible. If you come to our place now, I swear you'll be glad you did."

Eddie reconciled himself to the trip but still tried for more details.

"Okay, if you tell me I should drop everything and come I shall do, but at least you can tell me what kind of venture we'll be discussing, can't you?"

Abbas sighed in his expressive way, then paused before continuing.

"Eddie, I don't like discussing business when you're tired, but promise me you'll phone Robert as soon as we're through, and send him the love of our entire family, especially from the Sand Sheikh, he'll know who I mean and he'll explain the joke to you. The Sand Sheikh is a favourite relative of us both. Goodbye, Mr. Eddie."

Eddie's goodbye was unheard by Abbas who had already disconnected. Eddie got out of bed and padded into his den. He switched on the desk lamp and dialed Robert Falcon's number. It rang once and was answered by the lawyer.

"Hello, who is it?"

"It's me, Eddie. I'm sorry to phone you at this hour, Robert, and wake you."

"No, I was awake," Robert lied sleepily. "What is it, is something wrong?"

"No, I just heard from your Uncle Abbas, he's well."

Eddie then relayed to his now fully awake friend the entire conversation verbatim. "Tell me Robert who's the mysterious Sand Sheikh uncle of yours?"

Robert didn't reply immediately, which was in itself unusual for the man.

"I'm going to come round. Have some coffee ready."

Before Eddie could say anything, nephew Robert repeated the actions of Uncle Abbas and hung up.

"I'm surrounded by goddamned crazy men!"

Eddie muttered to himself and slammed down the phone.

Before the coffee was ready, there was a quiet tap on the front door. Eddie opened the door and found Robert, dressed in traditional Arabian Thobi, waiting for him. He ushered him in.

"Why are you dressed like that?"

Robert, quite out of character, almost regally took a seat on the Chesterfield armchair in Eddie's den. "It is unusual for me to dress like a Westerner when I don't have to, Eddie. At three-thirty a.m. I don't have to. Coffee?"

Eddie brought in the tray and watched his lawyer pour them a cup each.

"O.K. where's the fire, Robert? What made Abbas ring me at bloody three a.m. and got you off some poor woman's tits in the middle of the night?"

Robert smiled, his bearing and entire demeanor somehow more compelling now he was dressed in traditional costume. "Eddie, you know that to make any call from Jeddah is particularly difficult presently. No cell phones have worked in the Kingdom since they turned off the transponders and blew the masts to stop the rebels connecting to co-ordinate their riots and demonstrations. No tweets, social networks or internet. So it's back to centrally-controlled landlines, and to make a call during the night when you're a couple of hours ahead of London, you must bribe an operator. In the day it is twice as costly, and if you expect to book a call for a specific time, it'll be three times as much or more. When the place is going crazy and monitoring of all calls becomes the norm, you can imagine what it costs to jump ahead of the line. It would take thousands of dollars and much time to get through. Do you see now how important it was for Abbas to reach you any way he could. I can only explain the things I understand. I know my uncle well enough to know he'd not waste that much time and effort, plus big money, to get hold of you unless it was necessary and urgent!"

Robert was nearly shouting when he finished.

"Okay, Robert. Cool it, will you? Barry's asleep inside." Eddie said with quiet authority.

"I'm sorry, Eddie. I didn't mean to be so loud but I'm concerned for my uncle and anxious to make you understand that on certain matters, I'm no desert clown."

"Okay that's understood. We've both been a bit out of line. I'm sorry as well. So tell me, who's this Sandy Sheikh relative of yours?"

Robert finished his black coffee in one gulp and paced the room as he explained.

"Firstly, I must tell you I have no relative who is a sheikh, sandy or otherwise, my uncle Abbas was using a code that I alone would understand. Anyone listening to the call would think he was using a family nickname. In fact he was answering your questions without you realizing it. The sandy Sheikh is Prince Aziz. He's the adopted son of the King and he owns a large parcel of land in Abu Dhabi, near the city. It's got some equipment on it, plant and machinery for crushing rocks and cleaning sand. He used to sell it to people in construction before he got more interested in gambling in Las Vegas and let the business disintegrate. He used to do quite well."

Eddie laughed, tickled by the irony in this situation. "You're telling me that we're going to sell sand to the Arabs. So why the hurry for me to go out there? I know nothing about rock crushing Robert, you know that."

Robert vigorously shook his head.

"I know also that you're a gifted businessman who is now trusted by a cross section of Arabs, who equally know nothing about rock crushing and if I'm correct in reading between the lines, Abbas is telling us that the Palestinian Army is involved, somehow with the Saudi Royal Family's plans in Abu Dhabi, and possibly elsewhere in the Gulf as well. If they're going to move into a takeover of Abu Dhabi, why should they stop there? They could probably take Qatar, Oman, Kuwait, Bahrain, the United Arab Emirates, the whole bloody lot, and if that happens, they're going to need a whole mass of things, including sand and aggregate when they start building. It would be the biggest and most rapid construction, industrialization and military building programme the world has ever seen. Now, don't you think a trip to Uncle Abbas might be worthwhile?"

Eddie's reply was spontaneous and instant. "Book me the ticket, Robert. Your argument sounds good enough to me."

Robert smiled in triumph.

"I took the liberty of telephoning the airline when we'd finished talking earlier. You're on the plane, first class, of course, in four hours with an open return."

Chapter Thirty-four

Burj Al-Arab Hotel, Dubai
15th. October 2020 – 11.00 hrs.

The complimentary Rolls-Royce limousine containing Eddie glided to a sedate halt outside the seven-star hotel built on the island, which was, in turn, created four hundred metres out into the impossibly-blue sea. The building was over a quarter of a mile high, the second tallest building in the country after the royal family owned Al Haj complex less than a couple of kilometres distant.

The bellboy ushered Eddie into the plush marble elegance of the huge glass-domed atrium that formed part of the luxurious lobby of the hotel, as the porter carried his bags. Eddie was used to being surrounded by the very best but he had never seen a hotel as visually stunning as this.

A glass elevator whisked him up to the one hundred and thirteenth floor of the building with views of the entire desert and the city. He was ushered to his three-roomed suite. Eddie whistled to himself as he settled in then phoned Barry to tell him about the astonishing place, but a recorded message responded instead.

"Your call cannot be completed due to technical difficulties."

He realized that this was probably due to the local authorities taking the decision to cut off all social media, the internet and mobile communications. It was strange to be cut off from the instant gratification this would have allowed him. It had been many years since he wasn't able to speak with anyone on the planet, virtually for free, within seconds of having the desire to do so. Just as he was thinking this, the room telephone rang, and five minutes later he was being ushered into a meeting with Pierre Montcalm.

The Frenchman was tall and very thin, dressed in what looked like the latest Paris fashion, but was actually immaculate British Saville Row tailoring. The man's manners were on a par with his clothing; smooth, practiced and charming. He was every inch the aristocrat, and there was, Eddie thought, something almost professorial about his demeanour.

"Monsieur Roman, what a pleasure, I have heard only wonderful things about you." He extended his hand and Eddie shook it.

"Please take a seat."

Montcalm indicated the antique rosewood boardroom table and chairs. Eddie sat down and Montcalm sat opposite. "Is it OK if I call you Eddie?"

"Of course, Pierre?'

The two men smiled.

"Have our colleagues explained the situation to you, Eddie? It is very important that we; How do you say? All sing from the same hymn book, yes?"

He smiled again, and this time Eddie watched to see if the smile travelled from the man's handsome mouth to his eyes, and decided it didn't. Eddie liked to group people as if they were animals, and he mentally placed his host as either a snake or a lizard, he wasn't sure which it was, but he knew it was cold- blooded, and possibly very dangerous. He kept his own smile open and receptive. Let him think I'm stupid, Eddie thought. He liked it when people under-estimated him.

"I know what they told me, but why don't you tell me again, just in case I might have misunderstood something."

Montcalm had used the moment to sip from his glass of iced water.

"My pleasure, and by the way, this suite, she is secure. She was swept for listening devices again just before this meeting. Would you like some?"

He pointed to his glass. Eddie's smile broadened momentarily when he heard the man's English was less than perfect.

"No, I don't drink water. Fish fornicate in it."

Pierre didn't quite understand Eddie's little joke, so he continued. "What we discuss here, it is very delicate, so I have to ask you to sign our standard non-disclosure document as a pre-condition."

He pushed over a brief one-page document in front of Eddie, together with a pen. Eddie read the agreement and shook his head apologetically.

"I can't sign this."

He stood up and extended his hand toward Montcalm who was clearly disconcerted.

"There is a misunderstanding, my friend?" he asked Eddie.

"No misunderstanding, I don't have a lawyer with me, and you knew that in advance, and you also knew you were going to ask me to sign this binding legal document before I ever got on a plane, so why didn't you send it to me before I travelled thousands of miles to this shit heap in the sand?"

Montcalm rushed around the table seeking to settle Eddie's nerves. He didn't realize that the younger man was faking his righteous anger, using it to gain any slight advantage available to him.

"But it is a standard non-disclosure document. It is my company's standard policy for her to require everyone she does the business with to sign her."

He quickly became exasperated as Eddie shook his head.

"And it is my company's policy that we don't sign anything without legal representation present, and advice being given. So it seems that we have an impasse, Monsieur Montcalm."

The Frenchman picked up the offending document and ostentatiously ripped it into progressively smaller pieces.

"If this is the problem, she is now eliminated, but you must understand we all have a paramount need to keep this between us. It must never be anywhere seen or known by anyone. Do I have your hand on this, as one gentleman to another?"

He now extended his hand to Eddie who shook it ceremoniously.

"Of course, Pierre. This is one secret I wouldn't ever want anyone to know about. Now, do you have a proper drink?"

Montcalm smiled and opened a bottle of tonic water and poured it for Eddie.

"This is the very finest tonic water, Eddie. It is bottled especially for this part of the world, very expensive, but just what you need."

Eddie drank deeply and appreciated the very best gin and tonic. He raised his glass in salute. "As is evidenced in a variety of different ways,"

Pierre continued,

"The culture here and in Europe, she is very different. What is all right in America, here it is not permissible, and some things that she does here, they are not good in some other place. That's just how it is, we make no judgments."

"Are you trying to tell me how to behave?"

Montcalm shrugged with expressive Gallic charm.

"What we all do in the privacy of our own space is for our own conscience. No, I was talking about business ethics, they are as different as our own moral code and that of our hosts. We see things differently, not right or wrong, but differently. The way it will work here is pre-arranged, and it our turn to win the contract, but it has to follow a certain path."

"Which is?"

"Which is that there are five companies licenced to bid for this particular contract, ourselves and you, a division of the American conglomerate, Shechtel, a company from Germany, Kruger, and our friends from China, Shanghai Civil Construction.

The way it works is that one company, the agreed one, gets to make the lowest bid this time around, and that's your company."

Eddie shifted in his seat.

"We actually get to win the contract, and then what do we do? We're just a paper consortium, in reality there's me and my assistant and that's it." Montcalm continued almost as if Eddie's comment was so stupid that it wasn't worth his while responding. He picked up a beautiful brown calfskin briefcase and placed it on the table. Eddie watched as the Frenchman carefully applied a code number to each of the locks on the case as he talked.

"Naturally we are most happy to make the gesture we think is appropriate for your co-operation."

He opened the case and Eddie saw that it was full of neat piles of cash in U.S. dollars. "This is one million dollars, Eddie. It is yours now, and all we expect is your continued collaboration."

Eddie restrained himself from touching the cash. Whatever amount of money you have, he thought, it isn't the same as cold, hard cash!

"Naturally," continued Montcalm, "We supply you with all the drawings, supporting documentation, schedules, working papers, budgets, everything, and all you will have to do is possibly attend one or two more meetings after today. When our Arab friends evaluate the bids they will ask to see you on behalf of your company and the second cheapest bid, which is my organization. At that point you will allow it to become known how over-stretched your company is and we will win the bid. When that has been officially signed, we will pay you a very generous second payment of a further two-and-a-half million dollars, and we all get on with our happy, more prosperous lives. Is this good?"

Eddie did his best to conceal his excitement, the small twitch of his jaw being the only visible sign of the huge grin he was doing his best to hide. He'd just heard that for doing nothing he would end up with more than two million pounds dollars, not bad for a couple of meetings. It was simply too good to be true!

"Two things will make it better Pierre, another one million dollars at the back end, and some kind of additional guarantee to ensure that I'll get it. You seem a nice enough guy, I'm sure you're a correct and honourable man, but who knows what will happen to my money if something happened to you. More to the point where would my money go if something happened to me?"

Montcalm smiled and again this didn't reach his cold eyes.

"We can make certain that your money will go to wherever you tell us it should go. But don't worry, nothing is going to happen to you. It's in our interests to make sure it doesn't."

Eddie interrupted the smooth man.

"I listen and I am almost convinced and then I think, why does anyone ever give someone else millions of dollars if there's no risk. I don't think so. Be honest with me, I can deal with danger better if I know what I'm facing."

"I'm sure we can reach a compromise. What do you say to an additional half a million dollars?" Montcalm said, the smile never leaving his face.

"I would say 'no'."

Eddie closed the case full of cash and pushed it back toward Montcalm who ignored the gesture.

"Unless I know what I'm dealing with, I don't want anything to do with this.

Even for an extra million dollars."

Montcalm's smile was nailed into place thought Eddie. "Voila, we have a deal then, Eddie. An additional one million dollars makes it three-and-a-half million dollars payable at the successful conclusion of our bid, agreed?"

"Payable in cash, directly to me, and what about the guarantee I asked for?"

Montcalm looked at Eddie with increasing impatience tinged with respect. "Not a problem. The cash, we will give it to you personally, to your hand, and as for the guarantee, well, Eddie, what better proof of our good faith do you have than this million dollars? We are a big company but even we do not walk away from a million dollars. Once you have this, we will not rest until we complete this deal and there is only one way this deal can go, and that's to us. It is, as you say, a done deal. Is this satisfactory?"

"I want to know what the danger is." Eddie demanded. "I'm not agreeing anything unless and until I know what the problem is."

Montcalm made a decision.

"OK, but the danger doesn't come from where you might expect. In fact, you have danger if you do what I ask, and perhaps more danger if you don't. You obviously are not yet aware that you already have a sleeping partner, an Arab who has the title Prince Mohammed Aziz, and believe me you would much prefer it if he stayed asleep, he is a very unpredictable man. Apparently one of the adopted sons of his majesty, the King of Saudi Arabia. He doesn't care for any arrangement where he is not in total command. He will be very excited by this deal, and won't understand it if you don't get the deal. That's the danger. But you're a resourceful man. Do you think you can overcome just one crazy Arab Prince?"

Eddie stood and shook hands with the Frenchman.

"We'll never know until I try. How crazy can he be. We have a deal."

Montcalm gripped Eddie's hand in both of his. The beaming smile on both of their faces remained absent from their eyes.

Chapter Thirty-five

Arranged around the circular table in the subterranean room were six very self-satisfied military men. Secret contingency plans, conceived long ago in private rooms like this, had matured to succulent ripeness. Now was the moment to savor the celebratory meal's fine smell and its alluring visual appeal, then and only then would the victory be complete.

General Mordechai Ben Zvi, officer in command of Israel's defence forces, the Chief of Staff, sat next to Motti Hopel, the mysterious Chief of Israel's Mossad, the intelligence and counter espionage unit. He, like his unit, was both feared and respected by friend and foe. Hopel's frail, bespectacled, homely, buck-toothed, smiling countenance concealed a man widely regarded by intelligence analysts as the most deadly spymaster since Beria or Himmler.

On the other side of the General, sat Israel's Air Force supremo General Dov Eytan, a ginger curly-haired man who had reached his rank one-year before, at the age of forty. His prowess as a pilot had been legendary, and he had matured well into his new position of authority, seemingly leaving behind his meteoric temper tantrums and overt dalliances with internationally famous ladies.

Facing the Israelis were their American counterparts: General Omar Keynes, Chief of Staff, a robust fifty-five-year-old, widely known by his cherished nickname 'Redbuster'. His florid cheeks and bull neck sat squarely on an ex-athlete's run to fat body, his cornflower-blue eyes never rested, never seemed to focus. An impatient man who didn't suffer fools gladly, he had a bloated historical perspective of his own importance, determined to make events suit this vision.

"Good day to you all, and a special welcome to our very good friends from Israel."

He banged the table, applauding the Israeli contingent. Soon followed by the other Americans in the room, all clapping their hands or banging on the table.

To his right, lounged Milton Braschin who then spoke in his unique accent; a mixture of his Czechoslovakian birthplace and New Jersey where he'd lived from the age of nine. Even his appearance was hard to define; a man of blurred edges,

"You've done what our political masters should have done years ago. Let me add a hearty mazel tov!"

Although his words were warm his watery eyes behind thick tortoiseshell eyeglasses were of indeterminate colour and betrayed no emotion. He was a hard man to read. He had a tendency to gain and lose weight rapidly, thinking little of a weight change of forty pounds in under two months. The last time he was so overweight his gut had spilled over his tight pants and he found himself slouching forward, shambling around his Langley office in carpet slippers, his double chin spilling over his restraining shirt collar. At that time, he had met Brandy, a cocktail waitress with a super-white smile, big blonde hair and boobs to get lost in. Just thirty-four, she told him that she wasn't interested unless he lost seventy-five pounds, bought her a nice condo and put a diamond ring on her finger. At the time, he had looked like a man in his late sixties but that was before she had spent just the one night with him, showing him what was on his a la carte menu if he got his act together, and kept taking the Viagra.

Presently, the now exceedingly-slim Braschin was enjoying the effects of the successful gastric band surgery he had undergone, and stood an almost emaciated one hundred and fifty-eight pounds spread very sparingly on his now straight-backed six-feet-two frame. Since the surgical procedure, he looked about ten years older but his former enormous intake of food was reduced to the one power drink four or five times a day. Containing root vegetables, fruits, and a blended New York steak for breakfast; Brandy made sure he consumed nothing else except gallons of water, and a vitamin power drink, during the rest of the day. His diet made him miserable, but his reflection in the mirror cheered him up again. He was a most unusual, singular, man, even in the annals of the idiosyncratic C.I.A. that he ran. He was also the first director to be promoted from within the company's ranks to his present exalted position for over two decades. The rank and file of the firm loved him for his seeming humanity and warmth, which was mostly fake. He was a good boss and like a spook version of the late President Reagan, he made the team feel great, even if there was little to sustain the feeling.

He addressed his next remarks to the last man present, the elegant beribboned Chief of Staff of the US Air Force, General Robert Wisehart, an officer more suited to fighting wars than keeping the peace.

"I assure you all, this room is secure. Now Robert, we'll use first names if you don't mind, avoid ranks and surnames, just in case, you understand yes?"

Braschin lectured the Air Force Chief as if he were a brash recruit.

Wisehart either didn't notice or didn't care to notice the putdown. The only sign that betrayed his annoyance was the way his eyes nervously twitched, like a series of double- barreled winks to his counterpart Dov Eytan who he now addressed in his rasping, vodka riddled, Texan drawl.

"It sure appears you've punched a big hole in the Arabs defences, Dov. From our surveillance satellites data you've shot the shit out of them six ways to hell!"

Eytan, the Israeli Air Force general recognized what he'd heard as a compliment but wasn't expert enough in American slang to follow anything more than the gist of a conversation carried on in English. He lamely tried to repay the compliment.

"Robert is kindness. Without no weapons is not possible, thank you."

Hopel, the intelligence man, interjected in his flawless, though monotone, English. "I think we can all be gratified by our success so far, but any amount of battles won still does not necessarily mean the war is ours. We are here to ask you but one question. When do you take out Saudi Arabia as per our agreement?"

The Americans shuffled uncomfortably in their seats under their allies' implacable stare. They didn't answer, so General Zvi, Chief of Staff for the IDF, repeated the question in his bass growl.

"It's a simple question, gentlemen. When are you going to fill your part of the bargain and take out Saudi, or are you going to renege on your deal with us just like the British and French did over Suez? Without the Saudis taken out, we will have won yet another meaningless battle. So when do you stop with the talking and start to help us with the heavy lifting?"

General Omar Keynes, Commander of the US Central Command, smiled without any mirth, then cleared his throat and addressed them almost as if he were again lecturing dumb WestPoint rookies.

"Mordechai, there ain't no percentage in you guys blasting off at us. We're all with you guys a hundred and ten per cent, you know that. Shit, fella, we even sanctioned the removal of that Irish garbage, along with your own fellow traveler and pointed the finger at the Palestinians. We can't understand what's with the big hurry up.

We'll take them Saudis any day now, easy as sliding down a greased pole. We keep our promises. Anyhow, we've done the whole thing in just a few months, and we did it with very little collateral damage. Great result all over the board."

Mordechai Ben Zvi gravely shook his head. "Omar, you have sent us weapons and intelligence. In return, we have the blood of our dead young men and women. How do you compare these two things? We do it because we believe it gives us a chance at a real peace afterwards, but you, why do you do it? Will you be satisfied with their oil, or do you want more?"

Milton Braschin nervously removed his spectacles and methodically cleaned them with his checked necktie.

"Omar, Mordechai, why are we arguing? We're all in this together, irrevocably. It's obvious that you want to de-stabilize and split the Arabs, so do we, but your reasons are primarily political, and ours, and in this room I'll admit it, are primarily economic. You have to understand our difficulties. We cannot be seen to be controlling or subverting our democratically-elected leaders, all that Arab Spring democracy shit. However we can create a situation where Madam President has only one option; to use the military to impose America's will. It's almost done, we're at the end game, and her patience is cracking. For the first time since those half-assed wars in Iraq and Afghanistan, after we re-armed under that fat ass Trump, America has the means available to regain its rightful place on centre stage. We can fight on three continents simultaneously again. We have the boots on the ground and the weapons. Soon we'll even have the draft back. These are great days! We have geared for this conflict because of the rehearsals we had in Iraq, Afghanistan and Kuwait. You Israelites don't seem to get it."

He sighed and paused for dramatic effect.

"This isn't about you, you know we like you, always have and always will, but you're the sideshow and we're the main event. We like you guys, better than almost anyone, and I'd include our own Jews in that reckoning. I wish they could be more like you guys. But the key factors are that we increased our military spending so that we now spend about twenty five per cent more than the rest of the world combined. We are back on top and we intend to show the world that we are. But the last twenty years did teach us something. We did learn not to start something we can't finish and we limit ourselves to one-and-a-half wars, major wars anywhere in the world even if we have double that capacity. In future, we don't go in anywhere without enough boots on the ground. Now the machine is ready, we're ready to crush anyone who stands in our way, and we will show anyone who is top dog.

We're back! Do you seriously expect even this President to miss an opportunity to secure our oil supplies and guarantee her re-election in one hit? This is her golden opportunity; a nice little war we're guaranteed to win without too many body bags coming home, and her election is a slam-dunk. Come on, you know even big time liberals like her. She has no alternative but to do it, and once she green lights this, we'll never have to look back for a hundred years. You'll get your peace and we'll have the ultimate super economy, self-sufficient in energy, industry and food, the Chinese can go and fuck themselves. We're still number one."

He held up one finger to emphasize the point, like a triumphant sportsman who just scored. The Israelis looked to one another, exasperated at his simplistic rhetoric.

"The American people are pushing her as hard as we are, and they are the ultimate weapon in our hands. Because of our manipulations, the Saudis got wind of normal shipments of arms to you and reduced oil production and increased prices. Americans just hate being told what to do, especially by a bunch of rag heads. It was only a small step from there by the President to freeze all Saudi's assets in America.

Everything has gone according to plan, a little behind schedule perhaps, but still according to plan."

Motti Hopel turned to his commander, Ben Zvi, and spoke in a hissing, sibilant tone, "May I be entirely frank with our friends?"

The general nodded.

Hopel continued, "We have good reason to believe that large formations of Palestinian Army units are already in Saudi Arabia. We have intelligence reports from several sources that verify this..."

Keynes interrupted.

"Are you suggesting that the goddamned Palestinians are going to fight our marines? You have to be kidding me. We'll wipe the mothers out in one week!"

Hopel's disparaging glare would have been enough to shut up anyone who knew him well; unfortunately the American Chief of Staff did not. He continued.

"Shit, we'll have ourselves the biggest turkey shoot since the Little Big Horn!"

Hopel resumed, his deep commanding voice brooked no further interruptions.

"Forgive me, Omar. I don't suggest the Palestinians are going to fight you, but if I remember my history, your side lost at the Little Big Horn, didn't it?"

He let the silence command yet more attention for his next verbal volley.

"You Americans."

He sighed theatrically.

"Don't underestimate the Palestinians. They are the best educated, motivated,

trained and ruthless of our enemies. If their leadership hadn't been so dogmatic and divided, we would have had even graver difficulties coping with them. They're our very own Viet Cong."

His smile was glacial as he continued.

"We asked for this meeting to stress this new urgency to you. There are only hours or days at the most standing between you either achieving a brilliant victory or suffering a humiliating fiasco, even worse than your Bay of Pigs invasion of Cuba.

Now do you understand?

Before Keynes could answer, Milton Braschin again tried to calm things down. "Can we ask our Israeli friends for more details? Not to put too fine a point on it, how come you know about this alleged move by the Palestinians and we don't? You can't exactly hide regiments from our spies in the sky and we've not seen a thing, have we, Russell?"

He asked the Air Force man.

"Not a thing." Wisehart answered, than added. "And with the new Falcon Image Transformer Mark 3, we can see an ant fart from three hundred and fifty miles up in space." Braschin stopped him by raising his hand.

"Thank you,. Let's not cloud the issue with technicalities, but you see why it's hard for us to understand how a whole army can get into Saudi and you can see it, but we can't. Satisfy us on that score, we'll not think we're being parlayed into a corner."

Mordechai jumped from his seat, shouting. "What kind of idiots are you people? Do you imagine we would simply identify our agents hand them over to your gentle care just so you'll be satisfied? If we tell you we have facts then you will have to choose to believe us or not, your choice. Have we lied to you about such things before? You might not care about your men in the field but we do! If our people tell you something, you'd better believe it or there's no point in our continuing with this farce. You have turned the CIA from an efficient intelligence gathering organization into a glorified hunt and kill terrorists machine, and as a consequence you've lost the capacity to run human spies. You've decapitated your entire operations in Lebanon, Syria, Iran and most of Iraq, and you would love it if we let you have a free ride on the backs of our boys. Well, it isn't going to happen."

He turned to Hopel and Eytan, and signaled towards the door.

"Come on, these friends of ours still don't trust us. Let's go home and fight our own wars like we always do."

Both men rose to go, but were stopped by Braschin's plea to stay.

"I apologize, honestly I apologize, and I meant no offence. Please sit down, gentlemen. My English is easily misunderstood. Let me rephrase my question. At least, listen."

The Israelis grumpily resumed their seats.

"Okay, so we'll listen." said Mordechai.

"We've all gotten off on the wrong foot here. We aren't questioning your integrity or any stuff like that, simply the accuracy of your information and where it came from.

Now that ain't such a terrible thing to ask, is it? Listen up here, you know we're talking about the whole ball of wax. We don't need no problems now, do we?"

Everyone turned to Motti Hopel as Omar Keynes finished. So it all depends on how I reply, thought the man from Mossad, didn't it always? He mentally shrugged off the responsibility and tension. His brain worked best when it was analytical and cold, neither emotion nor personalities had any toehold in his decision making process, unlike the politicians and generals. He never made what he considered the mistake of identifying closely with the men who effectively were the blind instruments of their policies.

"We have our men infiltrated deep within both the Palestinian command structure and with influence in the Saudi royal family. Any further information I gave you would be a dereliction of my duty to these brave men, but you do have my solemn oath that this is the truth. Through these men we know our information to be accurate, timely and critical. Whatever you see or don't see from your spy in the sky cameras. Ours is primarily human intelligence gathered at great personal risk and I attest to its accuracy."

The Americans knew this meant the Saudi intelligence service had failed to wipe out Israel's spy network in that country despite their ruthless efforts to achieve this. It was Braschin who spoke again.

"How can you be sure your people on the ground haven't been turned, perhaps become double agents feeding you false information. There's a lot of money available down in those parts to make a man forget his conscience?"

Hopel didn't even seem to think before replying.

"I could talk about loyalty, about being a Jewish fish in an anti Semitic ocean, but that wouldn't convince you, because you're pragmatic people. We test them ourselves. Agents are offered very lucrative inducements to see if they'll turn."

"What action do you take if they accept?"

Asked General Wisehart, fascinated by these revelations. Hopel's tongue was coated in acid as he replied.

"Why, Bob, we eliminate them, of course."

There was a stillness in the room, interrupted only by the C.I.A. man unconsciously humming approbation. That was the proper way to do business, he thought, and wished his political masters had let him off the leash more often to fight the Russians' much-vaunted K.G.B. and their successors, the F.S.B. in the same manner. Say what you like about these Israelis, they know how to operate efficiently in the spy business.

General Keynes pressed a white button on the table's control console and anticipated the enjoyment of watching the Israeli's open-mouthed amazement as the walls of the room became glass, affording them a view of the futuristically-styled Strategic Air Command's secondary headquarters in Colorado. But they simply smiled and nodded to each other. Motti said.

"This is almost identical to our own H.Q. in Tel Aviv, General, before we finished the upgrade and re-decoration?"

Keynes stilled his response, and looked on as the American command and control's vast technological resources spread below them in an enormous oyster shell-shaped man made cave fanning out from the narrowest point beneath them to its broadest some three hundred feet away. On the immense curved surface was a map that seemed almost alive.

"What you're seeing is, we believe, the first real three-dimensional situation map ever conceived. It's a pictorial relay of the Earth beamed down from our Communication satellites continually and married by the computers, so's you don't even see the join. Actually, we're using a random computer scrambler to confuse any spies because we're playing this picture to you by de-coding millions of numbers that represent the different contours and colours etc. It's much the same technique N.A.S.A. perfected on the Mars probe, and because no one else has this kind of Nanotechnology yet, we use it for almost every type of communication. In the event of anyone picking a fight with us, we're fairly certain they'll try and take out our important communication space stations first, and as they don't know which is sending orders to open fire and which is relaying baseball scores to a submarine's crew in some Scottish dry dock, they'll be forced to attack the whole bunch, and since we've started we've been putting up about twenty a month, some for virtually nothing, and half of those are dummies putting out gobbledygook. In other words, the chances are nil that they could take away our eyes before we could respond.

Neat, eh?"

He walked to the window and with a proprietary wave of his arm, encompassed the amazingly sophisticated H.Q.

"Is fantastical"!" Crowed General Dov Eytan, who was now being instructed by Wisehart in the complex's capabilities. Hopel and his counterpart Braschin also paired off to discuss their grey brotherhood. The only two men who still clung stubbornly to their task were Mordechai Zvi and Keynes whose mutual respect and friendship had been the catalyst for this desperate military gamble.

"Mordechai, if you'd tell me where those fucking terrorists are on that map and what they're up to, I'll blow their asses clear to Kingdom come, I swear I will."

The Israeli general put his big powerful hands on Keynes' shoulders then stared at him dead in the eye.

"Omar, I know where they're not and I know where they were a day or so ago. I also think we know where they're going. Maybe sometimes not getting so much information so quick means we have more time to evaluate what we do get. The Palestinians have been drifting into Saudi in fairly small groups for about five days.

They've used a bunch of different routes mainly via Amman in Jordan, some used the Jeddah Road which, as you know, is virtually due south, many other units seem to be using Baghdad as a staging post then hopping down across the Saudi border via Basra to Kuwait. More still are grouping near Riyadh near Al Hufuf, but the biggest concentrations by far, about thirty thousand men we guess, are somewhere in the southern desert wilderness, wedged between the United Arab Emirates, Qatar and Oman. In the daytime, they've been disguised as truckers, businessmen, busloads of tourists or pilgrims who are really soldiers. You name it they're doing it.

At night they're pouring over the desert on the smaller back routes and getting back together at pre-set points."

The American general considered the implications thoughtfully. Despite his obvious vanity, he had a first-rate military mind that he'd learnt was best camouflaged in a country-boy innocence if he wanted to progress upwards in Washington's rarefied, sometimes poisonous, political air.

"Looking at our big board over there, what would you say they're aiming to do?"

The Jewish general smiled innocently.

"I can only guess, Omar. My guess is they like you about as much as they like us. If you accept that argument you can draw your own pictures. As you would say, I think they'll try to fuck you up in Saudi."

Keynes pulled a briar pipe from the side pocket of his rumpled uniform and ceremoniously lit the sweet smelling tobacco.

"Friend, tell me," he said at last, between puffs. "Are you giving me all your information, or just the bits that suit you?"

The Israeli's face went red as his blood pressure rose.

"If we weren't good friends, personally good friends, our whole partnership could be ruined by such a remark. For the last time, I'm telling you we're here not only for ourselves and our selfish interests, but also to help you. For once, we're in a position to help and you won't grasp our hand in friendship."

It was Omar Keynes' turn to be the peacemaker, as both the military leaders gazed down onto the calm efficiency of the computers churning out their endless permutations of information to human drones whose function was purely to receive, leaving the blessed giving to that revered and select group, the programmers.

Strange, thought Mordechai, the Americans seem not to understand that their own famed computer processors were designed and manufactured by young Jewish geniuses on an Israeli high-tech campus close to Tel Aviv. Almost every one of them had previously served in Israel's cyber defence team, the best in the world. So we know everything the Americans know as soon as it appears on the American super computers.

"Why are you people so goddamned stiff necked and obstinate?"

Mordechai felt the colour rush to his cheeks as the anger he fought so hard to suppress nearly boiled to the surface again. "Oh, Omar, you're not going to say some of your best friends are Jewish, are you? I wouldn't do that if you don't want me to make you eat that pipe!"

"You see what I mean! Before I can finish apologizing the first time round, you're demanding a second apology. Your pleasure lies in behaving impossibly. I don't care whether you think I'm a goddamned anti Semite, because I ain't. Anyone who's a true southern Baptist like me just can't be, but you people have got to be the lousiest public relations people in the world. You're your own worst enemies. Don't you give a fuck for the world's opinion?"

"No, I don't." Mordechai laughed.

"No, we don't care for the world's opinion. We would love the world to like us but whatever we do that doesn't happen so we care for ourselves not our own opinion poll ratings. If we go under, it'll be because we ran out of God's help not because some Jew-hater says he doesn't like us. He doesn't need a reason to hate, his hate feeds upon itself like a terrible cancer; like my speech is starting to go round upon its own tail in the never-ending circle of a logical man grappling with the insanity of an illogical world. After all isn't anti-Semitism the only racism accepted in your polite society?"

The two friends smiled at one another.

"Alright, you crazy fucker, you'll get your American cavalry charge even if I have to tell that dumb bitch President of ours; and I never even said that; a whole pack of lies to do it,"

Keynes said, happy now that he'd reached a decision, be it wrong or right. Like most clever men in clouded areas, the difficulty lay in deciding what to do rather than in the execution of the deed itself. The generals shook hands to seal their understanding.

"That's if you can keep anything from that witch. She's some piece of work, all pretty tits, pert ass, perfect teeth and a mind like a computer."

The American knew that in the White House in a sealed and totally secure communications room the whole conversation was being overheard by the United States President. He enjoyed the fact that she'd be smiling as he described her. In fact she was a little upset as she listened in to the conversations that the handsome Israeli hadn't joined in with a lusty description of her physical attributes. She enjoyed the vicarious thrill.

General Wisehart pressed a button marked 'read out' on the computer terminal by which he stood with General Eytan. The green electrical lines came up instantly, an impersonal bank balance made up of statistics from the latest Middle Eastern war, already nicknamed by the world and this computer's programmer, "Code name 'Israel Blitzkrieg'."

Wisehart read the first line and then followed its awful lists:

Syria - estimates of damage – Military
Men killed in action 17,000 (approx.)
Wounded 42,500 (approx.)
Captured 72,387
Aircraft destroyed - estimated 308
Aircraft unserviceable - estimated 58 . . . . .
Tanks destroyed - estimated 1,600
Tanks damaged - estimated 2,000 . . . . .
Air missile defences -estimated 30% effective . . . . .
Anti aircraft defences general - estimated 75% operative but ineffectual . . . . .

Civilian casualties

Damascus
killed 6,812
injured 12,308

Aleppo
killed 8,612
injured 4,219

Homs
killed 1,237
injured 3,297

Hama
killed 928
injured 2,022

Other targeted areas
killed 6,325
injured 17,412

Economic impact report
Euphrates Dam destroyed
Flooding approx. 1 million acres
82% of country's generation of electricity cut
Civilian casualties reported low, population sparse in region
Principal rail lines destroyed at junctions
Oil pipeline destroyed at Homs
Many buildings ruined by bombing in cities
Total estimated cost of damages sustained - Approx. 83 billion dollars U.S

"How do you like them apples, Dov?"

Wisehart asked, turning from the hypnotic parade of statistics flashing across the screen, but the Israeli had shaken his head and gone, leaving the American alone with his numbers and his thoughts. Why's he so antsy? he wondered, pressing for the figures on Egypt. "Now, they're really impressive kill ratios," he said to himself as he forgot the ingratitude of General Eytan and re-focused his attention on those all-important numbers.

The Israeli knew too well that under those statistics was the torn flesh and bone, the spilt blood of hundreds of thousands of people, just like him and his family.

Chapter Thirty-six

King Ibn Saud Royal Hospital, Riyadh, Saudi Arabia
15th. Oct 2020 – 16.30 hrs.

His Excellency Prince Mohammed Aziz leaned with his back against the door, his legs spread wide apart. He held up the hem of his gold-edged black Thobi in his left hand, waiting patiently, confident. In his right hand he held a plain brown paper bag, which he shook enticingly. There was a heavy clinking sound as bottles rattled against each other. Mo looked contemptuously at the Englishwoman, Angela Simmonds, across the office of the senior consultant she worked for as a part-time secretary. Angela was peroxide blonde, thirtyish and still attractive in a prematurely-ageing body that had already seen too much booze. She licked her lips when she heard the sound of the bottles; she needed a drink and it had to be soon. The price was her sickening debasement for the Prince's pleasure. It had started when she arrived in Saudi to be with her husband, a structural engineer out on a three-year construction project, but instead of being with him she had spent every night alone in their company villa while he was more than a hundred miles away, working on the desert site of his project. Always a heavy drinker, she turned to alcohol for solace. In a country with no western-style entertainment or social life the bottle became her haven.

One of the company's other bored housewives told Angela about the job opportunities at the hospital and she had easily captured the position she now held. It was there that she'd met the Prince when he'd come to the hospital to visit a sick friend. Their mutual physical attraction was instant. He lusted after her ivory skin and open sexuality, she was lonely and foolishly imagined him as her personal desert Prince. The first weeks of their affair had been passionate until she told him one night that she loved him. He turned to ice. He met her endearments with insults and her tears were met by his never-ending supply of torrent of booze. Quickly her love turned to loathing as he made it plain that their arrangement was now purely business. He liked screwing European women especially now he was spending his time in the desert and he made sure she was hooked on his booze. She felt she was in his power and had no alternative but to give in to his every degrading wish. Alcohol was prohibited under the Islamic code and black market supplies were far too expensive for her limited means. He treated her with ever more contempt as he forced her down to new depths of depravity, now supplying her with crack cocaine until he called her his crack cocaine whore forcing her to bear his now loathsome touch with shuddering revulsion.

Angela looked at him with hate as he stood at the door stroking his distended member, but she needed a drink and a jolt of cocaine, and he had both. Her last supplies had been drained in the days before, and now she felt that involuntary twitching of muscles, her nerve ends begin to tingle. Worse than the physical signs, was the knowledge that there was no more drink or drugs, except by giving herself to the Prince to do whatever he wanted. Her eye caught the glint of sun as it played across some surgical instruments on the desk between them. She thought of killing herself, she thought of killing him.

"It's my period, your Excellency. Let me have a drink and we can do whatever you want next time."

He dropped his Thobi and turned to go.

"No, don't go. Please don't go. At least give me a little taster. Give me a drink."

She pleaded, but he had no compassion. "My husband might come in at any minute."

The Prince turned from the door. "You're lying, he's in Riyadh."

Angela knew to beg him further for a drink would be useless, she who had never previously been to bed with anyone other than her husband and had never experienced anything with him resembling excitement, had become trapped by the sexuality this pervert had unleashed in her, unleashed for his own purpose, which had become his obsession and her torment.

"Alright, I'll do whatever you want."

Mo smiled and signaled her to him. She started to walk towards him but he signaled her to stop. "On your knees, crawl to me!"

She knew resistance was futile. She dropped to her knees and crawled until she reached him. He cupped her breasts and squeezed her nipples through her clothing but she stopped him.

"First a drink."

She pleased. He hesitated, looking from her eyes to the bag.

"I won't do it without a drink."

He handed her a bottle of Glennivet whisky. There were three more left in the bag, each one worth seventy-five pounds. As she greedily undid the bottle cap, he slipped his hands past her white nylon uniform and brassiere, squeezing her bosoms together as she swigged from the bottle.

"You pig!" she screamed. "It's been watered down, the bloody seals are broken."

"Drink it, whore!"

He shouted, squeezing her ever harder and as tears of pain and humiliation welled up, she swigged the Scotch straight from the bottle until half of it was in her. He wrenched the bottle from her hands.

"Now, get down bitch!"

He forced her to turn and kicked her viciously behind the knees. She collapsed forward onto the floor. Before she could move, he forced up the rear of her uniform exposing her scanty black lace knickers. He ripped them into shreds as she felt his huge machine tear into and plow her dry rectum. She nearly blacked out from the searing agony. He forced her to arch her back into him by jamming the whisky bottle into her mouth. She gagged on it but such was her need for booze it became more important than the pain. Without thought, she began to frenetically grind her ass to his rhythm as with every forward thrust, he let her throat have more of the precious amber liquid until it was gone and she felt the fires rage within her as he brutally used the bottle in her vagina, bringing her to a purely physical orgasm that nevertheless sent uncontrollable spasms through her.

Still he bucked into her, shouting:

"English whore, you love it. Go on, say you love it!"

As she felt the pain surface, she screamed: "I love it, I love it!"

At last he climaxed like a wild beast, snorting great breathes as his eyes rolled back in his head. He pulled himself from her and rolled her body roughly over, swiftly he reached down and pulled her head up by the hair until she took him in the mouth. She heard his high-pitched giggle and tasted her total debasement as he held the back of her head and thrust himself down her throat. She choked and fought to free herself, but he was too strong. He held her firmly, thrusting again and again. Thrust, choke, thrust, choke, thrust and then, without warning he was forced over her head and sprawling across the floor beyond, his Thobi about his waist and the scotch bottles rolling around his feet. Aziz furiously turned on the man who'd forced open the door. The small, normally placid man was Angela's husband, David, now shattered by what he found.

"Jesus Christ, Angela, what the hell's going on?"

Angela, coughing and spluttering looked up at her husband's astonished face. He saw the whisky and Mo's half-naked body then he understood.

"You filthy slut!"

His rage erupted from volcanic depths. Lunging for Angela, he dragged her to her feet and threw her into the wall.

"Why? Why? Why?"

He roared the question at her again and again.

Mo clutched the desk and pulled himself up. Simmonds spun round to face him. "You filthy animal! I'll teach you..."

Dave Simmonds never finished the threat, Mo grabbed a surgical scalpel from the desk and with the speed of a cornered rat, lunged at the Englishman's throat, tearing and ripping in a torrent of Simmonds's lifeblood. Finally, the small man fell forwards convulsively clutching his throat, and gasping horribly, he crashed to the ground leaving his back undefended which Mo struck repeatedly until there was no life to kill.

"Stop it, stop it, you're killing him, stop it!"

Angela Simmonds screamed as she pushed Mo aside with the strength of the demented and fell sobbing across the body of her butchered husband. The Prince paused as he struggled to catch his breath, still gripping the bloody weapon. The door was shut. He put his ear to it, but the only sound was the woman's sobbing, his own jagged breaths and the loud whirr of the air conditioner, no running feet or shouts of alarm. The woman's body heaved in quiet hysteria, no longer aware of the King's son standing above her. His brain, now operated only at the basest level. Only semi-conscious, the woman noticed nothing as he ripped up her white medical overall but when he fell on her back and ravished her inflamed vulva, she screamed a wild continuous wail, like someone falling from a cliff, on and on she screamed. He leapt from her and desperately looked for the scalpel; only death would shut her up. He raised the weapon but his downward thrust froze as a military boot kicked the door open and two Saudi soldiers charged into their room their automatic rifles leveled at him.

"She tried to kill me, men! That western devil tried to kill me!

A tall red-haired American pushed his way through the crowd that had gathered by the door.

"What's going on here?" he asked the soldiers. Some of them turned on him sharply.

"Who are you, Are you involved in this?"

"I'm Dr. Chuck Harris, senior consultant here, and this is my office. Now will someone tell me what the hell's going on?"

"They tried to kill me." blustered the Prince trying to move around the soldiers to the door, but a sharp meaningful gesture by one of the soldiers with his rifle halted any thought of escape. The doctor was on his haunches examining the couple on the floor. The woman sat up, mouthing indistinct words between sobs.

Harris looked at her husband.

"This man's been butchered, his head's nearly cut clean off his shoulders."

Angela screamed and leapt at the Prince. "This bastard did it, he killed my Dave and raped me!"

She tried to scratch at the Prince's face but the doctor held her back. Four more soldiers, dressed in combat fatigues appeared through the milling throng. They joined their comrades and began to argue furiously amongst themselves in confusion and alarm. One of them was yelling into his walkie-talkie radio for instructions and very swiftly, the electronic wail of a siren announced its approach. Several more uniformed men barged down the corridor led by an officer. The crowd of nosy onlookers evaporated and the consultant's room filled with imposing uniforms.

The officer saw Mo and at once his surly attitude was transformed to that of humble supplicant. "Your Excellency, can I be of service?"

The Prince, relieved by this turn of events, gushed forth his version of the story to the mustachioed officer, who ignored Angela's screamed protestations of the truth.

The officer's English was imperfect but adequate as he turned to the doctor.

"Mr. Consultant, this man is His Excellency Prince Mohammed Aziz."

He said this more as an explanation than as any introduction.

"He says on his royal oath to Allah that the dead man tried to force him to buy some prohibited alcohol, whisky, and that when he correctly refused this man attacked him; naturally the Prince defended himself."

Defended himself is it?" questioned Harris incredulously.

"For God's sake look at the body. He's been savagely attacked, and his wife has been brutally raped!"

The officer turned from Harris in disgust. He snapped an order at his soldiers in rapid Arabic. Even in the chaos of the bloodied room, many of the men had been openly leering at Angela Simmons. Harris took off his overall and put it on her. A single soldier politely escorted Aziz from the room while the other men formed a circle around Angela Simmonds and hustled her out.

"But she hasn't done anything!" protested Harris.

"Mr. Doctor," said the officer, "We don't know what happened here, but it will be tidied up at the police station."

Harris was not a man to be easily deterred.

"Well can you explain to me how getting raped by that drug addict murderer makes her liable for arrest. She was bloody well raped, I tell you!"

"Mr. Doctor, white women should not provoke attacks. Under Islamic law, rape can only be proved if the alleged rapist confesses or if there are four male witnesses. Women who allege rape without the benefit of the act having been witnessed by four men are actually confessing to having illicit sex. If they or the accused happens to be married, then it is considered to be adultery."

"What?" exploded Harris.

"It is well known," the officer continued. "Certain white-skinned women come here to behave in an improper manner, flaunting themselves for sexual thrills. It is natural a man should be tempted, even an exalted man like the Prince."

Harris leaned towards the officer so that their faces were inches apart. "I demand to go with her to safeguard her interests," he said with as much authority as he could muster.

"You will, Mr. Doctor," the officer replied to the doctor's surprise and satisfaction. "You are also under arrest."

The doctor's pleasure at his small victory turned into ashes of bile as he asked. "For God's sake what for?"

"This is your office, yes?" the soldier asked.

"Yes, you know it is. What's that got to do with anything?"

The Saudi officer bent over and picked up one of the bottles of whisky still lying on the floor.

"It is strictly prohibited by our laws to be in possession of alcohols."

He held up his hand to quell Harris's protests. "Please, Mr. Consultant Doctor Sir Harris, let us go quietly to the police station, everything will be made clear there, of this I am sure."

As Harris was handcuffed and led down the now deserted corridors, he called out several times.

"Call the American Consulate, for Christ's sake, someone call the Consulate!"

The Saudi officer, who had seemed indifferent to his shouts, responded.

"And I promise I shall bring this matter to the personal attention of the American consulate immediately."

He then led the American to an enclosed V.W. microbus parked in the hospital's barren forecourt. The rear doors were opened by a burly, wide-shouldered soldier as broad as he was tall. He casually punched the American's belly to wind him and shut him up as he manacled him to the iron rail that ran the entire length of the bus's centre.

In the stifling heat and gloom, Harris saw there was another figure incarcerated with him. As the doctor's eyes adjusted to the darkness he saw his fellow sufferer was a blonde man, probably in his mid-thirties, although the beating he'd taken on his face made it hard to judge. Harris slid his shackles down the bar, which dissected the vehicle's interior until he was directly opposite the other man.

"Hi, I'm Chuck Harris, you?"

The man looked up and smiled painfully, despite his swollen and cut face. "Yeah, I'm Richard Slobodan. We've met."

His voice was familiar, West Coast, but the face wasn't.

"I'm sorry, Richard, I don't recall."

The other man chuckled mirthlessly. "This is kind of silly, don't you think, Chuck? A medical consultant and the American Consul exchanging tidbits in the back of a mobile jail?"

"Jesus!" exclaimed Harris, only now realizing why the Saudi officer was so sanguine about his desperate shouts for his Consul. The man was in a worse situation than himself.

"How in hell did you get arrested, you're the Consul, for Christ sake?"

"Hey till we get split up call me Dick, would you? I'd take it as a personal favour if I could forget our State Department for a while, especially the fact I'm the boy on the spot who gets the shit dumped on his head."

The government man wiped his sweating head with his shoulder, reminding Harris just how uncomfortable and hot he himself felt. "Apart from not liking the State Department, what other crimes did you commit to get yourself locked in here; Don't you guys get diplomatic immunity?"

Slobodian shook his head.

"Haven't you heard the good old USA just invaded this fair country?"

The doctor's mouth dropped open. A veteran of Iraq, he'd never envisaged his country going to war in the Middle East again, other than for self-defence. "American soldiers here?" he asked the U.S. government representative.

"Well, not here. That's reserved for suckers like us who nobody warns, but certainly our brave boys are hitting the beaches." Slobodian said with the kind of cynicism that two men unsure of their immediate fate shared, then again shook his head, the perspiration spraying off him in twin rivulets as the microbus finally started its motor and pulled into the noisy traffic.

"I thought it was all the usual bluff." the doctor said, more to himself than the American consul, whose cynical attitude was starting to upset him.

"Listen buddy, if we ain't lucky, we're going to find ourselves in another Iranian situation. You remember those hostages, nearly two years they waited with a death sentence hanging over them. Hey listen, man, I'm sorry. At least we have company in the crapper. In a country that's as crazy as this, that's no bad thing."

Harris nodded glumly, reluctantly agreeing with the official's gloomy prediction. This could easily end up with them being blindfolded and stood against a wall, shot #as American agents.

"Maybe with our boys all over them they weren't so paranoid after all," the doctor said, remembering his many arguments with Saudis who had doubted his conjecture that America's foreign policy thrust under the President Obama had shifted from imperial to moral and with Trump from moral to total indifference. It seemed as if his Arab friends were right and he was wrong. Now he and his new acquaintance might soon both pay the ultimate price.

"So we're here just because we're Yanks?" he asked the Consul.

"Sure, but I expect they'll have a million phony reasons just in case things get out of hand and the marines get into town ahead of schedule."

It was the doctor's turn to laugh bitterly. "Knowing from experience how our generals think, I wouldn't hold your breath. We're in the crapper."

As the vehicle sped through the modern town, they saw nothing of the panic the American landings was causing the Saudi population. The rich had already gone;

the new and growing middle classes were thrashing their BMWs, Mercedes and Cadillacs down highways in every direction, chickens without heads, and their routes sometimes taking them directly to the enemy.

The only people still on the streets were the poor, and they were all foreigners or soldiers; there are hardly any poor native Saudi Arabians. The poor were Pakistani labourers, Yemeni manual workers and their Turkish foremen and all their multi-national colleagues who had automatically stopped work in the oilfields and construction sites when their Saudi bosses vanished and heavily-censored news of American landings filtered down to them. But they didn't have any escape route planned or readily available to them. They vainly waited for reliable news or instructions, or some international agency to rescue them. Their first priority became survival, as they only had a couple of weeks of provisions at their far-flung desert oil installations, and were also concerned that the local tribes-people might just take what little they did have.

"Listen, Doc," said Slobodian, "I heard the soldiers talking so I know what happened, and as I'm still the Consul, I'd best give you a rundown of the facts of life round here – you might still have some chance if you play the game by their rules. Remember under Muslim law, being a rape victim means you the victim are guilty of moral turpitude, and if you're an infidel woman and he happens to be a Muslim man who also happens to be a member of the Royal family. We all know why he was here because it was a real badly kept secret so, you got yourself a big problem. The alcohol thing's also got an angle; they read the code how it suits them – if they really want you they can get you. As a medic, you probably already know there's even alcohol in a whole pile of cosmetics right down to baby lotions, so they don't even need to catch you with a bottle of booze – a wrong aftershave or hand cream are just as illegal."

They both felt the vehicle slowing down as the driver went down to second gear and turned right.

"Tell me what help any of this is to me, what can I do?" the doctor asked.

"Remember your single most influential defence witness is your wallet."

The Consul managed to reply. As the rear doors swung open, two men, silhouetted by the bright sun, beckoned in badly disjointed English for the prisoners to exit.

The guards each escorted one man from the small truck. When both men were out in the sunlight, Harris only just managed to see the true extent of facial injury to the Consul before they were separated; He was in a mess.

"Good luck, Chuck!"

He called from the doorway he was being pushed into. As Harris began to reply, he saw the soldier guarding Slobodian casually swing his club across the bridge of the diplomat's nose and the blood gush from it. Harris wanted to go and help, but his own guard held him firmly by the elbow. He whispered to the American. "We are not all like this doctor, but don't be foolish or I cannot help you to live."

Harris started to stammer a surprised question when the same guard bundled him into an office built of grey concrete frieze blocks.

Already standing there were Angela Simmonds and Prince Mohammed Aziz. It was a bare room except for a small filing cabinet, and a cheap whitewood table. Behind it sat a short, hugely-overweight soldier in a stained officer's uniform. His face in contrast to the rest of his appearance was that of a Renaissance cherub. Behind him in a corner sat an intimidating and silent giant in traditional clothing. It was Nafti who stared at the Westerners with seeming contempt.

The officer opened up a children's exercise book that apparently served as the station's registrar.

"Name?" he asked in Arabic. Mo immediately, and with great relief recognized the brooding presence of Nafti. Ignoring the officer, he told his man his version of events, fervently protesting his innocence. The officer ignored him in turn and simply wrote his name in the book and turned his attention to the others.

Angela Simmons no longer cried but seemed indifferent to everything, gazing lifelessly into the middle distance, her mind lost in a web of self-protection. Harris gave her name, and then his own. The officer came from behind the desk and perfunctorily searched the Prince as he was nervous around this man of obvious importance and rank. He then frisked Harris much more thoroughly, then he turned his attention to the woman.

Harris tried to block him but was hit by a guard in between the shoulder blades with a rifle butt. The officer searched her body minutely and Harris, feeling other eyes behind him, turned and saw a gaggle of soldiers ogling the scene. Only the silent giant in the corner and the woman herself seemed oblivious to this new indignity.

"What am I and Mrs. Simmonds being charged with?" asked Harris, but he was ignored. There was some Arabic conversation between the officer and the giant man in the dimly-lit corner. Their discussion concluded, one of the soldiers moved to the middle of the room and opened a large rusting door in the corner opposite the giant who stood, revealing his enormous size. As the door swung wide, a fetid stench slammed into the room, hitting everyone in the lungs.

Harris and Angela Simmonds were ushered beyond the doorway down into an underground basement area that had been divided by bars into two lines of cells separated by a narrow central corridor. As they stumbled down the stairs, rats scampered aside, and some of the prisoners already underground shouted insults at the guards. Angela and Harris were placed into individual cells but Harris noticed that none of these doors were locked; only the outer door was firmly bolted. For a short while, there was silence, except for the sound of the ever-hungry rats across the floor, which was littered with every form of human excretion from bloody vomit to faeces. Each cell's furniture consisted only of a few boards on the damp, fetid concrete floor pretending to be a bed. There was no running water and the toilet facilities were represented by a mound of stinking turds in a shallow ditch at the end of the corridor which was infested by rats and huge insects, similar to millipedes, but several inches long bloated with their sickening nourishment.

Hours of darkness passed in this black hole before the door of Harris's cell opened again and several men entered. They swiftly and silently surrounded Harris. He was unable to resist as two men pinned his arms behind him. The others, he couldn't tell how many, systematically beat his face and body until his grunts of pain became shouts of agony. When he thought that he could take no more, they forced him on his face to the floor and he knew what was to happen next as they made him lift his ass in the air and they ripped off his trousers. He felt hands very roughly probe his ass and he cried in pain and anger at them and his helplessness. His attackers laughed as he felt something enter him.

Before the attack could continue, there was some shouting in Arabic, and Harris was half-pulled, half-dragged out to the upstairs office where someone's unseen hands pulled his clothes together for him. The giant he'd seen earlier stood with the officer as Harris adjusted his eyes to the light.

"Do you know what your fucking men just did to me?" Harris shouted at the officer. "Those bastards beat me up and raped me!"

The officer didn't smile.

Nafti answered in perfect-but-accented English. "There were no police officers in the cells I can assure you. Anything that happened was the work of your fellow prisoners. Can you describe your attackers?"

Harris said nothing, realizing that he was again powerless.

"I work for the royal family" said Nafti.

"Congratulations." Harris responded.

Nafti ignored the interruption. "Do you understand the situation you are in, you and the woman?"

Harris tried to bluster. "What the hell are you talking about? We're innocent. I don't even drink!"

The Prince's bodyguard came closer, talking quietly, almost confidentially. "Was there whisky in your room?"

"Are you all mad? I've told you time after time that bastard was feeding booze and drugs to that poor Englishwoman in exchange for sex and when she didn't play ball he raped her then murdered her husband!"

Nafti came still closer, making Harris even more scared, the sheer bulk so intimidating. "What evidence do you have against the Prince?"

"What?"

Harris took a step back, feeling the wall behind him. Nafti came forward again closing the gap. "Evidence. His Excellency insists the alcohol was already there, the man Simmonds wanted to sell it to him. Many westerners try to make money by such methods."

The American felt the big man's hot breath in his own mouth as he tried to answer. "The Simmonds woman will make a statement supporting me!"

Nafti was almost whispering into the doctor's ear. "The Prince will call you both liars. Understand me well. This is not America. Who do you think will be believed, the son of the King or an alcoholic whore?"

Harris turned his face so that he was looking straight up into the bigger man's eyes. "You know she was raped."

He protested weakly.

"Raped!" smiled the big olive skinned man.

"Rape is no defence. The question is why? Thousands of women live here without being raped. It is obvious she provoked the Prince. Only children can be raped. A grown woman brings it on herself, by dressing provocatively, by the way she talks to a man, the way she looks at him. Women know these things, and that their no means yes. All men have experienced such things."

"This is crazy. A woman can say no at any time, and it means no, and you stop. What can I do?" Harris implored, his resolve disintegrating now that he understood his comfortable Western concepts of morality and justice didn't apply in this place. Nafti took a step back abruptly, he seemed more friend than persecutor.

"There is very little that can be done."

He said it like a sad uncle says to a nephew that he can't have any more candy. "Look, can't you pull some strings? You work for them. She's locked in there with thirty guys, she can't crap without an audience, she's been raped and seen her husband killed. If she's not already insane it'll be a miracle."

Nafti shrugged, the universal gesture of helplessness. "What can I do for her? She'll have to make do with it. It will probably be three or four months before she stands trial, the same for you. Ask yourself what happens if an Arab breaks the law in your country or in England. Do you change your laws to set them free? All normal diplomatic doors slammed shut when your forces invaded our country today. Why should we allow such people to accuse our Royal family of lying? Do you assume your western values are superior to Islamic justice founded over fourteen hundred years ago?

He turned his back on Harris before he could respond and spoke swiftly in Arabic to the fat prison officer who shuffled from the office with a wide grin on his face.

"What's going on?" asked Harris.

"There is one way out for both of you but only if you are willing to be sensible" Nafti told him in return. The doctor became even more nervous at the other man's abrupt change of attitude.

"Sure, yes, sure I'm interested," he replied cautiously, wary of some new trap.

"First you must write a medical report stating the Simmonds woman was not raped."

"But..." Harris tried to interject but was cut off.

"Do exactly what I say or stay here and rot. Next the whisky, it belonged to the husband. He's dead, he can't be charged so he won't be worried. The woman simply signs a statement admitting her husband was a bootlegger, tried to press whisky on the Prince who had innocently gone to hospital seeking medical advice. There was an argument, the Prince justifiably defended himself. Everyone will live more happily this way, I'm certain you agree."

Harris shook his head, this complex nightmare web of deceit and the terrible knowledge of his own fears and weaknesses forced him to argue against his natural instincts. "Have you seen the man's body; Do you think anyone can believe the story you're concocting if they see the body?"

"Nobody will see the body. There is a ban about to be invoked that an infidel cannot be buried in this holy Islamic soil, and the British Consulate will take possession of the man's remains and quietly ship it out."

Harris stayed silent. The big man continued.

"Don't worry about dead men. You and the woman will do what I say. My way you'll be safely out of the country. If you persist and go to trial, you'll both be changed for life by your year's wait in a Saudi jail. You might survive, but the woman will be fucked to death, if not by the other prisoners then surely by the guards. You don't want her to suffer further, do you?"

Harris looked at the other man's face, seeking truth and finding it. "Why are you telling me this: Why don't you just let us rot? You work for that psychotic bastard. Is this one of his tortures? Watching me beg then doing what he wants anyway, walking away from this free as a bird, laughing at us?"

It was the giant's turn to shake his head. "My loyalty is to the royal family not to any one man. You have my word he will not escape justice. Bit by bit, he will be stripped of his money, his power, his positions of authority. He will be exiled and if he resists, he will suffer more, trust me. For all his deeds, he shall be punished."

Strangely, Harris trusted this man, although he hadn't any reason to do so. "What you've told me doesn't sound like much of a punishment."

"For him it is. His father and all his family will never again talk to him, a black sheep. He'll watch younger relatives become ever more rich and powerful but he will be treated as dirt. He will lose face. For a proud Arab man, this is a terrible punishment."

Nafti was tempted to continue but knew he couldn't.

Harris wanted to argue more, but knew he mustn't.

The two men stood like this, in silence, until the American spoke. "I'll play ball as long as you personally guarantee to get me and the woman straight out of this country, today." In response Nafti pulled some money from his tunic and shoved it into the doctor's shirt pocket.

"Don't ask questions, consider it a loan."

Nafti cut off any protests when he shouted something in Arabic and the fat officer appeared. He looked at this man who had a deadly reputation, questioning him with raised eyebrows; the giant's brooding face was adequate reply.

"We managed to make the doctor understand our system of justice."

The officer commented. "Yes, an exchange of official papers is in order." Nafti replied.

The squat soldier pulled a sweat-stained envelope from the breast pocket of his tunic which was two sizes too small. From the envelope he extracted some creased papers written in Arabic script which he pressed flat on the desk and bellowed for his men. Two guards rushed in and entered the cells, reappearing in seconds with Angela Simmonds supported between them. Her eyes didn't focus on her surroundings as she meekly signed the statement papers without reading them.

Harris noticed that she had been cleaned up as much as possible in the circumstances; she had been washed and was now wearing clean police overalls. He tried to catch her eye but there was no reaction from her. He also signed the papers where indicated. The officer gave an order to the guards who then left the office.

Harris perched Mrs. Simmonds on the edge of the desk, but was pushed aside by the soldier who gently led her to his own seat. Nafti pointed to the doctor's pocket who understood, took out the wad of money he'd just been given and handed it to the now avuncular officer. The man counted the money.

"Ten thousand dollars American!" he concluded cheerfully. He gave Nafti five thousand and kept the balance.

Nafti counted his money as if he'd never seen it before. "Come with me. We must go to the airport. The last plane for England leaves soon."

Nafti led Angela and the Doctor out of the claustrophobic room into a black Cadillac. The car headed towards the airport with Nafti driving through the near-deserted streets, not stopping for anything as he jumped a red stop light Harris turned to him.

"We haven't got our papers, passports and stuff. We'll have to go back." Nafti didn't take his eyes from the road. "You'll be okay, it's arranged."

"You mean we don't need anything, just go past all the formalities onto what has to be the last plane out of this place while it's at war?"

Nafti drove the car relentlessly onwards, ignoring the questions. "What about the landings, how are they going, what happened to Slobodian, the American Consul?"

The car neared the ultra modern airport and was halted by military police at a hastily- erected roadblock. Nafti pressed the electric window control and as it came down an excitable army sergeant poked his head into the car. He recognized Nafti and waved the car through. The huge man smoothly manoeuvred the wheel left, right and left again between the portable steel tank traps and onto the terminal. He parked the car in a row made up of hundreds of abandoned Rolls-Royces, Cadillacs and Mercedes, their proud owners having deserted them in favour of speedier outward-bound aircraft. Harris followed Nafti's lead and jumped out of the car. The Arab picked up Angela Simmonds as if she were a child, and Harris trailed them into the main departure concourse.

The scene that greeted them was incredible. Men, women and children were being dispossessed of all their valuables by a grimly-efficient team of Palestinian soldiers who had taken over border guard duties.

As Nafti barged through the crowds, an old lady was arguing fiercely with one of the soldiers who had demanded her jewellery.

"You give me everything you have!" he screamed. The woman was not easily cowed.

"You touch me again, you Palestinian scum, and I'll..."

Before she could finish the soldier smashed the butt of his rifle into her face, the crowd swirled back from the woman as she crashed, unconscious to the harsh, unforgiving ground. Nafti used his bulk and speed to crash through. In one movement, he handed Angela Simmonds to Harris and attacked the Palestinian's back with his hands balled, clubbing both sides of the soldier's kidneys making him drop his gun onto the prostrate old woman. Before he could turn, Nafti's right hand, now open, chopped into the exposed skin between neck and shoulder. As the soldier fell to his knees, Nafti cupped his chin between his hands and forced his foot into the small of the man's back. The man gasped for mercy as his comrades rushed to his aid, their automatic guns leveled at the giant.

"One more step and I break his back!" roared Nafti. The men froze except for a lieutenant who walked closer. He looked at the soldier then at the sobbing woman, now being treated by Harris.

"I mean you no harm." he said to Nafti, and calmly raised his revolver. The giant stretched the man's back into a bow of agony, as the shot rang out it was the soldier who died, his blood spilling into Nafti's hands, his brains blowing out onto the crowd from the exit wound. Nafti dropped the corpse onto the floor, ignoring the hysteria surrounding the officer who was calmly appraising him. The Palestinian seemed to make his decision in that frozen instant, speaking in whispered guttural English.

"Golda had great legs." Nafti knew he was listening to a fellow Israeli agent or a plant. He had seconds to decide which because the tumult around them was decreasing. Emotion was not part of his training but years living under deep cover had armed him with good instincts. "But she has thunder thighs."

He used the ridiculous, but therefore probably secure response.

"How did you know?" Nafti asked, "There aren't many Saudi soldiers more than six feet six inches tall. Call it a good guess." came the reply.

The Palestinian officer was also an Israeli agent and he allowed the briefest of smiles to fill his normally serious face. "The Palestinians attack southward towards Kuwait at 06:00 tomorrow," he whispered to Nafti. "Tell control."

The big man nodded. The officer pointed his gun at the baying crowd and reverted to Arabic.

"Alright, you imperialist pigs. The next person who moves is dead!"

The noise of shrieking women and shouting men was stilled as the officer fired into the ceiling.

"I said shut up. Now, get back into line or die."

The mob shuffled swiftly into line. The man pretending to be a Palestinian officer ordered his troops back to their positions that ringed the terminal and, like a giant human funnel, led to a booth at which all documents and exit permits were being methodically checked by four plainly-terrified Saudi customs officers.

Harris helped the now conscious and loudly protesting elderly Saudi woman to her feet. Two other Palestinian soldiers escorted Angela Simmonds while others unceremoniously dragged the corpse of their fallen comrade out of sight.

"Come, follow me," said the officer to Nafti and his small group. He led them past the long lines of disgruntled Saudis and into the curtained exit booth. As he addressed the customs men, Nafti saw five or six enormous black plastic bags full of jewellery being dragged away by the soldiers.

Nafti returned his attention to the customs man who was addressing him. "Can we see your papers?"

Nafti laughed. "Shut up, idiot. If you tell me where the royal party can be found, I might forget your insolence. Quick now, where are they?"

The group were let through the booth as if they were royalty themselves. Nafti shook hands with the Palestinian officer, their eyes saying much more than the words spoken by either. Harris watched the officer return to the terminal and then observed the brief, almost wistful look on the giant's hard face. It vanished as Nafti felt his eyes on him.

"How's the woman?" he asked Harris, who was still supporting her with his right arm.

"She'll die if we don't get her to a hospital soon. She's hemorrhaging heavily. I'd say a womb infection, and as you can see for yourself, mentally she's someplace altogether different."

Nafti looked down the long-deserted marble corridors for any sign that would indicate where aircraft might be leaving from.

"Follow me," he said, taking a guess and heading left, to yet more trouble.

Chapter Thirty-seven

Saudi Airlines 'Super-Jumbo' Flight SA 030, London To Abu Dhabi
16th. October 2020 – 21.00 hrs.

Eddie Roman looked at his watch yet again. The plane was already two hours late and there had not been a single word of explanation. The steward caught sight of his signal and walked over to him across the roomy cabin.

"Can I get you anything, sir?" he asked pleasantly.

"Yeah, how about a brown paper bag,. I'm tired of coke."

The steward smiled broadly. This was proving to be a lucrative journey selling illicit booze to thirsty passengers. "If you follow me to the lounge, sir..."

He led Eddie from his seat through the first class cabin, then up the spiral stairway that brought them to the lounge area. Eddie sat by the port window looking down on the Mediterranean sparkling far below. The steward appeared, placed a glass on the table, next to a carafe of mineral water, then like a conjurer, handed Eddie a brown sealed package, and winked conspiratorially. Eddie gave the man a one hundred dollar note and opened the package; a bottle of Bells Whisky. He poured himself a double and took a long pull.

The plane, which had been heading due south, banked slowly to the right. Eddie at last understood; they were turning in a series of huge circles avoiding the African landmass always keeping the sea below.

"Why are we going in circles?" he asked the steward.

"I am simply an airborne 'trolley dolly', Sir. I don't even know what you're drinking so how do I know why we're circling?" he answered, taking the seat opposite Eddie in the otherwise-empty lounge.

"Would fifty dollars help you discover the reason?" asked Eddie.

"Yes, I'm sure it would," answered the steward, leaving his seat and walking to the cockpit door. He knocked politely and went in. Moments later, he was back by Eddie's side.

"I have the answer to your question sir. We're being cleared to divert southwest over Libyan airspace, then due south into Africa. When we reach Ethiopia, we'll head east over the Gulf of Aden and then up through the Straits of Hormuz and inland to Abu Dhabi."

"Jesus, how long will this little diversion take?" Eddie asked.

The steward shrugged expressively. "About six hours if we don't have to land for re- fuelling."

"Jesus!" Eddie repeated.

"Why the hell are we going on this magical mystery tour?"

Before the steward could respond, the aircraft banked steeply to the right and went almost straight up, throwing the steward like a rag doll into the bulkhead, his surprised face crashing into its steel frame. Eddie fought to securely fasten his seatbelt against enormous gravitational forces. Through his porthole, he glimpsed a flash of metal followed by another, a warplane with its cannons blazing. Eddie realized that their super jumbo had accidentally wandered into the Arab Israeli war.

His plane leveled off above the two warring jets and as the fasten seatbelts sign came alight, he saw with shock that the airplane being chased below was American, its pursuer had markings that he didn't recognize. The American plane spiraled down but seemed unable to shake off its enemy which gained speed, closing the distance rapidly. Eddie found himself shouting encouragement to his adopted countryman as the American F16 looped upwards still followed by the faster, but more cumbersome, Russian-built MIG 25 Foxbat. The American plane completed its manoeuvre and was now behind the MIG, prey becoming the hunter. The MIG's superior speed started to create a gap but the plane wasn't fast enough to escape the American's heat-seeking air-to-air missiles which shot forward and exploded the MIG into a million floating pieces of expensive scrap.

Eddie, cheering wildly, watched the remaining aircraft complete a barrel roll, celebrating its victory just as the airline pilot's voice came over the speakers. "I'm sorry about that, ladies and gentlemen," said the laconic French accented voice of the airliner's Captain, "But as I'm sure you've already understood, we have wandered accidentally into a war zone. We just received news indicating that forces of the U.S.A. have invaded Saudi Arabia's eastern coast. As your captain, I have decided to land at Jeddah which is on Saudi Arabia's west coast because to make for Abu Dhabi under circumstances like this would be extremely unwise. You will keep your seatbelts fastened at all times until we are stationary on the ground. Once again, I apologize on behalf of the airline for any inconvenience caused, but I'm sure you would prefer to arrive safe but late rather than take any unnecessary risks and not arrive at all. Thank you."

Eddie pulled his safety belt tighter, took an enormous gulp from his whisky bottle and prayed, wishing he were anywhere but here. A place where he could control his own fate.

Chapter Thirty-eight

Jeddah International Airport, Saudi Arabia
16th. October – 21.25 hrs.

The small V.I.P. lounge was crowded to its padded red leather doors. Seated on an ornate wing chair was King Ibin Saud, his lean face framed by his plain white headdress and neatly trimmed black goatee beard. Before him on a low footstool, knelt Prince Mohammed Aziz, his jet eyes swimming with tears of self-pity. The King looked from the prostrate young man across the room to the seven elderly Mullahs who constituted the Islamic Court that now sat in judgment.

The oldest of the judges, known only as Karim, was handing down the holy men's decision on the case.

"Your Highness will recognize the difficulty of the court's position; if we turn in one direction we risk your anger, if we turn in another direction we could be derelict in our duty to Allah."

He paused for dramatic effect, then raised his arm and pointed his finger at the terrified young Prince.

"But this man, this aberration, this offal, cannot be allowed to defile our people further without punishment. He is diseased in his mind, he is contaminated by western decadence. Therefore, your Highness, we are left no alternative. If no person present has anything to say in mitigation for this man, we will pass sentence."

Karim stopped. He was content that he'd made his position clear without personal affront to the King, an extremely important factor since he and the other Mullahs present had become very closely identified with the royal family, and would either escape with them or face a new regime's revenge. Mo openly cried.

"Father, please don't throw me to the wolves. I have always been a faithful son. I'll do whatever you say, but don't reject me!"

The King pushed his son's hands away. Once again a man who is my father pushes me away, thought Mo.

"You hear Karim. This person who calls himself my son, who dishonours the House of Saud is still more worried about rejection than death. Perhaps for such a person, we should reflect on the most suitable punishment."

He let the words be considered by Karim who responded swiftly. "It is unusual for anyone other than a Mullah to concern himself with decisions of an Islamic court your Excellency."

The King's well-known temper was near breaking point.

"Of course, Karim. As always in spiritual affairs, your wisdom is total and all Islam is grateful to Allah for your presence amongst us."

The King truly hated and despised Karim. However, the old goat lent his regime religious legitimacy and continuity of this factor would be crucial in the coming months. He continued. "But as necessity dictated this matter should come before you in this strange, turbulent moment in our history, it has forced changes in our behaviour; what usually you would deliberate upon for weeks, you have accomplished, with brilliance, in hours. Brothers, I implore you not to think this humble worshipper is critical of your decision. These are difficult times. We all wish for continual guidance from Allah.

Who of us knows what strengths we might need in the future? All of us, from the lowest peasant to the mightiest warrior, will look to all his brothers for assistance..."

The King hesitated, and looked from Karim's intelligent, hard face to that of his unworthy adopted son.

"Even offal is worth more than the price than the price of the blunted executioner's blade," intoned the King. Karim understood the King's offer; in return for a sum of money, would mercy be shown. The holy man was, in addition to his truly-held deep beliefs, also a pragmatist. A reasonable amount of blood money could well be considered a suitable conclusion to the matter, as long as this out of control, possibly mad Prince did no more harm.

"The Koran teaches us to dispense appropriate justice, your Excellency. Knowing this, we are yet to see any evidence of true repentance from the culprit."

The young Prince turned to face Karim. "I have told you repeatedly that I'm innocent, what more do you want from me?"

The King barked an order to the four guards standing behind him. "Remove him to another room. If he utters even one word cut out his tongue."

The guards frog-marched the prisoner from the room. He watched as his son was taken away, utter contempt and disdain apparent on the King's expressive face.

However, he still loved his wayward son.

"Gentlemen, Allah would forgive you for speedy dispensation of his justice on this occasion. We must go from this place now or become American puppets. Before you decide on the punishment, I implore you to believe that although my son is guilty he has secretly, but to my certain knowledge, been repeatedly of great service to our beloved country. Those good actions must be weighed in the balance and carefully measured; in his favour."

After the King finished what was for him a deeply humiliating speech, he silently prayed that Mo was worthy of placing him in this embarrassing position of having to plead with these self important, pompous religious leaders. Whatever punishment the young man received was nothing to what suffering he, the King would inflict on these Mullahs should the opportunity ever present itself to him.

The Mullahs talked amongst themselves. Their plain black Thobis drawn together by the intimacy of their consultations formed a wall as if they were a flock of crows sitting on a fence, thought the King. Finally, it was Karim who coughed delicately to attract his King's wandering attention.

"We are, as you know, modern and moderate men, your supreme Excellency, we do not wish to inflict torture, merely dispense justice. We first must ask you, an expert on legal matters, a question, with your permission?"

"Granted," replied the King impatiently.

"Your Excellency agrees that there are a range of punishments available to an Islamic court?"

The King nodded. "Of course."

He didn't trust himself to talk further to this cunning holy man, but he remained eager to save his favourite son. He believed that his country desperately needed such a man in their hour of need.

"Would you agree that your son is a very ambitious young man, even arrogant?" He nodded again. Karim continued.

"Then for him a punishment worse than death would be the blocking of his ambition, the removal of any possible reason to regard himself higher than the lowliest peasant. Our punishment is his banishment into exile for one year, plus forfeit of his entire estate as a religious tax to Islam, and His Majesty's agreement that he will be removed, forever, from any inheritance, title and estates. You, his father, will contribute an additional one tenth of all your future income on your son's behalf. If you wish to help your son, you must give Islam the same amount as you give him, Riyal for Riyal, for the next ten years..."

Karim saw the anger burning bright in the faces of the King.

"The Royal House of Saudi will become even stronger when the world knows of it's willingness to treat one of their own as if he were the son of a stranger. Might I suggest the Prince be returned so that he may hear of his punishment?"

Karim said this with such honeyed sweetness only those who knew him would perceive his joy. The King knew him well enough. He stood up to his full six feet three inches.

"Karim, we have finished this thing. Let the boy say his goodbyes in private. I suggest you, your men of God, go now."

The King thus dismissed Karim and his fellow Mullahs, and they obediently filed from the room without a backwards glance.

The King understood that Mo was no guiltier in this than he'd trained him to be; everything he'd ever demanded of his son had blood as its reward. He is the product of our own wishes and dreams. You cannot breed a flesh-eating lion and expect it to behave like a lamb. Why should we allow ourselves to be treated like peasant scum, like superstitious nomads? We were both educated at the world's best universities and yet, still we are forced listen to the idiotic superstitious ramblings of that witch Karim regarding the destiny of my son!

There will again come the day when we are so powerful we can dispense with the men like Karim, but until we reach that day, they are our only link with the masses of our people, without them agitating on our behalf, we may control the people's bodies but never their minds. We must remember what happened to our friend the Shah, and all those who led other, Arab lands, which now are no more than Islamic dictatorships, run by people just like our friend Karim. Let us thank Allah that Karim is no Khomeini. He, at least, is contented by money, which is the one thing we have in abundance. So be calm, be patient, our day will return, but until it dawns, you must adjust as I do to our new position. We are in the eye of a storm, to survive is our duty. Mo failed to see this but thankfully, he is still alive to make amends. Now let me explain this to my son.

His burly guards escorted Prince Mo back into the room. The spirit had gone from him, the spark of arrogant contempt extinguished in dull, downcast eyes.

Beneath his pathetic and abject appearance, the Prince was allowing himself the luxury of letting his imagination run riot, picturing the revenge he would wreak on them all; his father the King and the Mullahs who were no more than religious thieves and plunderers.

After all I've done for my country, this is my reward.

Wait Saudi Arabia, wait for the return of your Prince. I shall justly reward you.

Chapter Thirty-nine

Control Tower and Runways, Jeddah Airport, Saudi Arabia
17th. October 2020 – 21.25 Hrs.

Eddie Roman had dragged the comatose steward into the chair opposite and strapped the seatbelt across the man's blood-spattered shirtfront. The last few minutes had been a nightmare rollercoaster ride as the huge Boeing aircraft dived, climbed, then weaved crazily in the claustrophobic darkness of the night sky above the featureless desert.

Ever since the captain's terse announcement following the air battle, Eddie had understood the additional danger he was in. As an American citizen arriving in Saudi which his country had apparently just invaded was not terrific timing. The welcome he could expect might well be less than enthusiastic, that's if they arrived at all.

He kept staring out of the windows, praying not to see any more fighter planes of any kind or country. Even more scaring than this possibility was his fear that some trigger-happy lunatic below might fire off a few ground-to-air missiles at such a tempting piece of target practice as this lumbering monster which seemed to be much too slow at five hundred and fifty miles per hour. The pilot's frenetic manoeuvres only intensified his terror; the captain was apparently as anxious as he was.

At last Eddie's eyes caught some lights pulsing at ground level, their glow intermittently illuminating a swathe of unlit buildings; it had to be Jeddah Airport, the reasons for lack of lighting obvious in time of war. The giant aircraft, configured to carry over seven hundred passengers, banked steeply to the left, the pilot was now on the home straight. Just talk sweet nothings to the tower baby, willed Eddie, pulling his seatbelt even tighter, long-forgotten prayers sprang to his parched lips.

Over the sound of the jet engines, he heard women's high-pitched screaming from the main body of the plane. One way or another, life or death would be decided over the next few minutes.

On the ground below the first royal jet stood ready for its passengers, red carpet extended majestically down the glittering-white steps towards the private exit from the V.I.P. lounge, the aircraft's powerful twin tail engines idled.

His Excellency Prince Mohammed Aziz walked with as much dignity as he could muster to the second royal jet, a sleek blue Lear. He held his head erect as he mounted the stairs, ignoring the honour guard of battle dressed Palestinian soldiers encircling this part of the airport. Mo turned to look at his adopted homeland for perhaps the last time, inhaling a last lungful of its sweet night air, then entered the aircraft.

Karim and his group of religious leaders waited impatiently in the third executive Jet. Its smaller capacity cramped and stark interior a small price to pay for escape. Karim beckoned the pilot, a lanky, sandy haired, fresh-faced Englishman in his early thirties, widely known as the best and most reliable whisky smuggler in the country. Which customs official dare check a royal plane?

The man ambled over to Karim and respectfully removes his cap. "Yes?"

"When are we going, captain?"

"After the King, I expect," the Englishman replied without any inflection in his voice or look to his face, which, however, did not hide the fact that he was well known to Karim as a flouter of the Islamic code.

"Captain, then tell me when is the King due to depart?"

The captain looked genuinely hurt that he couldn't help.

"I'm sorry your Imperial Holiness, sir, but that's a state secret, no one knows the King's schedule. I dare say if we all patiently wait though, we'll find out."

Karim closed his eyes as the Englishman strolled back to his cockpit. Every member of the royal family, even distant relatives, had been safely airlifted out of the country and now he had to wait for the King to leave first. It was unforgivable!

Nafti shoved the protesting stewardess aside, and led Doctor Harris and Angela Simmonds through the empty departure lounge into the airbridge leading to the waiting Saudi Airlines Tri-Star. Two hulking men had already begun closing the aircraft's door when Nafti coldly ordered them to stop.

"Where's your authority?" asked the older of the two men, Nafti leveled his pistol at the man's face.

"Here !"

"Alright, alright. I'm not going anywhere myself. You take them on if you want, no one's trying to stop you!"

He and his companion rushed from the half-closed door, back into the main building. Nafti smiled to his two exhausted companions. "Follow me, keep close!"

With his enormous shoulder, he charged through the door to discover a surprised and motley crew of Saudi refugees. Men, women and children clogging every spare inch with an incredible array of their possessions, everything from a large Picasso to the latest DVD's and electronic games were stacked together in the aisles.

"There's no spare seats here. Let's go friend," said Harris, turning to leave. Nafti held his arm, forcing him to stay.

A blonde Germanic-looking stewardess shouted at them across the gangway. "What do you think you're doing? We're about to leave and there are no seats. You can see there are no seats!" Nafti followed her sweeping gesture and saw a fat little man and his fat little woman both feigning indifference. The man was familiar but was doing his best to become invisible. Nafti ignored the hysterical stewardess and clambered over a pile of luggage towards the fat man who had covered his face with a courtesy copy of the *Wall Street Journal*. Nafti lifted a corner of the newspaper.

"Your stocks just hit rock bottom, Mr. Prison Officer. Up you get."

The big man neatly tore the newspaper in half, revealing the wide-eyed officer.

"My wife has a weak heart. You don't understand, I have to be with her to look after her."

He pleaded. Nafti pulled him up. "Good news, you'll be together and able to look after your wife, here in Jeddah. Now back to your prison or I break your neck"!"

Swiftly the man led his woman away hushing her screamed protestations.

Harris sat Angela Simmonds, and turned to thank the strange giant, but he had already gone, hidden behind the aircraft door, which was being closed from the outside. Eddie Roman's aircraft made its last approach turn before landing. His body perspired and shook; when would it be over?

The Saudi Tri-Star containing more than three hundred and ten refugees including Doctor Harris and Angela Simmonds edged carefully away from the dark departures building. King Ibin Saud and his brother Prince Khaloof marched imperiously to their aircraft. It was royal tradition that those next in line of accession to the throne traveled with the monarch; no over-ambitious aspirant was likely to blow him up if they were to suffer the same fate.

Nafti entered the second royal jet. His royal companion, Prince Aziz, turned and when he saw the big dark shape, he came to him and hugged him, great sobs racking his body.

"I thought even you had deserted me. Forgive me, friend, I should know better."

Nafti returned the Prince's embrace, his face hidden in the darkness reflecting his total hatred.

"Your Excellency must never forget we are brothers, blood brothers."

Karim's Lear jet taxied slowly in the darkness. He led the group of Mullahs in wailing prayers. The English pilot slammed the cockpit door. The Airport's Control

Tower's last three air controllers, all experienced men from the U.K., used to a heavy pattern of traffic, spoke into their headsets, their trained eyes scanning their monitors constantly for any possibility of trouble. The three men had been offered a bonus of fifty thousand dollars each to stay at their desks until these last few aircraft were safely dispatched. They were proud professionals, trained years before by the Royal Air Force to do their jobs, whatever the circumstances.

The Palestinian officer, who had recently identified himself to Nafti as an Israeli agent, walked briskly to the control tower. He quietly removed the safety catch on his Shmausser machine pistol as he approached the two guards at the door, and called to them. "Good evening, brothers."

As the men returned the greeting, he shot them both dead with one long, traversing burst of withering fire. He fired at the door lock, shattering it and automatically triggering the alarm which wailed a warning as the officer kicked the door open, and rolled low and fast into the concrete hallway. No shots were fired at him as he warily ascended the metal stairway, the sound of the siren covering the noise of his steel-tipped army boots.

The steward opposite Eddie Roman began to regain consciousness as the wheels of the mighty jet feathered down onto the main runway.

The Tri-Star was about to make his turn into the takeoff spot at the crown of runway two when the pilot received orders to break off and cross to the main runway.

The King's jet took the Tri-Star's position at the head of runway two, the pilot demanding instant priority to be cleared for takeoff. Behind him in close echelon were the remaining royal aircraft numbers two and three.

The chief Air Traffic Controller saw the converging blips on his radar monitor screen as the landing jumbo screamed down the runway towards the Tri-Star which was slowly turning at the other end of the tarmac. The Israeli agent burst into the room firing wildly as the controllers began to scream warnings to all the pilots. The Saudi soldiers guarding the controllers instinctively returned fire, killing the agent even as they themselves died.

Eddie saw the steward's face screw up in horror at something he saw happening at the front of the airplane. He twisted in his seat in time to see the giant Tri-Star hurtling toward them. The steward screamed for less than a second before the piercing sound merged with the roar of the jumbo jet, burying, crashing and tearing into the other aircraft. Eddie felt himself catapult into the air, then bounce into something hard and searing with heat before he felt himself floating, seemingly in slow motion into the blackness.

Doc Harris patted Angela's hand reassuring the instant before the Tri-Star was rammed into oblivion.

The King's aircraft smoothly led the remaining royal jets safely into the air above the roaring inferno.

Below was chaos. Many people dying in unimaginable horror as flames enveloped them, while others, just feet away suffered no more than bumps and bruises. There was nothing fair or equitable as metal crushed bodies indiscriminately and flames burned flesh away from bone.

Among the chaos Eddie Roman was carried to safety by a medic.

Chapter Forty

The Lodge, Chamonix, France
27th. October 2020 09.30 hrs.

Eddie limped from his chauffeur driven limousine. He understood very well how unbelievably lucky he had been to only suffer minor burns, cuts and a broken leg.

He had decided he just wanted out, anything to get home away from this madness to some semblance of normality.

Whatever he could get from this deal would be great, even nothing and a safe ticket out of this madhouse would be better than living like this, flying between continents as people seemed determined to kill him and everyone else.

When he entered his French hotel suite, its telephone was ringing. He looked out of the room's window as heavy snow fell on to his picture-perfect view of Mont Blanc.

he picked up the receiver and pressed and a voice he vaguely recognized spoke.

"Welcome my brother, it's time we got together, it's been too long."

Eddie remembered the voice, but it was deeper now.

"You will meet my associates and we will be working together, and you will remember all that we were once to each other."

As it then dawned on Eddie, he sat down, shocked by the realization;

"Mo?"

There was a long pause, and then Mo spoke to him in Arabic, "In our own way, we've both made a mark, and now we shall do so together. I think you'd call that irony."

Eddie's sharp mind was still struggling with the reason for the call, how did Mo come to be involved in any deals in the new Saudi Kingdom? What was the connection?

"Why the phone call. What's wrong with a face-to-face after all this time?"

asked Eddie.

Mo chuckled. "I would enjoy seeing your face as you tried to work this out, but it's kismet and you can never work out kismet, it just is. Now you'll find there is no way out of this except in a box. We wouldn't want that to happen to you or your special friend Barry, would we?"

Eddie recognized this as a threat and was genuinely surprised. Mo continued, "We're playing for very big stakes, my brother, as big as it gets, and there is a price for failure, but now we are also partners, so we will both have opportunities to make up for lost time."

"You know I've wanted to apologize to you for many years; for what I did."

There was a pause as Mo enjoyed the moment, and the obvious discomfort of his old friend.

"Don't worry about it. I ended up with the better end of that deal. You'd never guess how it ended up for me. As you might put it, I guess I was born under a lucky star."

Before Eddie could ask Mo what he was talking about, he had disconnected. Eddie was disturbed by the fact that his old friend could still upset him after all the years since they'd lived as brothers. He felt winded, almost nauseous, and sat down. No-one could get to him like his old friend Mo, no one had the same ability to make him feel so guilty. Eddie had never been able to bury his guilt over what he'd done and looking back, he wished he could re-write history. Despite the fact that they both had a terrible relationship with their adopted father, he knew he should never have robbed Mo of his birthright with the same man. He still fondly remembered that up to the moment when he had betrayed Mo, they had grown up as brothers from different mothers.

He might have been a boy, but he had been old enough to know exactly what he was doing. But he didn't have long to ponder before he noticed the time on his watch, so showered and changed into fresh clothes.

He rushed to the elevator and was soon in the lush meeting room being greeted by Pierre Montcalm.

"Bonjour my friend, did you have a good flight?"

Eddie looked around the room and was greeted by a diverse group of men and women. There was a Chinese woman, tiny and birdlike with bright gimlet black eyes, her name was on a small nameplate on the immense glass table in front of her:

Madam B. Kim. She observed Eddie as if he were a piece of food, her lipstick smile broad, and unusually for an Asian woman, she allowed her teeth to show. They were very small and pointed, giving her an almost feral appearance, but doing nothing to conceal her intense interest in Eddie.

Eddie was, in turn, intrigued by the woman sitting to her left, her entire form concealed in a white traditional Arab costume with a silver edging. He could only see her eyes, which were large and luminous, likely of a younger woman, seeming to bore right into him. As a boy in Iraq, Eddie had always been fascinated by such women, trying to imagine what the person underneath the flowing robes was like.

The nameplate in front of her stated she was Princess Leila Aziz. She patted the chair to her right.

"Hello Mister Roman. It's good to meet you."

Eddie noticed that her English had a slight American accent as he moved over to the seat she indicated and sat down.

"It's good to meet you also. Which company do you represent?"

She chuckled throatily. He liked the sound. "We both work for your company, we are partners and colleagues."

Eddie smiled and thought this was going to be interesting and potentially very complicated. "Of course."

But before he could continue, Pierre Montcalm stood in front of them all. Now Eddie had enough time to look around the rest of the room and noticed a very blond man with bright blue eyes and a small neat goatee beard. Henrik Lassen, Eddie thought, couldn't have been more Scandinavian if he tried. The last person seated at the other end of the table was a very overweight American man, Eddie's guess, since the man was called James Marrow and wearing a large white cowboy hat.

Ranged behind the people at the table, were several young women who appeared to be assistants to the principals and, behind the Chinese lady, were three inscrutable Chinese young men, who Eddie thought were her security.

Pierre Montcalm held up his arms to quell the chatter in the room. "Welcome everyone. It is the pleasure of La Salle Industries to host this little get together. We are all aware of the purpose of this meeting, but to avoid any confusion, I shall be explicit. We form a loose, discrete association of companies with unparalleled capabilities to construct the new world of tomorrow from the ashes of yesterday's conflicts. We take no sides, we have no political agenda, we develop and build the cities, the industrial infrastructure and the defence umbrella for generations yet to be born. The politicians may spin wonderful dreams, but it is the people in this room who make it happen!"

Eddie looked around as Montcalm took a breath and a sip of water. It was clear that even these hard bitten cynical men and women were enraptured by the Frenchman's passion. Pierre continued...

"To move forward in an orderly fashion, without stumbling is our goal. To achieve this is good for us, and vital for the survival of our world order. There can be no chaos if our systems are to survive and prosper for the future. They mocked President Reagan many years ago when he talked about his trickle-down theory of economics, but he was right and they were wrong. Unless the strong remain rich and powerful, there is no hope for the poor and the weak. We have to prosper primarily for the good of all our fellow citizens of our world!"

The others in the room politely applauded as they heard what they all thought, but were usually too shy to repeat in public.

Montcalm held up his hand for silence. As he did so, Eddie found himself looking into the eyes of the Princess, who smiled at him.

"We will talk later, privately," she whispered. Eddie found himself smiling at the thought of spending time alone with her.

Montcalm continued. "Joining us today are the new leaders of our pre-approved companies. They deservedly inherit the position formerly occupied by their previous principal, and are represented today by two young and dynamic leaders: Her Excellency Princess Leila Aziz of the Royal House of Saud and Mr. Edward Roman of London and Wall Street. They are fully briefed regarding how our system of bidding works and are happy to maintain the status quo as long as their company has its moment in the sun, a little later, and is, of course, properly compensated in the agreed manner."

He smiled but noted carefully that nothing registered in the eyes of the Princess.

Eddie picked up the slight shake of the head from Montcalm but was unable, and perhaps a little unwilling, to stop the Princess from talking. He wanted to hear what she had to say even if the Frenchman didn't.

"Monsieur Montcalm, a moment please," she began. He sat down, allowing her to address the group. "Thank you. What I have to say will only take a moment. We are at a disadvantage since you all know your systems so well and have had plenty of time to adapt, whereas my colleague and I," she nodded toward Eddie, "Have been thrust into this situation virtually without notice or an opportunity to even converse. Of course, we wish to do nothing to disrupt the smooth running of the bidding process, but we do need an opportunity to assimilate all the new knowledge you've been generous enough to share with us each individually."

Montcalm tried to intervene, but the Princess held up her hand to silence him. "And therefore I respectfully request an adjournment to allow us a small opportunity to reflect together on this situation."

Montcalm rose to his feet, smiled, and turned to face the impatient group. "I think I can speak for everyone present when I say that we are all very busy and simply do not have the time for delays and hesitation. This has all been decided long before by the leaders of our companies and..."

Before he could finish, Eddie interrupted, "Previous leaders in our case, and all the Princess is asking for is a couple of hours. We're all reasonable people, so I'm confident we can all manage a couple of hours, can't we?"

Although phrased as a question, Montcalm recognized he would look unreasonable if he didn't allow the request.

"Of course, well..." He looked theatrically at his watch.

"Let us resume for lunch at noon, which allows you a little more than a couple of hours, OK?"

Everyone rose to their feet and broke into sub groups, chatting with each other, making it obvious that they weren't happy with this unscheduled break. Montcalm led some of them out of the room as the others tidied up their paperwork.

The Princess stood and turned to Eddie. She smiled and he returned the smile.

"So are you thinking the same as me?" she asked. His smile broadened.

"Well, I was thinking what are we going to talk about so much for a couple of hours, and you?"

She looked around the room and seeing no one else was watching or could overhear them she whispered. "I can think of other things we can do."

She let the thought linger, but Eddie pretended he didn't understand rather than add any fuel to the fire.

"Yes, I'm sure you have much to do. Would you prefer we had our talk here or in one of the other meeting rooms?"

"I have another idea," she said, reaching for his hand and pulling him after her. He hurried to keep up, unsure how to deal with this woman.

"Where are you taking me?" he asked as she playfully led him on.

"To my own little private cabin!"

When they got there, he saw that it was a magnificent wooden T-shaped building with large tinted windows, set in the snow, nestling between giant conifer trees, looking out over the magnificent view of Mont Blanc. She whisked them both into the luxurious interior and turned to face him giggling. He was uncertain how to react as she held both his hands in hers.

"Don't you want to see how ugly I am?" she teased.

"Princess, this is crazy. We just met, we have business to discuss, and..."

She laughed again. "And you're gay!" she said emphatically, but quietly.

He nodded. "And I'm gay."

She pulled away her face covering and he saw she wasn't so much beautiful as stunning, not conventionally pretty, her features were each too big for that. Her eyes were enormous and very dark, her lashes too black and arched, her nose strong and prominent, with flared nostrils, her lips too full, her jaw too firm, almost masculine, but her mouth was generous and seemed to almost be perpetually smiling.

"What do you think? If you were the other way inclined would you want me? She moved to stand very close to him, looking up at his face from just inches away, her body pressed against his. He could feel every one of her voluptuous curves pressing into him. Eddie didn't know how to respond, but his body reacted, he had never been this close to a sexually-alluring woman in his adult life.

She looked up into his eyes surprised to feel his manhood harden against her belly.

She reached down and felt his length through his trousers. "What a waste!"

As she said this he wrapped one arm around her and with his free hand, pulled her all-concealing clothing open and felt her hot, lithe body. They kissed passionately before he pulled back, just an inch or two.

"I don't think we should do this," he muttered between kisses.

"Don't worry about that." she undid his belt and trousers,

"We won't tell anyone."

She pulled his rock-hard penis out of his boxer shorts. Their kisses intensified as they were both now aroused beyond any reason. She guided his hands to undo the clasp of her lacy bra and as he undid it, he could see her generous but pert breasts, topped with large, jutting dark brown nipples. He felt them in his hands and she shuddered with intensified pleasure.

"Suck them," she demanded, and he bent his head to suck her breasts as she used her free hand to lift one then the other to his hungry mouth. Now, her breasts were wet with his saliva and she arched her back and curved one of her legs around his waist, rubbing her groin against him, using his torso and leg to excite her sex even more. He smelt her heat and she took his hand from her breast to her pussy, which he could feel was wet through her very brief lacy knickers. She knew this was where he might reject her for being a woman. She paused as his fingers discovered her through the fine silk material, and then smiled as he simply ripped her underwear apart as if it were paper.

"I'm sorry," he muttered, his fingers exploring every inch of her ripe, open and moist hairless pussy, inserting into her. She moaned.

"Don't stop," she implored, and his movements became more rapid and she began to pant with mounting passion.

"Take me, now!," she insisted as he pushed her onto the double sized sofa as they both pulled off their remaining clothes until they were naked.

"Are you sure you want me to make love to you?" he asked.

"No," she hissed, "I want you to fuck me!"

Without any more preamble, he pushed himself into her, unable to wait. It was as if a dam burst within him as he pounded into her with savage intensity, his cock piercing-deep within her as she matched his every move with her hips thrusting back at him, her legs wrapping around his muscular torso. They fucked like animals, no sounds except the slapping of his balls on her ass, and each of them gasping for breath as their sweat and juices mingled until he started to orgasm. She felt this and her pussy contracted around him, milking him and feeling her own multiple orgasm overcoming her. They clung to each to one another as their storm of passion overcame them.

Eventually they both subsided, and he kissed her mouth, eyes, cheeks and ears. The Princess smiled, content with him still locked in her. "You're my first gay lover, and if that's how it goes, I don't think I shall ever change back. But now we know that you're bi-sexual, at least, yes?" She stroked his hair, smoothing it, as if discovering how well-formed he was.

He looked at her and liked what he saw. "You're my first royalty of either sex, and it gets worse, my Princess."

She tilted her head to one side. "I'm Jewish."

She started to laugh and he joined her, and soon she was helpless. As they separated, she pointed at him.

"If they found me with anyone except a husband in my country they would chop of both our heads, but to be fucked by a Jewish gay man! For that I could really get in trouble!"

"What could they do. Chop your head off, then sew it back on to chop it off a second time?" He laughed, but realized the danger they were in if they were ever discovered. "I know why I did this, but you… why, you must be crazy!"

She looked at him, her eyes staring hard at his before she kissed him again, this time with less passion but more intimacy and friendship.

"Yes, perhaps I am a little, maybe I like danger a bit too much, but it's serious, if my brother or the family, in fact anyone, found out about us, there would be a whole line of people waiting to kill us both and it isn't a joke. Where I come from I'm not allowed to even drive a car so going to bed with a Jew wouldn't be good."

He sat up to look at her wonderful toned body, and thought of the strange fate that had brought him to this time and place.

"Seriously, why are you here, is it business or pleasure?"

She laughed again. "I like to mix it up a bit, but I arrived here for business then spotted an opportunity for pleasure, but yes, business. I was sent here for business, not because I'm so highly rated, but more because I think my brother doesn't think he can trust anyone else so completely."

Eddie thought for a moment, then responded. "I've heard some stories about your brother..." He let it hang for a moment.

She tilted her head, as if to say, if you've got something to say come on, out with it.

"What do you mean exactly?" she asked. He hesitated, so she continued, filling the otherwise silent gap.

"Yes, he is a bit volatile my brother. In fact, some say he's maybe a little crazy, but I would say he's crazy like a fox."

Eddie was happy to listen, he'd learned one lesson from his adoptive father, and that was to let others talk and you listen, that's how you discover information, what makes people tick. Most people, Max had taught him, learn nothing because they're too busy talking to listen and watch.

She lit a small black cigarette and much to Eddie's discomfort, blew the smoke out indiscriminately.

"We own twenty five percent of this company. We have every right to be here, and to have our views heard. Do you have some objection to that?"

She asked him. Eddie shook his head and stroked her hair.

"You're picking a fight with yourself. I love you being here, what could be nicer?"

She pushed his hand away and jumped up, standing by the bed and becoming progressively angrier. "Don't patronize me because I'm a woman!" she shouted. He raised his hand in a gesture of self-defence, but couldn't keep the smile from his face as he watched her berate him while they were both still naked.

"Don't you dare laugh at me, you pig!" she shouted, but the more she raised the volume, the harder he found it to restrain his laughter.

"Whatever you say, but it's very hard to take you too seriously when your lovely wobbly bits are waving in front of my face."

"It's true!" she shouted.

"What my mother said, you are all boys, and none of you ever become grown up men except in one department."

She moved her arm back to slap his smiling face, but he effortlessly caught her hands in his before she could strike him.

"There's really nothing to be angry about is there?" he asked her, encircling her with his long arms, and pulling her to him in a comfortable embrace. At first she playfully tried to pull away from him, but she liked the feeling and strength of his warm body. He kissed her shoulders and neck, while he whispered,

"Tell me what you want me to do and I will be happy to do it." she groaned with pleasure as he nuzzled her neck and stroked her back.

"This isn't fair, I want to talk about business."

But it was hard for her to concentrate as he let his hands wander, one stroking her strong, sleek rump and the other tracing a path from her tumescent nipples down across her breasts, stroking down her taut stomach to her sex. Despite herself, she felt her own wetness as she involuntarily responded to his touch.

"We can discuss business if you like," he suggested, but she held his hand to the smooth apex of her ripe sex.

"Shut up, you bastard."

All her resistance withered, she lay back on the bed, opening her legs and pulled him on to her, and without any help, his manhood found and entered her in one thrust of all-consuming pleasure.

"Now make love to me." she whispered.

This time their lovemaking was more languid, richer, and more fulfilling as their earlier sheer urgency and lust was replaced with shared intimacies and the beginnings of mutual knowledge of what gave the other pleasure.

Neither the Princess nor Eddie was aware of the concealed digital cameras and sound equipment that recorded their every movement. They would have been shocked and terrified had they seen her adopted brother, his boyhood friend Prince Mohammed Aziz, watching the action on his laptop computer from his own cabin less than one kilometre away.

"Got you, my precious little sister!" he said to himself as he smiled, checking to see the whole thing was being recorded for posterity on his hard drive.

Later Princess Aziz and Eddie lay in each other's arms, both aware that theirs was an explosive sexual chemistry rarely found in a lifetime. He wasn't sure how to deal with this new intimacy, having never previously shared himself so completely with a woman. The Princess was also confused. She had, after all, been assigned the duty of preserving the interests of the Royal family of Saudi Arabia. How could either of them have predicted that such an unlikely mating would happen? She was under no illusions. Despite her brother instructing her to do anything necessary to secure their position on the deal, he wouldn't have imagined that she would have behaved with such depraved recklessness. But she was a woman who was used to getting her way, and what her brother didn't know wouldn't hurt him. How could life be #exciting if there were no risks?

Eddie, on the other hand, was more pensive and withdrawn. He was confused by both his emotions and sexual self identification. For many years, he had been content in the knowledge that he was gay and proud. He had never thought about women sexually. In fact, he had been certain that he was going to spend his life with Barry. After all, he had loved him so completely that he had wanted their partnership solemnized in a civil ceremony, and yet here he was, in bed with a passionate and very womanly woman. But, as ever, Eddie forced himself to be pragmatic and to deal with the business issues before all else. His life had taught him one great lesson; if you had money, you had choices, so the first thing to consider was always how to get more money because that created power, freedom of choice, above all, the freedom from worry about the basic tools of life. Food, shelter, travel and the right to say what you want, when you want to whom you like.

"What does the Royal House of Saud want me to do with this little company?" he asked.

"What is your intention?" she asked by way of a reply. He considered this, then decided the truth might be unwise at this juncture, better to listen a little bit more. "I don't really have a plan, I was just going with the flow. You know they want me, I mean us, to let the French win the bid, and we get paid to vanish this time around and they get this deal, we get one of the next few deals. It might be a good idea really, we haven't got the infrastructure, we're property developers and they're talking about some facilities and a new town or suchlike, and we wouldn't know where to begin with a project like that, would we."

She propped herself up and pulled on a silk bathrobe while he talked.

When he finished she smiled and started to talk as if to a bright child.

"You have no idea, do you?" She let the question hang a moment before continuing. "This isn't about a town being built, although of course there will be whole new cities rising out of the desert, no, this is much bigger than that. This development is the biggest single military construction project in the world. It is going to be the hub of the new Saudi defence forces, a central platform for both the army and air force, with its own missile defence umbrella being developed, guess where?"

He shrugged.

"I don't know, but I'd guess America or Britain?"

She laughed again.

"Try again" she teased.

"I give in. There's only really France and Russia left with that kind of technology, or maybe China?"

She paused for effect, then moved closer to him, whispering in his ear. "This you're never going to believe, but it's the Israelis. They're selling us their three tier Steel Dome technology to protect us from a missile attack. I promise you, its true."

Eddie whistled between his teeth. "You're kidding me!"

He said quietly but emphatically. "Why would Israel give you, their avowed enemy, a missile umbrella?"

Now it was her turn to sound a little patronizing. "Have you never heard the phrase the Israelis and we sometimes use, a wisdom both our peoples share, 'the enemy of my enemy is my friend'?"

He was still unconvinced, but something about her claim struck him as a real possibility. "Look at the foreign policy of Saudi Arabia and Israel, and tell me the difference."

She stated with some venom.

He thought about this, then responded. "Even if this is true, what difference can we make to what's happening? We're too small to be of any interest to anyone. This whole thing is way over our level." Now it was her turn to pause. She sighed, then continued. "Normally yes, we would be of no consequence whatsoever. We're too small to be on anyone's radar, but sometimes there are accidents of history, and this is one of those. We're just in the right place at the right time—"

"Or..."

He interrupted: "The wrong place at the wrong time, depending on your point of view."

She smiled and nodded, her beautiful eyes focused on his face.

"Yes, but there is nothing written in anyone's bible saying we can't make a profit out of lucky circumstance, is there?"

He joined her laughter and pulled her to him. "I think we have time for us to enjoy something even better than conversation."

He kissed her, and they were lost in each other.

In the cabin nearby, Mo watched and listened, and shook his head in wry amusement.

"Who would have thought my brother could behave in such a way, and with my sister, a Princess of Islam. Isn't this nearly incest?"

He picked up the mobile satellite phone and placed the call to The Leader.

The call was received by the most feared terrorist in the world, The Leader was top of the wanted lists of every major democracy whose citizens he had murdered in his "holy war" against the non believing infidels. He was in his comfortable, well-guarded villa in the walled compound near the town of Peshawar in the Islamic Republic of Pakistan, not far from the road to Islamabad near the border with Afghanistan.

Chapter Forty-One

The Leader's Villa, Peshawar, Pakistan
29th. October 2020 – 13.00 hours.

The Americans had posted a one hundred million dollar reward for the Leader to be brought to justice, "Dead or Alive". But the picture they had of the man was thirty years out of date. He had carefully avoided the prying eyes of any camera lens, knowing that one day his life might depend on his anonymity. His plans had always been long-term and deadly. He was no longer the longhaired, clean-shaven student at the London School of Economics, the wild child of rich parents from the best parts of Beirut and Paris. He had changed his identity and appearance so many times even the Leader was not sure how he would have looked without his two face-altering surgical procedures. The first had shortened his originally rather hook nose, and fixed his teeth with a perfect Hollywood smile. He had decided that, as the voice of his people, he had needed to look his best. Then when he realized he couldn't let anyone know his true identity, he had the second surgery. This had changed the shape of his eyes, making them less hooded, and removing the bags underneath. He had grown his beard to a greater length, and dyed his facial hair a lighter golden brown. He had allowed the beard to grow not because of his religious beliefs, but because he wasn't happy how his cheeks looked after the surgeon had plumped his face where it had once looked gaunt. He thought he looked like a squirrel that had nuts in his mouth, and he had been very angry when he'd seen the results in a mirror in the private clinic in Switzerland. So angry that he had decided the surgeon should pay his own version of a penalty clause. He would never botch up anyone else's face now that his right hand had been hacked off.

The Leader believed in unremitting warfare, and it didn't matter if the battle lasted a hundred or a thousand years, he knew that eventually his brand of Islam would win against the decadent and disbelieving. He was already preparing for the day when the Great Satan, America, was destroyed, along with its British lackeys. Once those two were finally powerless, the rest of the Europeans would collapse as a viable enemy. Then the Zionist entity would have no friends left to help them and their destruction would be certain. Then and only then, could his attention shift to the ultimate battle, and the final victory, against Russia, India and China.

But, that would be in the years that followed and experience instructed the Leader that he had to remain calm for the many battles still yet to materialize. He quietly enjoyed being known simply as the Leader, happy that no other name was necessary. As his family of business people would have said, his was a brand identity that the whole world recognized. He had been the natural successor to that fool Bin Laden and his redundant, soft Al-Qaeda movement and the misguided, simple minded Islamic State in all its guises. They talked of changing the world order, but the Leader was actually doing it, and bring the infidels and unbelievers to their knees before the one true prophet.

The conversation was brief, the Leader kept his communications very short for fear of being traced. He was confident that no one knew his voice or where to look for him. The Americans and the British had repeatedly stated that they believed he was hiding in the wild tribal area between Afghanistan and Pakistan, and their search, he knew, had taken them recently to Wajiristan.

He had even had one of his body-doubles sleeping in different hovels and caves every night for months now, to give the American Navy Seals and British Special Boat Squadron a phantom to chase. He enjoyed the thought that he had outwitted them and all their sophistication.

Mo, or 'The Prince' as he was known in the movement, impressed The Leader. The Prince had risen high and fast in the newly-reorganized Al-Qaeda, and was now recognized as the top ranked of the next generation of freedom fighters. The Leader considered Mo extremely bright, knowledgeable in the methods and life styles of their enemies, and committed to their destruction, without any fear of consequence.

He admired the younger man's ruthless dedication to the cause, his ferocity and the fear he created in their enemies. He also appreciated the fact that the young man had limitless funds only a heartbeat away and the perfect cover story.

The Leader was only on the satellite telephone long enough to hear Mo say, "Everything is in place, the deal will go ahead as planned, if Allah pleases."

The Leader responded, "Allah be praised!"

Before disconnecting the call. He threw the instrument to his courier and trusted associate for instant disposal, since the Leader never used the same phone twice. But this time, his legendary caution was not enough. Due to the fact that the Americans had not been able to monitor his call directly, they had instead managed to plant a tiny tracking and recording device in his unwitting courier's thyroid pill container that had made it possible for the Americans to know, for the first time in many years, where the Leader was, and what he was doing and saying. He was unaware of this when he took another offered phone.

"Are you certain this is clean and untraceable?" he asked the young, nervous man who nodded. "My Leader, I swear it on my life."

The Leader stared into the younger man's eyes and stroked his own long black beard. He knew it made people around him very nervous when he stared at them, and that was the reason he had used this device. It never occurred to any of his devout and fanatical followers that he dyed his beard and under his snow-white turban his head was bald. The Leader had long since learned that his reputation for sudden and extreme violence was as effective in getting what he wanted as the actual use of torture. But those around him knew that the Leader would not hesitate to order mutilation, torture or decapitation if his plans for global Islamic domination were threatened. He was proud to be called a fanatic if that was how the world outside defined a true believer. He accepted only total obedience from those who followed him, from others he demanded either surrender or death.

"Place the call."

He instructed the courier, who did so nervously. He then handed the phone back to the Leader who waved his assistant away, leaving him alone in his office area, impatiently waiting for the connection.

"Remember, never more than five paces distant my friend," he hissed at the courier. They both knew what this meant. If there was an attempt on the Leader's life, he wanted those close to him to realize that they would also perish. On the third ring, a man with a high-pitched voice responded in perfect English, as if he was a broadcaster for the BBC World Service, which is where the President Rafsanjani of the Islamic Republic of Iran had in fact learned the language, as a young man listening to the broadcasts from London when he was in exile as a student in Pakistan and the hated Shah was still in power in Tehran.

"Is that you, my friend?"

The Leader grinned. After all this was his oldest friend, from the days when they studied together in the religious school in Islamabad, planning and plotting, so many years before.

"Yes it is."

They didn't need to swap names because they recognized each other.

"I wish I could look upon your face, my friend," The Leader said to the President. "It would be wonderful. But is there something I can do for my brother?"

There was no need for explanation because they had been working in harmony for so many years, they and their brothers in Hamas, Hezbollah and the Taliban, and of course all the Islamic Brotherhood members who recognized that their battle against the Zionist and Imperialists was to be the final battle, to the death.

"It appears as if the keys to the Kingdom have fallen into our hands." As the two men held their clandestine and coded conversation they considered secure, they were unaware that every word was being recorded, automatically transcribed and distributed among the combined secret intelligence agencies of their sworn enemies in the U.S.A. and U.K.

Two unmanned Predator drones were re-directed from their patrol areas, and flying unseen at four hundred miles per hour, some forty thousand feet in the sky above, they were quickly triangulated toward the Leader and the President in their two different locations. The two craft were flown by two very different remote pilots: one in Italy a Brit, Flight Lieutenant Greg Page was in charge of the aircraft high above Iran, and the other, a young American woman, Marine Sergeant Marie Rosenthal, was in a darkened room staring at her control screen in the Las Vegas military aviation centre.

Their Predators were in the air for up to two days at a time, and each was heavily armed with laser-guided cruise missiles. These robot craft never got tired or bored. In fact, they could stay aloft, their cameras taking perfect 4D pictures from high in the sky, and then, unseen and unheard, make their kill entirely without warning. But today they were instructed not to administer the kill order.

Greg Page sighed. He would love to have ruined the mad Mullah's day in Iran, but his was not to reason why, but simply to do or die. He was a fine young officer who did as he was told.

Marie Rosenthal the young Marine Sergeant operating in the Nevada desert had a different agenda. She was a fine technician, with an unblemished record which had her earmarked for a speedy promotion track, but that was going to change on this day. Before anyone realized what she was doing, she had confirmed the target co-ordinates and issued the fire and forget instructions to her Predator's Cruise Missile deployment. No one but Marie initially knew that her missile had launched and was targeted at the Leader. No one knew that she longed for just such an opportunity as she was a committed Zionist who was dedicated to the survival of Israel at any cost, and who considered the top echelon of the control and command infrastructure of the terrorist movement to be the head of the snake that had to be decapitated, as existential threats to the future of not only the Jewish state, but also of the western world she, and everybody she cared for, inhabited.

The Chinese space military tracking station carefully noted that the Americans had fired one of their cruise missiles in the direction of a target in Pakistan. Their technician passed the information to his commanding officer who, in turn, relayed this information to the High Command General in Bejing, who was in charge of this sector, via his secure phone line. The general simply thanked his junior officer and continued with his lunch, a superb duckling in a sweet sauce, prepared with some expertise by his favourite mistress, content in the knowledge that another Muslim terrorist was about to be blown into countless pieces, and that he, High Command General, was going to be pleasured by his delectable young mistress. This was turning into the perfect day. Another mad Muslim terrorist future enemy dead and the American Imperialists to be blamed by another future client state for China.

The Leader had inherited some of the tastes of Osama Bin Laden; the maximum number of four wives allowed a good practicing Muslim man. He sometimes found it difficult to please the needs of each of them every night as was their original habit. He blamed the high dosage of pills for high blood pressure he had been taking for the last five or six years. Sometimes he just didn't have the strength, or even the will, to want to be with any of his wives. Each of them was capable, in their unique way, of showing their displeasure. He had first tried some internet porn to spice up his waning interest, but the positive effect it had on him when he was watching didn't last while he was in an intimate position. What was more annoying, was that the women had gossiped and consulted with each other over the problem and had openly defied him. He was ready to make an example of Adiba, his first wife, when she showed him the packet of small blue pills and insisted he tried it with whichever of the wives he wanted that night. He couldn't admit he was nervous of the pill giving him a heart attack. He had no alternative so he took the pill with a glass of water and summoned Adiba to his room. After all if was going to die of a heart attack it would be while he was on top of the old bitch!

His wife entered the room and saw that he had taken the pill. She looked at her husband and smiled as he pulled up the sheet and revealed himself, proving that the pill had worked. Her smile broadened into a grin as she pulled off her nightdress to reveal she was still a desirable and voluptuous woman, perhaps a little more rounded than had been the case many years before, but still able to excite her man, one way or the other. She climbed into the bed and they embraced. "Welcome home to my arms." she whispered.

It was the final sound either of them heard as the missile tore through the window and evaporated everything and everyone within a fifteen-metre radius.

The Predator targeting the Iranian President was recalled. He would live a little longer.

Thousands of miles away in the Nevada desert, Marine Sergeant Marie Rosenthal was watching the images flash back from the nose cone camera of the cruise missile as it transmitted up to the moment of the detonation, delayed a couple of seconds by the distance of transmission. Although she was a trained technician, she couldn't restrain herself from a whoop of exhilaration as the missile exploded killing the Leader and his team of murderers. Marie thought for a fleeting moment about his family but then her attention turned to how she was going to file her report. She began typing into her computer log that she had a rogue missile release with unknown consequences, but she couldn't keep the smile from her face. At last, all her years of training and dedication had paid a dividend. An enemy of civilization had been eliminated and she wished she could shout it out to the world. Later tonight she would make the call to her contact in New York City and that woman, pretending to be her cousin, would relay the news to Tel Aviv. No one could be certain just yet, but another head of the monster had been cut off, and that was good.

The Prince was notified of the death of the Leader by telephone. He prayed briefly for the soul of the Leader but then smiled, his destiny now within his grasp. His destiny, to lead.

Chapter Forty-Two

Georges V Hotel, Paris, France
30th. October 2020 – 11.00 hrs.

Mo was exhilarated by the news coming from Pakistan. At last, his time had come.

Now he was to be The Leader, and the men entering the room over the last day had confirmed, one by one, that they were not going to challenge him. These were the inner circles of the High Command of the Warriors of Islam, and they understood strength, control, money and power. Of course, they also understood and agreed that the final outcome to be achieved was the coming global Caliphate in which Allah, the all merciful, would rule supreme over all the people of the world.

In the movement there were no elections, just measuring of strength, a test of survival, an ability to stay ahead of friends and enemies, a test he had always survived, and here he was, the perfect weapon for Al-Qaeda. Knowledgeable of the new methods and command systems, with intimate knowledge of the leading personnel of the western powers and how they controlled every aspect of their counter terrorism.

Above all, he was a recognized diplomat who was beyond suspicion, equipped with every code and access point for the entire hierarchy of the enemy. He was the perfect weapon to target at the hated enemies of Islam.

Now he would make sure that new funding would help the movement regain some of its lost prominence and he knew how to access money so vast that they would no longer be the under equipped underdogs. He hated the fact that the last few years had been marked by inefficient, corrupt fat accountants insisting that all the operatives presented receipts for all items of expenditure over ten dollars. What kind of revolution was this when the bean counters had control over strategy? This was one of his first steps; kick out the shyster lawyers and accountants and give power back to the warriors.

The symmetry of using the silly little company of his 'brother' to front the collection of Saudi Arabian money to fund the downfall of the west and all those who supported them, was perfect.

All he had to do was drive through the deal and quickly eliminate all opposition to it, and that would be his pleasure.

Chapter Forty-Three

Private Meeting Room, Chamonix, France
30ᵗʰ. October 2020 – 11.00 hours

The Princess sat at the board table looking calm, as if she knew all the moves. Montcalm was becoming exasperated, thought Eddie, as the Frenchman pointedly looked at his beautiful platinum Longines watch; number one of only five ever made to the same design.

"But your Highness, it seems as if there must be some misunderstanding. I already have an agreement with your company, reached with your principal, and major shareholder, Mister Roman here. Isn't this correct, Mister Roman?"

He made the question sound like a statement as he turned his attention to Eddie.

Eddie shrugged. "Well, we didn't actually sign on the dotted line. We had an understanding based on information you'd given me, which, quite frankly, we could call, how shall we say it, is less than full, n'est ce pas?"

Montcalm bristled, but the circumstances were too important for him to blow this deal based on his desire to ring the neck of these two amateurs. He turned on his Gallic charm full beam.

"Could a slightly larger inducement help you see it my way?" He asked, as if they were sharing some very sophisticated joke. Before Eddie could enquire how much larger, the Princess interjected. "This is a matter of Arabic unity. We believe we should be undertaking the large-scale reconstruction of our region ourselves. Why do we need your meddling, when you so clearly are the cause of our problems? No, we intend to honour our agreements, so the question becomes how much does it take to pay you all to go away?"

Eddie smiled at the sheer chutzpah of her attempt to turn the tables on the smooth Frenchman, who, in turn, was finding it almost impossible to contain his fury.

"This is an outrage your Highness. We have an agreement in..."

Before he could complete the sentence, Eddie interrupted him.

"But of course any such agreement would equate to your having formed a cartel and that would be illegal and improper. It would be our duty to report any such cartel as good friends of the House of Saud, now that it has been made clear to us, don't you agree?"

Montcalm sat down, deflating like a burst balloon. "We have only a very short time to make new arrangements. Tell me what you can accept and I shall see if I can sell it to the rest of the group. You know we have a system that works, we can't change it now, its way too late for that."

The Princess rose to her feet imperiously. What an actress, thought Eddie, as she faced Montcalm. "You know our room number."

Montcalm hadn't got to the top of a mighty international conglomerate without some guile and spirit of his own. He stood and faced her.

"You don't have the means to undertake such a project. You're two people from a paper company trying to make yourselves important, and your whole world is collapsing around you. Do you not understand this is not just trouble from a bunch of major companies. You're about to upset, how do you say, really piss off the most powerful and dangerous governments as well and they don't sue, they eliminate silly little problems such as you."

Eddie stood and confronted Montcalm. "Is that meant to be a threat?"

Montcalm simply smiled.

"No, it's a warning, from one business man to another. You don't want this, trust me, it is not your world."

Now it was Eddie's turn to smile. "Your homework is simply not good enough, is it? This is exactly my kind of trouble."

He turned to the Princess. "Come on, your Highness, it is time for us to leave." She smiled and stood to join her newfound partner as they walked to the door just as the other members of the cartel began to enter. Montcalm held up his elegantly-manicured hand, his annoying smile plastered to his face. As if he were the puppet master, in control of the situation, he addressed Eddie and the Princess.

"Do you want to explain what you're doing, or would you prefer me to do so on your behalf?"

The Princess suppressed her anger but her eyes narrowed. Eddie took the initiative. "We can talk for ourselves."

He turned to face the group, who looked at him inquisitively. "As you can see, ladies and gentlemen, the Princess and I are about to leave since the terms offered to us on the cartel's behalf are simply not acceptable."

Madam Kim, the Chinese lady, who was normally so silent, turned her staring catlike eyes from Montcalm past Eddie and settled on the Princess.

"Perhaps her Highness..." she made the word sound like an insult "...would like to inform the meeting exactly what she would find acceptable so that we might consider the position."

The Princess returned her stare, ignoring the men.

"That's simple, we want it all." And with that she turned and led Eddie from the room. There was a moment of stunned silence before the room erupted in an angry hubbub of voices.

Chapter Forty-Four

The Adeneaur Suite, The Adler Hotel, Berlin, Germany
3rd. November 2020 – 16.00 hours

Mo was now in full white silk Arabic clothes. He enjoyed the freedom of the costume, and the fact that the westerners who serviced the room showed some respect and perhaps a little fear when they brought his strictly Halal refreshments to him. His plan was working.

One-by-one, he was splitting the old European super powers out of the equation of terror. Sitting with him was the youthful Foreign Minister of Germany, the frumpy but famously brilliant, Eva Schwartz and the representative from France, the floppy haired, highly cultured, aristocratic Henri Le Conte. They had entered in disguise, out of cars that had pulled up outside the hidden, below-ground service entrance of the hotel, guarded by their large and discreet security teams who ushered them to the service elevators on up to the suite.

All diplomats for the western powers had extremely large additional security surrounding them since the recent assassinations of the Israeli and American diplomats in Washington. The irony of having additional Special Forces surrounding these diplomats when they were meeting the groups suspected of organizing the recent murders didn't escape the security men.

Mo rose to greet his guests, his hand extended to the Frenchman, who shook it, and then Mo moved to his seat facing his guests, studiously avoiding any physical contact with the German woman. They sat in the comfortable wing chairs assessing each other.

"Would you like some tea, coffee?" Mo asked his guests. Schwartz smiled as she raised her hand to decline, but Le Conte made no pretence at friendship, allowing his clear resentment at having to attend this meeting to show. The Frenchman looked at his watch somewhat theatrically and Mo smiled.

"You have somewhere more important to attend, Foreign Minister?" he asked, barely keeping the sarcasm from his voice.

Le Conte sighed and shook his handsome head. "No, monsieur, but our absence will be noticed by the media if we are not quick about this. Therefore, with the utmost courtesy, could you, as our American friends would express it, cut to the chase?"

Schwartz was almost unable to keep the triumphant look from her face, but she was a diplomat of the old fashioned sort, and didn't allow her emotions to show.

Personally she liked the courteous young Arab better than the prickly, arrogant, pompous Frenchman. Mo poured himself a cup of tea, and his guests noticed the label on the teabag it was English Breakfast Tea, and the German woman mentally filed this piece of information; anything might prove useful one day.

The Prince looked at them both and took a long sip of his drink before he spoke. "It's my habit to sum up a situation briefly as a starting point. You can no longer describe the Middle East as if it were one mass of Arab dictatorships. The Arab Spring in 2011 took care of that. After that, there came new dictatorships, some systems you would describe as democracies, and some Islamic republics. Almost all of them share many common belief and economic systems, young populations, backing for the Palestinian cause and non-acceptance of a Jewish-only state in Israel."

He paused, letting his words settle in, and then continued, "The classic saying states that one man's terrorist is another man's freedom fighter.

There was a time, very recently in fact, when your country," he indicated Le Conte, "...foolishly banned the wearing of traditional and religiously obligated clothing, as if this would hide the truth, which is in the war of ideas the old western Imperial powers were losing, and Islamic ideas and beliefs were winning. It is inevitable."

Frau Schwartz had always thought that the particular piece of legislation Mo was describing had been a retrograde mistake sure to cause repercussions, but she hadn't had herself smuggled to this place to have a political lecture in her country about an ally from a terrorist.

"That is all most interesting, but can you tell me what it is you want from this meeting today?"

Mo didn't like being interrupted, particularly by a woman, and it didn't matter how important the woman might think she is. He held up his hand to stop her, but she pretended not to notice.

"I speak for my country," said Le Conte, but was ignored by the other two people both of whom considered irrelevant. Frau Schwartz stared hard at Mo and asked.

"And what, exactly is your role within your… organization?"

Mo's grip was so tight on the arms of his chair that his knuckles had turned white.

The German lady noticed this with satisfaction. The French Minister reluctantly admired her, despite the fact that he disliked being judged so obviously unimportant in this conversation.

"I speak for the organization!"

He responded, hating the fact that his voice had risen, and was almost comically high.

"You are the leader of the organization?" she asked, drilling down. He nodded almost imperceptibly, but it could have been read more than one way; like everything he appeared to say or do, it was nebulous, shifting with the sands of time, whereas his actions appeared so definite.

"Was that a yes? You are the leader? We need to know, the world wants to know."

Mo enjoyed the moment. "You need to know so you can arrange a drone to kill me here, in nice civilized Paris?"

His guests looked to one another and then Frau Schwartz spoke.

"You know that neither of our governments had anything whatsoever to do with any of the political killings of the organization's leadership."

"We didn't hear you condemning these murders at the United Nations, did we?" he asked, before continuing. "But these are, as you intimate, stale arguments, and we all want to move forward, don't we?"

His guests smiled and nodded.

"I offer a new vision," Mo continued, "One we can work together on, isn't that what we all desire? We need to take smaller steps, not seek to find instant solutions to long- term problems. We all agree on this. From our organization, this is a new perspective. We don't change our goals, but we are changing the route to get to our destination."

"What exactly does this mean?" the German woman asked. Mo smiled again, he had expected detailed questions from her, and knew it was vital to his cause that he convince the woman, and if he managed to do this the French would follow, and therefore most of Europe. The British were, as always, a contrary nation, they would be work for another day.

"We still desire and will create an Islamic Caliphate across the borders of such countries as Afghanistan and Pakistan, but we are prepared to participate in an orderly transition, one in which we take part in shared governments. We can work this way, together, you and we, in Syria, Egypt, Turkey, and Saudi Arabia. We can even work together with the Jews in a federation of Palestine and Israel, in a one state, secular final solution to the Jewish question. That way, there is to be no problems in sharing the ground between the sea and the river Jordan, no one would have a problem with Jerusalem being the capital of this new country, the settlements could house both Arab and Jewish people, and the law of return for all the Jews and all the Palestinians would be shared."

The Frenchman and the German woman were silent, just as Mo wanted. "The rich countries will contribute the money they currently invest in aid, and providing defence presently to the two entities and instead this cash will be an investment in the future, helping to fund the building of new cities, industries and infrastructure."

"You can sell this to the Palestinians?" asked Frau Schwartz.

He answered quickly. "If you can sell it to the Americans so that they can make the Israelis fall into line, yes, I will deliver the Palestinians."

The French Foreign Minister could barely contain himself. He was, he thought, in the room while history was being made. He had always wanted his place in history to be more than a footnote and here was the opportunity. "

We can deal with the Americans and the Israelis," he assured Mo, but the German woman was less easy to convince.

"Why do you change course like this, after so many years of hate and intransigence?"

Mo stood and looked down at the two foreign ministers. "Perhaps after our most recent conflict, we have learned from your two countries. It wasn't so long ago that two great world wars started here, in the heart of Europe, and your two countries still managed to find a way to become friends with open borders and common policies. How can you deny us the same opportunity? Why would you want to? Do we have an understanding?"

After agreeing general deal terms, the two foreign Ministers left with the promise that they would prepare an outline agreement that would be presented to the Americans, Israelis and Palestinians for discussion and ratification.

The two diplomats left the hotel suite exhilarated by their meeting, not realizing for a second that like many others they had been fooled by the plausible new leader of Al- Qaeda. In his mind they were simply useful idiots. He had no intention of sharing anything with the Jews who would be eliminated from the future Palestine. No Jew would ever be allowed to live there. The Caliphate would engulf all the infidels. Mo's aide Nafti entered the room after their guests had left.

"A call, my Leader!"

He extracted a cell phone from his pocket. Mo knew it was a one time pre-paid instrument that would be discarded after this call, untraceable even by the cyber war experts that the Americans employed at their National Security Agency or the British GCHQ in Cheltenham. What he didn't know was that the young Turkish Cypriot man who supplied their throw away phones at a considerable price via a small shop in London's Finsbury Park was actually an Israeli intelligence operative.

The cell telephone equipment that Mo was using came direct from a very smart lab full of brilliant young women and men working at the Israel Defence Forces Operations Department in Tel Aviv, the real hub of that country's cyber warfare effort, not a back street in Turkish Cyprus

Mo issued carefully coded instructions to his contact about picking up a table from their old district in Basra, Iraq.

The listeners in Tel Aviv decoded Mo's words almost immediately and, disregarded the information referring to something written under God's table, thinking that the Prince was simply being somewhat nostalgic or wistful, as he brought the world to the brink of catastrophe, threatening the world with dirty nuclear bombs that, with wonderful irony, had been conceived, created and buried in the desert by Saddam Hussein.

Mo held the world in the palm of his hand, and the realization made him aware that greatness awaited him.. It all depended on what secrets were under the table God had given to Noah to build his ark. All anyone had to do was find the ancient table and follow the directions and then nothing would protect his chosen people from being completely destroyed by this deluge.

Chapter Forty-Five

Israel Intelligence H.Q., Tel Aviv, Israel
4th. November 06.00 hours

The Israelis continued recording both sides of the Prince's conversation since video and sound recording was continuous once the phone was live. The instant Mo started speaking, the computers in a subterranean room, about one hundred feet beneath the nondescript building in a street near Dizengoff Square, Tel Aviv, had activated, summoning well-trained human intelligence officers to come and listen. The Israeli intelligence officers knew that such calls were routinely encoded.

Daniel shrugged. He was a young, slim, wispily bearded man habitually dressed in a white long sleeved shirt and black trousers. He was just back from gaining his PhDin America's Harvard University.

"It's heavily encoded." he announced to the three-person team of analysts who had rushed over to his area, each one of them with their own Doctoral qualifications and ever eager to prove their genius.

"How long to decode it, Danny?" asked Shimon, his commanding officer. Dan shrugged again. He liked being a little enigmatic, he thought it made him mysterious and attractive to his female colleague Rivkah. He didn't like being called Danny which he thought made him sound like a kid, and that wouldn't impress Rivkah. She was a blonde woman with corkscrew curly hair, deep blue eyes and an incredibly lush body. They were both the same rank and although younger than him, clearly more worldly. She never seemed to notice anything about him other than his work. Today, she was going to be impressed, he thought, as he realized he could break the code quite easily.

"Give me ten minutes," he said. He thought he saw Rivkah look in his direction for a moment and he liked the attention which was clear as he flashed his best smile, full of contrived confidence toward the group.

Shimon witnessed his young protégé Danny preening like a peacock as he sought to impress the girl rather than focusing his attention on the conversation he was decoding. Shimon preferred obtaining results efficiently and fast. He was a young man in a hurry. Everyone in the room was aware that their department, like their British and American counterparts were supposedly only collecting meta data with information relating to patterns of calls, duration and telephone systems used, together with the sending and receiving numbers.

In fact they had all moved way beyond their legal authority and were listening in on all calls of interest, anywhere in the world. When there was a possible breach of law in one of the other loosely allied countries, the other country would handle the matter for them and simple information swapping was happening round the clock. Using this simple trick they had, so far, avoided breaking their own laws, or better put, dodged the application of those laws.

This time Israel didn't need or want to share their information yet, and within ten minutes their team were listening to the two leaders of their sworn enemies, Iran and Al-Qaeda, plotting how to plant three dirty nuclear weapons in Tel Aviv. The Israeli intelligence and political establishments had long been bracing themselves for just such an eventuality but now it was becoming a reality it was still shocking. The estimates on the explosive power and fallout from these weapons varied wildly, but the least they expected was huge damage with tens of thousands of casualties and wherever was hit would be uninhabitable for many years to come.

Within five minutes Shira Lipna, Prime Minister of Israel received the dreaded phone call notifying her of this new threat.

"Is it possible they knew we were listening?" she asked, realizing that this could have been a double bluff on the part of Israel's enemies. She listened to the assurances of her intelligence chief that the call was genuine and the voices of the two men had been run through the stress analysis computer software, which had determined that there was a ninety-six percent probability that the men meant what they had said.

"Do we know when, or the source of the weapons?" she asked Motti Hopel, the legendary Head of Israel's secret service, Mossad. He was seated in his office communicating with her by video link, she noticed that he was lit so that he appeared to have a halo of light around his head. He spoke with the deep, throaty voice of a man now smoking his fortieth cigarette of the day despite the ban. Not a man bothered with rules except his own, he responded, "No, Prime Minister."

She paused, then decided to press the point. "...I thought we had eliminated the threat from Iran."

It was a rhetorical question but valid.

"If we can find the source, we can eliminate it before the threat becomes a reality, yes?" she asked.

The Intelligence veteran nodded. "Agreed, and we're tracking the possible sources back to their roots now, and when we find them they will be eliminated, but for now I suggest, most strongly, we go to Condition Red at once."

The Prime Minister smiled, thinking how bizarre it was that a country already under deadly attack from every one of its neighbours was now in jeopardy from an existential threat to its very survival.

"You need a politician to say the words? Condition Red, make it so," she said, not able to think of any alternative and knowing the potential consequences.

"As we have had this security conversation outside the war cabinet, will you be recording this conversation, Prime Minister?" Motti asked her.

"It's all recorded for posterity, my friend. You have a couple of hours, get started," she responded, and cut the connection. The Prime Minister wondered if this was to be the end game, when her people could no longer dodge the bullet. What had she left undone to save her people?

Chapter Forty-Six

Basra and The Desert, Iraq
4th. November 2020 – 07.15

The Rent Collector and his family had just returned from their day's work and were sitting at their old wooden table, waiting impatiently for their evening meal. They still lived in their working class suburb but the wars and tribulations had been kind to the Rent Collector and his large, extended family of four wives, thirteen children and various other family members who had attached themselves to his rising star.

He enjoyed his leadership position at the head of this table. At least here no one doubted his authority or they felt the back of his hand. There were no property owners to remind him that he would never reach their status. He enjoyed his special table even more now that his worthless camel of a son-in-law had eventually sanded it down and rid it of its blemishes, then varnishing over its imperfections. It was almost like new!

No one in the noisy family heard the big jeep roll to a stop outside the house. The first moment they understood there was a problem was when the group of six heavily-armed men dressed in military style uniforms ran towards the house. The invaders wore balaclavas to hide their faces, and this made them appear even more terrifying. Despite this two of the Rent Collector's sons tried to protest but one was shot in the stomach and the other was ruthlessly clubbed back into a seat.

The Rent Collector knew better than to resist such men and simply said, "Welcome to our home, gentlemen such an entrance is unnecessary. How can we, in this humble home, be of assistance as we are always more than willing to co-operate with the authorities?"

The man who appeared to lead the group turned to the Rent Collector. "Is this the old table you took from the Jews?"

The Rent Collector pointed to his wounded son, "May one of my women attend to my son's wounds, Sir?"

The man turned to the wounded young man and then his brother, he nodded to the soldier with the gun, "Now that one!"

The soldier shot the Rent Collector's second son, killing him instantly.

"The Table?"

The man pointed his gun at the Rent Collector's favourite young wife. The old man immediately indicated the table with a shrug.

"If you require Noah's Table, it is yours. We were just custodians."

The man turned to his soldiers. "Looks like junk, but take it."

His men swept the food from the table, making a mess on the floor and on the people sitting around the table. Several of them protested and as they did so the leader and another of his men opened fire with their semi-automatic weapons, leaving no one in the large family alive to bear witness. The last thing the Rent Collector ever saw was the old table being removed from amongst the carnage, and was left wondering why he and his family should be killed for the sake of such a thing.

The armed gang ran out with the table and loaded it carefully on to the back of their second open truck then sped away. Their leader positioned himself next to the table with his cell phone, sending images of it back to his high command. He couldn't see what was so special about the odd bit of furniture. Even though he was very quick to disconnect once he was sure the message had been transmitted, he hadn't been fast enough to evade either the Israeli or American geo-synchronous general Eytan satellites constantly watching for unusual communications in this tumultuous part of the world.

Both the Israelis and Americans deciphered the images almost instantly, but whereas the Israelis understood what they were seeing, the Americans would take longer to do so, the information having to travel through so many layers of analysis, bureaucracy and redundant duplication of inter-departmental management.

"From here on in we must presume they have the location of all the buried weapons of mass destruction from the table. Can we get there quickly enough to stop them getting the nukes?" Israel's Prime Minister asked the Commander of the Air Force, General Eytan

He shook his head.

"We have to overfly several hostile countries and the Americans still control the airspace over Iraq. We have to collaborate or end up in a dogfight with them."

"So after all this fighting, it comes down to Iranian backed terrorists getting their hands on nuclear weapons. I will not accept this situation. How much is buried there, and can we get to it. What do we do? Ideas please, now, gentlemen."

She looked around the war cabinet, at her military leaders, at the real leaders of her country.

"You wanted to take the lead, now is your chance. Why don't you tell us what we should do?"

There was silence as the implications of the situation shocked the others in the room.

"OK," she continued. "The only way forward is to enlist the help of our friends in America."

There was a general grumble of discontent. Motti Hopel puffed at his unlit pipe and raised his hand for attention. "Madam Prime Minister, if we tell the Americans this information they will know for certain that we have satellite, rocket and space technology way beyond anything we've ever made known previously. We've convinced them our birds are just weather satellites."

Eytan, the Air Force Chief took this as his cue.

"We can reach this target within three to four hours, but without co-operation, we might have to shoot down American birds, and we would also suffer large losses. But I swear, we would eliminate the targets, no one could stop us getting to them."

"Why waste time fighting our friends when we have so many enemies available," she smiled, but they all understood and couldn't dispute her logic,

"We need to combine with the Americans to deal with this. We need assets with a specific targeting capacity right here, right now. If you can't give me that solution this minute get out of my way."

Other people around the table began shouting to be heard but were silenced by the Prime Minister banging the table with the palm of her hand.

"We face an existential threat to our nation. Now is not the time to worry about tactics and secrets. Do you really believe the Americans don't know our technical capacity?"

She didn't wait for a reply.

"Get me President Pollaci right now."

In less than a minute, the two women were talking on a secure video link, and within a further few moments the Israeli technicians passed the relevant information to their American counterparts who targeted four advanced Predator drones with special facial recognition technology attached toward the target area in the soft belly of Israel, armed with air to ground missiles targeted at co-ordinates they'd intercepted during Prince Mohammed's telephone read out to his followers in Iraq.

Chapter Forty-Seven

Under the Old City, Jerusalem
4th. November 2020 – 10.20 hours

Prince Mo smiled as Nafti checked the co-ordinates from the table against a large contour map of the region.

"Quick, before we lose the connection. Where is it?"

Nafti located the map references and narrowed them down to the spot on the map matching the required longitude and latitude. Neither realized that the Israelis had already routed the American remotely-controlled attack drones to the same location.

Mo enjoyed the fact that he had been able to re-enter Jerusalem via the West Bank after being smuggled across the River Jordan. It had been easier than he thought it would be. Perhaps this was because the Jews were distracted with the wars they had caused by their presence as a cuckoo in the nest raging all around them. Now was the time, the moment the Islamic world had dreamed about. This was to be the final solution to the Zionist's unrealistic dreams of continuing to exist in an Islamic sea.

He looked around the dark, cavernous space buried deep beneath the Church of the Rock. The torches providing a flickering light as he sat with the leaders of Hamas and Hezbollah. He enjoyed being the power broker, the link between all these factions. He had proved that he was the first man able to bring them together to fight the common enemy. His weapon that allowed him to achieve this was to first weaken those regimes which might have been against his aims, and he had been brilliant in using his prime enemies' own strength to achieve this goal. Once the Iranians and others he considered western stooges had been neutralized, it left the field open for his more direct form of warfare against the Zionist entity.

Sheikh Younis, the elderly leader of Hamas, sighed theatrically.

"So, here we sit, in the belly of the beast, waiting for our forces to unleash a nuclear device, and you think the Jews will not retaliate?" he asked as he stroked his long red beard, his snow-white turban sitting at a jaunty slant on his large head.

"Retaliate against who?" replied Mo, trying hard to maintain a serious demeanor, although he wanted to laugh.

"You don't understand. These people doing this thing, they are not our people, and they are as Jewish as any of our enemy. What Stalin used to call 'useful idiots'. We have Jews to kill Jews. What could be any better than this?"

The other two men looked at each other, then Abu Arafat, the extreme hardline leader of Hezbollah, shook his head. "This is certain, these are real Jews. You will be able to prove it afterwards?"

Mo turned on the big-screen Apple monitor, and on the screen appeared three men and a woman seated behind a trestle table.

"Look at the definition on this screen, you just couldn't count the number of pixels in that image. Perfect!" At the centre of the group was Landau, the same man who had supported the British Nazis in their fight against their enemies, the Islamists in that country.

"Hello, shalom, my name is Landau. I run a group called the Zionist Opposition Group – some of you might know it better by the name, ZOG – and the three people sitting next to me are also members of the same organization. Their names are Hetty Miller, Baruch Goldstein and Mendel Blum."

The camera panned across the unremarkable group.

"...And together we have become martyrs for the cause of Zionism, the right of Jews to live in a free and democratic country of their own."

He paused for effect.

"...When you see this film, we will have already taken direct action to eliminate the Islamic curse from our country once and for all, and we shall be safe in the arms of the Lord. We do this not to kill or maim but to make the world understand that we, like our enemies, are also capable of any action to achieve our ends, just like our enemies, and we will not hesitate to take any further actions necessary to bring the return to Zion of all the Jews of the world so that the prophecies are fulfilled in readiness for the Messiah."

The watching group were happy

"Allah has been generous in supplying us with such fools." said Sheikh Younis.

"This video was made by the Jewish suicide bombers before they set out on their mission to wipe out the centres of Tel Aviv and Haifa. We will have incontrovertible medical evidence, including DNA samples from each of them, since afterwards, there won't be much to see. But now we have to be patient just a few hours more, and we will have finally won our war."

He stood to signal that their meeting was over and smiled as the other men indicated that he was now the first among equals; both a Prince and the new Leader.

"Brothers, we have made arrangements for you to wait in more comfort in the home of a noted local friend, where you can safely pray and make yourselves ready for the important and triumphant days ahead."

The two leaders from Gaza and Lebanon stood to take their leave of Mo, smiling warmly and embracing him as a brother, showing respect and humility. The younger man had no idea that the two men had no intention of staying in the area with him, as they knew exactly what was going to happen, and now knew for sure that he didn't.

Nafti then ushered out both the leaders of Hamas and Hezbollah. The giant was desperately seeking to find an excuse to leave the presence of Mo so he could contact his superior officers in the Mossad and issue an emergency warning to protect Tel Aviv and Haifa, and he was forming a backup plan in case no opportunity presented itself. He was shocked when Eddie, his long lost son, was escorted to the entrance of the subterranean meeting place, accompanied by Princess Leila Aziz.

Nafti had been so long under deep cover that he sometimes forgot he was really a Jew called Benjamin. He had never been able to spend any time with his son after he was a baby. He had snatched moments to monitor his progress through life and he knew who he was the instant he saw him. He also knew that the only reason Mo, the Prince, would have Eddie here was to seek his destruction, because Nafti realized that today was the end game.

Eddie was disturbed by the way the giant was staring at him and there was something about the man, other than his sheer size, that made his gaze pause on his face. There had been so many years since he was a small boy in Basra and had stared at the picture of his father who had vanished before he became just a cloudy, obscure legend. He didn't make the connection and the moment passed.

Nafti watched as the Prince looked up and smiled at the Princess and Eddie. "Welcome my sister, and Ehud, its good to see you after all these years, and back more or less where it all began. Please sit down."

Eddie and the Princess sat down opposite Mo, on the other side of the coffee table.

"We could have done our business on the telephone. What's the point in going over old ground? You know I regret what happened. I've already admitted it was a terrible mistake."

Mo looked between his sister and Eddie, and something in their body language made him smile as he turned to the Princess.

"Don't tell me, let me guess, oh yes, you've dishonoured the royal family of Saudi Arabia with a Jew!"

Before either the Princess or Eddie could respond Mo grinned, but without any warmth. "Do you suppose I really care about what you do in bed? Do you, Eddie, suppose I would simply, politely accept an apology? Just like that? No pain, no suffering?

Come on, Ehud. We're alike you and I. We have the same background. You're from the people with ancient ways, so am I. An eye for an eye and a tooth for a tooth. You know your Bible, Ehud, I know you do."

The Princess interrupted her adopted brother.

"Stop it, Mo. He's here under my protection. You promised me there would be no trouble, just business. What is all this nonsense?"

"Ask him," Mo snarled.

"I understand he has become a very honest man as he matured."

Eddie looked at Mo hard, trying to see the young boy he had once known. "There's no degree in honesty, Mo, a person is either honest or dishonest. It took me a long time to learn that and to find on which side of the line I wanted to live."

Mo stood up and was already losing his temper. "Always the Jew, clever with words and twisting the truth. But it was you who lied and robbed me of my family, not the other way around. Isn't that the truth?"

Eddie remained calm. "No, it isn't. I told the truth, and I always regretted it. But I don't understand the point of you getting us here just to have the same fight over again. Why have you got us here, to show us how powerful you are?"

"I'm The Leader now, and I have the power of life and death, and I have something you treasure and now you're finally going to pay the price for what you did to me".

"What do you mean?" asked Eddie, worried but unable to figure out what Mo had in mind.

Then Mo raised his cell phone with a triumphant grin on his face. "These things are amazing. 3D and high definition images with almost perfect sound recorded and transmitted from anywhere on the planet to anywhere else. Amazing isn't it? And look at the little film we recorded in London for you last night. But I'll put it on the big screen here because then you won't miss a thing."

Mo turned on the big computer monitor. Eddie saw the living room of his flat and then watched in horror as his partner Barry was frog-marched by several men into vision. He was then bound by his hands and feet, and had a gag forced into his mouth. Four men forced Barry to his knees. He was now trembling and crying as one of the men pulled a large scimitar sword from a gym bag as another forced Barry's head forward, exposing his neck to the blade.

Mo paused the playback of the recording and turned to Eddie. "Sadly the blade was not as sharp as it should have been. I have told my men to be more humane in future, but you know how it is, you can't get the help these days."

They all watched as Barry was slowly decapitated, his severed head held aloft for the camera as his body slumped to the floor.

Eddie jumped at Mo and before anyone could react, he had him by the throat, choking him. Nafti didn't know what to do as he saw Mo turn to him for help. The Princess was screaming at the horror of the last few minutes and no one was listening. Nafti instinctively sought to protect both Mo and Eddie, pulling them apart. He then held Mo down on the floor with one huge hand clasped around his throat to silence him as Eddie staggered to his feet. The young man shook his head.

"What are you doing, I don't understand?"

"You, take this gun and guard the door. Shoot anyone that tries to get in." Nafti instructed the Princess as he threw her his revolver with his free hand.

"You."

He turned to Eddie. "Grab Mo's phone and call this number, 555-1920, and say Benjamin is home and needs to talk immediately. Hundreds of thousands of lives depend on it!"

Eddie did as he was told. In the meantime, Nafti manhandled Mo into one of the leather seats, his huge hand still choking off any attempts Mo made to speak.

Eddie made the telephone connection and repeated the message exactly as Nafti had instructed. Within seconds he passed the phone to the giant.

"Are you ready?"

There was a few moments while the people at the other end readied their voice recognition technology. "Ready, go ahead caller." said the electronic sounding woman's voice.

"This is Benjamin returning to base, I need to speak urgently, priority one to the chief!"

There was another pause as the technology analysed Benjamin's voice, and further checked to see if he was under stress, and the answer to both questions was yes. Benjamin used the pause to slightly release the pressure on Mo's neck and as he gasped for air, he stared with disbelief at the giant he had always called Nafti. He spat in the giant's face, and Nafti slapped him as if admonishing a child.

"Tell me when and where the attacks will take place. I will remove each of your eyes with my fingers while you consider your answer."

He increased his grip around Mo's neck then pointed his giant forefinger at Mo's left eye and gouged it out. Mo screamed in agony as the eyeball fell on his chest. "Now the other one." said Nafti calmly, but before he could take out Mo's right eye, Mo begged for mercy.

"Stop, stop, I'll tell you. It's Dizengoff Square at noon in Tel Aviv and at the same time, Ben Gurion Avenue just below the Bahai Gardens in Haifa."

Seconds later, Motti Hoppel, Head of Mossad, was on the other end of the line, "Welcome home, Benjamin. Tell me what you have."

"I am in Jerusalem with Mo, The Leader, as my prisoner. There are four Jewish terrorists from a group called ZOG en route with dirty nuclear devices originating in Iraq to destroy the centres of Tel Aviv and Haifa. The targets are Dizengoff Square and the area below the Bahai Gardens on Ben Gurion Avenue in Haifa. This is for real, Condition Ultra. What should I do?"

Motti Hoppel was a man who liked to think, to contemplate all the options, but knew today there was no time to consider all the angles. Today he just had to react, and in his experience, Israel's most hidden agent, Benjamin, had an irreproachable record in intelligence gathering.

"Are you sure of your facts?"

Benjamin looked at Mo who was still whimpering in agony.

"I'm certain."

"Then secure our friend and wait where you are. We've located your position, our boys will pick you up. You've done enough. Leave the heavy lifting to us. We never leave our people behind."

Motti was right about everything, except on this occasion there were two facts that Benjamin had got wrong, and they were the location of the attacks and their timing.

Chapter Forty-Eight

The West Bank and Gaza, Israel
4th. November 2020 - 12.00 hours

Israeli security personnel took less than two hours to sweep into action within the Arabic population of Israel plus the West Bank and Gaza. Heavy fighting was reported by the international media which the Israeli military spokesperson, usually so talkative, refused to explain.

Information about the attack being planned for Tel Aviv and Haifa was passed to the security forces who flooded into those two locations, but they were unable to find anything.

The tension became almost unbearable as the search failed.

The Hamas fighters in Gaza put up a suicidal, brave but ultimately futile resistance swiftly overwhelmed by massively superior firepower. The Israeli forces included fluent Arabic- speaking snatch squads that made mass arrests of a long list of all known and potential threats to their country.

This tactic had been long-practiced in rigorous and repeated training for such a day, and thanks to heavy infiltration of the various Palestinian factions by Arab agents willing to sell out either for loyalty to their country of birth, money or blackmail, the Israelis knew where almost all of their targets were when they burst through the Palestinian defences.

But the Israelis had never imagined the possibility that the men and a woman carrying the dirty bombs to their targets would be fellow Jews. Genuine zealots ready to unleash hell to release their vision of heaven. They were acting not because of money or blackmail but because they believed in a secular, non Jewish, non Arab federation of Israel and Palestine, and thought the only way this could be achieved was to shock the world into forcing it to happen with a nuclear attack of three small nuclear dirty bombs.

In Iran, the Ayatollah stroked his white beard and exchanged smiles with the President of Iran, his chosen political acolyte. "Everything is in place?" he asked the younger man, who nodded and responded, "It is, Allah be praised."

The Ayatollah smiled again, satisfied that at last the world would be rid of the Jewish infestation in the Zionist entity they called Israel, just as he had been predicting all his adult life.

In an orthodox Jewish section of Jerusalem called Mea Sharim Nancy Roman sat in her comfortable apartment smiling as she looked at the photographs of her boys when they were youngsters growing up back home, when everything was good.

How she loved her Eddie and Mo, and remembering how they loved her. Will I ever see my boys again? she wondered.

The three men and one woman, followers of ZOG, dressed as American Evangelical Christian tourists got off their coach in Jerusalem at that moment, each clutching a suicide bag containing enough explosives and nuclear material to make four Hiroshima bombs. They kissed and hugged one another then went their separate ways. It was now too late for any power on earth to stop them as they entered the

Old City, the only holy place on earth where Jews, Christians and Muslims prayed to their God.

The American President watched the images being flashed back to her via the watching satellites, hoping that the Predators would destroy their targets in time.

Mo was managing his pain and despite his hands being tied firmly behind his back with his own trousers belt, he waited for the next scheduled communication, confirming that the additional target, Israel's nuclear reactor in Dimona had been obliterated. He looked at the digital clock on the big computer monitor.

A huge security sweep mobilized in Jerusalem; thousands of men and women setting up emergency barriers, and stop and search positions. The ancient city ground to a halt almost immediately, but the men and women of ZOG were already within the first perimeter area, fast approaching their targets.

Rigorously trained to observe and analyse, Benjamin knew there was something wrong with the behaviour of his prisoner. Mo shouldn't be this calm in the face of such a major setback, he should be going crazy that things weren't going his way but he appeared fine, praying to himself. Benjamin grabbed him by his shoulders and shook him. But he got no reaction.

"Mo, the first training session I ever had they asked me would I murder one man, or a woman, or an animal if it meant saving a bigger number of people." He pulled his combat knife and aimed it at the praying man. "Can you guess what my answer was?"

The threat was real and Mo realized it. "You can call yourself Benjamin now, but you're still mine Nafti, and you're a traitor to me."

Mo smiled. "You bastard,"

Benjamin, who was finding it difficult not to think of himself as Nafti continued, "I know you. You never smile unless you're going to pull some shit!"

Eddie looked at Mo and agreed.

"He's changed the targets, I tell you he's changed the targets!"

Mo looked at Eddie and laughed, the hole where his eye had been removed seemed to stare malevolently.

"I haven't changed anything and this monster can do what he wants to me. I have nothing to fear because in the end, I shall win, and do you know why?"

"Go on, tell us," Eddie responded.

"Because we love death more than you love life!" Mo mumbled this, but it was all the more emphatic for the quiet venom with which he said it.

"Nancy should see us now." Eddie said with obvious sincerity. Mo turned his good eye toward his old friend, now deadly enemy.

"She's home safe, tucked up, she's the one good thing I remember from America.""No she's not, she's right here in the Old City, less than a mile from here."

There was a terrible moment as an awful thought crossed Mo's mind.

American Predator drones flew over the most densely populated areas of Israel's busiest commercial and industrial areas, unaware and coldly uncaring that there had been an almost total communications breakdown between the military, political and intelligence communities.

President Polacci watched from the military situation room, her nervous despair apparent from the way she paced up and down.

"Are we in communications with the Israelis?" she asked. Just at that moment, a young female White House member of staff got her attention,

"Yes?" The President asked.

"Ma'am, there are calls from the British Prime Minister, the German Chancellor and the French and Russian Presidents."

"I'll call back, tell them, but not right now."

The President answered impatiently.

"What's with our drones? Why can't they get a lock on these people? Right now the drones seem to be taking a scenic tour of Israel.'

General Russell Wisehart, the crew cut Head of the United States Air Force, bristled with indignation that any damned fool civilian would question the amazing technology being employed.

"Ma'am, automatic tracking systems are ineffective when they're looking in the wrong direction. I think we need to co-ordinate better with our Israeli allies and check their intelligence or we run the risk of losing our drones and their targets."

As he made the statement, one of the four television images went blank, and then, after a few moments, two of the other screens darkened, leaving just one image.

Milton Braschin, the Director of the CIA added, "Just like the general said,

Madam President. These are not rag heads with no technology, these are super bright people, and they're experienced fighters, we must find a way to talk with them."

The President drew in a deep breath and spoke as she sat down, "Fanatics always fail when they underestimate the determination of democracies."

Braschin didn't listen to political speeches he thought were said just for future memoirs. He preferred not to say anything that could later be attributed to him, and that way he'd outlasted several Presidents,. This was just plain dumb.

"We're running all over the atlas like headless chickens, Madam President, when what we need is time to think."

"Don't you get it? There is no more fucking time!" said the President, almost shouting, pulling her hair back in a severe bun and clipping it in position with a rubber band she found on the table. There was shock in the room, no one had ever heard the President use profanity before and it stirred the air of crisis even further.

In Israel, the Prime Minister turned to her military commander in chief, Mordecai Zvi,

"Why did you shoot down the American drones? They were trying to help."

He almost sneered, unable to totally conceal his disdain of the Prime Minister, who he considered a well-intentioned but ignorant leader, an amateur when a professional was required.

"While I serve as head of this country's defence forces, Prime Minister, I control the ground, the sea and the skies over this country, no one else, not even the Americans."

As Israel's leaders argued, the four members of the Zionist Opposition Group reached their primary target. There was no security at the entrance to the Temple on the Mount in Jerusalem. The normal security detail on this special site were usually supplied by the Jordanian Ministry of Awqaf in Amman but on this day they had been replaced by other men wearing identical uniforms. But these weren't Palestinians or Jordanians, they were not even Arabs, although they looked right, and spoke the language fluently. There the similarity ended because these were a special detachment from the Iranian special forces group known as Quds.

They had been smuggled in from Jordan and their task was simple, to export Iran's Islamic revolution to the world.

Today, they were to insure that the four people each carrying large red and black Manchester United football tote bags were allowed through to the Temple without anyone stopping them.

The Quds warriors were chosen not just because they were tough and bright, but also because they had proven they were devout followers of Islam. None of them knew that they were escorting Jews who were going to obliterate one of the most holy and sacred sites for Muslims all over the world, the Rock from which the Prophet Mohammed ascended to the heavens.

The Jewish fanatic Landau was almost unable to hide the elation he felt as he led his small group through the crowds of worshippers towards the building, which housed the Holy Rock, accompanied by eight guards. He was smiling and praying very quietly in Hebrew, muttering words of praise to the Lord.

He was aware that they were causing attention, but he wasn't nervous because he believed that he was wrapped in the arms of the Lord, protected by Him to do his holy work.

Before this mission Landau had received special dispensation from Rabbi Werner to enter the area normally forbidden to Jews both by the Muslim guardians of the site and their own holy men. The ultra religious Jews claimed that no Jew should enter the site since they might accidentally enter the most holy of areas, the inviolate space where the original Ark of the Covenant had stood, before the First and Second Temples were destroyed and the ruins converted by subsequent Christians and Muslim conquerors for use by their religions.

Far below, in the caverns burrowed thousands of years previously by the then-Jewish rulers of Jerusalem, Benjamin turned to his son Eddie.

"Whatever happens now, I want you to know I'm proud of you, Ehud."

Eddie stared at him. "What do you mean?"

He asked, and finally, after so many years, Benjamin showed his son the locket he had worn for so long around his neck. Eddie saw the picture of his mother and felt for the matching locket around his own neck, knowing the two photographs would match perfectly.

"Ehud, I'm Benjamin, your father."

The four members of the Zionist Opposition Group placed their bags at the four corners of the Rock from which the Prophet Mohammed had ascended. To the consternation of their Iranian guards who kept curious Muslim worshippers back several yards, the four Jews started to utter an ancient Jewish prayer in unison,

"Hear oh Israel, the Lord our God, the Lord is One."

It was the first and last time Jews had prayed at the exact site of the Second Temple's Ark of the Covenant for over two thousand years.

At the end of the prayer, Landau looked to the other three members of his group and held a mezuzah containing the central Jewish law, the Torah, in a tiny rolled up scroll and they each kissed it, to show their deep respect and love for the law. He held up five fingers, then four, three, two and finally one.

Chapter Forty-Nine

Jerusalem
4th. November 2020 – 13.00 hours

Four huge explosions hammered out their message deep, punching through to hell itself and they were so close that they merged into one dreadful, tearing cacophony of grinding noise, rocking and piercing the ground far below, dispassionately searching out victims to incinerate and evaporate into shadowed memories as the shock waves traveled outwards, the destruction crashing, roaring and slicing through the ancient ground like some great beast. In an instant tens of thousands of people vanished into the thin air along with more than three thousand years of history.

Far above, impervious watching satellites and high -lying unmanned drones witnessed the explosion in the heart of Jerusalem. Initially analysts in the war rooms of the world couldn't decipher what they were watching.

Moments later as the world seemed to hold its collective breath, and then the first interpretations surfaced on the Arabic news channel.

"We are getting reliable reports that a huge explosion has destroyed the ancient city of Jerusalem and the epicentre appears to be at the Dome of the Rock. We will bring you breaking news as soon as we have it. This is not yet confirmed."

Where once there were ancient temples, churches and mosques, now there was just a jagged giant crater, measuring fifty feet deep at its centre and more than three hundred across. Inside the hole there was nothing to show that human beings had ever been there, the people, the Rock, the history had been wiped out as if by a petulant giant.

Beneath the site of the explosion, protected by fate and topography the Wailing Wall still stood. But all the people who had been standing there praying or just looking at the ancient site had also been obliterated. Of them there were just memories, some shadows blasted into the stone.

From the outer perimeter of the plateau on which the Golden Dome had so recently existed, came men and women, Jews and Christians and Muslims to do what they could to help the survivors, unaware of the fact that the main danger came not from the explosions but from the release of the fall out from nuclear waste into the atmosphere. Many of them realized that all those helping the injured would be contaminated by the deadly radioactivity, but still they came, their humanity overcoming their fear. It didn't matter who they were, just that they needed each other. Their faith or race simply didn't matter

In Iran, the Ayatollah called his war cabinet to prayer, content with the outcome of his strategy. The President of Iran realized he would have to be patient if he was ever going to become the pre-eminent power in his country and in this region of the world. The successful purging of the Jews and the Arabs who didn't follow the true path would make the Ayatollah too powerful to usurp.

In Tel Aviv, the Israeli Prime Minister and her war cabinet were too stunned to react for a very long moment. In silence they watched the Arabic news service, funded out of Iran. It was playing a loop of Landau and the other followers of ZOG. It was their final message. The fanatic looked into the camera and said.

"When you see this video I shall be sitting on the right hand of the Lord, and the sacred ground of the Second Temple will have been purged of the Muslim blemish and be readied for the future Third Temple to be built. I shall never see it, but I have done his work for the ingathering when the Messiah shall call us all home. Shalom."

The screen went blank. Motti Hoppel was whispering into his cell phone and sighed, "It isn't a fake, he's one of our own, a lunatic, Prime Minister. I think, on balance, it's genuine."

She shook her head.

"Every Muslim in the world will want to kill every Jew. Meanwhile thousands of us and them lay dead, side by side."

"That's nothing much new there. Maybe it's time to break the circle, Prime Minister." Motti replied. "Perhaps something good can come out of this madness."

In Jerusalem, sirens sounded, breaking the momentary silence after the explosions.

The survivors realized that these warned of some new danger but no one stopped in their search for signs of life.

Eddie found himself lying on the ground in the dark cavern that had been decompressed when the shock wave had hit it. The layers of many tons of solid rock had protected him from the blast and initial radiation fallout. He couldn't see anything in the blackness nor could he hear after his eardrums had been blown out.

He realized that there had been some kind of catastrophic explosion, but he couldn't figure out where it had originated. He tried to get up but found that he was trapped under a large metal support beam. He remembered that the cell phone in his hand had a torch application, which he managed to turn on. In the dim light, he could see the Princess. She was seemingly asleep but there was something wrong, and then

Eddie realized she wasn't breathing. In the awful stillness of the moment he called to her,

"Leila, Leila, can you hear me, come on Leila, speak to me." But she would never respond, her beautiful face frozen in perfect slumber.

Out of the darkness, there was another sound, a slithering and shifting, and rising like an awful apparition straight from hell Mo appeared, covered in mud, gore and filth, just a few inches from Eddie. "Well, here we are, two fools together," he said, the words coming painfully.

"I think that someone has made idiots of us all. Are you hurt, my brother, can I help you?" he asked Eddie, who remembered the moment a lifetime ago when they had last said these words,

"No my friend, we'll be OK, nothing can stop us when we have each other."

Mo smiled with genuine warmth towards Eddie. "You know I always loved you. Always, sometimes I also hated you, but I loved you always, all my life."

Eddie returned the smile, and put out his free hand to Mo's cheek. "Remember when we used to fish, and you were scared of the sea monsters?"

"Yes I do."

"There never were any monsters there, except the ones in your head. You know that there's where they all live, the monsters, in our heads, if we're very lucky they're not in our hearts." The two men held each other's hands,

"What did I do?" said Mo looking at the heavy debris across the chest of his old friend, but he couldn't move any of it, his own body was too weak even though he used every ounce of his remaining strength.

Benjamin appeared out of the darkness, grabbed the metal covering his son and began to lift. At first there was no movement despite Benjamin's enormous strength, but, shaking with the effort, his grip never loosening, Benjamin started to straighten his legs, the metal inching up.

"Come on, Ehud, move!"

Benjamin didn't allow his own pain to stop his lift, and Mo helped pull Eddie clear of the metal spar. He was free but felt the pain as the pressure on his chest was released. Eddie now helped Mo to his feet.

"Don't bother, Ehud, I'm a walking dead man. Save yourself. Get out of here with your father. He's a good man."

Benjamin was breathing deeply from his exertions, but now it was Eddie's turn to look forlorn and negative.

"There's no way out of here. We're buried, unless someone comes to look but they're going to be too busy to even think about us."

"They'll come," said Benjamin.

"My homing device is on, and we don't leave our fallen. We're expert at dealing with disasters, we've had so much experience."

And they did come and that's how they were found; two days later. The three men: one dead, one barely alive and one unharmed.

Epilogue

Benjamin walked out of the ruins with his son Eddie cradled in his powerful arms, supported by the soldiers. They weren't able to pry his fingers loose from the young man until they were both in the ambulance en route to the Shaare Zedek Medical Center, one of Jerusalem's major hospitals.

Prince Mo and Princess Leila Aziz, were declared dead at the scene and their remains were dispatched, with due ceremony, as a diplomatic dignitary and a member of the Royal Family of Saudi Arabia to that country's new capital in Manama, the former Kingdom of Bahrain.

No one would ever know who they were, the twenty men dressed in black uniforms abseiling down ropes suspended from their three black helicopters out of the inky darkness into the small military compound in Iraq's western desert. They fired their silenced weapons and very quickly overpowered the guards. Shortly after there was a huge explosion and the hidden weapons of mass destruction were finally destroyed. It registered on the Richter Scale as if it was a moderately sized earthquake.

The healing process for Israel and the Palestinians surprised the entire world. They now shared a common suffering that transcended everything that had preceded it. The centre of the eternal city was declared a permanently uninhabitable holy site for all religions and the capital of both Palestine to its east and Israel to the west.

The real capital of Israel was now Tel Aviv that, like almost all of the rest of the country, had been left physically unscathed by the explosions and the fall out cloud, which had dissipated in the hills and valleys from the Mount of Olives through the prevailing winds to the area beyond Mount Scopus. With the collapse of the Kingdom of Jordan, that country's capital, Amman, was now also the operational capital of all the Palestinian people.

The Israeli political leaders found themselves back in control when the military elite's General Staff formally submitted itself for arrest and was charged with High Treason. To avoid a potential civil war the Government declared a general amnesty for these men and women but they were stripped of their ranks, privileges and pensions. The Chiefs of the General Staff were all put under long term house arrest.

The government of Israel declared the Zionist Opposition Group a banned terrorist group and many of its members were rounded up and were soon undergoing due legal process.

In Palestine, there was a similar crackdown on all the terrorist groups who might de-stabilize the fragile peace process, which had almost miraculously materialized from the smoke and disaster of the great catastrophe.

The Americans and Chinese governments had underwritten the cost of a multinational peace-keeping force which now patrolled the new border which, with some minor land swaps, ran along the line of the old security fence which the Israelis had voluntarily torn down.

In Iran, the leadership plotted long-term for the time when they would eventually remove Israel from the face of the earth.

In Israel, Eddie became Ehud once more, finding comfort and love with his newly-discovered father, Benjamin. He found time for himself, and joined a local six a side football team and occasionally he dreamt of playing for far away Manchester United. With practice he could now keep the ball up over one hundred times.

THE END

הסוף

النهاية

Acknowledgements

Special thanks are due to many people who helped me with this book. Other than my wonderfully supportive and endlessly patient family I would like to pay special tribute to my friend and trusted military expert, Seth Milstein, a credit to the American military he has served so well and with such distinction in many parts of our troubled world. Without his advice and guidance I would have made innumerable military mistakes, and any that remain are entirely my fault for errors that my research was unable to uncover.

In addition I wish to pay public tribute to my excellent editor Morgen Bailey, who is kind but firm, quick but accurate and charming at all times.Special thanks are also due to Jonathan Downes at Gonzo for his tireless efforts to keep me on the straight and narrow with regard to correcting my many errors and making some great suggestions. I reiterate, any mistakes are all mine."

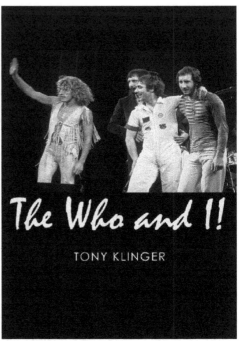

CURRENTLY AVAILABLE FROM TONY KLINGER AT GONZO

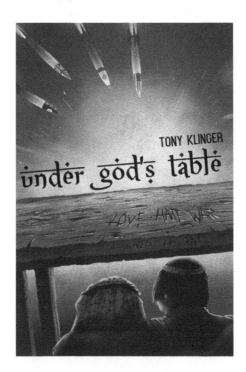

GONZO Books

There is still such a thing as alternative Publishing

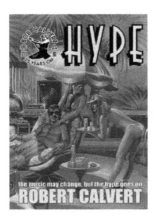

Robert Newton Calvert: Born 9 March 1945, Died 14 August 1988 after suffering a heart attack. Contributed poetry, lyrics and vocals to legendary space rock band Hawkwind intermittently on five of their most critically acclaimed albums, including Space Ritual (1973), Quark, Strangeness & Charm (1977) and Hawklords (1978). He also recorded a number of solo albums in the mid 1970s. CENTIGRADE 232 was Robert Calvert's first collection of poems.

Hype   'And now, for all you speeding street smarties out there, the one you've all been waiting for, the one that'll pierce your laid back ears, decoke your sinuses, cut clean thru the schlock rock, MOR/crossover, techno flash mind mush. It's the new Number One with a bullet ... with a bullet ... It's Tom, Supernova, Mahler with a pan galactic biggie ...' And the Hype goes on. And on. Hype, an amphetamine hit of a story by Hawkwind collaborator Robert Calvert. Who's been there and made it back again. The debriefing session starts here.

Rick Wakeman is the world's most unusual rock star, a genius who has pushed back the barriers of electronic rock. He has had some of the world's top orchestras perform his music, has owned eight Rolls Royces at one time, and has broken all the rules of composing and horrified his tutors at the Royal College of Music. Yet he has delighted his millions of fans. This frank book, authorised by Wakeman himself, tells the moving tale of his larger than life career.

"So many books, so little time."
Frank Zappa

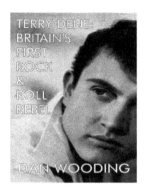

There are nine Henrys, pur ported to be the world's first cloned cartoon charac ter. They live in a strange lo fi domestic surrealist world peopled by talking rock buns and elephants on wobbly stilts.

They mooch around in their minimalist universe suffer ing from an existential crisis with some genetically modified humour thrown in.

Marty Wilde on Terry Dene: "Whatever happened to Terry becomes a great deal more comprehensible as you read of the callous way in which he was treated by people who should have known better many of whom, frankly, will never know better of the sad little shadows of the past who eased themselves into Terry's life, took everything they could get and, when it seemed that all was lost, quietly left him ... Dan Wood ing's book tells it all."

Rick Wakeman: "There have always been certain 'careers' that have fascinated the public, newspapers, and the media in general. Such include musicians, actors, sportsmen, police, and not surprisingly, the people who give the police their employ ment: The criminal. For the man in the street, all these careers have one thing in common: they are seemingly beyond both his reach and, in many cases, understanding and as such, his only associ ation can be through the media of newspapers or tele vision. The police, however, will always require the ser vices of the grass, the squealer, the snitch, (call him what you will), in order to assist in their investiga tions and arrests; and amaz ingly, this is the area that seldom gets written about."

"Outside of a dog, a book is man's best friend. Inside of a dog it's too dark to read."
Groucho Marx

Bill Harkleroad joined Captain Beef heart's Magic Band at a time when they were changing from a straight ahead blues band into something completely dif ferent. Through the vision of Don Van Vliet (Captain Beefheart) they created a new form of music which many at the time considered atonal and difficult, but which over the years has continued to exert a powerful influence. Beefheart re christened Harkleroad as Zoot Horn Rollo, and they embarked on recording one of the classic rock albums of all time Trout Mask Replica - a work of unequalled daring and inventiveness.

Politics, paganism and .... Vlad the Impaler. Selected stories from CJ Stone from 2003 to the present. Meet Ivor Coles, a British Tommy killed in action in September 1915, lost, and then found again. Visit Mothers Club in Erdington, the best psyche delic music club in the UK in the '60s. Celebrate Robin Hood's Day and find out what a huckle duckle is. Travel to Stonehenge at the Summer Solstice and carouse with the hippies. Find out what a Ranter is, and why CJ Stone thinks that he's one. Take LSD with Dr Lilly, the psychedelic scientist. Meet a headless soldier or the ghost of Elvis Presley in Gabalfa, Cardiff. Journey to Whitstable, to New York, to Malta and to Transylvania, and to many other places, real and imagined, polit ical and spiritual, transcendent and mundane. As The Independent says, Chris is "The best guide to the underground since Charon ferried dead souls across the Styx."

This is is the first in the highly acclaimed vampire novels of the late Mick Farren. Victor Renquist, a surprisingly urbane and likable leader of a colony of vampires which has existed for centuries in New York is faced with both admin istrative and emotional prob lems. And when you are a vampire, administration is not a thing which one takes lightly.

"The person, be it gentleman or lady, who has not pleasure in a good novel, must be intolerably stupid."

Jane Austen

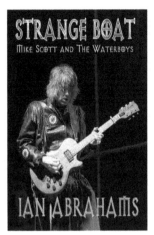

Los Angeles   City of Angels, city of dreams. But sometimes the dreams become nightmares. Having fled New York, Victor Renquist and his small group of Nosferatu are striving to re establish their colony. They have become a deeper, darker part of the city's nightlife. And Hollywood's glitterati are hot on the scent of a new thrill, one that outshines all others   immortality. But someone, somewhere, is med dling with even darker powers, powers that even the Nosferatu fear. Someone is attempting to summon the entity of ancient evil known as Cthulhu. And Ren quist must overcome dissent in his own colony, solve the riddle of the Darklost (a being brought part way along the Nosferatu path and then abandoned) and combat powerful enemies to save the world   of humans!

Canadian born Corky Laing is probably best known as the drummer with Mountain. Corky joined the band shortly after Mountain played at the famous Woodstock Festival, although he did receive a gold disc for sales of the soundtrack album after over dubbing drums on Ten Years After's performance. Whilst with Mountain Corky Laing recorded three studio albums with them before the band split. Follow ing the split Corky, along with Mountain gui tarist Leslie West, formed a rock three piece with former Cream bassist Jack Bruce. West, Bruce and Laing recorded two studio albums and a live album before West and Laing re formed Mountain, along with Felix Pappalardi. Since 1974 Corky and Leslie have led Mountain through various line ups and recordings, and continue to record and perform today at numer ous concerts across the world. In addition to his work with Mountain, Corky Laing has recorded one solo album and formed the band Cork with former Spin Doctors guitarist Eric Shenkman, and recorded a further two studio albums with the band, which has also featured former Jimi Hendrix bassist Noel Redding. The stories are told in an incredibly frank, engaging and amusing manner, and will appeal also to those people who may not necessarily be fans of

To me there's no difference between Mike Scott and The Waterboys; they both mean the same thing. They mean myself and whoever are my current travel ling musical companions." Mike Scott Strange Boat charts the twisting and meandering journey of Mike Scott, describing the literary and spiritual references that inform his songwriting and explor ing the multitude of locations and cultures in which The Waterboys have assembled and reflected in their recordings. From his early forays into the music scene in Scotland at the end of the 1970s, to his creation of a 'Big Music' that peaked with the hit single 'The Whole of the Moon' and onto the Irish adventure which spawned the classic Fisher man's Blues, his constantly restless creativity has led him through a myriad of changes. With his revolving cast of troubadours at his side, he's created some of the most era defining records of the 1980s, reeled and jigged across the Celtic heartlands, reinvented himself as an electric rocker in New York, and sought out personal renewal in the spiritual calm of Findhorn's Scot tish highland retreat. Mike Scott's life has been a tale of continual musical exploration entwined with an ever evolving spirituality. "An intriguing portrait of a modern musician" (Record Collector).

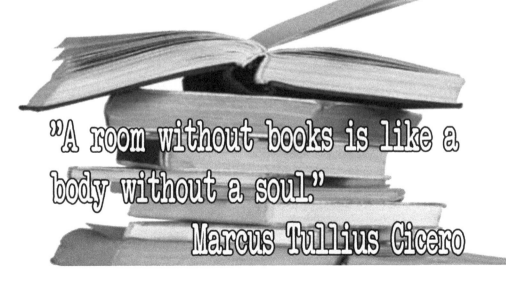

"A room without books is like a body without a soul."
Marcus Tullius Cicero

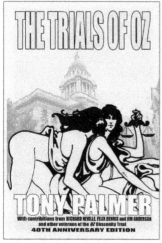

The OZ trial was the longest obscenity trial in history. It was also one of the worst reported. With minor exceptions, the Press chose to rewrite what had occurred, presumably to fit in with what seemed to them the acceptable prejudices of the times. Perhaps this was inevitable. The proceedings dragged on for nearly six weeks in the hot summer of 1971 when there were, no doubt, a great many other events more worthy of attention. Against the background of murder in Ulster, for example, the OZ affair probably fades into its proper insignificance. Even so, after the trial, when some newspapers realised that maybe something important had happened, it became more and more apparent that what was essential was for anyone who wished to be able to read what had actually been said. Trial and judgment by a badly informed press became the order of the day. This 40th Anniversary edition includes new material by all three of the original defendants, the prosecuting barrister, one of the OZ schoolkids, and even the daughters of the judge. There are also many illustrations including unseen material from Feliz Dennis' own collection…

Merrell Fankhauser has led one of the most diverse and interesting careers in music. He was born in Louisville, Kentucky, and moved to California when he was 13 years old. Merrell went on to become one of the innovators of surf music and psychedelic folk rock. His travels from Hollywood to his 15 year jungle experience on the island of Maui have been documented in numerous music books and magazines in the United States and Europe. Merrell has gained legendary international status throughout the field of rock music; his credits include over 250 songs published and released. He is a multi talented singer/songwriter and unique guitar player whose sound has delighted listeners for over 35 years. This extraordinary book tells a unique story of one of the founding fathers of surf rock, who went on to play in a succession of progressive and psychedelic bands and to meet some of the greatest names in the business, including Captain Beefheart, Randy California, The Beach Boys, Jan and Dean… and there is even a run in with the notorious Manson family.

On September 19, 1985, Frank Zappa testified before the United States Senate Commerce, Technology, and Transportation committee, attacking the Parents Music Resource Center or PMRC, a music organization co founded by Tipper Gore, wife of then senator Al Gore. The PMRC consisted of many wives of politicians, including the wives of five members of the committee, and was founded to address the issue of song lyrics with sexual or satanic content. Zappa saw their activities as on a path towards censor shipyand called their proposal for voluntary labelling of records with explicit content "extortion" of the music industry. This is what happened.

"Good friends, good books, and a sleepy conscience: this is the ideal life."
Mark Twain

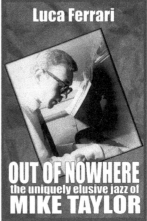

An erudite catalogue of some of the most peculiar records ever made. We have lined up, described and put into context 500 "albums" in the expectation that those of you who can't help yourselves when it comes to finding and collecting music will benefit from these efforts in two ways. Firstly, you'll know you are not alone. Secondly, we hope that some of the work covering the following pages leads you to new discoveries, and makes your life slightly better as a result.

Roy Weard was born in Barking, then a part of Essex, in 1948. He spent most of the mid-sixties through to the mid seventies involved first in folk music and then in the psychedelic hippie scene. He toured with many bands in various capacities from T-Shirt seller to sound engineer, production manager and tour manager. He was involved in several bands of his own, played at many of the iconic free festivals, made three full length albums and two singles, wrote for music magazines, computer magazines and produced copious MySpace blogs. He has lived all over London, spent four years in Hamburg, Germany and finally settled in Brighton where he now resides. He still sings in a rock and roll band, promotes gigs, does a weekly radio show and steadfastly refuses to act his age. This is his story.

Michael Ronald Taylor (1938 - 1969) was a British jazz composer, pianist and co-song-writer for the band Cream.

Mike Taylor drowned in the River Thames near Leigh-on-Sea, Essex in January 1969, following years of heavy drug use (principally hashish and LSD). He had been homeless for three years, and his death was almost entirely unre-marked. This is the first biography written about him.